99 COFFINS

A Historical Vampire Tale

99 COFFINS

DAVID WELLINGTON

THREE RIVERS PRESS
NEW YORK

Copyright © 2007 by David Wellington

Published in the United States by Three Rivers Press,
an imprint of the Crown Publishing Group,
a division of Random House, Inc., New York.
www.crownpublishing.com

Three Rivers Press and the Tugboat design are registered trademarks of Random House, Inc.

Library of Congress Cataloging-in-Publication Data
Wellington, David.
   99 coffins : a historical vampire tale / David Wellington. —
1st ed.
   1. Vampires—Fiction. 2. Women detectives—Fiction.
3. Pennsylvania—Fiction. 4. Gettysburg National
Military Park (Pa.)—Fiction. I. Title. II. Title: Ninety-
nine coffins.
PS3623.E468A616 2007
813'.6—dc22   2007027621

ISBN 978-0-307-38171-2

Printed in the United States of America

DESIGN BY BARBARA STURMAN

10 9 8 7 6 5 4 3 2 1

First Edition

For Alex

She is older than the rocks among which she sits; like the vampire, she has been dead many times, and learned the secrets of the grave.

—Walter Pater, Studies in the History of the Renaissance

CHESS

1.

Fifty thousand men had died or been wounded on this broad valley, Montrose told himself. It must have been a scene out of hell—the injured lying sprawled across the corpses, the cannon still firing from the top of one hill at the top of another. The horses screaming, the smoke, the utter desperation. This was where the country could have fallen apart—instead, this place had saved it from utter ruin.

Of course, that had been a century and a half ago. Now as he stared out over the dewy Gettysburg battlefield all he saw were the trees shimmering in the wind that swept down between two ridges and stirred the long green grass. The blood had dried up long ago and the bodies all had been taken away to be buried. Off in one corner of the field he could just make out the scrupulously period-authentic tents of a band of reenactors, but it looked like even they were sleeping in.

He rubbed his face to try to wake himself up, forgetting for the third time that morning that he still had kohl daubed around his eyes from the previous night's clubbing. Jeff Montrose was not a morning person. He preferred to think of himself as a creature of the night.

Of course, when Professor John Geistdoerfer called you at six A.M. on a Sunday morning and asked if you'd supervise a student dig until he could arrive, you made your voice as chipper as possible and you got dressed in a hurry. The professor was the hottest thing going in the field of Civil War Era Studies, one of the most influential people at Gettysburg College. Staying on his good side was mandatory for a grad student like Montrose, if he ever wanted to have a career of his own someday.

And when the student dig turned out to be something special—well, even the most hard-core night owl could make an exception. Montrose ran down through the trees to the road and waved at the professor's Buick as it nosed its way toward him. The car pulled onto the side of the road where Montrose indicated.

Geistdoerfer was a tall man with a shock of silver hair and a neatly combed mustache. He climbed out of the car and started up the track, not waiting to hear what his student had to say.

"I called you the second we found it," Montrose tried to explain, chasing after the professor. "Nobody's gone down inside yet—I made sure of it."

Geistdoerfer nodded but said nothing as the two of them hurried toward the site. His eyes tracked back and forth across the main trench, a ragged opening in the earth made by inexpert hands. At the bottom, still mostly buried in dark earth, was a floor of decayed wooden planking. The undergrads who excavated it had come only for extra credit and none of them were CWES majors. They stood around the trench now in their bright clothes, looking either bored or scared, holding their trowels and shovels at their sides. Geistdoerfer was a popular teacher, but he could be a harsh grader, and none of them wanted to incur his wrath.

The site had been chosen for student work because it was supposed to be of only passing interest to history. Once it had been a powder magazine, a narrow pit dug in the earth where the Confederates had stored barrels of black gunpowder. At the end of the battle, when the soldiers had beat a hasty retreat, they had blown up the magazine to keep it out of the hands of the victorious Union troops. Geistdoerfer hadn't expected to find anything in the dig other than maybe some shards of burned barrels and a few whitened lead minié balls identical to the ones you could buy at any gift shop in town.

For the first few hours of the dig they hadn't even turned up that much. Then things got more interesting. Marcy Jackson, a criminal justice major, had been digging in the bottom of the trench when she uncovered the magazine's floorboards about an hour before Geistdoerfer arrived. Now Montrose motioned for her to step forward. Her hands were shoved deeply into her pockets.

"Marcy hit one of the floorboards with her trowel and thought it sounded hollow. Like there was an open space underneath," Montrose said. "She, um, she hit the boards a couple of times and they broke away. There was an open space beneath, maybe a big one." Which meant the site was more than just another powder magazine, though what else it had been used for was anybody's guess.

"I just wanted to see what was down there," she said. "We're supposed to be curious. You said that in class."

"Yes, I did." Geistdoerfer studied her for a moment. "I also told you, young lady, that it's traditional, at a dig, to not destroy anything before the senior academic on-site can have a look," he said.

Montrose could see Jackson's shoulders trembling as she stared down at her shoes.

The professor's stare didn't waver. "Considering the result, however, I think we can let this one slide." Then he smiled, warmly and invitingly. "Will you show me what you found?"

The student bit her lip and climbed down into the trench, with Geistdoerfer following. Together they examined the hole in the boards. The professor called up for Montrose to fetch some flashlights and a ladder. Geistdoerfer went down first, with Montrose and Jackson following. At the bottom they waved their lights around with no idea what they might find.

The powder magazine had been built on top of a natural cavern, they soon decided. Pennsylvania had plenty of them, though most of the big caves were north of Gettysburg. It looked like the Confederates had known it was there, since in several places the ceiling of the cave was shored up with timbers. Jagged stalactites hung from the ceiling, but some effort had been made to even out the floor. Their flashlights did little to cut through the almost perfect darkness in the cave, but they could see it wasn't empty. A number of long, low shapes huddled in the gloom, maybe large crates of some kind.

Jackson played her light over one of them and then squeaked like a mouse. The two men turned their lights on her face and she blinked in annoyance. "I'm okay. I just wasn't expecting a coffin."

Montrose dropped to his knees next to the box she'd examined and saw she was right. "Oh my God," he whispered. When they'd discovered the cave he'd assumed it would hold old weaponry or perhaps long-rotten foodstuffs and general supplies. The thought it might be a crypt had never occurred to him.

He started to shake with excitement. Every archaeologist at heart wants to dig up old burial sites. They may get excited about flint arrowheads or ancient kitchen middens, but the reason they got into the field in the first place was because they wanted to find the next King Tut or the next stash of terra-cotta warriors. He waved his light around at some of the other boxes and saw they were all the same. Long, octagonal in shape. They were plain wooden coffins with simple lids held on by rusting hinges.

His mind raced with the possibilities. Inside would be bones, of course, which were of great interest, but maybe also the remains of clothing, maybe Civil War–era jewelry. There was so much to be done, so much cataloging and descriptive work, the entire cavern had to be plotted and diagrams drawn up—

His train of thought was derailed instantly when Jackson reached down and lifted the lid of the nearest coffin. "Hey, don't—" he shouted, but she already had it open.

"Young lady," the professor sighed, but then he just shook his head. Montrose went to take a look. How could he not?

Inside the coffin lay a skeleton in almost perfect preservation. All the bones were intact, though strangely enough they were also completely bare of flesh. Even after a hundred and forty years you would expect to see some remains of hair or desiccated skin, but these were as clean as a museum specimen. Far more surprising, though, was that the skull was deformed. The jaws were larger than they should have been. They also had more teeth than they should. Far more teeth, and none of them were bicuspids or molars. They were wicked-looking triangular teeth, slightly translucent, like those of a shark. Montrose recognized those teeth from somewhere, but he couldn't quite place where.

Apparently Geistdoerfer had a better memory. Montrose could feel the professor's body go rigid beside him. "Miss Jackson, I'm going to ask you to leave now," he said. "This is no longer an appropriate site for undergraduate students. In fact, Mister Montrose, would you be good enough to go up top and send all of the students home?"

"Of course," Montrose said. He led Jackson back to the ladder and did as the professor had asked. Some of the students grumbled and some had questions he couldn't answer. He promised them all he'd explain at the next class meeting. When they were gone he hurried back down the ladder, desperate to get to work.

What he found at the bottom didn't make any sense to him. The professor was kneeling next to the coffin and had something in his hand, a black object about the size of his fist. He laid it quite gently and carefully inside the skeleton's rib cage, then leaned back as if in surprise.

Jeff started to ask what was going on, but the professor held up one hand for silence. "I'd appreciate it if you went home too, Jeff. I'd like to be alone with this find for a while."

"Don't you need someone to help start cataloging all this?" Montrose asked.

The professor's eyes were very bright in his flashlight beam. Jeff didn't need more than one look to know the answer.

"Yeah, sure," the student said. "I'll see you later, then."

Geistdoerfer was already staring down into the coffin again. He made no reply.

2.

I met with General Hancock for the last time in 1886, on Governors Island in the harbor of New York City. He was in ill health then, and much reduced in his duties as Commander of the Atlantic Division, and I waited in the anterooms of his office for several hours in the cold, with only a small stove to warm me. When he came in he walked with much difficulty, and some pain, yet gave me the warm felicitations we two have always shared.

We had some matters of small business to conclude. Last of these was the thin sheaf of documents I had compiled, about my work at Gettysburg in July 1863. "I think they should be burned," the general told me, without a glance at them. His eyes were fixed on my face instead, and as sharp and clear as I remembered, from the third day of the battle. The pain had not then touched his fierce intellect, nor his spirit. "These papers offer nothing to posterity save moral terror, and would ruin many a fine career should they be published now. What benefits any of us to stir up old memories?"

One does not question a man of Winfield Scott Hancock's authority. I bowed over the papers and gathered them again into my valise. He turned to reach for a glass of tea, which steamed in the icy room.

"And what of the soldiers?" I asked. "They are veterans, all."

But his answer was immediate. "They are dead, sir," he told me, putting his feet up on the stove. "It is better for them to remain so." His voice sank lower as he added, "and best for our sacred Conscience, as well."

A week later he was brought to Pennsylvania, and buried there, having died of a very old wound that never healed.

—THE PAPERS OF COLONEL WILLIAM PITTENGER

3.

The unmarked car sat screened by a row of trees only a hundred yards from the barn. The same barn she'd been looking at for so long—just a big unkempt pile of weather-eaten wood planks, with here and there a broken window. It looked like it ought to be deserted, or even condemned, yet she knew it was full to capacity with the fifteen members of the Godwin family, every single one of whom had a criminal record. As far as she could tell they were all asleep. A gray squirrel ran up the side of a drainpipe and she nearly jumped out of her seat. Getting control of herself, she scribbled some notes on her spiral pad. *Sept. 29, 2004, continuing surveillance outside of Godwin residence near Lairdsville, Pennsylvania.* This was it, she thought. The day of the raid had finally come. She looked up. The dashboard clock ticked over to 5:47 A.M. and she made a note.

"I count five vehicles out front," Corporal Painter said. "That's all of them—the whole family's in there. We can get everybody in one sweep." As the junior officer on the investigation, Caxton had been assigned to shadow one of the more experienced troopers. Painter had been doing this for years. He sipped at an iced coffee and squinted through the windshield. "This is your first taste of real police work, right?"

"I guess you could say that," she replied. Once upon a time she had worked on a kind of investigation. She had fought for her life against vampires far more deadly than any bad guy Painter might have tracked down in his career. The vampire case had gotten her promoted, but it didn't appear anywhere on her permanent record. It had been nearly a full year since she'd moved up from the Bureau of Patrol to the Bureau of Criminal Investigation. In that time she'd taken endless classes at the academy in Hershey, qualified on tests both written and oral, passed polygraph and background checks and full psychological, medical, and physical fitness evaluations, including a urinalysis for drug screening, before she was actually permitted to work a real investigation in the field. Then had come the hard part, the actual work. For the last two months she had been pulling twelve-hour shifts in the car, watching the barn that they believed contained one of the biggest meth labs in the Commonwealth. She hadn't made a single collar yet, nor confiscated any evidence, nor interviewed a person of interest. This raid would prove whether or not she was cut out for criminal investigations, and she wanted to do everything perfectly.

"Here's a tip, then. You don't have to write down the time every five minutes if nothing happens." He smiled and gestured at her notepad with his coffee cup.

She smiled back and shoved the pad into her pocket. She kept her eyes on the barn. She wanted to say something funny, something to make Painter think she was one of the guys. Before she could think of anything, though, the car radio lit up and the voice of Captain Horace, their superior, came through.

"All cars, all cars. The warrant just came through. Hazmat and firefighters in place. All cars are on scene. Let's wake 'em up!"

Caxton's body surged with adrenaline. It was time.

Painter twisted the key in the ignition and threw the car into gear. They lurched forward onto the road, then swung into the broad unpaved driveway in front of the barn, their tires squealing. All around them other cars—hidden until that exact moment—came tearing out of the woods, and armored cops spilled out onto the gravel. Beside her a pair of troopers brought up a breeching device—a length of PVC pipe filled with concrete that could knock down even a steel-core door. Another trooper ran toward the door to knock and announce—to give the legally required warning he had to shout out before they could bust in and serve the warrant. Everyone was armored, and everyone was masked up. She grabbed her own gas mask off her belt and strapped it over her face. Meth labs churned out some pretty nasty chemicals, including phosphine gas that could kill you in seconds. She couldn't see very well through the faceplate, but she ran forward anyway, drawing her weapon and keeping it down near her hip. Her heart pounded in her chest. Everything was happening so fast.

"Team one to the left, team two with me. Go, go, go!" Captain Horace shouted, coming up from behind her. "Team three"—that was her team—"get some distance. Team three," he called, "get back, get—heads down!"

A window had opened up in the second story of the barn. A man with a shaved head and sores on his face leaned out and started firing at them with a hunting rifle. Damn it, she thought, they were supposed to have been asleep! She ran forward, seeking shelter on the porch of the barn, a narrow roofed porch that would give her cover.

"You! Get back, get back!" Horace shouted. Gunshots smashed into the gravel and struck the hood of her car as if it had been hit with a hammer. "Caxton, get back!"

In her twenty-seven years of life no one had ever shot at her before. Her brain stopped working and her kidneys hurt as her adrenal glands poured fire into her veins. She tried to think. She had to follow the order. She tried to spin on her heel and run back. The cars were so far away, though. She was out in the open and the porch was so close—

Without warning a high-velocity bullet smashed into her sternum, knocking her backward.

Her vision went red, then black, but only for a moment.

Her feet couldn't seem to grip the loose gravel, and her head collided jarringly with the ground. She could hear nothing at all. Her entire body felt like a bell that had been struck.

Gloved hands grabbed her ankles and pulled her backward, away from the barn, her legs bouncing wildly. She couldn't feel her left arm. Faces stared down into hers, faces in helmets and gas masks. She could hear a buzzing noise that slowly resolved into a human voice demanding to know if she was still alive.

"Vest," she said. "The vest took it." Hands grabbed at her chest and pulled and tugged. Someone got the bullet free, a shiny lump of distorted metal. Someone else pulled at her helmet, but she batted the hands away. "I'm okay," she shouted, again and again.

She could hear a little better by that point. She could hear the unrhythmic barking of hunting rifles and the more stately reply of automatic weapons fire.

"Get her out of here," the captain shouted.

"No, I'm good!" she shouted back. Her body begged to differ. *You're not as fragile as you think,* she told it, repeating words an old colleague had once said to her. They wouldn't let her get up—they were still dragging her, even as she fought them.

"What the fuck happened?" a trooper asked, pressing his shoulder against the side of a car. He leaned out a little, into the open, then jumped back as rifle fire chewed up the gravel ahead of him. "They were supposed to all be asleep!"

Captain Horace tore off his gas mask and scowled at the barn. "I guess they use their own shit. Meth freaks get up earlier than normal people."

Hands reached down and helped her sit up against the side of a car. She couldn't see anything through her mask. She couldn't breathe. "Let me up," she shouted. "I can still shoot!"

"Stay *down,*" Horace shouted, pushing down hard on her shoulder. "I don't have time for this. I'm giving you an order.

You disobeyed the last one. You don't get to do that twice. You stay here, stay down, and stay out of the goddamned way."

Caxton wanted to protest, but she knew he wasn't interested in her opinion. "Yes, sir," she said. He nodded and jumped up to run to the back of another car. She struggled to take off her gas mask and drop it on the gravel beside her, then settled in to get comfortable.

It was hours before the shooting was done and they'd carted off the last suspect. After that she could only watch as the other troopers came parading out of the house carrying pieces of the meth lab wrapped in plastic and plastered with biohazard stickers. Ambulances carried away the wounded and almost as an afterthought a paramedic was sent to take a look at her bruised chest. He took off her vest, opened up her shirt, and took one look at her before handing her an ice pack and telling her she was fine. While she was being discharged Corporal Painter came by to check up on her. "You missed all the fun," he said, grinning. He leaned down and gave her a hand to help get her back on her feet. Her rib cage creaked a little as she rose, but she knew she was fine. "Not quite what you signed on for, was it?" he asked.

She shook her head. "I'm going home," she told him. She dug her notepad out of her pants pocket and threw it to him. "Here, you can write up the report."

4.

They asked I tell my tale. I should like it not, save the War Department demands it of me, & no man, no living man can call me SHIRKER, so I will write down on these pages what happened to me & to the men of my charge, & what horrors I have seen & what tragedies did occur. Also, of those trespasses we committed. So be it.

Let me begin after the battle of Chancellorsville, for what happened there is of no matter to my present narrative. Suffice to say the Third Maine Volunteer Infantry was the last to flee that hell of cannon fire and muddy death. When at last the order came to retreat, we made all due speed away. On June 21st, 1863, after some marching, we made camp in a place called Gum Spring, Virginia. Before we were allowed to rest, however, the sergeant came down the line with a candle in his hand and beating on a small drum with new orders. We were to stand Picket Duty, which is no soldier's desire. The six of us, which were one quarter of the remains of Company H, marched out about one mile from the lines, there to look for & make contact with the enemy, should he present himself. Hiram Morse, who I have called a malingerer & worse, liked it least. "This is dog's duty," he muttered, & often. "To send us into the heart of the Confederacy in the middle of the night! Do they want us dead, truly?"

I should, as my duty as corporal requires, have struck him & made him silent but it was good old Bill who saved me from such an unwelcome task. "Maybe you'd like to ride back to camp & ask our Colonel that question," he whispered. "I'm sure he'd love to hear your thoughts."

—THE STATEMENT OF ALVA GRIEST

5.

The next morning Caxton was finally getting some sleep when sunlight flooded into the room and burned her cheek. She tried to roll away from it but the heat and light followed her. She clenched her eyes tight and grabbed hard at her pillow.

Something soft and feathery brushed across her mouth. Caxton nearly screamed as she bolted upright, her eyelids flashing open.

"Time to get up, beautiful," Clara said. She had a white rose in her small hand and she'd been running its delicate petals across Laura's lips.

Caxton took a deep breath and forced a smile. After a tense moment Clara's face turned up with a wry grin. Clara had already showered, and her wet hair hung in spiky bangs across her forehead. She was wearing her uniform shirt and not much else.

"Too much, so early?" Clara asked. Her eyes were bright. She held out the rose and Laura took it. Then she picked up a glass of orange juice from the bedside table and held that out, too.

Caxton forced herself to calm down, to push away the darkness of the night. There had been bad dreams, as always. She was, over time, learning ways to forget them when she woke up. Clara had learned ways to help.

"Just perfect," Caxton said. She drained half the glass of juice. "What time is it?"

"Almost eight. I have to go." Clara was a police photographer for the sheriff's department in Lancaster County. It was nearly an hour's commute from the house they shared near Harrisburg. Caxton had been trying to convince Clara for months to join the state police so they could work out of the same building, but so far she had resisted.

Caxton drank her juice while Clara finished getting dressed. "I have to get moving, too," she said.

Clara kissed her on the cheek. "Call me if you want to meet for lunch, okay?"

And with that she left. Caxton padded into the kitchen, the floor freezing cold against her bare feet, and watched through the window as Clara drove away in her unmarked Crown Victoria. She craned her neck, leaning hard on the sink, to catch an extra little moment. Then Clara was really gone, and Caxton was all alone.

She didn't waste much time getting ready. She had come to not like her own house when there was no one else in it. Some very bad things had happened there, and she was a little surprised it wasn't actually haunted.

Deanna, Caxton's lover before Clara, had died there. Not right away. It had been ugly, and Caxton herself had been involved in a very bad way. She had inherited the house and her car from Deanna, but the dead woman's legacy went a lot deeper than that. It threatened to destroy her mind every night. After moving in, Clara had redecorated the place completely, but the velvet curtains and the hanging strands of lights shaped to look like chili peppers only went so far.

She took a long shower, which felt very good. She ran a comb through her short hair and brushed her teeth. She ran a wet washcloth over her face and smeared on deodorant. Back in the bedroom she pulled on black dress slacks, a white button-down man's shirt, and her best knit tie. Standard dress for criminal investigations and not too aggressively butch. It looked cold outside, appropriately cold for the season, so she grabbed a knee-length black coat and rushed outside to feed the dogs.

Her greyhounds were excited to see her, as usual, and started singing as soon as she pulled open the door of their heated kennel. Fifi, her newest acquisition, had to lick her hand for a long time before she would allow Caxton to change her water. The dog had been abused at her former home and she still didn't trust anyone, even if they were carrying treats.

The dogs all wanted to play, to get out and run, but she didn't have time. Food and water supplied, a little love spread around the three dogs in the kennel, she moved on. In the driveway she popped open the door of her Mazda and climbed inside.

She took out her BlackBerry and scrolled through her email. After yesterday's shooting she was on medical leave from work, but there was still something she had to do. She'd been putting it off—frankly, she'd been avoiding it in hopes that it would just go away. It wasn't exactly something she would enjoy, but it was important. She could go and visit a crippled old man to whom she owed her life several times over.

Jameson Arkeley had been her mentor, once, or at least she had wanted him to play that role. She'd been useful to him in his crusade to drive vampires to extinction. She'd worked with him closely and as a result terrible, truly horrible things had happened to her life. A year later she was just starting to recover from them.

He'd been badly injured back then, so much so that he had been forced to retire from the U.S. Marshals Service. He'd been in the hospital for months having his battered body put back together. Caxton had tried to visit him once, only to be told he didn't want to see her. That seemed harsh, but not surprising. He was a tough old bastard and he didn't waste a lot of time on sentimentality. Since then she hadn't seen him or heard from him. Then out of nowhere he had emailed her, asking her to come and see him at a hotel in Hanover. There was no other information in the email, just a request for her presence.

Now seemed like the perfect opportunity. She took the car out onto the highway and headed south, down toward the border with Maryland. It was a good hour's drive, but felt longer. Back when she'd worked on the highway patrol she had thought nothing of being in a car for eight hours a day, driving endless distances up and down the Turnpike. In one short year she'd lost that, and now an hour's drive seemed to take forever.

In Hanover she pulled into the lot of a Hampton Inn and walked into the lobby. A blue-vested clerk at the reception desk smiled broadly as she walked up and leaned on his counter. "Hi," she said, "I'm—"

"Officer Caxton, you don't need to introduce yourself," he said. "I'm a huge fan."

Caxton smiled but couldn't contain a little sigh. Another fan of the TV movie. They all seemed to think that she'd personally had something to do with the production. She hadn't even seen any money out of it, much less worked on the set. She could barely watch it, herself, because it brought back too many memories.

"Mr. Arkeley is expecting you, of course," the clerk told her. "Isn't he great?"

"Are we talking about Jameson Arkeley?" She couldn't imagine anyone calling the grizzled old vampire killer "great." It just didn't fit.

The clerk nodded, though. "Just exactly like they showed him. I remember thinking when I watched the movie that nobody could be that big a jerk, that they must have broadened his character, but—well. I suppose I don't need to tell you. He's in room 112. Could you just sign this?"

"Sure," she said, and looked down, expecting to see a guest registry. Instead the clerk held out a copy of the DVD release of *Teeth: The Pennsylvania Vampire Killings*. Underneath the title was a picture of the actress who had played Caxton. Nearly a perfect match, except the woman on the cover had blue eyes and bright red lipstick. It looked ridiculous, since she was also wearing a state trooper's uniform and shooting a giant pistol from the hip.

Caxton shook her head a little but took the pen the clerk offered and scribbled her name across the picture. Another name was already inscribed near the bottom. It was Arkeley's signature, an almost angry-looking letter *A* followed by a simple dash. She wondered how many times the clerk had been forced to ask before Arkeley had consented to that.

"You," the clerk said, "have just made my day. If you guys need anything, complimentary room service, free cable, whatever, just call this desk and ask for Frank, okay?"

"Okay," she said, and handed him the DVD. Then she turned and headed down a short hallway to the guest rooms. Room 112 was near the end, across from the laundry room. She knocked lightly on the door and then stood back, her hands in her pockets. She would stay an hour, she told herself. No more than that.

The door opened and Arkeley looked out at her. She almost gasped, but covered her shock in time. He had changed considerably since the last time she'd seen him. Back then he was in his early sixties but looked eighty. Killing vampires had left him wizened and with a face so full of wrinkles that his eyes seemed to get lost in the folds.

Now he looked ghastly. The undead servants of the teen-aged vampire Kevin Scapegrace had left their mark on him, and even a year later silvery scars covered most of the left half of his face. His left eyelid drooped low over the eye and the left half of his mouth was a J-shaped mass of scar tissue. His buzzed hair was missing in a big swath across the top of his head, where a reddish fissure dug through his scalp.

She looked down, away from his face, but that was almost worse. His left hand was a club of flesh with no fingers. Scapegrace himself had bitten them off, she remembered. Just grabbed them with his teeth and tore them right off. She'd always imagined that they could have been reattached. Apparently she'd been wrong.

The worst change to his appearance, though, didn't stem from his injuries or his scars. It came from time, and distance. She remembered him, whenever she did think of him, as a giant of a man. He'd been considerably taller than her and much broader through the shoulders. Or at least she remembered him that way. The man standing before her was a little old man, a badly, horribly injured little old man who couldn't have fought off a teenaged delinquent, much less a rapacious vampire. It seemed impossible that this was the same man she'd once known. Then he opened his mouth and proved her wrong.

"Too long, Trooper," he said. "You took too damned long getting here. It might already be too late."

"I was busy," she said, almost reflexively. She softened a little and tried greeting him again. "Nice to see you, too, Jameson," she said, and followed him into the hotel room.

6.

It was uneasy work to cross those fields. There was but little moon, & yet starlight was enough to see by. All of us had the fear, for this was the land of partisans and rangers, who would shoot a man's back should he step away from his fellows & only long enough to heed the call of nature. At the least we could see something. Away from the line & the endless dust of marching the air was almost preternaturally clear. Perhaps that is how Eben Nudd spotted the white demon so easily, though it took pains to hide itself.

Nudd grabbed my arm, without warning, & I nearly jumped. In the darkness every motion was an enemy, & every sound the hoofbeats of a regiment of Reb cavalry. Nudd did not call out, though, or make any sign. He lifted one finger & pointed toward a stand of trees at perhaps twenty-five yards.

For myself I saw but a certain pallor in those woods, at least at first, like a snake of mist coiled up. I squatted down & squinted & thought maybe I saw a pair of eyes there, like the last embers of a campfire. I did not care for their expression. "Is that man watching us?" I asked Eben Nudd, my voice a barest exhalation of air.

"Ayup," he said, which I sometimes think is half of his vocabulary. Eben Nudd is the very type of a downeaster, formerly a lobsterman, with a craggy face like leather & eyes as pale & clear as morning dew, & he was born, it sometimes seems, with no passion in his breast at all. Many times on many battlefields his coldness had served us well & I trusted him now, even when I liked not what he had to say. "Longer than we seen him, I figger."

—THE STATEMENT OF ALVA GRIEST

7.

Arkeley moved slowly, one leg dragging behind the other. Caxton shuffled along behind him as respectfully as she could. Once he turned to glare back at her, but he said nothing. With a deep grunt he dropped to sit on the edge of a single bed and then ran his good hand over his face as if he were wiping away sweat.

"How have you been?" she asked. "How's your family? Have you seen them much lately?" He had a wife and two children, she knew, though she'd never met them. She believed he was estranged from his family, though not in any kind of dramatic way. He had just become so obsessed with his work that they had fallen by the wayside, immaterial to what he considered important.

"Everyone's fine." She expected him to say something more but he didn't.

She glanced around the room. She'd been trained to always make a note of her surroundings when she entered a new place, and though she didn't expect to find any criminals lurking in the corners, she did get a big surprise. The room was nice enough, a small double furnished tastefully though cheaply. There was a big television in a cabinet on one wall, an open closet with a pair of suits hanging from its rack. A door at the far end of the room led to a darkened bathroom. A thin muslin curtain had been drawn across the windows, leaving the room in semidarkness. Arkeley's suitcase stood open and mostly packed on the other bed. Beyond that bed, near the windows, two metal luggage stands had been erected. Balanced on top of them stood a simple wooden coffin.

Caxton's guts clenched at the sight of it. She had no doubt that it was occupied.

The coffin could belong only to one creature, the vampire who had destroyed Caxton's life and turned every one of her nights into a parade of nightmares. Justinia Malvern, a three-hundred-year-old monster with a pedigree of cunning and deceit.

Even a year later Caxton felt the urge to go over to the coffin, throw back the lid, and tear out Malvern's heart. It was daytime, and she knew that if she did open the casket she would find little but bones and maggots in there. Even by night the vampire was a decrepit wreck, a rotten body with one eye and little else but a diabolical will to continue her blighted existence. Like all vampires she was immortal, but she required blood to maintain her bodily health. The older a vampire got the more blood they needed every night just to be able to walk. A long, long time ago Malvern had passed the point where she could hunt for herself, and now she was doomed to an eternity in her coffin, barely able to move at all. If she could get enough blood—and she would need gallons of it every night—she could have revivified, but Arkeley had made sure that never happened.

Caxton walked over and set her hand on the coffin. The wood was cold as ice, and her skin prickled when it got too close. Malvern, like all vampires, was an unnatural freak, something that shouldn't exist. She warped reality around herself, and every living thing recognized the wrongness, the unclean nature of her. Maggots didn't seem to mind, but dogs and horses would go crazy if she came close to them. Caxton's urge to destroy her was a perfectly rational reaction. Yet if she did it, if she ended so much trouble then and there, she knew she would go to jail. Malvern was a mastermind of vampires, a schemer and conspirator, but she had never harmed an American citizen as far as anyone could prove. The courts had decided after long deliberation that she was still human and still deserving of the protection of the law. Arkeley had spent much of his adult life fighting that ruling and trying to get a warrant for her execution. He had so far failed at every turn.

"Jesus," Caxton said. "You're traveling with her?"

"After the debacle at Arabella Furnace I decided I didn't trust her with anyone else." Arkeley nodded at the coffin and then at a laptop computer set on the nightstand next to it.

Caxton opened the lid of the laptop and watched the screen flicker to life. A mostly blank window opened, a document created by a word processor. Malvern was too far decayed to be able to talk or even gesture much, but she could hunt and peck on a computer keyboard, sometimes taking hours to tap out a few characters. If left alone all night with the computer sometimes she tried to communicate with the world outside her coffin. It was rare that she had anything worthwhile to say—mostly she wasted her time on idle threats and dark imprecations. The message Caxton found on the screen was a little more cryptic than usual:

comformeh

"Any idea what this means?" Caxton asked Arkeley.

He shook his head. "It's not any language I recognize. I think she may have reached the point where she can't even form words anymore and she's just stabbing at random keys."

Caxton shoved her hands back in her pockets. She felt vaguely ill, as if the air in the room had been tainted.

She turned to look at him with sad eyes. She expected to find him combative and scolding, but instead he took her glance as a spur to action. He straightened up and his eyes positively glowed. He fastened the top button of his shirt with one hand and struggled into a jacket. Then he scuttled up off the bed and took a pair of black leather gloves from out of his suitcase. With his good hand and then with his teeth he pulled them on. One glove covered the lump of flesh at the end of his left arm. The fingers of that glove splayed out pointlessly, but at least they looked somewhat normal.

"Why didn't you get a prosthetic?" she asked.

"Too much nerve damage. Now, if you're done playing nurse, we need to get started," he told her. "There's much work to be done and we've already wasted two crucial days because apparently you don't check your email anymore. I need you to call your captain and tell him you'll be working on a new case for an indefinite time period. I'm sure they'll understand in Harrisburg and if they don't, I really don't care. I still have enough clout to get you reassigned as necessary."

"No," she said.

He stared at her, his eyes frozen and unblinking. "No," he repeated. "That's not acceptable."

"I helped you once. I was nearly killed. People I cared about were . . . killed." She closed her eyes and let a wave of grief pass through her. When it had receded she looked at him again. "That ought to be enough."

"It's never over," he told her.

"No? We killed all the vampires. Except her, of course. I've moved on. I've got a real job, doing real police work now."

"And how is that working out?" he asked. "I was a real cop once, you'll remember. I know what that's like. It's pointless. You chase around the same criminals you chased around the year before. You put them away for a while and then they get out and they repeat the same squalid little crimes. This is different. It's far more important."

Arkeley's life had been taken over by the vampires. Every minute of his day he spent thinking about them, planning their destruction. She couldn't let herself get sucked in like that. "What I do is important, too," she said. She didn't want to go into the details. She didn't want to say what she was really thinking. Her first raid might not have gone how she'd hoped, but she had survived it. When she was down and hurt people had worked to save her. He would never have dragged her out of the line of fire, she knew. He would have pushed her further into danger. Was her resistance to his plea based solely on fear? Was she fighting him just because she didn't want to get killed? She said, half trying to convince herself, "I protect the people of this state. I'm working drug law enforcement right now, keeping methamphetamines away from schoolkids."

He shook his head. "Forget about that. When you hear what I've found you'll—"

She interrupted him. "I don't want to know."

He looked as if he couldn't understand what she was saying.

Caxton sighed, deep and long. She had no idea what he wanted from her, but she knew she wanted no part of it. "I'm glad you're doing okay, and I'm sure whatever's got you so worked up is important, really," she said. "But I don't have time to help you right now."

"You don't? Something else more important calling for your attention?" he asked. "Maybe you need to spend more time with your girlfriend? One of your dogs got sick? Well, that's too bad. You're needed elsewhere right now. In Gettysburg, to be exact. You're driving."

"No," she said.

"No?"

The word lost all meaning when he repeated it like that. It would be easy to raise her hands in surrender and say yes instead—as she always had before. But she was a normal person now. If she wanted to stay normal, she had to stay strong.

He grimaced horribly and asked, "Why on earth not? You know me, Trooper. You know I don't waste my time on trivialities. If I say this is important you should know by now that it is absolutely crucial."

"Yeah, well," she said, but couldn't, for a moment, finish that thought. He was right—she knew he was right. He wouldn't have summoned her just to catch up on old times. He had something for her to do, and it was probably something dangerous.

"I need you right now. I need you to drive me to Gettysburg today."

She could say no to him. She was sure that she had the strength to do it. He was a weak old man now. Yet she felt like she had to give him something. "I'll tell you what," she said. "I'll give you a ride. But that's all."

He frowned but he didn't fight her. She knew him well enough to realize that was a bad sign, but she didn't know how to react. "Very well. Let me get my coat." He struggled as he walked around the side of the bed toward the closet.

"What about her?" Caxton asked, looking at the coffin.

"As long as I'm back by nightfall she shouldn't be any trouble," he said.

8.

The life of a spymaster for the War Department had its consolations. For one thing, I was appointed a horse to ride, while it seemed every other man in the world must walk. All that day I rode while the Army of the Potomac moved past me in a never-ending line, a human chain that stretched as far south as vision permitted, and went away from me to the north just as far. The dust they stirred up with their boots made a pall that rose on the air and hung there, like some spirit host of Araby made of sand. All day they tramped by, with calls and halloos from the drivers of the mule trains, and some singing, though not much.

This was just after Chancellorsville, when all hope seemed vain. Though outnumbered, Lee had trounced us yet again without breaking a sweat. He seemed invincible; surely that was the common belief. The Union has never known a darker day. The war had turned against us and even I believed the dream of a unified Union was doomed. Perhaps this helps explain what we did, and what we dared.

I was headed deep into Maryland, and away from Virginia, for which I was glad. I'd learned much from my contacts behind the lines, and needed promptly to report. From some runaway slaves who'd been attached to Jeb Stuart's supply lines, I'd heard that Lee was moving again, and this time the enemy was headed north.

A very charming Southern belle, who was in secret a hater of slavery, had told me even more. Lee was headed for Pennsylvania. For the first time he intended to bring the war to us, to the North. Already the democrats in Congress were howling for an end to this war. Well, it looked as if they might get it, but on Jeff Davis's terms.

—THE PAPERS OF WILLIAM PITTENGER

9.

She followed him out to the parking lot. The clerk at the front desk gave them a cheery wave, which Arkeley completely ignored. The old Fed shoved himself into her little Mazda and in a minute they were off. It wasn't a long drive to Gettysburg—it was the next town over from Hanover. Though they didn't talk any more along the way, the atmosphere in the car never got too unbearable. She was just doing a favor for an old friend, she told herself. Well, *friend* was probably the wrong word.

He cleared his throat as they neared Gettysburg, but only to give her directions. "It's on the far side of town," he said.

She drove through the center of Gettysburg, a town given over almost entirely to history. She knew very little about the Civil War, but like most kids raised in central Pennsylvania she'd been dragged through Gettysburg on class trips as a child, so she knew it had been the location of a particularly important battle, the turning point of the war. Now it was a tourist destination.

Not necessarily a tourist *trap*, though. She had seen plenty of those: soulless little towns comprised entirely of T-shirt shops and gaudy ice cream parlors. Instead Gettysburg was a well-preserved Victorian town, full of brick buildings with slate roofs that hadn't changed much in a hundred and forty years. It was almost tasteful—at least at its center. She drove through a traffic circle called Lincoln Square, past small museums and antiques shops, banks, and hotels. The town was crowded with tourists, families with herds of children carrying plastic replicas of Civil War–era rifles and felt forage caps with plastic brims. The real things were in evidence as well, in some profusion: it seemed every corner had at least one reenactor in blue or gray, clad in authentic but itchy-looking uniforms, most of them with beards and long sideburns.

She sighed as she stopped at a crosswalk to let a gaggle of schoolchildren pass. "Okay," she said. "I'll bite."

"Hmm?" he asked.

"What's here?" she asked. "What kind of horror could there possibly be in a place like this?"

He shifted painfully in his seat. "Something old. I got a call a couple days ago from a student at the college here. An archaeologist was digging up some old Civil War ruins and found some evidence of vampire activity."

"No," Caxton exhaled, "we got them all!"

He waved one impatient hand at her. "Old vampire activity," he said. "More than a century old. They found the bones of a number of vampires, still in their coffins. It's almost certainly nothing."

"But you won't rest easy until you check it out," she said.

"I never rest easy," he told her. It wasn't what she wanted to hear. She didn't want to have anything in common with him, not anymore.

Caxton stared straight ahead at the crosswalk, ready to get moving again. Eventually some adults herded up the children and moved them on. They drove in silence until she'd reached the far end of town. He had her turn off into the military park, up to the top of Seminary Ridge, a zone of quiet green hills studded everywhere by endless monuments—obelisks, arches, huge marble statues. There were fewer tourists out that way but a lot more reenactors, some of them having set up elaborate period-accurate tent camps. They drilled in formation or stood around polishing cannon and mortars that looked like they could actually be fired. Arkeley told her to turn off on a poorly marked gravel road, and the car rumbled along for about half a mile into a thick clump of trees. Three cars, late-model cheap Japanese sedans, sat in a crook of the road, and a foot trail led deeper into the woods. Caxton pulled up beside a red Nissan Sentra and switched off the ignition. She had no idea where she was or what Arkeley wanted there, and she told herself she didn't care.

He cleared his throat again. "Aren't you going to take off your seat belt?" he asked.

"No," she told him. "I'm not staying."

"Alright," he told her. "If you're determined to be unhelpful, so be it. Maybe you'll do me one last favor, though." He reached into his inside jacket pocket and drew out a long length of rumpled knit cloth. It was soon revealed as a necktie that was probably twenty-five years old. "There is a way to tie one of these with only one hand, but I haven't mastered it yet."

She squinted at him. Did he really want her to tie it on for him? Did he really want her to touch him? It would certainly be a first.

"I've never gone into an official interview in my life where I wasn't properly dressed," he explained. "I'm not allowed to wear my badge anymore, but I can at least look like a cop."

She stared at him for a long time. Jameson Arkeley, vampire

killer emeritus, needed somebody else to tie his tie. She fought back the wave of bitter sadness that gave her but she couldn't quite swallow her pity.

"Alright," she said. She unfastened her seat belt. It was easy enough to get the tie on him. She'd tied Clara's tie plenty of times. When the knot was tight enough for him he grunted in satisfaction.

"Good. Now. Please help me get out of the car."

She could hardly refuse him that. She got out of the car and gave him a hand climbing out of his seat and suddenly they were both standing there, just like they used to. Like partners.

"Tell me, honestly, that you aren't even curious," he said, looking at the trail.

She started to do just that. The words didn't come easily, though.

"Tell me you don't even want to take a look. What do you have to do today that is so much more important than this?" he asked.

She would have said no just on principle. She would have refused. But he was right—she was curious, even though her life wasn't about vampires anymore. Especially not their moldering bones. He was right about another thing, too. She had nothing else to do.

Arkeley's body might be ruined, but he still knew how to push her buttons. Then and there she knew she had to at least take a look.

She locked up the car and together they headed down the trail. It ran through a field of wildly profuse grass for about two hundred yards, then ended in a simple campsite with a cluster of nylon tents and a big fire ring. There were no reenactors around, but a man in a hooded sweatshirt and jeans was waiting for them. He shook Arkeley's hand eagerly enough, then turned and smiled at Caxton as if he was waiting to be introduced.

"Trooper, meet Jeff Montrose. He's from the archaeology department of Gettysburg College."

Caxton raised an eyebrow, but held out a hand for Montrose to shake. He was of average height, and maybe a little pudgy. His brown hair was thinning on top and he had a long and elaborate goatee that he had dyed so blond it was almost white. There was something weird about his eyes, she thought, which worried her—but then she realized he was just wearing eyeliner. "Civil War Era Studies is what we're calling it, but we get our hands dirty whenever we can."

"Hi," she said. His appearance didn't bother her, but it wasn't what she expected from an archaeologist. He didn't recognize her or ask her for her autograph, which was one thing in his favor. "Are you a professor?" she asked. She'd never finished college, but she didn't remember her professors wearing eye makeup.

"A grad student. Running Wolf's technically in charge here, but he had classes all day, so he asked me to help you out."

"Who's Running Wolf?" she asked, confused.

He laughed. "Sorry. That's what we call Professor Geistdoerfer. He got the name because he jogs through campus every day. He's a fixture around here—I forget sometimes that people in the real world might not know him. The whole college does." Montrose could not mask the boyish enthusiasm on his face, though every time he looked over at Arkeley he stopped smiling, as if that scarred face had reminded him this was a police investigation. "I've sent all the diggers out for lunch, so we have the place to ourselves." He turned and walked to the largest of the tents and lifted its flap. "This is so exciting. We'd really like to get back to work, so if you don't mind, I think I'll just show you what we've got."

The three of them entered the tent, an enclosed space maybe twenty feet by ten. Long tables had been set up inside and covered with white paper. Muddy-looking bits of metal and deformed white bullets were laid out for inspection, with handwritten notes penciled around them. They didn't interest her as much as the hole in the ground in the middle of the tent. A wide pit had been carved out of the earth there with a bright yellow ladder leading down into the ground. The walls of the pit had been shored up with timbers. In some places the pit had been excavated down to the level of wooden floorboards. Had it been the cellar of a house long since demolished?

Montrose went down first without any ceremony. Caxton followed and then Arkeley struggled his way down. He had trouble on the ladder, but he didn't complain and he brushed her hands away whenever she tried to help him.

Montrose gestured at the pit around them. It was about six feet deep and Caxton couldn't really see out. A weird earthy smell made her eyes water. "We found this magazine site years ago but just now got the approval to open it up. The Park Service doesn't care much for relic hunting, even when it's done the right way. Too many people came through here with metal detectors over the years, digging up sacred soil." He shrugged. "I figure that the best way to honor history is to learn about it, but I guess not everybody agrees with me. This was a Confederate powder magazine originally, a place where they stored barrels of gunpowder for the cannon. They kept them underground where it was cool and where if they blew up accidentally nobody would get hurt. There are magazines like this all over Gettysburg, most of them constructed very quickly and then filled in with earth after they were no longer needed. Sometimes you find pieces of barrels or maybe some broken hardware from a winch or a pulley, but that's about it. This wasn't supposed to be a particularly interesting dig, but you always look, just in case."

He headed over to the far end of the pit and Caxton saw another ladder there, leading farther down into the earth. Electric light streamed up from a hole cut in the floorboards.

"After the Battle of Gettysburg they intentionally blew it up. That's not too surprising—the Confederates tore out of here in a real hurry when they realized they'd lost the battle, and they didn't want the Union to get the powder they left behind. Except now we think they might have had another reason, as well." He moved to the second ladder and crouched down as if to peer inside. "We were almost done here. We found some artifacts and maybe we could have gotten a paper out of this place in one of the lesser journals. I think we were all glad to be done so we could move on to more interesting stuff. Then one of my fellow students—Marcy Jackson is her name," he said, waiting for Caxton to write it down, "told Professor Geistdoerfer that she thought the floor here sounded hollow. You're not supposed to ruin the integrity of a site by digging just because somebody had a hunch but like I said, this place wasn't very important. So Marcy took a chance."

He headed down the ladder. Caxton started to follow but stopped when she saw Arkeley leaning on a support beam and looking bored. "Aren't you coming?" she asked.

"In this condition I'll never get down there," he told her, grimacing as he looked down at his stiff legs.

She nodded and turned to head down the ladder. This, then, was the real reason he'd talked her into coming with him. How much had it cost him to admit that he couldn't do this alone?

The ladder went down about fifteen feet. At the bottom Caxton found herself in a large natural cavern, maybe a hundred feet from end to end and twenty-five feet wide. There were caves like it all over the Commonwealth, but this one was unlike the tourist caves Caxton had visited. Electric lights hung from the ceiling on thick cables, though they were clearly put there recently by the archaeologists. The cavern's walls were rough and the ceiling was thick with stalactites. The floor was almost invisible. Almost every square inch of the space had been filled with coffins.

10.

It is with some abruptness I break the flow of my narrative, but it cannot match the speed with which things happened then. There was some shooting, even as John Tyler's neck was torn open by invisible claws. Eben Nudd dropped to a crouch, & dug inside his pack, while Hiram Morse pushed past me, running for the hills like the Yellow Dog we'd always thought him to be.

John Tyler had been an undistinguished soldier but he hardly deserved to lose his life in such a way. The pale phantom I'd seen in the woods was at his throat, his, or rather its, mouth incarnadine & buried in the wound. I raised my own weapon, & knowing I'd never have time to load a shot, I charged with my bayonet, & stabbed the demon ruthlessly again & again, but to no effect. Eben Nudd came up behind me with something in his hand, some small piece of wood, & I saw it was a crucifix of the kind some Roman Catholics carry. He thrust this holy symbol forward as if it were a firebrand, chanting a simple prayer the whole time, his eyes blazing as if he would turn back the total Host of Hell.

The beast dropped John Tyler on the ground, & stepped forward, & grabbed the cross from Eben Nudd's hand. The downeaster looked surprised, & that alone shocked me. With one hand the demon crushed the whittled Christ into pieces, & cast them over his shoulder. I raised my weapon again but before I could strike the demon had dissolved, once more, into shadows & was gone.

—THE STATEMENT OF ALVA GRIEST

11.

Caxton tried to breathe calmly. The electric bulbs overhead only dimly lit the cavern, but it was still daytime. There was no immediate danger of the coffins opening, lid after lid, and death climbing out.

"Isn't this awesome?" Montrose asked her.

She shook her head in incomprehension.

"I love this stuff," he said. "Ghosts and vampires and things that go bump in the night. It's why I wanted to study this era in the first place—the nineteenth century was just so morbid. I pay for my tuition by giving ghost tours of the town. I have this velvet cape I wear, you know? And I tell people scary stories for tips. I never in a million years thought I'd see the real thing."

"Ghost tours," she said, distractedly. She was not a big fan of ghosts, but at least they couldn't hurt you physically. Vampires were another story. "Jesus."

She moved down the ranks of coffins. She knelt down and drifted her hand over the top of one. A lumpy stalagmite had grown on its lid where water dripping from above had left mineral deposits over the years. Her hand felt cold and clammy as it passed over the weathered wood of the lid, and she felt her stomach churn as she stepped closer. It wasn't like when she'd approached Malvern's coffin back in the hotel room, however. The feeling wasn't as strong. This felt more like an echo of evil that had passed by long ago.

"You must know the history of this town pretty well," she said. "You ever hear any stories about vampires at the Battle of Gettysburg?"

He shook his head. "No, nothing like that."

"I take it this is the first time anyone's found a vampire crypt here, then."

He laughed at the idea. "Yes, and we never expected to. Most of the battlefield's been played out for decades. You don't expect to find anything anymore except the occasional bullet or maybe the tin badge off some dead guy's hat. There aren't a lot of mysteries left here, which is what makes this so incredible."

She had to open the coffin. She had to see what was inside. She didn't want to—she had to. There were so many of them. If there were vampires in all of the coffins, what could they possibly do? How could they possibly fight back? She did a quick count. The coffins were laid out in long, neat rows, five of them across and ten . . . fifteen . . . twenty deep. That made an even hundred. A hundred vampires wouldn't just be a problem. They would be an army. An army of blood-fueled killing machines.

A year earlier Caxton had helped Arkeley destroy four vampires and it had cost both of them dearly. It had destroyed his body and nearly taken her sanity. She had done things—horrible things—that she tried to never think about, but that she relived endlessly in her dreams. She had been infected with the vampiric curse. She had nearly become one of them herself. The four vampires had done so much evil in just a few short days while Arkeley had played a deadly game of catch-up, following them from one bloodbath to another, walking right into the fiendish traps they left for him, with Caxton held out like squirming bait for them the whole time.

Four—just four—had destroyed both their lives. A hundred vampires would have torn them to pieces without blinking.

A wave of unreality passed through her, a feeling of sheer impossibility. This couldn't be happening. It might be a dream or some kind of hallucination. She counted the coffins again and got the same number.

"Isn't it just gorgeous? Professor Geistdoerfer made sure he was the first one down here," Montrose said, looking at her sheepishly. "He wanted to make sure it was his name at the top of the paper when he wrote this place up. I'm just glad to be part of this—I love a good juicy mystery."

She stared at him. What was he babbling about? Did he even know what a real living vampire was capable of? Most people didn't. Most people seemed to think they were like paler versions of Romantic poets. That they dressed in lace shirts and sipped red wine. That they would deign, from time to time, to nibble at somebody's neck with delicate little fangs.

She grasped the edge of the nearest coffin lid. It felt like ice in her hands. She lifted and heaved and the battered old wood started to give way.

"Hey! You can't do that! That has to be fully cataloged before we open it up."

She grunted and threw the lid back on its rusted hinges. The lid shrieked and the metal hardware snapped. With a clatter that echoed around the cavern the lid smashed to the floor. Caxton leaned over the open coffin and stared down at its contents.

A skull looked back at her, its mouth open in a dreadful grin. The eye sockets and cheekbones looked mostly human, but the mouth was filled with sharp triangular teeth lined up in deep rows. Much like the teeth of a shark. Caxton had seen such teeth before, seen what they were capable of. A vampire could tear a man's arm off at the socket with one bite. With another it could take his head. Vampires, real vampires, didn't nibble on the necks of nubile young virgins. They tore people to pieces and sucked blood out of the chunks.

The lower jaw had fallen away from the rest of the skull and dropped to one side. Caxton glanced down and saw the rest of the bones lying jumbled in the bottom of the coffin, only approximately in the positions they'd once held. She grabbed at the intact rib cage and lifted it up even as Montrose grabbed at her arms and tried to pull her away.

"What the hell do you think you're doing? That's College property!"

She glared at him. She was trained in hand-to-hand combat and could easily have broken his wrists to get free of his grasp, but it didn't come to that. When he saw the look in her eyes he took an involuntary step back. She didn't have to work hard to summon up real, blistering anger. She had only to think about Malvern and her brood.

He tried to match her withering gaze, but didn't have it in him. Eventually he looked away, his eyes darting to the left, and she knew he wouldn't interfere again. She reached back into the coffin and lifted the rib cage once more. She reached between the cold bones, her fingers tracing the lines of the sternum and the xiphoid process, tapping on the knobby vertebrae. She didn't find what she was looking for.

Oh, thank God, she thought, and let out a long relieved sigh.

The heart was missing.

Vampires possessed many gifts the living could not match. They were stronger, much faster, and they were nearly invulnerable to physical damage. If you cut a vampire's arm off he could grow a new one while you watched. If you fired an entire clip of bullets into his face he would just laugh and hold you down while his teeth and eyes grew back. The heart of a vampire was its only weak spot. It took blood, the stolen blood of humans, to regrow damaged tissues and heal those injuries, and without a heart a vampire could not regenerate. When the heart was destroyed the vampire was dead.

Whoever had buried so many vampires under Gettysburg had been smart enough to make sure they stayed buried.

In the cold cavern her relief felt like warmth spreading through her numb fingers and toes. It felt like coming back to life, to reality, like waking up from a nightmare. She would need to check every coffin, of course, defile every piece of College property in the cavern, because she had to make sure. But it looked like the world was safe again.

Thank God.

She rubbed at her face with her hands. Her whole body tingled with adrenaline. Slowly she stood up straight and looked at Montrose again.

"Listen," he said, "I've tried to be helpful here. But I really do need to bring my people back and start the real work of cataloging this place and—"

Caxton held up one hand. "We won't keep you much longer. I just have to make sure these bodies are truly dead. That means looking at all of them." She walked down one of the rows, holding out her hand over each of the coffins she passed. Each of them gave her the same cold feeling she'd gotten from the first. It seemed vampire bones were unnatural even in true death. She wondered if Montrose could feel it or if it was something only she could perceive. "I'll try to be gentler with the other ones."

Something occurred to her then. She looked back and counted coffins, then looked to either side. Four of the rows had twenty coffins each. The row she was looking at was short a coffin. It had only nineteen.

"There are ninety-nine coffins here," she said. It irked her, but just a little. Why weren't there an even hundred? Of course she had no idea why the coffins were there in the first place, or how many vampires there had once been. It just seemed a little odd. "I count ninety-nine."

"Ninety-nine intact, yeah," Montrose said. He waved her over to the other side of the cavern. She stepped over a coffin to reach him and couldn't help but feel a little jolt of fear that it would open as she passed overhead and that the skeleton inside would rear up to grab her. She walked over to meet him and looked down at the end of the row. There had been another coffin there at some time, for an even hundred. Now there was just a pile of broken wood. The lid was reduced nearly to splinters, while the sides of the coffin looked as if they'd been smashed apart with a sledgehammer. There were no bones inside, nor any sign of occupation. The wood did not register cold when she ran her hand over it.

"Did you find it like this?" she asked.

He nodded. "We were surprised we didn't find more of them like it. If this place really is a hundred and forty-one years old, you'd expect a lot more damage over time. Normally with a big tomb like this you find signs of animals breaking in and gnawing at the bones, or at the very least you'd think groundwater would have gotten in at some point and flooded the chamber. We think that's probably what happened to this one."

"If animals had come for the bones, wouldn't you have found chewed-up fragments of them, or something?" she asked.

He shrugged once more. "This is an inexact science a lot of the time. If you have a better explanation I'd love to hear it."

Caxton thought she might have another explanation. Certainly not a better one. But no, it was impossible. Even if one of the vampires had been buried with his heart intact he wouldn't have had the strength left after so much time to break his way out of the coffin. He wouldn't have had the strength to sit up.

There was another possibility, but it didn't merit thinking about. That someone else might have come down into the cavern and removed one of the skeletons. But why on earth would anyone do that?

She didn't like thinking about the possibilities. She didn't like that a skeleton was missing. Still, she had work to do—she had to check the intact coffins. Worrying could wait until that was done.

12.

Hiram Morse had run off in the scuffle, & John Tyler was dead. Worst of all, my Bill was gone missing. I sought him everywhere to no avail. I could hardly fit this fact into my head. We had been so close all our lives, & it was rare a day would go by that I had not spoken with him. Much more rare since the war began & we signed on together. My father had forbidden it of me, but Bill had chosen a man's path, & I could do naught but follow. Through battle & cannon & smoke & war we had been together. In but a moment the white demon had changed that.

"Corporal Griest," someone spoke, & I turned to see who it might be. Had it been our enemy returned I would not have flinched. Yet instead it was German Pete who was tugging at my pant leg. His hands were smeared with blood & his face was hard. "John Tyler's dead, Corporal," he told me. "Do we bury him, now?"

I shook my body as if some ghost had possessed me.

"Supposed to head back to the line," Eben Nudd said, reminding me of my duty, & he was right. We were standing picket, my handful of men & I. Our duty was not to engage the enemy, nor to put ourselves in greater danger, but only to return & report.

Yet my Bill was gone! Two years he & I had slept in the same tent, shared the same maggoty meat in camp. Since I was a child he had been the only friend I counted in the wide world.

"Did any man see what happened to Bill?" I asked.

"He's not here," Eben Nudd said, in his fashion. "Might expect him to be dead, too."

"No one saw him get hurt, though." I stared at German Pete, who shook his head in negation. "Then he still lives. We don't leave him here, not with that demon running loose."

"Weren't no demon," Eben Nudd said. I scowled at him but

he showed me the broken pieces of his wooden cross. "No demon can stand the sight of Our Lord."

"That thing was a VAMPIRE," German Pete insisted, "& ye all know it." He spat on the ground, too close, I thought, to where John Tyler lay. "Bill's food for it now as well. A vampire! A Reb vampire, at that."

"We should report," Eben Nudd told me, his face very still.

—THE STATEMENT OF ALVA GRIEST

13.

It took Caxton hours to check all the intact coffins. Her legs grew cramped from squatting down all the time and her arms ached with stirring up the bones, but she didn't want to go back and face Arkeley until the job was complete. As she worked her fear was slowly replaced by boredom. To help pass the time she quizzed Montrose. "How old is this place?" she asked.

Montrose shrugged. "There's no good way to tell without a lot of lab work, but the powder magazine was chemically dated back to 1863. The coffins can't be any later than that. This place definitely hasn't been opened since then."

Caxton nodded. Even if the vampires had still had their hearts intact, there was no way they could have gotten out of their coffins. Vampires theoretically lived forever, but like Justinia Malvern, the older they got the more blood they required just to stand upright, much less to maraud and pillage. Any vampire old enough to have been buried in the cavern would have been far too old to be a danger in the twenty-first century.

"Do you have any idea who put them down here?"

"None. There's no evidence down here that would tell us something like that and I can't find anything in the archives to explain it, either. We opened the cavern three days ago and since then I've been hitting the Internet pretty hard, searching databases of Civil War–era documents. That's just good fieldwork. If you find something like this you want to know everything you can before you start opening things up." He shrugged. "There's no record of this place, though that's hardly surprising."

"Why?"

Montrose shrugged. "This was the nineteenth century we're talking about. People didn't save every email and scrap of correspondence the way we do now. A lot of records from the war were destroyed, either when libraries and archives burned down or when somebody was just cleaning house and threw out tons of old paper."

She finished her search shortly thereafter. Of the ninety-nine skeletons in the tomb not a single one still had its heart. That was something. "Okay," she said. "I don't see any reason why we need to delay your work any further. Give me your phone number in case we have any more questions."

He gave her his info and started up the ladder ahead of her. Before she followed she took one last look back at the cavern. The silence of the place and its long shadows were enough to make it eerie. The perfect stillness of the air inside and the sporadic dripping of water from the ceiling didn't help. It was the skeletons themselves, though, that made the place so creepy. Their combined chill was enough to set her hair on end.

The place was a mystery. How had the skeletons gotten there? Why were they buried in an open space, in individual coffins? Someone had been careful enough to kill the vampires properly. Somebody had been scared enough to seal the place off by detonating a gunpowder magazine on top of it. Why, though, hadn't they gone farther? Why not crush the bones to powder and dump the powder in the sea?

Perhaps some long-dead predecessor of Arkeley, some nineteenth-century vampire hunter, had filled the cavern. Perhaps he had thought the dead deserved a proper burial. Perhaps the hundredth coffin had been placed there as she'd found it, empty and broken. Perhaps there had never been a hundredth vampire.

She knew it wouldn't be that simple.

As she climbed up the ladder Montrose cut the power to the lights below. Caxton froze in place on the rungs and felt the darkness beneath her swell as if the cavern had been holding its breath, waiting for her to leave it in peace.

She wasted no further time getting back up top.

Arkeley waited for her there. "Now are you interested?" he asked.

"I suppose you could say my curiosity is piqued," she admitted, "but I don't think we have anything to worry about. That tomb has been untouched for over a century. How did you even find out about this?" she asked. "Ancient crypts aren't exactly your style."

"One of Geistdoerfer's students wants to be a police officer," he told her. She looked over at the archaeologist, who just shrugged. "That's what she's studying toward, anyway."

Caxton checked her notebook. "Is her name Marcy Jackson?"

Arkeley nodded. "When they opened the first coffin and found a vampire inside she called the Marshals Service and asked to talk to me. I'm officially retired but they still had my number. I've left explicit instructions that I'm to be notified whenever a case like this comes up."

He asked her what she'd thought of the cavern. He grunted his approval when she told him she'd checked all the skeletons and that all the hearts were gone.

"What about the other one?" he asked.

"The empty coffin?" She turned and asked Montrose, "Has anyone been down there other than your team?"

"Of course not," he replied. "And we're all under strict instructions not to talk about it. The professor was very upset with Marcy when she called you in—though of course, we're happy to cooperate with your investigation in any way we can."

Caxton nodded. "And the coffin was empty when you found it."

The grad student concurred.

"That doesn't mean it's always been empty. It doesn't mean there wasn't a vampire inside it at some point," Arkeley insisted.

"Okay, but what of it? You know as well as I do that a vampire buried underground that long with no blood couldn't possibly be active."

He grunted again, less agreeably. "I also know better than to underestimate them."

She sighed, but she'd known it would come to this. Arkeley had spent twenty years of his life chasing down every vampire legend and rumor he could find. He'd turned up real vampires twice in that time—but only because he never tired of the search. He considered his hobby to be vital to the public safety and had frittered away his life with endless investigations. No doubt they had all been crucial, had all been fraught with danger, at least until he'd actually done the legwork and found a cold trail or a long-dead monster who had grown in time into a local myth.

Arkeley had become obsessed a long time ago, and now he had nothing else to occupy his time. She wouldn't let that happen to her. She wouldn't let vampires define her life.

"This is a dead end," she said. "Something bad was here, but that was a long time ago. You should go home. You should call your wife."

"You don't want to open an investigation, then?"

She turned to look right at him. The scars on his face didn't bother her as much as they had before. "I'm not authorized to do that. This isn't my job. It's not even my jurisdiction. I'll put in some calls. I'll alert the proper authorities, get a bulletin out for people to keep their eyes open. Just in case. After that I'm done. Now, come on. I'll give you a ride back to Hanover."

"Don't bother," he said. "Montrose will take me into town and I'll get a bus from there."

"That's ridiculous, Jameson. My car is right here and—"

He had already turned to leave the tent. "You've made yourself clear. I can't count on you. So be it."

Her chest burned with the rejection, but she let him go. Montrose gave her what might have been a sympathetic glance and then filed out after the old Fed, leaving her alone. She stood in silence for a minute until she'd heard them drive away, then went out to the Mazda and headed back toward town. Halfway there her stomach started to grumble and she realized she hadn't eaten all day. It was five-thirty, about when Clara would be getting home, but Caxton needed to eat before she went back to Harrisburg. She parked in a public lot in Gettysburg and went into a little café that wasn't completely overrun with tourists.

She ordered a ham croissant and a diet Coke and sat down to eat, but the food was tasteless. She took two or three bites and pushed the rest aside.

14.

"If he's hurt, I can track him, ja," German Pete said, & reached for his haversack. From this reeking bag he took out a measure of black powder, some small greasy pieces of hollow bone that might have belonged to some unfortunate bird once, & a couple of hawthorn leaves. "It's madness," he told me, "to go traipsing in the dark when vampires are about, but I'll do what you say, Corporal." He ground his ingredients together in a tiny pestle with some spit, then rubbed the resulting paste into the blood that still stained his hands. He asked for a match & Eben Nudd broke one off his block, then snapped it to life. German Pete took the flame

between his cupped palms & cursed liberally as the gunpowder there flared up. He put his breath into the fire, however, & the flame which had been yellow turned a dull & flickering red.

All around his feet the same hellish light licked at the grass & the fallen leaves. Wherever John Tyler had lost his life's blood the light shone, & much of it on his corpse & shirt as well, & everywhere we looked, though not as much of it as I expected. I've seen so many men die in this war, & always the blood splashed on the ground like a pitcher of water being poured out. Yet here only a few drops & splatters remained.

German Pete had claimed our demon was a vampire, & I knew vampires sip blood as their repast. Perhaps I did not wish to believe it before; I had no choice now.

"There, look ye," German Pete said, & pointed with his glowing hands. A trace of dim fire led away from where we stood. Small drops of it could be seen heading off to our right. That was the same direction from which the vampire had first come.

"Is that Bill's blood?" I demanded. I was terrified, if the War Department must know.

"Ye'll have to have a chance. This charm's for tracking a wounded deer, as such it was taught to me, & I've never seen it used otherwise. Might be Hiram Morse's," German Pete told me. "Might be the vampire's own. Yet it's a track, & that's what ye asked for."

—THE STATEMENT OF ALVA GRIEST

15.

Night had fallen, just barely—the sky still showed a burning yellow through the black silhouettes of the trees. The streetlights were on, but some were still glowing a doubtful orange, occasionally flickering into life just to wink out again. In the street the air had gotten colder, far colder than she'd expected. She'd left her coat in the Mazda, and she wrapped her arms around herself for warmth as she headed toward the car.

The very last thing she wanted to do was spend another minute in Gettysburg. It was time to go home. She thought of Clara, probably already waiting for her back at the house. She could go home, feed the dogs, and then spend the evening curled up on the couch with Clara while the TV put them both to sleep. It sounded just about perfect.

Maybe Clara would let her sleep with the light on for once. After the chill she'd gotten from the mass vampire grave she didn't feel the need to be frightened again for a long time.

It was only a few blocks between the café and where she'd parked. She walked quickly, keeping her head down. She didn't look up at the windows of the houses-turned-souvenir-stores that she passed. When she reached the Mazda, though, a sound made her look up.

An alarm bell rang somewhere nearby. The harsh panicky sound might have come from blocks away, but it was one of the sounds she was trained to notice and identify. It was a burglar alarm. Not her area of expertise, she told herself.

She was who she was, however. She was a cop. She stepped away from the Mazda and back into the tree-lined street. The alarm was around a corner, she thought, away from the main tourist areas, deeper into the actual town. It would only take a second to check it out. She wasn't supposed to do that, of course. The state police didn't intervene in municipal criminal investigations. According to standard operating procedure, she should call it in and let the local police take care of it.

She was right there, though. It couldn't be more than a minute away on foot. She would just take a look, get the street address where the bell was ringing.

Half-jogging, she headed around the corner and up the block beyond. The alarm came from a nondescript building across the street from the Gettysburg College campus. The shrill noise bounced off the big brick buildings of the college and rattled down the deserted street, which had been mobbed with tourists just a few hours before. She could see no one nearby. If the local police were on their way, she couldn't hear their sirens.

She moved closer, sticking to the shadows of the sidewalk. She couldn't hear anything except the alarm, which was loud enough to give her a headache. She was close enough to see the building's two wide plate-glass windows, obscured by heavy venetian blinds. A black awning over the doorway read MONTAGUE FUNERAL HOME. A placard above the doorknob read CLOSED.

The door stood slightly ajar. The doorknob had been wrenched sideways in its socket, and it looked like the lock had been forced.

Okay. That was all she needed to know. She dashed across the street to the cover of some trees and took out her cell phone. She called the Harrisburg office of the Pennsylvania State Police and asked the police communications operator on duty to patch her through to the Gettysburg police department. A woman's voice answered, "Police Department Dispatch. How may I direct your call?"

Caxton glanced at the building across the way. There was no sign of movement within. "This is Laura Caxton with the state police, Troop H. I'm at one-fifty-five Carlisle Street and I've got an activated burglar alarm."

"I've already registered that alarm and dispatched a patrol unit," the dispatcher told her. "But thanks. Are you available to assist if the chief requests it?"

Caxton frowned. "I'm off duty but, yeah. If you need help I'm here. What's the ETA on your unit?"

"Upward of five minutes. Have you spotted any subjects?"

"No. There's sign of forced entry, though. It's the mortuary down here. I don't see anyone outside or any suspicious vehicles, so—"

The alarm clanged wildly and then stopped. Caxton peered through the lamp-lit gloom but couldn't see any change in the building.

"There's definitely someone inside. They just disabled the alarm and—"

One of the plate glass windows exploded outward, sending jagged shards of glass skating across the street. The blinds fluttered and broke apart, and then a square wooden object protruded from the shattered window. It lurched out to drop with a heavy thud on the sidewalk.

No, no no, Caxton thought.

It was a casket, a big mahogany casket. A much more ornate version of the hundred coffins she'd seen that afternoon. Caxton knew better than to think some junkies had broken into the funeral home to steal something that would be so hard to sell on the street. She had a much better idea who was behind the break-in. Somebody who needed a coffin because his old one had gotten smashed.

"Trooper?" her phone chirped. "Trooper, are you there?"

She bit her lip and tried to think, but there was no time. "Cancel that patrol car, dispatch. No, don't cancel it—get as many people down here as you can, get them to clear out the vicinity. Get all the civilians off the street!"

"Trooper? I don't copy—what's going on?"

"Get everyone away from here!" Caxton shouted.

The vampire jumped up onto the jagged lower edge of the broken window and then leaped down into the street. His skin was the color of cold milk, his eyes red and dully glowing. He had no hair anywhere on his body, and his ears stood up in points. His mouth was full of row after row of sharp teeth.

He looked as if he hadn't fed in a century. His body was emaciated, pared down by hunger until he was thinner than any human being she'd ever seen. His skin stretched tight over prominent bones, and the muscles on his arms and legs were wasted away to thin cords. His ribs stuck out dramatically, and his cheeks were hollow with starvation. His skin was dotted with dark patches of decay and in some places had cracked open in weeping sores. He wore nothing but a pair of ragged gray pants that were falling apart at the seams.

He looked up the street, then back down as if he expected somebody to be there. Then he looked right across at Caxton and she knew he could see her blood, could see her veins and arteries lit up in the dark, her heart pounding in her chest.

Caxton's free hand went to her hip to draw her weapon. It didn't look like he'd fed that night. If she was fast enough maybe she could keep him from ripping her to pieces. Her hand touched her belt and found nothing, and she wasted a vital second looking down, only to realize her Beretta wasn't there. It was still in her car.

"Dispatch, I have a vampire over here—do you copy? I have a vampire!" she screamed into the phone. "Request immediate assistance!"

16.

After long searching I found my quarry & almost at once I regretted it. Bill lay curled on a tussock of grass & mud, his body twisted up & broken. His pack & musket were missing & nowhere to be found & his blue jacket had been torn open in the front, the buttons cast about him as if he'd torn them off in a frenzy. His neck & his hands were as pale as the belly of a fish, but that was not the worst of it. His face hung in ragged strips as if he'd been mauled by a bear. Flaps of skin hung loose on his cheeks & his nose was laid open, as completely as if it had been flayed in an anatomist's classroom.

I found his forage cap near his hand. I picked it up, &
wrapped it around & around my own hands, & wept for him, for
my Bill was dead.

Eben Nudd placed one hand upon my shoulder, which I was
most grateful for. German Pete sat down on his pack & drank
deep from his canteen.

I knelt down to kiss my friend's brow one last time, & it was
then I had the worst shock of my life. For though I could feel no
heat in him, nor did he breathe or show other sign of life; yet
Bill moved. He winced away from my touch.

"Alva," he said. He stirred, too weak it seemed to sit up, yet
desperate to get away. "Alva, he's calling me."

"Who is, Bill? Who calls you? Come, let's get you up & back
to camp. The surgeons will do something for you." They could
hardly repair his torn face, I thought, but plenty of men in this
war have been disfigured, & yet lived to fight again. "Come."

"No!" he screamed, his voice as high & thin as a whistle. He
struck me on the shoulder & knocked me backward onto my fun-
dament. "No, none of you get closer! Leave me! He's calling, O,
can you not hear him? He calls even now!"

With that he leapt up, & ran off, calling over his shoulder
that I should not follow. That I should give him up for dead.

—THE STATEMENT OF ALVA GRIEST

17.

The vampire saw her. His red eyes bored right into her. She
tried to look away, but she couldn't.

In an offhand, very casual way, she knew exactly
what was happening. He was mesmerizing her. It had happened
before. Had she been capable of it she would have screamed,
run away, at least tried to move her eyes. But she couldn't. The

vampire had the power to compel her. The amulet at her throat grew warm as it fought that influence, but it had little power of its own. Its purpose was to focus her own mental energies, to give her the clarity to fight the vampire's psychic attack. Unless she could reach up and grab it, turn her thoughts toward it, it was useless. And until the vampire looked away from her she could do nothing but stare at him, her rational mind disconnected from her body.

The cell phone in her hand made loud buzzing noises. Most likely it was the dispatcher on the other end asking her frantic questions. She opened her fingers and the phone slid to the ground. It bounced off the sidewalk, but she couldn't look down to see where it had gone. She couldn't look anywhere except into the vampire's eyes.

And those eyes—they were cold, even though they were the color of fiery embers. They were vacant of any emotion. They were locked on hers with an unmatchable strength. He could hold her there forever if he wanted to. He could come over and tear her throat out with his hands and she would not be able to turn away or move an inch.

She heard police sirens coming closer but lacked the presence of mind to even hope for rescue.

He padded lightly into the street, coming closer. He had all the time in the world and he knew it. Unable to break his gaze, she did not see the police car approaching. Focused intently on her, perhaps seeing nothing but the blood in her body, the vampire didn't see the car either.

Whether or not the driver of the car saw him she didn't know. He came around the corner at high speed, his tires shrieking on the asphalt (she heard a plaintive cry from far off, that was all), and barreled down the street right into the vampire's side, knocking him down and dragging him half a block as the car's brakes howled and smoked.

Instantly the spell was broken. A stale breath burst out of Caxton's lungs—she'd been holding it in the whole time—and she bent double, nausea and fear wracking her body. She reached into her collar and grabbed the charm there, almost scalding herself on its stored heat. Strength rushed back through her, making her blood surge.

"Is he dead?" someone yelled. "Please tell me he's dead."

"Who?" she asked, before realizing the question was not directed at her. She looked up to see two local police officers circling the vampire's inert body in the street. They had their weapons out but held upward, at a safe ready.

"He's not moving," one of them said. They were both male, dressed in identical uniforms. One of them, the one who had last spoken, was broad through the shoulders but no taller than Caxton. He prodded the vampire's arm with his shoe. The other one, a big wall of a man, stood back to cover his partner.

She knew with a dread familiarity that they would be dead in seconds if she didn't act. "State Police!" she shouted, and ran toward them as fast as her body would allow. She felt drained and unsteady. "Get back!"

The taller policeman looked up at her, his mouth forming around a word. The other bent down to take a closer look at the vampire. It happened then all in a flash. The vampire lifted himself up on his elbows and twisted his head to the side. His mouth opened, revealing his sharp, translucent teeth. They dug into the crouching policeman's leg and bit down hard.

Blood slapped the front of the car, the legs of the standing policeman, the dark surface of the street. The vampire must have bitten right through a major artery. The crouching policeman screamed and tried to bring his gun down to shoot the vampire, but before he got it halfway down he was dead. He slumped backward and his skull smacked the asphalt with a noise that made Caxton wince.

The surviving policeman jumped back, wheeling his pistol

around. Caxton came up to the side of the car and grabbed at his arm, pulling him back still farther.

The vampire dragged himself out from under the car. His mouth and most of his chest were covered in gore. His skin looked less luminously white, had in fact taken on a vague pinkish cast. He looked no less wasted and emaciated than before, but Caxton knew that he would be a dozen times stronger with the officer's blood in him.

The remaining cop bent his knees and grabbed his weapon in both hands. He sighted down the barrel and put a bullet right into the back of the vampire's bald head. Caxton watched the vampire's skin buckle and open, saw the skull underneath crack under the bullet's impact. The wound closed over as quickly and smoothly as if the bullet had been fired into a bucket full of milk. If the vampire even felt the shot, he showed no sign.

"The heart," Caxton had time to say. "You have to destroy the heart." Even as she was speaking, though, the vampire turned slowly around to stare at the local cop. The man's face convulsed in fear and loathing and then suddenly went slack. His body trembled and his arms fell loose at his sides, his gun forgotten in his hand.

It would have been easy for the vampire to kill Caxton and the other officer just then. He might have done it just to keep them from following him—she'd seen vampires do that before. Instead he rushed over to where the coffin lay just outside of the mortuary's window. He grabbed up the coffin, turned away from them, and dashed across the street and into the campus of the college.

In the distance a siren started to howl with a series of short wavering cries.

"What's that?" Caxton asked.

The cop looked around him as if he couldn't remember where he was. "Tornado alarm," he said. "They wanted to get the people off the streets in a hurry. It'll just scare the tourists, but the locals will know to get them to shelter."

Caxton breathed a sigh of relief. The dispatcher had taken her seriously. There was no danger of a real tornado—the sky was clear and full of stars—but the siren would serve its purpose. "That's good. Now, what we do next is—"

"Oh, God," the cop said. "Oh, sweet Jesus—Garrity!" He rushed to his fallen partner's side and grabbed at his wrists, feeling for a pulse. "He's dead!"

"Yes," Caxton said, as gently as she could. "We have to get the thing that killed him."

"Negative," the cop said. He reached for his radio and called for an ambulance. Then he switched bands and shouted, "Officer down, one-five-five Carlisle!"

"Good, good," Caxton said. He was following standing orders, she knew. You didn't just abandon a dead policeman in the street. But unless they hurried they were going to lose the vampire. "Now let's go."

He stared up at her. "Garrity's been my partner for eight years," he said, apparently thinking that ended the discussion. Under any other circumstances it probably would have.

Caxton knew she couldn't afford to wait for the ambulance. "Give me the car keys, then, and you stay here," she insisted. "I'm a state trooper. Come on! He's getting away!"

The cop stared at her with wondering eyes for far too long. She could almost see the fog of grief and fear and anger swirling in his brain. Finally he reached down into Garrity's blood-stained trouser pocket and yanked out a set of car keys. He pressed them into her hand without a word.

Caxton turned on her heel and jumped into the open door of the patrol car. She backed away from the horrible scene in the street—one more chilling vision to give her nightmares for years to come, she thought—and wheeled the car around to face the campus. A narrow road ran through a cluster of long, low buildings. She looked between them as she shot by but couldn't find any sign of the vampire. A few terrified-looking students were milling on the sidewalks, but they paid little attention to her. They were listening to the tornado siren, which was pulsing out its call faster and faster.

Up ahead the road widened. The signs said CONSTITUTION AVENUE, but that meant little to Caxton. She pressed down on the gas pedal and the cruiser jumped forward, pushing her back in her seat. The vampire could have turned off any of the side streets she passed, but all she could do was trust her luck and hope she caught sight of him. She had only started to despair when she caught a glimpse of a thin white shape bobbing in the darkness ahead of her. Yes, there—the vampire was still carrying the coffin, running right in the middle of the road ahead of her, his feet flashing and pushing him along far faster than any human could run. Caxton poured on as much speed as she could and slowly gained on him. He was so fast—how was it possible? He had to be a hundred and fifty years old, at least. Vampires that age should be stuck in their coffins, unable to rise, just like Justinia Malvern. It was impossible. Impossible, and yet clearly it was happening.

18.

Bill had bade me not follow him further. Yet what else could I do & call myself his friend? Through the dark, following still his trail, we gave chase along a narrow track. In time this gave way at a clearing in which stood a house & some outbuildings. Of the house there is much to say, so I shall put it aside for the moment, & speak of the outliers. These were tumbledown shacks, & a number of sheds, which flanked the house so close they near leaned on it. They were of the worst construction & looked very shabby, & hurt the house by comparison.

Ah, yes, the house! The house had been painted white once, &
perhaps even had looked grand. Six thick columns fronted it, &
it was topped by a generous cupola. The broad windows were
of clearest glass & I could see the remains of white curtains
beyond. Remains only, for the house had died & was surrendered
to corruption.

Is it correct, or even possible to say a HOUSE *has* DIED*? That*
was my first impression. The paint was peeling from its façade in
long pale tongues that revealed worm-eaten wood beneath. Some
half of the windows were broken out, with those of the upper
story boarded over in haste. The cupola dome had partially caved
in, & one end of the house entire was lower than the other, as if it
had shifted on its foundations, & would soon collapse.

The front door stood open or perhaps was missing. That
entrance was no more than a black rectangle leading into mys-
tery; splintered bullet holes around the jamb explained little. It
was through that portal I was certain Bill had run & I made to
follow, my musket & my haversack bouncing on my shoulders &
back, my breath ragged in my throat.

—THE STATEMENT OF ALVA GRIEST

19.

The vampire's white back glowed in her headlights. He
looked behind him now and again but never slowed
down. Caxton had her foot on the accelerator, but even as
parking lots and tree-studded quads flashed by her on either
side he was nearly keeping pace on foot.

Her best bet, she decided, was to run him down with the
car. If she could get it on top of him, pin him underneath it, she
might be able to hold him in place long enough to summon reinforcements. The idea of taking him on by herself was suicidal,
especially since she'd left her weapon in her own car. She

spared a single glance down and saw a riot shotgun bolted to the dashboard. That was something, though shotguns were almost useless against a vampire who had already fed. It might slow him down, and that was all she could hope for.

She roared after the vampire as fast as she could. Constitution Avenue swung north around the far edge of the campus, and she lost some ground as she had to turn to match the curve. Ahead of her the vampire lifted up his stolen coffin in both hands and then pivoted to sling it at her. She tried to veer out of the way as the massive wooden missile filled up her windshield. Shrieking, she stamped on the brake as the glass in front of her cracked and buckled on impact. The car rocked on its suspension and spun out, whirling around and nearly going up on its side. One of the tires, then another burst with a noise like gunshots, and the car fell back down onto the rims, listing hard to the side. The air bag deployed with a screeching hiss, then almost instantly collapsed though the car was still moving. Caxton was thrown sideways, colliding painfully with her door. Her seat belt yanked her back down into her seat as the car bounced to an unsteady stop.

Through the starred windshield she could see a big football stadium ahead of her. She had slalomed into its parking lot—fitting enough, since the car wasn't going anywhere else that night.

She fought to get her equilibrium back. There was no time to check herself for whiplash or other injuries—she had to move. The vampire was still close by and she still had some slim chance of catching him. She grabbed the shotgun from its rack, checked to make sure it was loaded, then pushed open her door and stumbled out onto the concrete. She staggered to her feet and looked around but couldn't see the vampire.

This monster's behavior puzzled her somewhat. She'd never seen a vampire run away from a fight before, especially after he'd fed. A normal vampire should have been more than a match for the meager police response. Yet she'd never seen a vampire so starved-looking before, either, at least not one that could stand up straight.

The shotgun cradled in her arms, she dashed back toward the road—then turned as she caught a flash of movement to her side. Yes, there, she saw a pale shadow flitting between trees on the far side of the stadium. She would never catch up with him on foot if he could run as fast as he had while she'd pursued him in the car. She couldn't just give up, though. Her legs burned as she pounded toward the side of the stadium. She reached for her cell phone, but it was gone, and now she recalled dropping it while he had her hypnotized. She hadn't thought to pick it back up. She was on her own.

Beyond the stadium lay a practice field. She could see the vampire streaking across the close-clipped grass. Beyond that lay trees and green hills lit only by the stars. That was part of the national military park, she thought, part of the battlefield that contained nothing but marble obelisks and heavy monuments to fallen soldiers. It would get dark out there pretty fast between the trees, and she didn't have a flashlight.

She kept running.

She stopped at the top of the hill and tried to catch her breath. She knew she should turn back. There was no question. Let the vampire go, let him get away. It would disappoint Arkeley. Once that had meant something to her, but she had a life now. She had Clara to think of, and the dogs. If she were killed here—

She didn't get a chance to finish the thought. As Caxton turned around to head back to the campus behind her, the vampire was there. He stood perfectly still behind her, as if he'd been watching the back of her head the whole time. His eyes burned in their sockets like the glowing ends of two lit cigarettes.

Caxton pried her own gaze away from those eyes and grabbed at the amulet around her neck. She tried to bring the shotgun up, thinking only to blast those damned eyes right out of his head. With an easy, swooping motion he closed the distance between them and knocked the weapon out of her hand, sending it spiraling down the side of the hill. It slid away on the wet grass.

He grabbed her head in both of his hands and brought his face within inches of her own. She could smell the blood of the dead policeman on his breath. His eyes went wide and his stare bored right into her, but with the charm in her hand he couldn't quite connect. With a grunt of disgust he let go of her.

"I am a gentleman, Miss, and I was taught to never raise my hand against a lady's person." His voice was steely beneath the mushy growl that distorted every vampire's voice. Steely and brittle. He frowned around his sharp teeth. "I do not know what the etiquette books would say about a lady dressed in a man's attire."

Maybe he wasn't going to kill her, at least not right away. Caxton was too stunned to really comprehend what that meant. She glanced down and saw her white shirt and her tie. "This is my uniform," she said. "I'm with the state police."

"I've killed once tonight, and that's all I want, I think," he said. "But I warn you to leave me be. I'll not show mercy again, if our paths continue to cross." Then he threw her through the air, through darkness. She felt wet grass smack the side of her face as hard as a concrete wall, and then she felt nothing at all.

The darkness enveloped her as if she were enclosed inside a giant clenched fist. Then light burst into her world again and she convulsed violently.

"No!" she screamed, her eyes flicking open. The light had changed. The air was warmer. Where was she? Where was— who was in front of her? Was it the vampire? Her hands shot out and she grabbed for the thing in front of her, grabbed for its throat, not caring if it would prove as hard as stone, and then she had it, she had her hands around its windpipe and it was solid, solid flesh, solid warm flesh—

"Oh, God, no," Laura shrieked, letting go instantly. The

woman in front of her had black hair that fell in cute bangs across her eyebrows. Her eyes were a rich brown, wet eyes that reflected Laura's own screaming face.

It was Clara she had attacked. Clara who was coughing and sputtering for breath.

20.

Before I could enter said house, a shot called out, and buried itself between my feet. I stood stock-still, as if paralyzed, and thought my number must be up. The shootist who waved at me from a nearby tree, however, proved to be no Johnny Reb. Instead he was dressed in dark green with black rubber buttons. His weapon lay draped over a thick limb of the tree & it appeared to me as a mechanical python almost. It was a custom-made target rifle, a weapon I'd seen only once at a beef shoot before the commencement of hostilities. It looked like a good length of octagonal pipe with a batwing stock & a spyglass mounted on the top for good measure. I knew that rifle could have punched a hole right through me, especially at such proximity, & I also knew its master had been aiming to warn & not wound me. His strange uniform was meant to help him blend into the foliage, & I recognized it as the habiliments of the U.S. Sharpshooters. He was a Unionist, then, & good thing or I would have already been dead. He had a fringe of hair around the sides of his face & skin the color of walnut shells. What he was doing up in that tree I did not hazard to guess.

"My friend is in there!" I called back to him, but my voice faltered as he shushed me.

With his free hand he beckoned me closer to his position, then made me lie down in the tall grass there. "Rebs comin'," he hissed. Despite my furor I was still a soldier & I still understood what that meant. I made myself as discreet as possible.

—THE STATEMENT OF ALVA GRIEST

21.

Caxton lay back in her hospital bed and stared at the ceiling, unable to get comfortable. She'd been found at dawn crawling around in the military park. The park rangers had at first thought she was blasted on drugs, and had rushed her to Gettysburg's very modern hospital. The doctors had tested her and found no drugs at all in her system, but they still wanted her to rest. Fat chance. "I thought it was the vampire. Oh, God—I nearly killed Clara because I thought she was the vampire!"

"Yes." Vesta Polder placed her hands on Caxton's cheeks. The older woman wore dozens of plain gold rings on her fingers and the metal was cool and welcome against Laura's burning skin. She left her hands there while she studied Laura's eyes. "That's true. But there's no need to be so dramatic about it."

Laura licked her dry lips. She felt feverish and drained, like she was coming down from a bad case of the flu. "I could have killed her!"

Vesta Polder shrugged and took her hands away. "You didn't, though, and life is far too short for us to worry about the evil we *might* have done." The older woman had waves of frizzy blond hair that stuck nearly straight out from her head. She wore a long black dress buttoned tightly at the throat. She was a friend of Arkeley's—though perhaps it was better to call her an ally—and she was some kind of witch or medium or something. Caxton had never been quite clear on where Vesta's powers came from, but they were considerable. It had been Arkeley's idea to bring Vesta Polder in to the hospital, a strangely caring gesture on his part. She didn't choose to look a gift horse in the mouth by wondering about his true motivations. "Do you need a sedative, or do you think you can settle down, now?"

Caxton swallowed. Her throat was thick and scratchy, as if she'd been shouting for hours. "I'll try," she promised. She felt like she'd been scolded by an elementary schoolteacher. "Is she okay, though?"

"She'll be fine. I gave her some tea to soothe her hurt." Vesta Polder caught Caxton's look of alarm and shook her head. "Just plain old herbal tea. Much more effective than any potion for what ails her. She's frightened, of course, but I've already explained things to her and she isn't angry with you. This one," she said, looking down her sharp nose, "is worth keeping. She's smart enough and she's grounded in reality."

Caxton nodded. A lot of people wouldn't have described Clara that way, but Vesta saw people the way they truly were, not how they presented themselves. "Am I okay?" she asked.

Vesta Polder straightened up until she loomed over the hospital bed. "You could use a long rest. You should get away from this town, get as far away as possible. I can't say I like this place myself. Too many vibrations, good and bad. The ether here is sorely clouded. I'll be heading home now to where I can think properly. You should do the same." She reached into a pocket of her dress and drew something out. She opened her hand and the spiral pendant tumbled out, dangling on its torn ribbon. "The police found this near where they picked you up. Try to hold on to it better from now on, hmm?"

Caxton promised. She took the amulet gladly and held it tight in her hand. It felt cool like Vesta Polder's rings, and even more reassuring. The older woman patted her arm and left. As soon as the door of Caxton's room was open her next visitor entered. Clara sat down heavily in a chair next to the bed and smiled broadly at Caxton without saying a word. She had some red bruises on her throat that Caxton couldn't stand to look at.

"You scared me, you!" Clara said. "Stop doing that! When I got the call that they'd picked you up I was sure that the vampire'd gotten you. They told me it got that other guy, the local cop." Clara wore a black T-shirt and jeans—she must have taken the day off. "His family must be so upset right now but I just feel relieved. Does that make me a terrible person? Don't answer that. I'm just glad you're alive."

Caxton opened her mouth to speak, but only a raw creaking sound came out.

Clara's eyes widened. She shook her head. "Listen, the dogs are fine. I watered and fed them just like you showed me. Fifi doesn't like me, I think, but that's just got to mean she doesn't know me yet, right? Everybody likes me once they get to know me."

Laura closed her mouth and nodded against her pillow.

"The doctors say you can go home whenever you're ready. I put a new quilt on our bed—it was really cold last night, especially when I was all alone—and I saw a place on my way down here selling Macoun apples. Those are my favorite! I thought I'd make you a pie. Would you like that? I've never made one before, but . . . but . . ."

Clara was staring at her face. Something wet dribbled across the side of Caxton's mouth. She reached up and found that she was weeping copiously. She tried to apologize, but a wordless sob came out instead.

"Oh, Laura," Clara said, softly. She climbed out of her chair and into the bed, shoving Laura to the side. "It's okay. I'm here." She pressed her small body against Caxton's side, her chest. Her perfect soft mouth touched Caxton's greasy forehead.

She was rocking back and forth slowly, her arms wrapped around Caxton's limp body, when the door opened again.

"Ahem," Arkeley said.

Caxton didn't move. Clara sat up just enough to tell him to go away.

The old crippled Fed didn't obey her. Instead he came farther into the room to stand at the foot of the bed.

"Get out!" Clara said, louder this time. There was bad

blood between her and Arkeley—she'd even threatened to hit him, once, though she'd backed down when she realized it would have cost her her job just to punch a U.S. Marshal.

Caxton closed her eyes. She didn't know what to say. She didn't want to see Arkeley. At the very least, though, she owed him an apology. She swallowed heavily and shifted herself upright in the bed.

"My girlfriend and I," Clara said, "are kind of busy at the moment."

Arkeley's face contorted gruesomely, his scars bunching up and turning white. His eyes were shining. Was he smiling? It looked like it hurt him to do so. "Officer Hsu, why don't you go wait out in the hall?" he asked.

"Why don't you sit and spin?" Clara asked, throwing him the finger.

His smile didn't shift.

Caxton cleared her throat noisily. The two of them looked at her as if waiting for her to settle the differences between them. She didn't think she could do that, but at least she could try to take charge of the situation.

"You were right and I was wrong," she said, finally, looking into Arkeley's eyes. They didn't change; he hadn't come to gloat. "There was, in fact, a vampire in that last coffin. An active one."

"Yes. I've read the report filed by the survivor of last night's attack." He looked her up and down as if searching her for wounds. "The other survivor. His prose style was a little too emotional for proper police work, but I got the gist."

"How are you going to proceed?" she asked.

"Who? Me?" Arkeley's face went wide with surprise. It again made all his scars turn white. "I can't fight this vampire."

"Why not?"

The old man grimaced and looked away from her. "Are you really going to make me say it? I'm a cripple." His shoulders tensed. How much did it hurt him to admit his weakness, she wondered? How much had it humiliated him when he'd asked her to tie his tie for him? "My body doesn't work well enough anymore. I can advise you. That's all. This case is yours."

Caxton's mouth opened as if she were about to laugh. But she knew he was quite serious. "I can't," she tried.

"If you don't," he said, slowly, deliberately, "someone else will have to take your place. Most likely a local cop who has never dealt with a worse villain than a drunk driver. You know exactly what will happen to said cop. He'll die. He won't know what he's up against, he will underestimate the vampire, and he'll be ripped to shreds the first time he draws down on this monster."

Caxton thought of a hundred arguments against what Arkeley was saying. There was only one problem with them: He was right. She'd had horrible, perfect proof of that the night before. Arkeley was right—this was going to be her case.

22.

He proved as good an oracle of future events as he was a crack shot. Within moments of my concealing myself I began to hear hoofbeats approach. Within the space of a minute a horde of Secesh cavalry reined in before the house. Their leader, an officer of some distinction by the look of his insignia, wore leather gauntlets & a dusty slouch hat & good gray cotton tailored to his frame. Many of his men were in butternut though, which is to say, uniforms made at home & undyed. We'd seen plenty like them at Chancellorsville, where some men fought with no shoes on their feet, & some without even rifles of their own.

We were defeated at Chancellorsville, as we have been defeated every time we strove against Robbie Lee. I took this fact to heart & tried not to breathe too loudly.

"*Marse Obediah,*" *the cavalry commander shouted, as if he were hallooing an old friend.* "*Can you hear me in there? I've come from Richmond thirty miles. Can you hear me? The Cause requires your services once more. The Yanks are all over this part of creation & we must drive them back. General Lee commands it!*"

The officer wheeled his horse as if expecting an attack to come from any direction.

An answer came at last, however, in a voice that chilled my blood. There was very little human in that voice though the words were good English. It sounded more like a violin had been scraped with the neck of a broken bottle, & words had somehow come out.

"*You have been heard,*" *the voice announced.*

—THE STATEMENT OF ALVA GRIEST

23.

Caxton got out of the bed feeling like she'd been beaten up the night before. Her joints ached and there was a truly foul taste in her mouth. It couldn't be helped. Clara had brought her a change of clothes, which she got into painfully. It felt good to have a crisp new shirt on her back, though. She slipped on her coat and shoved her notebook and her cell phone in the pockets. The local police had been kind enough to return the latter after she dropped it in the street outside the mortuary.

"You're on the case," Arkeley said. It wasn't a question.

It had been, the day before, and the answer had been no. Now everything had changed. She had watched a fellow cop die because of a moment's hesitation. She had gone chasing after a vampire she had no chance of killing. It had all been so crystal clear. It had all made sense—the way nothing much had since the last time. Since the last vampire she'd fought.

"Yes," she said. Clara turned to look up at her, but Caxton didn't even meet her lover's eyes. What choice did she have?

Arkeley couldn't fight active vampires anymore. Not when he couldn't tie his own tie. There were plenty of other cops in the world, but none of them had her experience. In fact, none of them had any experience with vampires. If she left this job to other cops, they would almost certainly get themselves killed.

Of course there was no guarantee Caxton would survive, either. But that was part of who she was. Her father had been the only cop in a coal mining patch up north. His father had been a Pinkerton. What would her father say now, she wondered, if he were still alive? She knew exactly what he would say. He would tell her it was about damn time.

"I've made a lot of mistakes already," she said, and Arkeley just nodded. He'd never been big on reassurance. Still, the fact that he'd come to her for help—that he thought of her as the one best to find and destroy the vampire—meant something. She just hoped she could convince her superiors in Harrisburg. "We should start doing things right, then. We should start now."

He nodded again.

"That starts with getting some idea of what we're fighting. Vampires don't age well—that's been a constant so far. The older they get the more blood they need just to maintain, and after fifty or sixty years they can't even climb out of their coffins. This guy's different. I wish we knew how that was even possible. I saw him last night. He looked like he'd been starved of blood for a very long time. He looked terrible. Still, he almost outran a car."

"There's a lot we don't know about this one," Arkeley concurred. "I might be able to do something about that."

Caxton grunted in encouragement.

"It might be nothing. But I have a lead of sorts. I have a contact at the College of Physicians in Philadelphia—"

Clara laughed. "You mean at the Mütter Museum? Why am I not surprised an old fossil like you has an in with that place?"

Caxton frowned. She knew about the Mütter Museum, of

course. She'd been there on a class trip when she was a kid. It was the world's largest collection of medical anomalies. Two-headed babies in jars, the skeleton of the world's tallest man. Lots of skeletons, actually. She thought about the bones in the cave. The vampires that hadn't made it to the twenty-first century. "Hold on, Clara. Arkeley, what do they have there that would interest us?"

He shrugged, looking a little miffed at being interrupted. "As I was saying, my contact there got in touch with me recently. He'd turned up something in a storage room he knew I would want to see. They have the bones of a vampire in their collection. Bones which are dated to 1863."

Caxton's eyes went wide. "You think there's a connection."

"You don't?" he asked. "I should go and take a look, anyway. It might tell us something about who we're fighting."

Caxton nodded eagerly. She was less concerned by who the vampire might be than by what he might do next, however. "Okay. Find out what you can. The most important thing for me right now is to catch the active one. I'll head up to HQ and see what I can do about getting some people down here so we can start searching for this vampire's lair."

He left without another word. Caxton checked her pocket and found her car keys. Turning to Clara, she said, "You drove down here, right? You can take me back to where I left the Mazda and then—"

"Yeah," Clara said, standing up. She threw her arms around Caxton, pressed her face into the crook of Caxton's neck. "Anything I can do to help," she said. "Just promise me you won't get killed."

Caxton hugged her back, hard, and promised. When she let go she saw the red bruises on Clara's neck, however, and made a promise to herself.

The last time she fought vampires people had been hurt—people she cared about. That wasn't going to happen again.

They went out into the hospital's parking lot, where a stiff wind was whirling up great spirals of fallen orange leaves. Clara drove her back to the Mazda and left her there with one deep, meaningful kiss. She promised she would take care of the dogs.

"Don't expect me home tonight." Caxton didn't plan on coming home until the vampire was destroyed.

"Keep me informed," Clara insisted. Then she drove away.

Caxton watched the patrol cruiser go, watched the sweep of leaves it kicked up in its wake. Then she unlocked the Mazda and reached inside for the Beretta and its magazine, checked the action, and put the weapon in her coat pocket. Just having her familiar sidearm on her person made her feel better.

She wanted to get started right away, wanted to start liaising with the local cops and start an investigation folder. It wasn't that easy, though. First she had to drive back to Harrisburg and beg her superiors at the Bureau of Criminal Investigation to allow her to be reassigned and to give her some kind of jurisdiction for Gettysburg.

A thick layer of clouds lay over Route 15 as she hurried northward. She listened to the radio and tried not to think about much until she saw the aqueduct bridges of the state capital appear before her between two ridges. The dome of the capitol looked greenish under the overcast sky, but she was glad to see it. A few miles farther on, she pulled into the parking lot of the state police headquarters, a brick building with a big flag out front. She parked the Mazda and rushed inside to the lobby.

She had planned on speaking with her captain, but when she arrived she was told to go straight up to the Commissioner's office. At his door she introduced herself to his assistant. She expected to be kept waiting while her superior finished whatever he might be working on at that moment, but instead she was just waved in.

"Trooper Caxton," the Commissioner said, standing up from behind his desk. His office walls were lined with the antlers of twelve-point bucks, and there were antique rifles lined up behind his desk as if he wanted to be ready to shoot anyone who came through his door with bad news.

"Sir," she said.

"Do you know why I asked you to come up here?" he inquired.

She licked her lips and began. "There's evidence of a vampire pattern in Gettysburg," she said. "I mean, there's a vampire there. I've seen him." She cursed herself for not having rehearsed this speech before. She'd had plenty of time in the car. "I'd like to be assigned to special duty. If that's alright."

"Yes," he said.

She wasn't sure exactly what that meant. "Sir, I—"

"You want to be assigned special jurisdiction for this case. To be reassigned from your current duties. I'm agreeing with you. That's exactly what should happen now. And I'm not the only one." His eyes twinkled. "The doughnut munchers have spoken. This morning the police chief of Gettysburg called and asked to speak with me personally. I listened to what was going on and then I promised whatever assistance Gettysburg required. Do you know what the chief asked for?"

"No, sir."

"He asked for Laura Caxton, the famous vampire killer. The star of *Teeth*. They asked for you by name, Trooper."

Her hands were shaking. Was it that easy? Could it be that easy? The Commissioner came out from behind his desk and squeezed her bicep, then started walking toward his office door. She stood still until she realized she was being dismissed, then rushed to follow him.

"Sir," she said, "I want to thank—"

"Me? No need," the Commissioner said, smiling widely. "Like I said, I've read the reports on your work on the Godwin investigation. You got yourself shot and two troopers had to risk their lives pulling you out of the action." He smiled at her, but his eyes were already looking down at his desk. "I'd just as soon have you on special duty and away from the rest of my people."

Caxton did then what she'd learned a long time before was the only suitable reaction to such a backhanded compliment. She put her heels together, saluted, then turned and walked out the door.

24.

We crowded into the covered wagon and found room for knees and elbows around the dial. For light we had a single candle, but he assured me that was enough. It was a few minutes past midnight and I was anxious to be unburdened of my bad news.

The telegrapher, though, took his time getting set up, and even with his machine in operation, was much delayed. Cursing and fussing, he turned the indicator back and forth on the face of his dial, which was inscribed with two rounds of letters and numbers, and some few commands such as WAIT and STOP. He could not seem to get a good signal out, for messages kept coming in. He assured me this was normal, and set back to his work, but again with little success. I produced a small bottle from inside my coat and offered it to him, and this did much for his disposition, but did not help his machine.

"It's these new electro-magnetos, they're s'posed to be better than an honest man's telegraph key, but I don't see it. No fluids or acids to burn me, no salts to keep straight, that's fine and well. But this type picks up too many ghosts."

I must have raised an eyebrow.

"Oh, sure," he said. "After every battle we get 'em. They crowd the wires, you see. Dead men breathing out their last."

I watched in amazement as the indicator moved on the dial, of its own accord. The messages were picked out letter by letter so that even I could read them. The missives were never long or overly complex. M-O-T-H-E-R was the most common, and L-O-R-D-J-E-S-U-S, and S-A-V-E-M-Y-S-O-U-L and W-A-T-E-R. All the cries of the battlefield, tapped out in an invisible hand.

We managed to get my urgent news out, eventually, though two o'clock had come and gone. I was climbing out of the wagon, glad to be shut of that cramped and eerie conveyance, when the telegrapher called me back. "Another message, sir."

"What now, more news from the other side?"

"No, sir, this one's got your name on it. 'Received in full,' it says, and then, 'New orders. Gum Spring forthwith.' Where's that, then?"

"I'm sure I don't know," I said. It was the first I'd heard of the place.

—THE PAPERS OF WILLIAM PITTENGER

25.

A faint misty rain was falling by the time Caxton got back to Gettysburg. The afternoon was already half over, and it would be dark before she knew it. She wheeled into the parking lot of the town's sole police station, on High Street just south of Lincoln Square. She finished the takeout food that littered the Mazda's passenger seat; she needed to keep her strength up, especially as lousy as she felt after the previous night's exertions. Then she stepped out of the car and through the glass doors at the front of the cop shop. The sergeant at the front desk stood up when he saw her and pointed her through a pair of swinging doors. Beyond she found the bullpen, a dimly lit room full of cubicles, each with a PC and a couple of office chairs. Policemen in gray and black uniforms stood up all around the room as she walked in. She stopped short as every man in the room turned to face her.

They were patrolmen, not detectives. They were cops who spent every day walking the streets, keeping order. They were tall men, mostly, and most of them were a few pounds overweight. They wore bristly mustaches and their hair was short and neat. In other words, they looked a lot like her father had in his prime. She knew enough cops to recognize the look they were giving her. Their eyes were empty, the same way they'd look while they were interviewing suspects, willing to give nothing away for free.

One of them she actually recognized. A huge guy with broad shoulders and a hunched head, as if he was afraid of banging it on the ceiling. He was one of the cops who had responded to the mortuary burglary, the one who had survived. The one who stayed with his dead partner while she raced off in his borrowed cruiser. His name tag read GLAUER, and he stepped forward to stand in front of her, his immense bulk blocking her path. She wasn't sure what he wanted, but she was ready to defend herself if he wanted to call her out.

"Officer," she said, by way of greeting.

"Trooper," he said. His lips barely moved as he spoke. "Every man here was a friend of Brad Garrity. He was the one who—"

"Who died in service last night. I remember," Caxton said. She tried to keep her eyes as blank as his. Was he going to puff himself up next, and tell her how much he resented her walking into this office like she could just take over? Maybe he would accuse her of being an accomplice in Garrity's death. The vampire was to blame; everyone knew that, but she was a much more convenient target for his rage and grief. If he wanted to blow some steam at her, she supposed she could take it.

"You didn't know him," Glauer said. "We did. He had a wife and two kids, just little kids. He wasn't a smart guy, but people liked him. He was honest and hardworking, and he loved the job. He loved this town. He grew up here."

"I'm sorry," she said, permitting herself a frown of compassion.

Glauer shook his head, though. He didn't want her apologies. "When he died I followed procedure. I stuck with him until the ambulance arrived, even though I knew he was gone. I called it in. Afterward I came back here and filled out the paperwork. You, on the other hand, went tearing off after the perp who killed him."

She nodded. There were rules to this game and she would follow them.

"We heard what happened to you. I saw what happened to my cruiser, when they towed it out of the Musselman Stadium parking lot. We all," he said, glancing backward at the men standing behind him, "just wanted to say something."

Here it comes, Caxton thought. She would take it, whatever it was.

"We wanted to say thanks. You didn't know Brad, but you put your life on the line to catch his killer. That kind of courage is something we respect."

One of the men at the side of the room started to clap. The others followed suit immediately. The applause was hardly deafening, but it was real.

"Whatever you need to get this thing, whatever it takes, we're with you," Glauer said over the noise. He held out a hand and grasped hers hard, pumping it repeatedly. "Just next time, try to wreck Finster's car instead. It's a real shitbox."

Another man—it had to be Finster—said, "Hey," and everyone laughed, Caxton included. She took her hand back from Glauer and let him point the way to a glassed-in office at the back of the room.

Inside the local police chief waited for her, dozens of manila folders lined up neatly on his desk. He stood up promptly as she entered and shook her hand, then sat back down. "Trooper Caxton. I cannot tell you how glad I am to see you here. How

glad the borough of Gettysburg is that you could help us out."
The nameplate on his desk read CHIEF VICENTE and there was
no dust on it. The walls behind him held framed photos of policemen from years gone by, some of the photos looking sixty or
eighty years old. They showed cops who looked almost identical to the men out in the bullpen, just with different uniforms.

Vicente himself stood out, by contrast. He was young,
maybe ten years older than Caxton, and though he wore a
mustache it was thin and neatly trimmed. He was relatively
short and his eyes were bright and clear and full of optimism.
He had a faint Puerto Rican accent when he talked. He didn't
look anything like the cops in his bullpen. He looked a little like
a politician.

She sized him up in one professional once-over. He must
have worked damned hard to get where he was, to be chief of the
men outside his office. He must have put up with a lot of crap
along the way.

Caxton knew that story because it was a lot like her own.
This was a man she could work with, she thought. Somebody
she could understand. "I want to thank you for inviting me
down here," she said, by way of opening.

"Are you kidding? I think the luckiest thing that ever happened to the 'Burg was you being here last night." He opened
one of his manila folders and took out a map of the town. Portions of the map had been highlighted in yellow ink and a number of handwritten notes crowded the margins. "This town has a
population of about seventy-five hundred, and most days this
time of year we have twice that many tourists in town. I have
twenty sworn patrolmen to take care of those people, and a
couple dozen auxiliary officers I can call in for homecoming
or the bigger reenactments. Normally that's enough. Normally
our biggest problem is frat parties getting out of control up at
the college, or tourists who don't know how to drive and make
our traffic patterns a real mess." He looked up from the map

and smiled at her. "We had forty-three violent crimes reported last year. None of them resulted in a death."

"None?" Caxton repeated, a little stunned. "You had no murders at all last year?" Even in the sleepiest of backwater towns you normally got a couple of abused women killing their husbands or kids playing with guns blowing each other away. Then there were vehicular fatalities to consider. In the era of road rage, more and more people were realizing that a three-ton SUV made a great murder weapon.

Vicente shook his head, though. "This is one of the safest towns in Pennsylvania. We're very proud of that, and we'd like to keep it that way. My men aren't trained to respond to what happened last night. We had to download the correct forms to report a death in service because we didn't have any on hand. Trooper Caxton, you tell us what to do, okay? You tell us how to keep our people safe and we will listen."

Caxton sat back in her chair and inhaled deeply. "I haven't had time to prepare a formal action plan," she said.

Vicente raised his hands an inch or two off the desk and then lowered them again. "I'll take your best off-the-cuff suggestions, too."

She nodded and thought about it. She was trained for this. She had been training in criminal investigations for a year. "Yeah. Well, we start by looking for where he's sleeping. Vampires don't just dislike sunlight. They literally cannot get out of their coffins until the sun goes down. This one doesn't even have a coffin—he tried stealing one last night, but I screwed up his plan. He can sleep in a barrel or even a Dumpster if he has to, but he needs someplace dark and enclosed. If we can find where he is now, we can pull his heart out and be done without any further violence."

"Do you think that's a likely scenario?" Vicente asked, his eyes brightening.

"Unfortunately, no. There are too many places he could be

hiding and we don't have enough manpower to search the entire town today. It's going to be dark in a couple of hours. The vampire will need blood tonight—he looked emaciated, and they're worse than junkies, they need blood the way we need oxygen. If—when—he attacks somebody, we need to know about it so we can respond instantly. So we should put out an APB. I can work up an Identi-Kit profile so your people will know what he looks like, but he's conspicuous enough that people will probably recognize him right away. I need to get the call when that happens."

"I don't want to just wait for someone to die before we take action," Vicente said. "People around here won't like that."

"No, of course not." Caxton licked her lips. Her mouth was getting dry. She'd never done this before, but she was the only one who knew how to fight the monsters. She kept having to remind herself of that. "Every car we can get on the streets should have two cops in it, and enough firepower to take down the vampire. There's a state police barracks a few miles from here, and another one in Arendtsville. You can request they send every available unit. We'll search every shadow, every street corner. Maybe we'll get lucky. Also, I'd like to open an official investigation, see what we can learn about this guy." That should have come first, she realized. It should have been her first suggestion. Vicente caught her self-doubt; she could see it in his eyes. She was making mistakes already.

What would Arkeley do? It had been so much easier when he'd been in charge and she'd just followed his orders. She had to remind herself she'd been trained for this.

"There's somebody I need to talk to, a professor at the college." She pulled out her notepad and flicked back to the first page. "Professor Geistdoerfer, in the, uh, Civil War Era Studies department."

"The Running Wolf?" Vicente exclaimed.

"You know him?"

The police chief laughed and then covered his mouth. "I'm an alum of the college. Class of ninety-one. Everybody there knows him. How is he possibly mixed up in all this?"

"He was the first person to enter the tomb," Caxton said. When Vicente's face clouded in confusion, she felt like her heart had stopped for a second. The chief didn't even know how this had all begun. Briefly she filled him in on Arkeley's discovery and the investigation she'd made of the cavern and the hundred coffins.

"We're—we're not going to see more of these things, are we?" he asked, when she'd finished. His eyes were very wide and his mouth was open. He was scared shitless.

Well, maybe he should be, she decided. Maybe it would keep him on his toes. As long as he didn't get so scared he stopped functioning. She needed him.

"The hearts were all missing. That means they're dead. So hopefully we won't see more than just the one. But that's more than enough. Can you have someone make an appointment for me with the professor?"

"Yes," he said, "of course." He took a pack of gum out of his desk and peeled off a stick. He offered her one, as well, and she took it gladly. "I'll make sure he sees you right after the press conference."

Caxton stopped with her stick of gum halfway to her mouth. "Press conference?" she asked.

26.

The Rebs left then, & I began to breathe once more.

Leg by leg, arm by arm, the marksman unwound himself from his perch. He dropped to the ground with the softest of thuds & squatted down next to my hiding place. He was a tall &

lanky man like our Commander in Chief, even more so in fact. I guessed him seven feet tall & as thin as a reed. He held out one lined hand & I shook it gratefully.

"Alva Griest," I whispered.

"Rudolph Storrow of Indiana." He slung the rifle over his shoulder like a rower shipping an oar. I saw he wore a sawed-off shotgun as well in a holster at his belt, where an officer will keep a pistol; on the other side, where a sword should go, he had an Indian-style hatchet with a long handle, what is sometimes called a Tomahawk. I was terribly glad he was on my side. "Listen, Griest, there are two men comin' our way on foot, runnin' the same course you did. They're tryin' to be subtle, yet ain't very good at it. They your'n?"

I nodded. Eben Nudd & German Pete, he meant. "They're good men," I swore.

"If they're dressed in blue, they need no other recommends with me. Just get 'em in here quiet like, will ya, so's we don't bring down half of the Army of Northern Virginia with 'em."

I blushed from pate to soles, but did not waste further time with idle talk. I found my men in the weeds of a nearby field, & brought them to order, & introduced them to our new ally.

—THE STATEMENT OF ALVA GRIEST

27.

Glauer drove Caxton back to the hospital—she had some important business there before she could get started organizing the night's patrols, and she wanted him with her to act as her liaison with the local authorities. They took a patrol cruiser, one of five the department had left, since Caxton had put one of them in the shop. It felt very strange to climb into the passenger seat—a literal shotgun seat, with a Mossberg

500 locked between her knees. A laptop computer mounted between the seats kept jabbing her in the thigh as they took the sharp corners.

There had been a time when she drove Arkeley around, listening to whatever pearls of wisdom he cared to drop. She had tried to learn everything she could from him, thinking that he had planned to make her his successor. Instead he'd just wanted her as bait for the vampires. The tables had turned, it seemed, and she wondered if Arkeley had ever been so uncomfortable in the passenger seat. Not just because of the various bits of hardware poking her, but because for the first time in her life Caxton was in charge. Vicente and Glauer looked to her to make all the decisions. Caxton had been far more comfortable the night before, chasing a vampire with her life at stake, than she was ordering cops around. What if she screwed up? She had already screwed up, many times. It would probably happen again—and eventually she would screw up enough that people would die. Unless she could take down the vampire first.

"Time," she said, as they waited at a stoplight, "is going to be our enemy here." Gettysburg's roads had been laid out for carriage traffic in the nineteenth century, back when it was a market town, before the Battle. The roads had not been widened since—they couldn't be, since that would mean moving or demolishing historical buildings. As a result, and with two million tourists coming through every year, the quaint little town of seventy-five hundred people saw some pretty heavy gridlock. She sighed and wondered if it would be faster to get out and walk. To pass the time she looked at Glauer and asked him, "What's the worst thing you've ever seen?" It was one of the questions state troopers used to get to know each other, nothing more.

Glauer looked back at her as if she'd asked how, when, where, and with whom he had lost his virginity. She squirmed in her seat, wishing she could take her question back. After a second, though, he shrugged and looked forward through the windshield again. "About ten years ago, some coed, some girl up at the college, took a header off the top of Pennsylvania Hall. It's supposed to be haunted—maybe she was running away from a ghost. Maybe she was just high on acid." He shrugged again. "I got called in to tape off the scene, keep the other kids away. I had to be there all day with her until they could get an ambulance in there to take her out."

"Was she pretty well splattered?" Caxton asked.

He flinched and shook his head. "Not so bad. There was a little blood, but she was lying on her side almost like she'd just lain down and taken a nap. Her face was turned away from me. That was why I didn't notice the birds at first. They were all over her, pigeons, crows, starlings. I eventually decided to shoo them away, even though I felt like an idiot doing it. I would have done it sooner if I'd realized they'd come for her eyes."

Good one, Caxton thought. In the barracks of Troop T, the highway patrol, that would have gotten the man a couple of high fives and maybe a free beer. She started to smile and opened her mouth to congratulate him, but when she looked over again he was shivering. She'd stirred up a memory in Glauer that he would have preferred not to visit again. *Shit*, she thought. In Troop T they had seen worse things almost every day. Traffic fatalities could be bad, really bad, especially when it rained. They had developed a thick skin about it, used gallows humor to cover up how much it shook them. Apparently when you were a cop in a town with zero homicides you didn't have to grow calluses on your heart.

They arrived at the hospital a few minutes later. Glauer led her down the stairs and to the morgue, where Garrity's wife was already waiting for them. She sat in an orange plastic chair in a waiting room on the far side of the autopsy suite. She had a kerchief around her hair and wore sunglasses, probably to hide how puffy her eyes had become with weeping. A forgotten Styrofoam cup of coffee rested on the seat next to her.

Caxton held her breath before she walked into the waiting room and promised herself that this time she would get it right. She had to be sensitive and understanding, but she couldn't let those things stop her getting what she needed.

They didn't have a course in how to do this at the academy. Maybe they should have. She walked in and crouched down next to the woman and offered her hands. "Hi," she said, and studied the other woman's face. She had sandy hair and thin lips and she might have been thirty or forty; Caxton couldn't say. She had that same pasty complexion that grief gives everyone, a pallor that sadness brings. "I'm Laura Caxton. I work for the state police. I was with your husband last night," she said. "I want you to know I'm very, very sorry for what happened."

"Thank you," the woman said. She squeezed Caxton's hands and then let them go. "The doctor here said you had called him and that I couldn't take Brad's body until I'd spoken with you. Is there some kind of form to fill out?"

Caxton shot a glance at Glauer. The local cop stood by the door as if he were guarding it. His eyes did not meet hers. Supposedly he had already told Garrity's widow why they had come. Clearly he hadn't been specific enough.

"Your husband was killed by a vampire," Caxton said. "There's a possibility—I'm not really sure how to say this."

The woman pulled the sunglasses off her face. Her eyes were bloodshot, but they showed far more composure than Caxton had expected. "Why don't you just say it, and we'll worry about my feelings later?"

Caxton nodded and looked down at her shoes. She had to force herself to meet the woman's gaze. "Vampires have a certain power over their victims. They can call them back from death. It's not—it's not something you would want to happen. They come back corrupted, with their souls damaged. They become slaves of the vampire. I'm sure your husband was a strong man, a good man—"

"Oh, for Christ's sake," the woman finally said. Her hands were shaking, but her eyes blazed. "What is it that you want? Will you just tell me?"

Caxton bit her lip. "Until we cremate his body, he can be forced to come back and serve the vampire. We have to burn him, all of him. It's the only way."

The widow's face turned deathly white. She stared up at Glauer and Caxton waited for her to say something. She didn't.

"It's the only way," Caxton repeated. "I understand there may be religious reasons you may not want to do this, but—"

"Bullshit," the widow said.

"Helena, she's not making this up," Glauer said.

The woman's name was Helena. Why hadn't Caxton even asked? Her cheeks burned, but she knew she had to get the permission before she could move on. "If you'll just say the word, we'll take care of all the details."

"Mike, this woman is talking about—about—" Helena Garrity stood up suddenly, so suddenly she swayed from side to side. She rushed over to Glauer, who pulled her into a bear hug. She nearly disappeared into the broad expanse of his jacket.

"Shh," Glauer said, stroking her hair. The woman collapsed against his chest. "Just say yes."

The woman shook her head against Glauer's chest, but then said yes. Caxton produced the proper form and the woman signed on the appropriate line. A doctor came in and started talking to the widow in low tones. He took the form and shoved it in his pocket.

Glauer led Caxton back upstairs. He didn't speak until they were in the parking lot. He put on a pair of mirrored sunglasses, then, and looked away, toward the road. "You're not really a people person," he suggested.

"I'm a cop," she replied.

He looked almost surprised. "You think those are two different things?"

She kept her mouth shut all the way to their next stop—a meeting room at the back of a church. Chief Vicente was there waiting for them, standing at a podium with one of his patrolmen on either side of him. They should have been out searching for the vampire's body, she thought, but she supposed he had his reasons for doing this instead.

Vicente wanted a press conference. A half-dozen reporters from the *Gettysburg Times* and other papers around Adams County sat in uncomfortable-looking chairs, while a lone TV crew had set up in the corner, their cables and battery packs in a pile on the floor. They had a pair of floodlights trained on the podium and it looked pretty hot up there. Caxton lingered at the back of the room. The reporters looked back at her, ignoring the chief as he read a prepared statement.

"The state police in Harrisburg have been good enough to provide us with an expert in just this kind of crime," Vicente said, and raised one hand to gesture at her. He wanted her to come up and say something, she realized. "I'd like to introduce you to Laura Caxton. Thank you." He waved at her again. She wasn't sure whether or not to expect applause. When none came she rushed down to the podium and cleared her throat.

The lights were bright enough to blind her. She held up one hand to cover her eyes and looked out at the reporters. "I don't have a prepared statement," she admitted. "Are there any questions?"

One of the reporters stood up. He was wearing a dark blue blazer, but she couldn't really see his face. "Do you have any leads as to the vampire's identity?" he asked.

She shook her head. That didn't seem to suffice, so she leaned closer to the microphone and said, "No, not at this time. We're looking into it."

Another reporter asked, without getting up, "Can you tell us about the policeman who died last night? Did he suffer much, or did he go peacefully?"

She felt like she was back at school. She felt like she was being quizzed. That one had to be a trick question. "I'm sorry, I can't comment on that," she said.

Over by the television camera a third reporter asked, "Officer Caxton, can you give us some idea of what to expect? Can you outline your plan for catching this creature and what you're going to do to protect Gettysburg?"

"I've basically just got here and I haven't had time to create an action plan. We're still working on that—"

The reporter held up his hands in disgust. "Can't you give us any details of your investigation at all? What's your best-case scenario? What should people do?"

She glanced over at Vicente. His face was very still, as if he were keeping it under perfect control. His shoulders, however, were inching upward toward his ears. He didn't like her performance.

Well, so be it, she thought. She certainly had better things to do. Maybe it wouldn't hurt to throw him a bone, though. "Well, I can tell you that everyone should stay indoors tonight. Don't go out for any reason, not unless it's a true emergency. Anyone who has a place to go outside of town should do so now, before sunset. I'd urge all the tourists to cut their trips short and go home."

Vicente smiled very broadly and started walking back toward the podium, his hands together as if he might start clapping.

The reporter wasn't done with her, though. "Are you actually suggesting that Gettysburg should shut down its tourist industry?"

"Definitely," she said. "We're dealing with a vampire. They drink blood. They'll kill anyone who gets in their way. If I could, I would evacuate the whole town."

Even through the haze of light she could see every eye in the room go wide when she said that.

28.

I fumed in impatience. Bill had been badly hurt when I'd seen him, perhaps near death. Every minute I delayed my rescue reduced his chances of survival.

"Now ya hold your horses, Griest. That's one virtue I've learnt, & it has served me well. For a long time I been runnin' after that Reb, e'er since he sup'rised my company in the Peninsula. He slaughtered a good score of men in their sleep. I was on sentry duty that night or I would have been one of them. When you came runnin' up I was waiting for him to ride by so I could spill his brains on his own beloved soil by way of thanks. Woulda had 'im, too, if'n I hadn't wasted my powder on getting yer attention."

"Who is this murderer?" I asked.

"The Ranger Simonon, & about the worst snake the Confederacy ever pulled out of a hole. He's a sneak killer and a horse thief, of the sort they raise out Bleeding Kansas way. Father Abraham wants him dead as much as I, & by God, I'll have it so. If I can help yer pal, I will, but not if it means missin' another shoot."

"I aim to go inside, at once," I said again.

Storrow placed a hand on my shoulder & squeezed it. "There's danger in there, y'know. Mortal danger."

"You didn't strike me as cowardly before," I said.

The man would have been in his rights to strike me then. Instead he only spit on the ground and said, "I seen a thing come out of there last night I wouldn't want to meet again. Ya know what I'm jawin' about?"

"The vampire," German Pete barked.

Storrow looked at the man long & hard & then nodded. "Thought it might be one."

"Do you know aught of vampires, then?" I asked.

His shoulders raised in a shrug. "Precious little. What man does? They're rare as honest politicians, & I thank Jesus for that. I saw one they caught & killed in Angola town, back in '53, when I was a boy. They took & laid him out in a warehouse for the public edification. My daddy took us all in for a look, & paid a half-dime for the pleasure. Ugliest critter I ever saw, & it scared me stiff, dead as it was. This one's still quick."

—THE STATEMENT OF ALVA GRIEST

29.

"He couldn't get me off that podium fast enough," Caxton said. She leaned back in the Mazda's driver seat and rubbed at her eyes. It felt strangely good to talk to Arkeley. She'd never thought she would say that before.

Calling him had taken some courage. After she left the press conference and Glauer had taken her back to the police station, she had been left all alone in the swirling leaves of the parking lot, with no idea what to do next. Or rather, she knew exactly what needed to be done but she didn't have time to do it. She should have been out on the streets with the other cops, searching for the vampire. She had only ten minutes, though, before she was supposed to go to her interview with Professor Geistdoerfer. She had considered getting something to eat—it was going to be a long night—but there really wasn't time. So instead she had taken out her cell phone and called Clara, but she only got the machine.

She had screwed up, and badly. She knew that. She'd traumatized Garrity's poor widow and outraged the local media. Vicente had been furious with her after the press conference and she still wasn't sure why, but she knew it would be a problem. Organizing the manhunt for the vampire was going to be harder than ever.

The phone in her hand contained Arkeley's number, she thought. If there was anybody in the world who could give her some decent advice it would be the old Fed. He had actually done this before, stood where she stood, made the decisions she was forced to make. He would be a great source of advice—though never sympathy. She could expect little but scorn for how she'd handled things so far.

She had opened her phone list and there he was, the first entry. The only person she knew whose name started with *A*. She had hit the send button before she could stop herself. He was in a truck ferrying Malvern to Philadelphia and the connection had been lousy, but when he answered she had just started talking, ostensibly just updating him as to everything that had happened. When she finished there was silence on the line.

"Hello, Arkeley? Are you there?" she asked. "What do you think?"

"I think," he said, "that if you had consciously planned out how to be bad at this job, you still might have come off better."

She shook her head from side to side. It was about what she'd expected. "But what did they want? I just told them what I thought."

"That was the last thing they wanted. Press conferences are a very specific variety of bullshit. They serve two functions: to tell people that no matter how dire things might look, it's not their fault, and that they need take no action at this time."

"We have a vampire here!" she said, sounding whiny to her own ears.

"Yes. The good people of Gettysburg know that. They're terrified. They wanted you to get up there and tell them that they're safe and that you'll clean up the mess for them." His voice changed, grew more weary. "They just wanted some reassurance. They wanted a symbolic father to tell them everything was going to be alright. It's why you were welcomed so warmly in the first place. The chief there doesn't know what to do next and he asked you in so he could pass the buck."

"I thought it had more to do with my experience and skills."

Arkeley grunted. It almost sounded like a laugh. "Well, you've now demonstrated exactly what those skills are worth."

She frowned. He couldn't see it, but it wouldn't have bothered him anyway. "I don't remember you having to do any press conferences, last time."

"That was only because I bullied my way out of them. Listen, Trooper, I have to go now. We're nearly at the museum. Maybe I'll have something for you later—if the bones here really do date to 1863, they must be related in some way to our suspect. I'll have my phone on me, so keep me posted, please." He broke the connection without another word. Caxton flipped her phone closed and shoved it in her pocket. Arkeley had been a jerk, as usual, but talking to him had made her feel strangely better. He hadn't dismissed her from duty or told her to let the local cops handle the case. On some level he still believed she was the right woman for the job.

The job—she checked her watch and saw she just had time to make her appointment with Geistdoerfer. She checked her annotated map of the town and started up the Mazda. It wasn't far to the college campus—nothing in Gettysburg was very far from anything else—but traffic was thick. It was late, almost sundown, and she cursed the tourists around her as they crawled through green lights and blocked intersections.

She was heading up Carlisle Street when she realized that the tourists in their cars were headed away from the center of town. Always before, the traffic had flowed toward Lincoln Square. They were leaving the borough, heading out in great flocks. Had her press conference gone out live? Or maybe people were just smart enough to get their kids away from a town haunted by a vampire. She could only hope.

She pulled into a parking lot near a classroom building and headed inside. The Civil War Era Studies department had classes on the third floor overlooking a student area with a fountain. Through the windows she could see the campus lit up and golden in twilight. It reminded her of her own year and a half in college, a time she'd spent learning who she was, if she hadn't learned much else. She found the door she wanted and knocked politely, then stepped inside. The classroom was all but deserted, row after row of black metal chairs lined up facing a whiteboard and a long table littered with books and bags. Three female students—they looked so young to Caxton, who was barely out of her mid-twenties herself—had congregated around a very tall, very striking man who could only be Geistdoerfer.

"Running Wolf," they called him, and she finally understood why. He was of average build, but his height made him look lean. He had a sharp nose and sharper eyes, and his head was crowned with a thick shock of silver hair that turned darker in the back. His mustache was thick and bristly, but he didn't look like one of the Pennsylvania cops she'd seen back at the station. He looked far more distinguished, like some European aristocrat maybe, but with a real streak of wildness. When he spoke to the girls he tilted his head back slightly and looked down at them along his long nose. The gesture didn't look haughty, however, but almost conspiratorial. He looked as if he were sharing dark secrets with them even as he discussed the topics for their term papers.

"Professor," Caxton said. "I hate to interrupt, but—"

"Trooper, ah, Caxton," he said airily. "Oh, yes, the police called to say you were coming over. You young ladies had best leave us." He smiled down at his students and one of them actually giggled. "And do be safe tonight, won't you? Lock your doors so the beasties don't get you."

The students promised to be good and left, shouldering

their bags and giving Caxton a once-over as they passed her. It was only when they were gone that Caxton saw that Geistdoerfer's arm was in a sling. "Shall we go to my office, where we can sit down?"

"Sure," Caxton said.

He started loading books and papers into a satchel with his one good hand. Caxton helped him and somehow ended up carrying the bag as well. He led her down a long hallway that was starting to get gloomy as the sun fell. His office was at the far end, a cozy room lined with books. He sat down behind a big desk piled with student papers while Caxton took a padded chair on the far side. She glanced around, taking in her surroundings, the way any cop would, but the room offered few secrets at first glance. A cavalry saber hung on one wall, its scabbard mounted just beneath it. The blade was polished to a high shine but still spotted with rust.

"A horseman of J. E. B. Stuart's acquaintance dropped that about half a mile south of where we stand," he told her, "one hundred and forty-one years ago. His head had just been taken off by a cannonball, so he no longer needed it. He was good enough to let it fall in the mud, where it was quickly buried, and in the heat of July the mud hardened to something like cement. The sword lay there for quite some time, almost perfectly preserved, until I had the pleasure of digging it up when I was just a lad. I was a tourist, you know, dragged here by my parents from Nebraska, where we lived. I thought this place was boring until I saw that sword. Now I can't imagine anywhere more exciting, anywhere else I'd rather live. It is funny, isn't it, the path things take through history? The way the past intersects with and shapes our so modern lives?"

Caxton knew a few things about how the past could catch up with you. She didn't have time for chitchat, though. The sun was down and the vampire would be waking up—hungry. Best to get this interview over with quickly.

"I apologize for taking up your time," she said. "I've already spoken with Jeff Montrose—"

Geistdoerfer's eyes went wide for a moment. "A promising student, though a bit bizarre looking."

"Yes," Caxton agreed. "He showed me the cavern, and the bones inside. I'm pretty sure the vampire I'm chasing came out of the empty coffin down there. Montrose said you were the first person to enter the cavern, and I thought you might have seen something everyone else missed. That you might have some idea how the vampire got out."

"You thought, perhaps, that I might have actually seen the vampire leaving the cavern?"

Caxton squirmed in her chair. "I hardly think that's likely, no, but I need to check up on every lead. I'm sure you understand, as an archaeologist."

"Oh, absolutely." He tried to gesture with his hurt arm, but the sling wouldn't allow him much freedom of motion. He grunted and closed his eyes for a moment, as if the pain of his injury had caught up with him.

He opened a drawer with his good hand and took out a bottle of pills. After fiddling with the cap, he knocked two of them back into his mouth and swallowed them dry. He grunted them down his throat, then sat staring at his desk for a long minute while she waited for him to recover enough to talk.

He leaned back in his swivel chair, leaned all the way back and looked up at the ceiling. "Well," he said, finally, "I suppose there's no point in trying to lie now."

"I'm sorry?" Caxton asked.

"I could feed you some line, and believe me, I'm enough of an orator to probably sell it. I could tell you the coffin in question was already ruined when I found it. Empty and . . . all that. But there's hardly any point. You've caught me, copper. Red-handed." He looked down at his arm. She studied the sling closely for the first time and saw a drop of red welling up through the bandage around his wrist. "Oh, that's kind of funny, isn't it?"

Then he started to laugh.

30.

It had been a fine house once, with paintings on the walls & plentiful lamps to provide illumination. Now only sunlight, slanting downward from the rent dome of the cupola, limned the place in a yellow radiance that hid as much as it revealed. I could see where the paper on the walls had peeled back, & where the floorboards were littered with the bodies of dead wasps, dry & brittle so they crunched as I trod on them.

The entrance gave on an elaborate spiral staircase that must once have risen majestically to a second floor. An enormous finial in the shape of a chess pawn stood at the bottom of the railing, & it remained in fine shape, but shortly past that point the stairs had collapsed, or been pulled down. They had been reduced to a heap of plaster & broken marble that filled much of the room.

Beyond these stairs I proceeded, & found a luxurious parlor, reduced to a shambles. Shattered mirrors lined the walls while elegant chairs had been shoved to the back of the room like so much rubbish, some broken down to kindling, some still showing satin upholstery. In the center of the room stood a raised platform, perhaps like an altar, but with a rounded top. It was made of alabaster & chased with gold. I stepped closer & saw that it was hinged on one side & would open like a chest. Then I sucked in a deep breath & tried not to sicken. It was a sepulcher I had found. A gilded coffin.

"They cain't hurt ya by daylight," Storrow hissed at me from behind. I looked back & saw the other men standing in the doorway, peering over each others' shoulders but unwilling to take one more step forward.

I screwed up my courage & grabbed the side of the sarcophagus & threw the lid open. It rose easily on springs & I let go & jumped back, ready for anything.

Inside I saw a lining of stained red velvet, & nothing more. Not so much as a mouldering bone or scrap of a shroud.

"Nothin' ever was that easy, I s'pose," Storrow said, sounding almost regretful. For myself I was glad enough to find the vampire missing. I did not look to tussle with it again, at least not so soon.

"Bill's not here," I told the others. "Come on, let us keep searching."

I grasped the lid again & tried to close it, but it felt as if it had locked into place & all my strength could not move the lid. There must be some hidden catch or a release lever, I thought, & I bent to look closer.

At that moment some hard metal object caught the back of my collar, & jarred the very bones of my spine. Had I not been leaning forward it would have caved in the back of my skull, I am sure. Stunned, my arms tingling, I turned as quick as I could to see my assailant bringing his weapon back for another blow. It was a gold candelabra, I saw, with white wax still clotted in its receptacles. The man who wielded this expensive club wore a long nightshirt & had a stocking cap on his head. His face hung in tatters, the skin peeled back from the grayish muscles underneath. Just as Bill had come to look.

There was a struggle; the short of it is, I lived, and he did not. I would have studied the dead man in more detail, I think, had we not at the moment heard footsteps scuttling on the floor above our heads.

—THE STATEMENT OF ALVA GRIEST

31.

axton squinted. "If you're making a joke I'm afraid I don't get it."

"Then allow me to explain. You were quite right to come here, quite right." He leaned forward again and opened his eyes, and they flashed with a wild light that made her flinch. "I'm your culprit. I opened that cavern not knowing what I would find inside, but once I saw those coffins, once I saw the first set of bones, I saw the potential. I sent Montrose and the rest of the students away. I don't think any of them even saw the heart."

Caxton sat up very straight in her chair. Her Beretta was holstered under her left arm and she was very much aware of it.

"If they did they probably didn't know what they saw. It looked like a lump of coal, because someone had been good enough to coat it in tar. I imagine they meant to preserve it, though for how long I could not tell you. It was sitting on top of one of the coffins. Just one out of the hundred but I understood. It was meant to go inside—there might as well have been written instructions. I opened the coffin and placed the heart in the center of the rib cage and it started to work almost instantly. You'll wonder why I did such a stupid thing, of course." He nodded at the saber on the wall. "I have longed, my entire life, to speak with the poor man who dropped that. I have spent decades imagining what he would say to me, and the questions I would ask him. I thought the fellow in that coffin would be quite forthcoming. And I was right, in a way. He had plenty to say. Of course, he asked most of the questions."

The temperature in the room had dropped ten degrees while Geistdoerfer spoke. Caxton reached for her handgun, but before she could get her hand up someone reached down from behind her and grabbed both her arms in an iron grip. She didn't have to look down to know that the hands holding her down would be as pale as snow. She could feel the vampire behind her, feel the way he made the hairs on the back of her neck stand up straight.

"I knew what I was doing. I knew that it was probably a mistake. I felt a certain compulsion, though he tells me he had no power over me at that time. It was pure curiosity that moved me, then. Exactly the thing that killed the cat."

Geistdoerfer started to remove the dressing on his arm. It took some doing, as he only had one free hand and his mouth to work with. The vampire didn't speak while Caxton waited to see what lay beneath. The vampire didn't even breathe on her neck.

The vampire didn't tear her head off, either, or suck out all her blood. That might mean he just wanted to play with her first. Vampires had very little inner life—they mostly spent their nights pursuing blood, thinking about the blood to come. Occasionally they played with the bodies of their victims, and occasionally they played with their food before they drank. Human death amused them. Corpses could provide them with hours of entertainment.

"It was quite something to see. As soon as I lay the heart among his bones it began. The heart started to shake and jump. The tar on the surface cracked and whitened, then it burst open, as if it were under considerable pressure from within. A kind of white smoke leaked out, except it wasn't quite smoke. It seemed alive, like it had a will of its own. It filled the coffin and a thin ribbon of it spilled over. I thought it might crawl across the floor and come after me. Then I saw the bones inside that tendril of vapor, the finger bones."

Caxton barely heard him. She was too busy thinking about what it would be like to be a vampire's toy. Another possibility, though, was more likely, and also far more chilling. It was possible the vampire didn't want to kill her because he wanted something from her. One vampire, Efrain Reyes, had wanted her to be his lover. Kevin Scapegrace, who came after, merely wanted her because Malvern had decided it would be ironic to turn her into the thing she had destroyed. Then there was Deanna—but she didn't want to think about Deanna.

A third possibility presented itself. The night before, this vampire, the emaciated creature that Geistdoerfer had awoken, had spared her life because she was a woman and he was sworn never to hurt a member of the fairer sex. It was possible he was going to let her go again.

She doubted it, though. She doubted it very much. Such niceties belonged to human beings. A vampire, drawn by the smell of blood, would shed gallantry and courtesy quickly enough. What had saved her once was very unlikely to save her twice.

"The smoke solidified as I watched. At first he was as transparent and wobbly as a man made of jelly. Then he sat up and roared, a long, hoarse noise I could barely stand to hear. His whole body shook, even as it grew more and more solid, more complete. Finally he leaped up out of the coffin and stood hunched over in the cavern, looking like he had no idea where he was. He picked up the coffin and smashed it against the wall. I still don't know whether he was aware for the whole time he was in that box, or whether it was like a long sleep. He didn't seem to want to spend another second inside it, however."

Eventually Geistdoerfer got the bandage loose. It fell in a bloody, sticky heap on his desk. What was revealed beneath looked less like a human arm than a raw leg of lamb after a dog got through with it. There were still three fingers on his hand, but most of his wrist and forearm had been gnawed away. His thumb was missing altogether. A little blood welled out of the wound as Geistdoerfer flexed the muscles remaining to him.

When the blood glistened in the open air, the hands holding down Caxton constricted. The grip on her arms grew stronger.

She did feel the vampire breathe then—a long, cold sigh of desire that drifted down her neck like a tendril of fog.

"He struck me as hungry, so I offered him a drink," Geistdoerfer explained. "He was a bit more eager than either of us expected. He has apologized, of course, but I'm not sure that will be enough. I want you to know something, Trooper. I want you to know I had no idea what he would be like. After being buried, tucked away for so long—and he looked so thin, so cadaverously thin. I had no idea if he could even walk under his own power, or how strong he could really be."

Most people didn't. It was one reason that people like Arkeley and Caxton had to exist, because most people had no idea what vampires were capable of. You underestimated them at your peril—more often than not, your mortal peril.

"After this happened I wanted to go to the hospital, naturally. I fear I screamed quite a bit. He wouldn't let me go. He didn't want to let me get that far out of his sight. I have a friend, a professor here, who gave me the pills I've been taking. She has a bad back, but it only bothers her sometimes, and for now she was willing to share. She had plenty of questions herself, but I knew how to fend her off." Geistdoerfer looked up at her. "You've gone very quiet," he noticed.

"She knows what's coming," the vampire said. His voice was a growl, an inhuman burr in her left ear. She closed her eyes as he moved his thick jaw across her neck. She could feel the hardness of his teeth, feel the cold triangular shapes of them pressing against her warm flesh. None of them pricked her, though. He was holding himself back. If he drew her blood, he might not be able to resist his unnatural urge to kill her. "Forgive me if I take a liberty, Miss," he said, much softer than before. His hand, cold and clammy, stole around the side of her neck. His fingers drew across her throat, then reached down into the collar of her shirt.

"I see you've not replaced your amulet," he said in her ear.

His breath stank, though not of blood. It smelled like an open grave. It filled up her nose and her mouth and made her want to pull away.

Still she said nothing.

She was far too scared to speak.

Geistdoerfer replaced his bandage with fresh linen, wrapping it carefully and not too tightly around his ruined arm. Halfway through he had to stop and take some more pills. Finally he slipped his arm back into its sling, and then he rose from the desk and came around to stand next to her.

"I'm going to take your sidearm, now," he told her. He sounded truly contrite, but she wasn't about to forgive Geistdoerfer for what he'd done. Garrity's widow wouldn't have forgiven him, she knew. With his good hand he drew her Beretta out of its holster and laid it on the desk, well away from her hands. He took the can of pepper spray from her belt and pushed it into his own pants pocket. His hand moved upward, touching the pockets of her coat. He took away her handcuffs and her flashlight. He found the lump of her cell phone next and squeezed it experimentally. He left it where it was. She glanced up, trying to catch his eyes, but his face revealed nothing.

32.

The fiends were thick inside the door frame presently, wasting no moment on startlement at seeing us again. They pushed through as if their divers bodies had become a single, gelatinous mass.

Storrow's shotgun blasted my senses as he fired two loads of buckshot deep into that host. Torn faces & flailing limbs shattered & fell away. There was no blood, which surprised me, but much tearing of flesh & grinding of bone. I had the presence of mind to discharge my own weapon into the fray & heard a distant popping sound which came from German Pete's revolver. To me, half deafened by the noise of the shotgun, it sounded like a man throwing stones at a wooden fence. Yet the bullets it fired cut down half the foemen before us . . .

An imp of hell with a ragged face came clambering over the sundered bodies of the dead, a fireplace poker in his hand. There was no time to reload, so I jabbed forward with my bayonet. The blade sank with sickening ease through his skull & brains & he fell away without making a sound. Two more came charging at the doorway then & Eben Nudd knocked them sideways with the butt of his weapon.

& as easy as that, the door was clear.

—THE STATEMENT OF ALVA GRIEST

33.

"You've been hiding him here since you found him. In these offices, somewhere," she said.

"Let me show you," Geistdoerfer said.

The vampire let go of her once she'd been disarmed. Geistdoerfer picked up the Beretta and gestured at her with it, like something out of an old black-and-white movie. She got the point, and stood up slowly, keeping her hands high and visible.

They walked out of the office and down a darkened corridor. Geistdoerfer lowered the pistol as he opened a door marked CWES LAB. She watched the gun bob back and forth in his hand, point at the floor. She could have made a grab for it. Then she looked at the vampire.

His face was thin and sharp, his eyes tiny and beadlike. His teeth glimmered in the half-darkness.

If she made any sudden moves, she knew, he could tear her to pieces in the space between two heartbeats.

Eventually Geistdoerfer got the door open.

The three of them walked inside, into a room full of tables. Bits of metal and whitened lead bullets lay spread out on the tables. One held an enormous barrel, a hogshead, Caxton believed it was called. Its wood was silver with age and its hoops had turned to dull rust, but a black crust of tar held it in one piece. Another table held a single pair of decaying pants. Probably the same pants the vampire had worn when she'd seen him the night before. They were laid out carefully, as if a team of archaeologists had been going over them all day with magnifying glasses and dental picks. Geistdoerfer might have done just that, she realized.

In the center of the room stood an enormous set sink made of brushed aluminum. It was as big as a bathtub. "We're set up here to handle human remains, though I doubt the kind alumnus who funded this lab had quite our distinguished guest in mind."

Caxton leaned over the tub and smelled something awful inside. She looked closer, but only found a few maggots crawling blindly across the bottom of the sink.

"You've been sleeping in this tub," she said to the vampire. Most animals bolted in terror at the first sign of a vampire. Insects, and especially maggots, were the most notorious exception. During the day a vampire's body didn't just slumber, it liquefied. Maggots knew a free meal when they saw one.

"He kept saying he needed something better, that he needed a real coffin. Last night he went out to find one. Unfortunately you happened to be there at just the wrong time."

Or the right time, she thought. The right time to discover the weird game the archaeologist was playing. That discovery was probably going to get her killed, but it meant the vampire wouldn't be able to hide much longer. How many people knew where she was? Half the police department knew she'd set up this appointment. When she failed to appear at the police station that night the local cops would start to put the pieces together. This was the first place they would come to look.

Of course, she'd be dead by then. A wave of horror rippled

down her back, hitting every muscle in turn as it went. She wanted to run away. She wanted to start screaming.

She kept control of herself, somehow.

He gestured with the gun again. Clearly he'd never held one before. She would have been a lot more nervous if the safety had been off, but even in the gloom she could see otherwise. She might have been prompted to try some heroic gesture like grabbing the gun away from him. If it hadn't been for the vampire behind her.

"What's your name?" she asked.

He only smiled at her, a gruesome parody of a human smile. His teeth looked very sharp in the dim light.

"Were you a soldier?" she asked. When he didn't answer, she turned to look at Geistdoerfer. "Was he a soldier in the Battle?"

Geistdoerfer lowered his head for a second but didn't answer her question. Apparently between the two of them they were smart enough to remember she was a cop, and that when she asked questions, she was digging for clues. They weren't about to give her anything.

The gun moved again and this time she moved, heading down the corridor to a stairwell. Orange light came in through the windows, cast by the sodium vapor lamps outside. The light passed through the leaves of a tree being torn at by the wind, and long daggerlike shadows glided across the steps as she went down. At the bottom she pushed open a door and cold night air billowed in. Beyond lay a parking lot. There were no students out there—maybe they'd been smart enough to take her warning and lock themselves away for the night.

Geistdoerfer's car was a burgundy-colored Buick Electra, a big old machine with hints of tail fins. He unlocked the driver's-side door and gestured for her to get in. "I'm driving?" she asked.

For once she was answered. "It doesn't have power steering, I'm afraid. It makes it frightfully difficult with one hand. Also, you're the only one who knows where we're going."

"I am?" she asked, a little stunned. She had thought the two of them merely intended to get out of town, away from the manhunt she had ordered. Then she felt as if a bucket of cold water had been thrown on her. They didn't want her to take them home with her, did they? Clara was there—

The vampire answered in his grunting, roaring voice. "You must know, I think, where she's been taken. I could sense her before at something of a closeness, but now she's gone. Somewhere to the east."

"I don't know—" Caxton stammered, but Geistdoerfer cut her off.

"Spare us the declarations of innocence. You must know where she is. I've seen your movie, Trooper. I know how closely your fate and hers are wound together. Now where, pray tell, has she gone?"

Caxton's body froze convulsively with fear. They would hurt Clara—they would kill her. Would they do worse? She knew they could. "Please. Please don't."

The vampire grabbed her shoulders. Not hard enough to do any real damage. "Where is Miss Malvern? I will not be stayed or halted, not after all this time!"

He didn't want Clara. Her blood started running again in her veins. He wanted Malvern. It made sense. Vampires held only one thing sacred. The young ones, the active ones, cared for their elders. It was how Malvern had stayed alive for three centuries, by preying on that reverence. Clearly this vampire wanted to take care of her in his turn. As old as he was, he was still a youth compared to Malvern. Caxton wondered what she should do. Would she actually let him get to Malvern? If he brought her blood, if he brought her back to some kind of active life, that would only make things doubly worse. She would have two vampires on her hands instead of one.

It wasn't like she had much choice, though.

Geistdoerfer pointed the Beretta at her. "I don't have much

experience with this sort of thing, but I think I grasp the finer points. We're going to sit in the back. I'll hold the gun, my colleague will sit there and be quietly menacing. You, my dear, will drive us to . . . to . . . ?"

She could lie. She could drive them somewhere random, she could drive them to the state police headquarters in Harrisburg. The vampire would know, though. He could sense Malvern even at this distance. If she didn't drive him where he wanted to go, he would just kill her. If she didn't behave herself, he would have no reason to keep her alive. She wasn't ready to sacrifice herself just to slow him down. "The Mütter Museum," she finally admitted, sagging back into the leather of the driver's seat.

"That's in Philadelphia, isn't it? Very good. You'll take us there now, at a reasonable rate of speed, and you'll do nothing to make us conspicuous, yes? If you drive off the side of the road or into traffic, I'll be very upset with you. I've spent a lot of time keeping this car in good condition. I'll also remind you that such dramatics might very well kill me, and your delightful self, but a crash would prove little more than an inconvenience to the boss here. So drive carefully. Okay?"

He raised the gun in his hand and pointed it directly at her forehead.

"Okay?" he asked again.

"Yes," she said.

"Take the Turnpike," Geistdoerfer said. "It'll be the fastest this time of day." He handed her the keys across the back of her seat and she started up the car.

When they got to Philadelphia, she wondered, how long would the vampire let her live? But at least for the moment she was still in one piece. For the moment she could still think, and try to form a plan.

Not a single idea whatsoever presented itself to her.

What choice did she have? She threw the car into gear and drove out of the lot.

34.

"Obediah?" someone called. It was the ranger Simonon! I looked out through the doorway & saw mounted men gathered in the clearing before the house. The Rebs had returned. "Obediah?" he hallooed. "Is something amiss in there? I swear I heard gunfire just now."

We were as rats, stuck inside a trap, & our time was limited. It seemed hopeless.

The Reb cavalry made camp outside the door & settled in as if prepared to wait for days if need be, lighting fires, tying up their horses to the trees, & breaking out what rations they had. We inside could do little but curse our luck; albeit quietly. We made no more noise than four church mice, I think.

The Ranger Simonon did not come in, nor send any man to so much as glance inside the door. Neither Storrow nor I was foolish enough to think of trying to fight our way out. We possessed amongst us some small number of firearms, but in our desperate state we would have marched through that door only to be slaughtered instantly. We stayed well back from the doorway & tried not to be seen.

— THE STATEMENT OF ALVA GRIEST

35.

Outside, through the windows, she watched rural Pennsylvania go by. Houses lit up yellow and orange from shaded lamps, or a flickering blue where the televisions were on. Cars sat in the driveways, or tucked away in garages. Normal people were sitting down to dinner, or they had already finished and were washing up. Good people, and the bad ones too. Normal people. The people she'd pledged her life to protect. "There are a lot of cops in Philadelphia. A lot more than we have out here. I don't know what you expect to do when you find Malvern," she said, though she was afraid she did know, "but you'll have to deal with them eventually. You'll want blood. Either for her or for you, so you'll have to feed. You can hide for a while, but—"

The muzzle of the Beretta touched the back of her head. Geistdoerfer snarled at her when he spoke. "You're in mortal danger, Trooper. Right now. It's going to get worse. I can hear the panic in your voice. Would you like me to put you out of your misery?"

"No," she said, through gritted teeth.

"You're not ready to die, then? You'd like to try to live awhile longer?"

She didn't want to give him even that much. "Yes," she said anyway.

"Then please don't talk about what's inevitable. It's going to ruin my digestion."

Was he trying to shut her up? Or was he trying to explain his own actions? The vampire depended on him. The monster couldn't have gotten this far without Geistdoerfer. Maybe he wanted her to understand him. To forgive him.

Unlikely, she thought, but she kept that to herself.

"Can I turn on the radio?" she asked. Music might drive the darkest thoughts out of her head.

"I don't see why not," Geistdoerfer said. "Just keep it low."

She nodded, then glanced down at the Buick's dashboard. The radio was original to the car and not very sophisticated. She switched it on and a little rock music came out, mostly swamped in static. She tried fiddling with the tuning knob. The first station to come in clearly was a Christian talk channel, and she switched away again almost immediately. She didn't want to hear about how she was going to burn in hell for eternity, not when death was so close. She eventually found a station playing classical music. Something light and happy. Caxton didn't know enough about classical to say who the composer might have been.

"Mozart," the vampire announced, as if he'd heard her thoughts. "By God. I know this piece. I heard it played in Augusta once, at a Christmas festival. How . . . is there a music box in this vehicle? Yet it sounds so rich, like a full orchestra playing."

She didn't understand what he was asking. She didn't want to speak unless her fear sounded in her voice.

"Just a bit after your time, I think," Geistdoerfer said, "a man named Thomas Edison invented a way to capture sound out of the air and record it on a wax cylinder. Later they developed a way to then transmit those sounds across great distances."

"Like the telegraph?" the vampire asked.

"A similar principle. Though it requires no wires."

The vampire was silent awhile. Then he said, "There's so much changed. The lights burning on this road, you see them? This would have been impenetrable darkness, in my time. All the world outside our little fires was darkness. You've pushed that back so far I don't think you two can even imagine it, now."

"You have so much to teach us," Geistdoerfer announced.

The vampire didn't seem up to giving a lesson just then, however. He didn't speak again until they left the Turnpike.

It wasn't much farther to the museum. They passed through the sweeping green lanes of Fairmount Park, where streetlights studded the gloom, then rolled into town beneath the high wall of the old state penitentiary. Philadelphia was a city of discreet zones, districts that had their own specific characters. It felt more like a collection of small towns than a metropolis. The neighborhood that housed the Mütter Museum was one of the more unusual sections.

The streets were not busy that night, though crowds gathered outside of pubs and small restaurants. The vampire kept his head down, invisible to anyone casually glancing through the car's windows. Outside of a brewpub a couple of college-age boys hooted at them, but they were just admiring the Buick, not questioning its occupants.

Caxton wheeled down Twenty-second Street, passed the College of Physicians building, then ducked down an alley toward a small parking lot enclosed by buildings on three sides. There was no attendant; if you wanted to park there you were expected to fold up a five-dollar bill and tuck it through a slot near the exit. Only a couple of other cars stood in the lot.

Caxton pulled into an empty space and then shifted into park. The Buick's engine thundered in complaint for a second and then died down to an idle. Her arm muscles twitched as she switched off the car and laid back in her seat. Her body wanted to cramp up into a single knot. She felt a horrible urge to just lie down on the seat and close her eyes. To accept whatever was coming.

It seemed the vampire wasn't going to let her do that. "Miss, if you please, get out first."

"Don't try to run away," Geistdoerfer added.

She let her head fall forward for a moment, slumped on her neck. She rubbed at her eyes. She couldn't seem to master the bodily coordination to open the door. But then she did. She got her legs out, stretched them, lunged up with her torso until she was standing in the parking lot. Her body twanged with tension and fear, but she was standing up. That was what you did, when faced with an impossible situation. You kept going.

She climbed out of the car, but before she could even think of running the vampire was behind her, clutching her wrist in his hand. The grip was light, though she knew it could tighten without warning, and if it did it could crush her bones.

"We should really get inside, away from the madding crowd," Geistdoerfer insisted. He took a step away from the car and they all heard the sound of fabric tearing. The professor looked down and Caxton did too. She saw that his bad arm had gotten snagged by the tail fin of the Buick and that his sling had torn.

"It doesn't matter," Geistdoerfer said. "I'll fix it later." His face was a mask of pain. Had he injured himself on the tail fin? He started to walk toward the museum, rubbing at his ruined wrist with his good hand. "Come on," he said.

The vampire didn't move. Caxton had no choice but to stand still.

There wasn't much light in the parking area. Just a few overhead lamps that left plenty of shadows. Still she could see a trail of small drops of blood, round and flat, following Geistdoerfer wherever he went. Blood had stained the torn end of his sling and as she watched it gathered there wetly, formed a hanging dome of shiny red. Then it detached and slid off to spatter on the oil-stained ground.

The vampire held her arm tight. "I've had to smell his life for hours now," he told her. His voice was a low dusky growl. The purr of a big cat just before it pounced on a zebra. "I've sat next to him and smelt it, and held back as best I might."

Caxton didn't move. She knew what the sight of blood could do to a vampire. "He's your only friend in the world," she said. "Please, don't—"

"I'll need strength for what I'm to do here."

Then he was off like a shot, closing the distance between himself and Geistdoerfer in one quick leap. Caxton was dragged behind, held fast by his soft grip on her wrist. She fought and kicked and tried to pry his fingers loose with her free hand, but it was no use. It was like fighting against an industrial vise.

The vampire didn't waste time tearing sling and sleeve away from the professor's arm. He just bit right through the layers of cloth and deep into the flesh beneath, his teeth grating on the bones. Geistdoerfer screamed, but the sound didn't get very far. The professor's eyes glazed over as pain and shock took him, as the vampire tore and rent at his skin and muscle and sucked out his blood. For a moment it looked as if Geistdoerfer would die quietly, almost peacefully. Then his body started to shake, his limbs seizing in a convulsion of pain and horror. His eyes were blind by then, but his mouth kept working, his lips trying to form words. Caxton couldn't decide what he was trying to say.

When it was done, when the last drop of blood had been sucked from his body, Geistdoerfer looked paler than the vampire. He hung limp and quite dead and the vampire stood holding them both, live woman and dead man, like a child playing with two mismatched dolls.

The beast's eyes burned in the darkness then. His body rippled as if it were made of pale fog and a breeze was coursing through him. His emaciated frame seemed to swell as if the stolen blood had filled him up, distended him. When it was done he looked almost human. Or at least as close as he was ever likely to get.

He dragged the two of them over to a Dumpster in the alley and threw Geistdoerfer's body inside without further ceremony. Caxton wasn't surprised. Vampires and their minions held no reverence for human death. When the body was disposed of he dragged her to her feet and finally let go of her. She didn't even think to run. With the blood in him the vampire would be even faster than before. Stronger. Much harder to kill.

"She's here," he said. "Miss Malvern." He wasn't looking at her for confirmation. He had his head up as if he could smell the other vampire on the air. "She's quite close. You did well, my friend, to bring me here."

It was then, of all times, that Caxton's cell phone chose to ring.

36.

In back of the pantry, we found the servants' stairs, & thought we might be better hid on an upper floor. Every one of those steps creaked, and might have given us away. With time, however, we found ourselves at the top, and in front of a row of wide windows. The marksman & I peeked out through said apertures & watched Simonon playing cards with a sergeant who wore no shoes at all. We could speak up there, if we were soft about it. "I could get off a shot from here," Storrow said, running one hand along the massive barrel of his target rifle, "that would do the Union much good."

"& get us all killed, in the bargain," Eben Nudd pointed out.

Storrow nodded in agreement, but added nothing. I truly think he would have given his life, & been glad to do it, if he could remove the Ranger from play.

Through gritted teeth I asked my next question. "Why is he here, though? What does he want with this Obediah he keeps calling to?"

"You haven't yet guessed it?" Storrow asked. He favored me with a grim smile. "Obediah Chess, he's the master of this place, or else, he was." He pointed at the oversized finial at the bottom of the stairs. It was in the shape of a pawn, as I have recounted earlier. "Don't ask me how he came to his change of estate, but now he's yer vampire. Simonon's come to draft 'im."

"The Confederacy is recruiting vampires now?" I could scarcely credit it, even from such villains.

—THE STATEMENT OF ALVA GRIEST

37.

The vampire stared at Caxton's coat as her cell phone rattled out the opening bars of a Pat Benatar song. She closed her eyes as the phone buzzed against her side. Would this be the thing that finally got her killed?

The vampire didn't stop her as she slowly reached into her pocket and took out the phone. It had stopped ringing. A moment later it chirped to tell her she had new voice mail. "It's," she said, about to tell him it was her phone. Then she stopped.

Geistdoerfer had frisked her back in Gettysburg. He had felt the cell phone in her pocket, had actually squeezed it. He hadn't taken it away from her, though. Why not? At the time she had just assumed he didn't consider it a threat. She had decided he was right—what use was it to her while he was watching her every move?

Maybe, though—maybe he had been trying to help her. He had seemed to want to aid the vampire in his plan, had in fact acted like he was part of it all. He must have known on some level, however, that it would end in his own death. Unless somebody stopped the vampire first. He couldn't have helped her directly, not with the vampire right there. Had he been trying to give her a chance without giving himself away?

She would never know, now. But maybe she had gained a momentary advantage. Maybe she could use this.

"It's a music box," she said. "Like the one in the car." She showed the phone to the vampire but he just shook his head. He wouldn't even know what he was looking at. They hadn't had LCD screens or keypads in his time.

"It plays music for you? Whenever you like?"

She had to think. She had to think what she could do. She couldn't very well call the police. He would realize what was happening before she'd gotten more than a few words out. She couldn't even listen to the message she'd just received—that would look too suspicious.

"I can make it play another tune," she said, after a second. "Can I show you?"

He shrugged. He had plenty of time—the night was still young.

Caxton bit her lip and worked the keypad with her thumb. As quickly as she could she texted a short message to Arkeley:

at mm w vamp no gun

It was all she could think of. Looking up at the vampire, she hit send. The phone burbled in her hand, a happy little crescendo telling her the message was sent.

"Delightful," the vampire said, actually smiling. "Perhaps later you'll play me some more. Now, alas, I have much to do. Ladies first, if you please."

She nodded and walked ahead of him. She could feel him behind her, his icy presence making her skin crawl. She walked around the corner to the museum entrance. The door was locked but the vampire just tugged at the handle until the lock mechanism groaned and snapped. A small torn piece of metal flew out and tapped Caxton's hand. She walked through the opened door and into a broad lobby lit only by the orange glow of the streetlights outside.

Caxton had been to the Mütter Museum before, years past on a school trip. Long before her life had been about vampires. The place had spooked her out even back then. That was when it was well-lit and full of teenagers and college kids looking for a nasty thrill.

In the dark, in utter silence, the place was like a haunted mausoleum. A whole new kind of fear gripped her. It helped a little that there were no skeletons in the lobby, no two-headed babies floating in alcohol, just a broad staircase leading up, closed off with a velvet rope, and doors leading to a gift shop, some offices, and finally the museum. The building actually housed the College of Physicians of Philadelphia, a meeting place for doctors and a sizable medical library. The museum was only a small part of the college tucked away in a corner of the building. Caxton headed through a doorway to her left, then walked through a maze of plasterboard walls housing a display of medical instruments used by Lewis and Clark. Beyond that lay another exhibit, this one about the great epidemics of the last two centuries. The great influenza of 1918 was well represented—the signs on the walls described it as the greatest health crisis in history, responsible for more than fifty million deaths. She came up to a picture of a pile of bodies waiting for interment in a mass grave and she stopped.

No vampire could ever hope to match that kind of destruction. Yet if Malvern were revived she would certainly give it a try. She would need blood, whole oceans of it, to keep her going. The older a vampire got the more she needed every night. Arkeley had estimated once that it would take five or six murders a night just to keep her on her feet—and that even then she would still be hungry. Starved as she was, she was unable to hunt, unable to kill. Yet if this vampire found a way to revive her, where would she stop? She would create new vampires to serve her, to protect her. She would slay indiscriminately, cutting a bloody swath through Pennsylvania. How many dead cops would it take before she was eventually brought down?

She couldn't let this new vampire finish his task. So far fear for her own life had driven her, a desperate need to live just a little longer. But there were limits on even that terror.

"Not much farther, I think," he said behind her.

Had Arkeley gotten her message? She truly hoped so. She walked away from the picture on the wall, walked farther into the building, and there it was. The Mütter Museum in all its awful glory.

It spanned two levels, a main floor below them and a broad gallery connected by a pair of carved wooden staircases. Every inch of wall space had been lined with cabinets, dark wood fronted in polished glass. Inside were bones, mostly—walls full of skulls showing variations in cranial anatomy, whole skeletons mounted on steel bars to show deformities of bone structure. On her left stood the casket of the saponified woman, a corpse the Mütter had bought to demonstrate how soil conditions could turn a human body into grave wax. On display around the room were a giant impacted colon, the brain of the assassin who killed President Garfield, the conjoined liver of Chang and Eng.

It was all very tastefully done.

Caxton walked out onto the gallery and looked down at the main floor below. There were a lot more skeletons down there, some in huge glass cases of their own. One held the bones of a giant, a man at least seven feet tall, standing next to the remains of a dwarf. They looked strangely like a parent walking with a child. Nearby stood a big wooden set of drawers which she remembered held thousands of objects that had been removed from human stomachs—coins, pins, broken pieces of lightbulbs.

Between those two displays stood a single wooden coffin on a pair of sawhorses. The lid was closed. It wasn't part of the museum's collection. "There," she said, because she knew that Malvern was inside.

"Yes, thank you, I can see for myself." The vampire grabbed her shoulder, not overly hard, and turned her to face him. "You'll stay here," he said, "and wait for me to finish."

Her hands were in her pockets. She'd thought this might be coming. Despite what he thought, she still had her amulet. Because the ribbon was broken she couldn't wear it around her neck—instead she'd put it in her pants pocket. Where she could reach it if she needed it. Out in the parking lot she hadn't had a chance to grab it, but now she held it tightly. She could feel it getting warm.

His eyes blazed into hers. He was trying to hypnotize her—to freeze her in her tracks. Surely, she thought, he would feel something when it didn't work. He would know she had some protection against him.

He said nothing, though. Maybe he hadn't felt anything. Maybe he was just in a hurry. He brushed past her and then leaped over the side of the gallery, not bothering to take the stairs. He landed with a barely audible thump and moved immediately to the side of the coffin. For a second he stood motionless before it, then passed his white hands over its top, his head tilted back.

Someone walked up behind Caxton and she nearly screamed. A fingerless hand touched her shoulder and she turned to see Arkeley standing there. His face was a mask of torture in the gloom. His good hand held his old reliable Glock 23. It looked like he'd received her message, though clearly he hadn't had time to really prepare.

He raised his ruined hand to his lips and she understood he wanted her to be quiet. What was he waiting for? She knew him well enough to believe he must have some plan, but she couldn't imagine what it might be.

Below them the vampire lifted the lid of the coffin. It opened noiselessly. Inside lay Malvern. She was withered and her skin was covered in sores, but she looked far more healthy than the last time Caxton had seen her. That didn't make sense—Arkeley had been starving her of blood for over a year, hoping she would eventually die of malnutrition. If anything it looked like she'd grown stronger. How was that even possible?

The vampire reached into the coffin and ran his fingertips across Malvern's mottled cheek. He said something, so low she couldn't make it out.

There was no more time—what was Arkeley waiting for?

The Gettysburg vampire had found some way to cheat time. What if he knew some magical spell to bring Malvern back to her former self as well? There was no time at all.

Her eyes wide, she stared at Arkeley, but he only shook his head. So she did the only thing she could think of. Grabbing the Glock out of his hand, she aimed down at the vampire and put three quick rounds into his back, into where his heart would be. One two three. The noise was immense in that hushed place—it sounded as if every glass case in the museum had shattered at once.

The vampire vanished into thin air. If she'd gotten him, if she had killed him, he would have just slumped to the floor. She must have missed the heart, or the blood that flowed in his veins, Geistdoerfer's stolen blood, must have protected him.

"You idiot," Arkeley said, his face congested with rage. "How could you screw everything up?" He didn't wait for an answer but ran off, into the shadows.

38.

I was set to search the upstairs rooms, in case more fiends lay in wait for us. The task loomed large. Whatever soothing balm the excitement of battle may bring, it wears off powerfully fast. Luckily the second floor was not so large, & the number of doors I faced small. Two were locked; a third led to a narrow stairs, by which one could access the cupola, which was ringed inside with a narrow iron gallery. I headed back, & tried the locked doors again. You can perhaps imagine my horrified surprise when I heard a muffled sound from behind one of them.

It might have been a pigeon, having found its way in through some broken window, I told myself. But it was not. The sound I heard was high pitched, a keening whine that I had heard before. It was the voice of one of the fiends.

"I have a minié ball for you if you make another sound," I said through the door, my voice just loud enough to carry through the wood. I knew I could dispatch the creature beyond that portal. I was worried more he would make some alarum that would rouse the cavalry outside.

"Alva?" the voice asked. *"Alva, is it you?"*

You will have already guessed the identity of my conversant, & you are correct. It was BILL. My horribly wounded & long-sought friend, found at last. So why then did my blood run cold to hear him?

—THE STATEMENT OF ALVA GRIEST

39.

Caxton thundered down the stairs, her feet blurring on the steps, her weapon held high and ready, pointed at the ceiling. The vampire could be waiting for her at the bottom, in the shadows there. She could feel his teeth tearing into her flesh, ripping through her skin. He could be lying in ambush and she could be running right into his maw.

At the bottom of the stairs she turned and extended her arms, weapon in firing position. She looked around for pale humanoid shapes—and suddenly realized there were far too many of them. The skeletons in their cases all looked like vampires in the dark. The vampire she was chasing, while he no longer looked like a famine victim, was still rail thin, and would pass for a skeleton if he stood very still in a corner of the room.

Caxton pivoted slowly, trying to cover the entire room. This was madness. The vampire could see her just fine. Their night vision wasn't supernatural by any means, but they could see blood—her blood—as if it glowed with its own red light. She was a walking neon sign as far as the vampire was concerned. At any moment he could spring on her, and he was fast, so fast she wouldn't have time to get her gun around to fire at him.

The only sensible thing to do in her situation was run. Get out, get to a safe distance. Try to seal off the museum's exits, then wait for dawn. Arkeley had taught her a long time ago, however, that whenever you tried to fight vampires in a sensible fashion they would just slip through your net. In the time it took her to lock the museum's doors the vampire would be long gone—or he would already have killed her.

The only effective way to hunt vampires, Arkeley had shown her, was to walk right into their traps. To give them exactly what they wanted. It confused them, made them think you had more up your sleeve than you actually did.

There—she rushed forward, thinking she'd seen something move. She jabbed her handgun out, lined up its sights on center mass, started to squeeze the trigger.

Then she stopped. The shape she'd almost shot was the skeleton of a man who had suffered from crippling spina bifida. His bones looked as twisted and worn as driftwood.

The vampire laughed at her. Then she heard a chuckling, echoing sound that made her skin crawl. The sound seemed to come from all around her, from nowhere in particular. Had it come from directly above? She looked up with a fright, but saw nothing over her except for the ceiling. She didn't feel much relieved, though. That laugh had crawled right in her ear and laid eggs in her brain. A dry, nasty, grating laugh that spun off into distorted echoes had chased off into the shadows.

She had no time to decide what that meant, if anything. She had a subject to collar. Caxton pressed backward, up against a display of pickled fetuses, some with heads, some without, some with more than the requisite number. Slowly, inching her way, covering the whole room before her, she headed back for the stairs. She was pretty sure the vampire wasn't on the lower level.

She was wrong.

A white blur leaped over the top of Malvern's coffin and barreled right at her. She brought her weapon around just fast enough to blast a hole in his face before he collided with her bodily, knocking her to the floor. He reared up, clutching his eyes, and she rolled to the side before he could strike downward with his fists. They connected with the floor hard enough to crack the wooden parquet.

"Shit," she said, the word just leaping out of her mouth. He turned to follow her voice and she saw she'd ruined the bridge of his nose. Most of the middle of his face was hanging down by a flap of skin and she saw splintered bone in the wound. Even as she watched, however, white vapor filled in the hole with snaky tendrils that knitted together. In the time it took him to stand upright again, his face was completely restored.

He glanced at the coffin in the middle of the room, his face dropping in regret, and then he was moving again.

Caxton barely had time to dodge before the vampire swept past and up the stairs. Cursing—silently this time—she lifted her weapon again and dashed up after him, though he had already disappeared into the gallery. At the top of the stairs she swung around, covering the corners of the room. She didn't see him. There were two exits from the gallery—back through the maze of pasteboard walls and the exhibits, or out through a clearly marked exit door that returned visitors to the lobby. She dashed through the latter, knowing she was falling behind, that he was getting away. The velvet rope across the staircase had been torn from its mountings and she knew he had gone up.

Where was Arkeley, she wondered? Hopefully he'd run for safety. As far as she knew he didn't have another weapon, and she didn't think he'd be stupid enough to try to stop the vampire with his bare hands. It was up to her.

She took the stairs two and three at a time, breath pounding out of her mouth, sighing back in. Her body felt tight and constricted and she knew her adrenaline was starting to wear off. That was alright—she could replace it with raw, cold fear.

At the top of the stairs she dashed into a library, which must have been a beautiful room by daylight. In the orange streetlight that streamed through its tall windows, the rows of books and leather-upholstered armchairs looked rotten and decayed, as if the room had been abandoned to the elements for hundreds of years. To her left a door still swung on its hinges and she raced through. Beyond was a corridor that ran the length of the building, windows lining one side, the other lined with doors. Small marble tables stood between the doors. A pair of black leather driving gloves lay forgotten on the table nearest to her.

Four doors, she counted, and another staircase at the far end, leading down. The vampire could have used any of them.

She kept her back to the windows as she crab-walked slowly down the length of the hall. If he had taken the far stairs he was already gone, she knew. He would have fled through a back exit and she would never catch him. If he had taken one of the doors he might still be in the building, might in fact have trapped himself in a dead end. At the first door she reached out, touched the polished wood, tapped the doorknob with trembling fingers. If the vampire had been there recently she thought the knob might feel cold to the touch or perhaps the fine downy hairs on her hand would stand up. She felt no sense of unnatural presence there, however.

The next door led into an office, with the word DIRECTOR in gold letters painted on the wood. Caxton touched the knob. Nothing; no sense of unease or disgust. She turned it slowly. It let out a sharp metallic creak and she stopped immediately. Had she felt something move nearby, something hidden in the dark? She held herself as perfectly still as she knew how, tried to not even breathe.

What was it? There, she thought, a puff of breeze had caressed her cheek. She whirled around, ready to fire instantly, only to see that one of the windows was open a crack. A very delicate draft was coming through, nothing more.

Caxton bit her lip and moved to the third doorway. Her feet made only very soft sounds on the carpet. She reached out her hand toward the knob, fear making her arm shake, and let her fingertips graze the brass knob ever so gently.

Nothing.

She breathed out, let go a little of her muscular tension. One more door to check. If there was nothing there then at least she would know she was safe, that the vampire was gone and that she wasn't going to die that night. She moved quickly toward the fourth door, reaching for its knob.

Behind her the window crashed open, glass cracking with a jarring sound. A white mass shot through like a giant cannonball and blasted down the hall right toward her. Before she could even think the vampire had one hand at her throat. He smashed her backward against one of the marble tables, its edge digging painfully into her left kidney. He lifted her up again and then smashed her against the floor until her bones rattled inside her flesh. Only the thick carpeting kept her leg and arm from snapping on impact. He picked her up again and held her in the air, crushing her neck muscles with his powerful fingers. It felt like she'd had a handful of knives jabbed down her throat. She couldn't talk—couldn't breathe. If he closed his hand even a fraction of an inch more, she would die. Blackness swam through her vision as if big blobs of oil were dancing on the surface of her eyes.

He had spared her life once because she was a woman. He'd let her live a second time because she was useful to him, because she could drive a car. Clearly his patience was all used up.

Laura Caxton would have died then and there if it hadn't been for the Mütter's night watchman. He stepped out of the fourth door just then, perhaps alerted by the gasping, choking noises Caxton was making, and shone his flashlight right into the vampire's eyes.

The vampire screamed in pain. He was a nocturnal creature, and that much light hurt him far more than bullets. He dropped her, his arms flying up to protect his sensitive eyes from the bright light. In another second he was gone, down the back stairs and away.

40.

I dropped to my knees & peered through the keyhole. The eye that looked back on me from the other side was shot with blood, & quite yellow where it should have been white. But I recognized the brown iris, the color of the rocks on Cadillac Mountain. It was Bill, indeed.

"Wait there, Bill, I have some others with me. We'll bring you out of this captivity," I swore.

"Alva, no, you have to leave. You can't be here."

"I won't leave without you," I told him. "I'm going to force this door, & the noise of it be damned."

"No." The high-pitched voice turned hard as flint. "I . . . can't let you come in. I'd have to stop you, Alva. I would hurt you if you tried. Don't make me do that."

"What nonsense you speak!" Yet I felt my heart jump. I knew what Bill had become. My neck still ached, my side still bled with the wounds the fiends had given me, & now Bill was one & the same. But it was Bill, my Bill! The only true friend I've ever had. A man I slept next to for two years in a tent too small for dogs to use. A man whose life & mine were wound together as tight as the strands of a little girl's braided hair.

& yet I knew. I understood. "We can help, Bill. We can get you to a surgeon."

"There's nothing you can do for me now, Alva. It's too late. You must forget our friendship, & leave me as I am. I beg you just to go! This is all I can do for you. Even as I speak my soul is writhing, my hands are reaching for a knife to stab through this keyhole!"

I fell back on my haunches, my brains reeling. "Oh, Bill, say it isn't so." But it was. He spoke no more, & a moment later, his eye disappeared from the keyhole.

—THE STATEMENT OF ALVA GRIEST

41.

The night watchman—his name tag read HAROLD—helped her sit up and lean back against the wall. Caxton rubbed at her throat, trying to get circulation back into the crushed muscles there. "You okay?" he asked her over and over, as if through sheer repetition he could make it so. "That guy coulda killed us both, and easy!"

That was true. The light had hurt the vampire, but only momentarily. He could have smashed it and then returned to his slaughter. He'd been too smart to take the chance, though. He couldn't have known if Harold was armed, or if a platoon of police were behind him. She tried to explain that to the night watchman, and found she couldn't. It felt as if her larynx were being rubbed against a cheese grater. She could breathe, though. Her lungs were heaving up and down just fine. So she nodded. She slipped the safety of Arkeley's Glock back on and shoved the heavy pistol into her empty holster. It didn't quite fit—the leather holster wasn't designed for that particular model of handgun. After trying to force it, she finally just let it hang out a little.

Caxton rubbed at her eyes, her mouth. She let her body calm down on its own, let it take its time in doing so. She'd been very, very close to death. Well, it wasn't the first time. She knew what to do, which was to try to take it as easy as possible. If there was any real damage to her throat, then running around and chasing vampires would probably just make it worse.

Besides, the vampire was already gone. Once again he'd escaped her. Once again she'd failed.

Harold disappeared for a while, but finally came back with a paper cone full of cold water. It felt very good going down and she thanked him, even managing to squeak out her appreciation in words that only felt like butter knives as they came out of her. "I'm," she said, and paused for a second. "I'm Trooper Laura Cax—"

"Oh, yeah, I know who you are," he said, a big goofy smile on his face. He was a short guy, maybe fifty years old with curly scraps of pale hair sticking out of the bottom of a navy blue baseball cap. He wore gray overalls and yellow Timberland boots.

"Did Ark—" she stopped. Trying to pronounce hard *k* sounds made her feel as if a nail was lodged in her esophagus. "Did the other officer tell you I was here?" she finally managed to ask. She glanced down at the paper cone in her hand. A single drop of water remained lodged in the fold at its bottom. She licked it out eagerly and wished she had more.

"What, Jameson? Aw, no. He didn't tell me about you. I just recognized you, is all. From that movie *Teeth*. That was awesome."

She wanted to roll her eyes. Instead she said, "Thanks." Then she grimaced. Another hard *k*.

"That one scene, where Clara kisses you for the first time? That was so fucking hot. I must've watched that like a hundred times."

Caxton rolled her eyes. That scene always embarrassed her when she watched it. Had she really been that easy? "I have to see something," she said. Slowly she rose to her feet, bracing herself against the wall behind her. When she was relatively certain she wouldn't fall over again, she made her way down the stairs at the end of the hall. At the bottom a fire door stood half open, cool air from outside billowing in. She pushed it open and stepped outside, the night feeling good on her face for once. She breathed in a deep lungful that soothed her throat, then looked around. She stood on the edge of the parking lot. The Buick stood just where she'd left it. She saw the Dumpsters as well, one of which held the dead body of Professor Geistdoerfer. "Harold," she called back over her shoulder, "I need your help."

It was not easy getting the corpse out of the Dumpster. It took real work to lift Geistdoerfer over the lip of the container. Harold took the weight from her so she didn't have to just dump the dead man on the asphalt. Once that was done they carried him inside the Mütter building, Harold holding his feet, Caxton carrying him with her hands laced under his armpits. Geistdoerfer's wounded hand dragged on the ground, but it didn't leave a trail of blood. Every drop had been drained from his body and none of it had gone to waste.

Caxton knew that the body was a possible threat. The vampire had killed him and by so doing had established a magical link between the two of them. It was within the vampire's power to call Geistdoerfer back from death, to literally raise him as a servant who could not fail to do the vampire's bidding. It could happen at any time, over enormous distances, so they had to watch the corpse every second. She needed a place to keep it while she decided what to do next.

The College of Physicians of Philadelphia was mostly a meeting place for doctors and researchers, with lecture halls and conference rooms taking up most of its space. In the basement, however, there was a suite of rooms used for preparing specimens for the museum. It looked remarkably similar to the facilities in the Civil War Era Studies department at Gettysburg College, though the equipment was much older and less shiny. They laid out Geistdoerfer on an autopsy table there. Caxton folded his arms across his chest to try to give him some dignity, then wondered what to do next. They would need an ambulance or a hearse to take him to a funeral home. She would have to try to locate his family to let them know where they could pick him up. Then she would also have to convince them to cremate him.

First, though, she needed to start coordinating with the Philadelphia police, let them know there was a vampire loose in their streets. Her cell phone didn't get any reception in the basement, so she left Harold in charge of watching the body while she went upstairs. Halfway there she ran into Arkeley coming down.

"He got away," she said.

"Of course he did." The scars that crisscrossed Arkeley's face didn't constrain him from throwing her a look of utter contempt. If anything, they made his sneer look worse. "You couldn't wait ten more seconds?"

She tried to ignore him. "I need to call the loc-c-cal c-, the c-, the authorities," she gargled, holding up her phone. She tried to push past him, but he stopped her.

"Don't bother. I contacted them when I got your text message. I had already warned them something like this might happen."

Of course he had. Arkeley had always been ready for bad things to happen. It was how he lived his life. It was his most basic philosophy. She let her shoulders sag and put her phone away.

"They'll have units all over this part of town by now. Cops flashing their lights down every alley and back lot, helicopters up and scanning the rooftops. Of course it won't come to anything."

No, she supposed it wouldn't. Vampires were smarter and faster than garden-variety criminals. They knew instinctively how to blend into the shadows, how to use the night to their advantage. The regular police had little chance of finding him.

Caxton glanced at her watch. It wasn't even midnight. This late in the year the vampire would have plenty of darkness to work with, maybe seven more hours. How far could he get in that time? Or perhaps he would stay nearby, find a good hiding place where he could sleep through the day. Then he could come back the next night to try to rescue Malvern again.

"You damned fool. I expect you to screw things up from time to time. But it looks like even I underestimated your ability to ruin a perfectly good plan."

Exhaustion pushed down on her shoulders, but anger lifted her up: sudden, hot anger. Indignation. "Shut up," she said, wishing she had thought of some better words. Like maybe, *How dare you?*

"I'm doing my best. You threw me into this shitty situation and I'm doing everything I c-can." The hard *k* sounds didn't hurt so much when she was pissed off, she realized. "I'm the one chasing this bloodsucker, not you. I think I deserve a little respect."

"Oh?" he asked.

"Yes. If I hadn't taken action he could have revived Malvern. He could have carried her out of here while you just watched."

Arkeley's deep-set eyes twinkled a little, even the one under his paralyzed eyelid. "Interesting," he said.

"Fucking fascinating," she replied, though she had no idea what he was talking about.

"You seem to be under the false impression that our pale friend came here to rescue her." Arkeley's mouth moved in a way that might have conveyed some kind of emotion on a normal face. On his features it just looked like a worm crawling from one cheek to the other. "Come with me."

42.

TIME it was that proved our undoing. We were in danger of our lives all that day. We dared not do anything to alleviate our fears, or to improve our situation. We periodically checked on Simonon & his men, but they did not stir or make any sign of decamping. I think we all guessed what they waited for. For night, & the return of the vampire, from wherever he had gone. We knew he was not in the house, for we had seen his coffin, & it was empty. If he did not return, would we be trapped for the next day as well, & the next? Simonon looked a patient man, for all the tales of his butchery Storrow could relate.

The day passed as they do. Soldiers know how to wait; it is what they learn best. We passed our time as we might. I longed to return to the door down the hall & speak again with Bill, but I did not.

As orange light tinctured the sky above the trees I think we all held our breath, uncertain whether to feel relieved, or affeared. There was some excitement in the Reb camp as well, of a not wholly different character, I think. The tension grew, & mounted, but it did not last long. We Yanks, German Pete, Storrow, Nudd, & me, crowded the window, & didn't worry who might see our faces there.

None of us saw him come, though the horses smelled him perhaps. They bucked & tore at their lines, & made as if to bolt. Their neighing was the loudest thing I'd heard that day, I thought. & then he was present, the vampire Obediah Chess, standing next to the fire as if warming his pale flesh. As if he'd been there all along.

—THE STATEMENT OF ALVA GRIEST

43.

Arkeley led her back to the museum, back to the lower level, where Malvern still lay in her coffin. As they approached Caxton looked down at the old vampire, trying to piece things together.

There wasn't much left of Malvern. Her skin had turned to paper, still snowy white but riddled with dark sores. It had pulled away in places, hanging in tatters. Most of her scalp was missing, revealing yellow bone underneath. Her triangular ears hung down ragged and limp. One of her eyes was missing—it always had been—and the other was just a milky blob of flesh that wobbled back and forth in its socket. Caxton doubted she could see anything with that eye.

That didn't mean she was gone, though. When Caxton leaned down over the coffin, Malvern's head craned forward on its spindly neck, her jaws opening in slow motion. She could sense Caxton's presence somehow, and was trying to bite her, to tear into her flesh and suck her blood.

When Caxton pulled back the jaws closed, just as slowly as they'd opened.

The vampire from Gettysburg, her vampire, should have looked like that. Any vampire over a hundred years old should be that decayed and weak. Though he had fed on Geistdoerfer's blood, that should not have been enough. They still had no idea how he was able to walk, even to stand up. Much less how he could outrun a police cruiser or throw her around like a rag doll.

Arkeley cleared his throat. Caxton turned and saw him standing next to a display case. Inside stood the head and shoulders of a man with his skin and part of his musculature removed. His blood vessels had been painstakingly exposed and plasticized, painted different colors to differentiate between the veins and arteries. On top of the case stood a cheap black laptop computer. Arkeley popped it open and raised the screen so she could see it.

"You'll remember that she warned us," he said. "She told us that he would come for her." He tapped the space bar and the computer woke from its sleep mode. On the screen a white window appeared, the text field of a word processing program. Malvern's original message was displayed there in large italic type, completed and therefore a little more legible now:

comformeheshall

"Come for me he shall. Right," Caxton said. "She was gloating. Laughing at us because she knew that soon enough he would come and take her away from all this. Bring her blood or—something. I thought maybe he knew some spell. She calls them orisons, right? Some orison to restore her."

"Yes, I thought that too. Then I realized that she wasn't that stupid." Arkeley stepped in front of the screen and scrolled down the page. "Why give us even a cryptic warning? We wouldn't have expected him to even know who she was. By telling us that he was coming for her she gave us plenty of time to prepare. I knew I needed more information so earlier this evening I set her up and let her type some more."

He stepped away so she could see the screen. The next message read:

proteckt me you must
it is your dutie laura

"Protect—" Caxton put a hand over her mouth.

"Ah. I think you've begun to get the point," Arkeley said.

Caxton nodded. Yeah, she was getting it. The vampire of Gettysburg hadn't dragged her all this way so he could revive

Malvern. He'd come to destroy her. "But—they don't fight among themselves. They cooperate."

"Don't ever assume that what you know about one vampire must be true of them all," Arkeley told her. "That's a sure way to get yourself killed." She knew that tone. She'd heard him use it a hundred times before. The tone of a schoolteacher correcting a student who could never seem to learn the most basic lesson.

"I couldn't know this," she said.

"I called you as soon as she was done typing. Didn't you get the message?"

Her cell phone—she had received a message while standing out in the parking lot. Right before they'd come inside. "I wasn't in a position to receive it," she said. "He was standing there watching everything I did. It was the best I could do to send you that text message."

He nodded but he didn't look like he'd forgiven her. "God-damn it," he muttered. "I've been looking for a way to kill her for more than twenty years. I've devoted my whole career to it. The courts always stayed my hand. This would have ended so much misery and torment, so easily. If you had just been patient."

Caxton's cheeks burned, but she wasn't going to take the guilt. "Your misery. Your torment." It was true that he had been trying tirelessly to find some way to end Malvern's scheming. To put an end to her existence. It was also true what Malvern had said. "This message," she said, pointing to the screen, "wasn't for you. It was for me." It was addressed to her directly, by name.

Arkeley snorted. "She knows better than to appeal to my kinder nature." He picked up the laptop and moved it closer to the coffin, placing it on a display case just within Malvern's reach.

The skeletal arm lifted slowly, very slowly, from the coffin, and the decayed fingers rested almost lifelessly on the key-board. With painful slowness Malvern's index finger tapped spastically at the *H* key. The hand fell back for a full minute, the fingers opening and closing slowly as if they were too weak to even lie still. Then the hand moved on, skittering across the keys like a dried-up leaf blown by an autumn breeze, moving up and to the left to touch the *E*.

Something about the way the hand moved bothered Caxton. As slowly as Malvern moved from letter to letter, she was actually making pretty good time. "She's speeding up," Caxton said, frowning. She looked at the message already on the screen, the one begging for her assistance. "And she seems to have remembered how to use the space bar." The first message, "*comformeheshall*," had been a lot less coherent. "What's going on here?" she demanded. "What did you do?" She was afraid she already knew the answer.

"It took her days to type that last message. She averaged about a keystroke every four hours. I didn't have that kind of time." Arkeley kept his eyes on the screen.

"So you sped things up." She was terrified that she knew how he'd done it, too. "Show me your arms," Caxton demanded.

Arkeley snorted again. She wasn't kidding around, though. She needed to know. She grabbed his arm, his left arm. The one with no fingers. He didn't fight her as she pushed up his sleeve. There was a thick bandage of clean white gauze around his wrist.

"You fed her," Caxton breathed, not believing it, not knowing what it meant. It was a bad thing, she knew that. "You bastard. You fed her!" When Malvern had first become a ward of the court there had been doctors who took care of her. There had been two of them and she had been responsible for both of their deaths. They had fed her this same way—with their own blood. Arkeley had worked for years to get a court order forbidding them from doing just that. And now he was doing it himself.

Caxton could only shake her head in disbelief.

44.

The vampire wore a gentleman's suit of clothes, & had a tarboosh upon his head worked with golden threads. His eyes burned with the light of the fire. His face was clean shaven & his white skin radiant in the darkness.

"You wished to speak with me?" he asked. Slowly, Simonon stood up from his camp table, & approached.

"I wish to beg your help," the Ranger said. He was no coward, that man, I'll say as much. "Jeff Davis wishes the pleasure of your company."

"You'd sign me up," the vampire chuckled. "You'd make me one of your privates. Or an officer, perhaps? I don't relish the prospect of taking orders."

"Then be a partisan like myself," Simonon offered. "Choose your own targets, it will be allowed."

"Really?" the vampire did not move at all, nor make any flourish of his hands. Yet we could see his muscles bunch, loose under skin that barely seemed to fit him. He was like a catamount about to spring on a deer. "& if I choose you?"

He lashed out then, with both hands, & his teeth fastened on Simonon's shoulder. The Ranger screamed as flesh & bone parted ways & hot blood splashed the vampire's mouth & cheeks.

Our surprise was matched only by the uproar amongst the Rebs below. Some raised weapons, & I saw sabers being drawn, but none rushed to aid their leader. He was dead already, & all present knew it. The vampire having finished his feast, he dropped his victim to the ground as a man might cast away the bones of a cooked and eaten chicken. Then he turned to look at the cavalry troopers who surrounded him.

"I am the master of this house, & have invited none of you to *be my guest! You go back to Jeff Davis & tell him I'll serve no man, nor God, nor the Devil himself. You go & tell him!"*

—THE STATEMENT OF ALVA GRIEST

45.

There were a million phone calls to be made while they waited for Malvern to spell out her next message. Far too many to keep straight. The local metropolitan police all wanted reassurances and advice. Arkeley took the brunt of that, nodding and yessing and confirming all the protocols. The Philadelphia Commissioner of Police spent half an hour of Caxton's time demanding to know why she'd brought so much trouble to his city and what she planned to do about it. She offered to give a statement to the press, taking all the blame on herself, not that she really had the time. He grew silent then and when he spoke next it was to tell her he would take things from there.

It was only after she'd ended the call that she understood. She'd been trying to help, but instead he'd taken her offer as a threat. He must have heard what had happened to the Gettysburg tourist trade after she spoke to the press there.

Gettysburg—there were more calls, calls she was embarrassed to make, to Chief Vicente. He didn't like being woken up. He sounded pleased to hear from her once she said where she was calling from, though, and why. "Don't hurry back," he said, with a little laugh to try to take the sting away. It didn't work. "Can I tell my men to stand down from alert, then?" he asked.

Caxton chewed on her lip. She hesitated long enough that he asked if she was still there or if her phone had cut out.

"Yeah," she said, finally. "I'm still here. I think your people are safe." It was what he wanted to hear—it was what he'd always wanted to hear. "We know what he wants and it's here. I think he'll try again tomorrow night." Something still worried her, though. She thought of what Arkeley would say. He would want them to stay on their guard, just in case. Would it really hurt Gettysburg that much to keep the town's cops on their toes? "I'm not going to guarantee anything, though. Can you keep the tourists away another day or two?"

"We don't have any choice. Ninety percent of all hotel bookings for this week have already been canceled. Your vampire is costing us millions of dollars a day and I don't see things changing until you give us the green light."

She thought about Garrity, and Geistdoerfer. If the vampire killed another human being and drank his blood, how many millions was that worth? "You brought me in as a consultant," she said, finally. "I can't tell you what to do, just give you advice. And my advice is to stay sharp until we have a confirmed kill here."

"You're just covering your ass," he said, almost making it a question. Or maybe an accusation.

Was she? Maybe. But just because he wanted to hear something didn't mean she had to say it. "I think it's for the best, Chief," she said, finally, a little steel in her voice. "Even if that means erring on the side of caution."

"I'm counting on you, Trooper," he said. "You kill this jerk already. It's your responsibility." With that he hung up on her.

Arkeley put away his own phone and gestured her to come over to where he stood. She had one more call to make, though, and it wouldn't wait.

When Clara answered, the line was full of weird echoes and distorted voices. Caxton's blood ran cold until she heard her lover laugh and say, "What? What? No, shut up! It's Laura. Hey, baby."

Caxton smiled despite herself. "Do you have the TV on or something?" she asked.

"Yeah—yeah. Stop that! Sorry. Angie and Myrna are over and we're having a Maggie Gyllenhaal film festival. *Donnie Darko* right now, and we already saw *Secretary*. Are you coming home? I'll send somebody out for more beer."

Caxton sighed and slumped down onto a wooden bench. A wave of jealousy washed through her like nausea. Clara had known Angie since high school. Every time Caxton had met her she had a different color hair. In her latest incarnation she was a little goth chick with dyed black hair and lots of lace shirts that never quite covered her belly button. She was supposedly straight, but everyone knew she had a crush on Clara. Myrna had well-defined arms and frosted blond hair that stuck out wildly from her head. She was an ex, the last woman Clara had been with before she met Caxton. If she had asked point blank Clara would have told her that they were just friends, but for some reason she didn't dare ask.

She didn't dare say any of the things she wanted to. She had thought she would find Clara alone, with nothing better to do than listen to Caxton talk about how scared she'd been in the car, about how badly the vampire had hurt her, about how she'd almost been killed. It wouldn't be the first time she'd used Clara as a sounding board. She couldn't bring herself to ruin the girls' movie night, though. "I'm in Philly," she finally said. "Probably will be all night. Maybe tomorrow night too. Can you feed the dogs?"

"Um, yeah, I can—are you okay? I mean, you're obviously alive."

"Yes." Caxton scratched at one eyebrow.

"Well, that's good. Because you know, I worry."

"I know."

Clara's voice changed. The background noise cut out and

the line got sharper, but it was more than that. She was suddenly quite serious. "I just walked out back so I could hear you better. It's cold out here. You're okay, right? I mean you're not hurt."

"Yeah." Caxton closed her eyes. "Go back to your movie." It was suddenly all she wanted. For Clara to be someplace safe and warm and to be surrounded by friends.

"Okay. Come home when you can."

"Don't doubt it," Caxton said, and then she switched off the phone.

In the silence, in the darkened museum, she felt something dark stretching out its wings. All the fear and the pain were about to catch up with her. If she let them. When they did, she would curl up in a corner and just rock back and forth and mutter to herself. She would stop functioning.

That was not an option. To dispel the darkness she went back to the coffin and read what Malvern had typed on the laptop:

he's been a soljer, 'tis most all i know
he was not grateful for what i gave him
some they like not the taste of blood

"Not particularly helpful," Arkeley said, coming up from behind her. "We already figured she was the one who made him a vampire, right? And the fact that he was a soldier was just common sense, considering where he was buried."

"Maybe we should try asking actual questions," Caxton suggested. "Tell us where you think he'll go to ground. Or what his name is. What I'd really like to know," she said, "is how he can cheat time like that. He's half as old as you are, but he has the strength of a newly created vampire. How the hell does he manage that?"

Malvern's hand reached for the keyboard. Caxton watched it drift across the keys, feeling their contours. Not for the first time she thought the hand moved like the planchette on a Ouija board.

Arkeley looked up at her. His mouth curled up on one side. "It'll take her a while to answer those. That gives us plenty of time to check out the bones I came here for." They left Malvern there tapping at the keys, and went deeper into the Mütter's basements.

46.

A poor white, a planter who swore he'd never owned a slave, nor wanted to, was my first informant. I nearly ran him down in the road. He had all his worldly possessions on his back and said he was heading to the home of his brother and could not tarry long. Still, when I gave him water and a mouthful of what the soldiers colorfully call embalmed beef, he proved quite loquacious.

He knew roughly where the Chess plantation was, though he would never go there himself. "Haunted by ghosts," he assured me, "or somewhat worse." His tone favored the latter. "Old Marse Josiah Chess built that place in the last century. Filled it up with all manner of unnatural things. Bones of great big lizards they dug up out the ground, and of elephants and tigers and the like. Human bones, too, or so I am told. They say he got himself killed for his peculiarities, either by a rebellious slave, or—"

I hazarded a guess. "Or somewhat worse."

My man nodded happily. "His son Zachariah took the place over, and made a fine living out of it. Died ten years ago. His son Obediah came next, but there'll never be another in that line. Obediah ain't been seen since 'fore the present unpleasantness."

I thanked the man and hurried on. I was no more than a mile from my destination when I was stopped by a sentry and then brought to a camp where the Third Maine Volunteer Infantry

were resting after many days of marching. I protested volumi-
nously but knew it was no use: I would have to be vetted by the
local Commanding Officer before I could move on. It's easier,
sometimes, moving behind enemy lines, I swear. The CO was a
nice enough fellow, one Moses Lakeman. I told him of my destination and he swore on the Creator's name. "I have a company
out there right now doing picket duty, man! Tell me I've not sent
them into the proverbial lion's den."

I could tell him nothing of the sort.

—THE PAPERS OF WILLIAM PITTENGER

47.

Following Arkeley, she passed down a short hallway with a
vaulted brick ceiling. Safety lights hung in cages every
few yards and long rusted pipes hissed on either side of
her. At the end of the corridor stood a large open room, sealed
off by a thick metal door. Inside, heavy-duty air conditioners
blasted cold air down from the ceiling, and Caxton started shivering instantly. The air felt weird in other ways, too. Very dry.
The brick walls had been coated in generation after generation
of whitewash, but there was a lot less light than in the hall and a
lot more shadows. The room was full of enameled metal cabinets. They stood in long rows with just enough room between
them for a person to pass sideways. Some were simple filing
cabinets, some were big enough to be wardrobes, big enough to
hold very large objects. Each cabinet had been labeled in a spi-
dery hand, some of the ink so old and eroded that she could
barely make out the strings of numbers and letters.

She had a feeling she knew what was in the cabinets. They
weren't as attractive or well polished as the display cases in the

museum, but they probably served the same purpose. This had to be the real collection of the Mütter—all the bones and biological oddities and antiquated medical equipment the directors had amassed since the 1780s. The stuff that wasn't fit for display, for one reason or another.

Arkeley stopped in front of a tall cabinet with three long sliding drawers. As he passed through the room he had picked up a leather-bound book, a big ledger with broken gold lettering on the front. It had to be a catalog of what was in the various cabinets. He bent to match the cabinet's label against something in the ledger, then pulled loose a sheaf of white paper that had been folded into the book.

"Are we supposed to be down here?" she asked.

"Harold said it was fine," he told her.

"Harold's the night watchman." She frowned. "He could very easily lose his job over this. What does he owe you?" she asked. Arkeley didn't have a lot of friends—it had to go deeper than that.

The old Fed sighed. He closed the book and laid it on top of a filing cabinet. "About twenty years ago, Harold used to have a family. He ran a hardware store in Liverpool, West Virginia. He had a pretty wife and a pretty little girl named Samantha."

Caxton's mind made the connection. "Liverpool was the place where you first discovered Lares." That had been Arkeley's first vampire case, the one that had shaped his entire life. "I remember the details. There was a kids' slumber party. Six little girls. Lares—"

"Shredded them." Arkeley looked right into her eyes. "I pulled Lares' heart out of his chest with my bare hands, but Harold's little girl didn't make it. Neither did his marriage. He started drinking and he lost his hardware store. Moved out of the state, took a series of odd jobs. He's never been right since. But he was good people then, as they say in Liverpool, and he's good people now. Harold will keep his mouth shut and he'll give us good warning before we're caught down here. Now, help me with this. It might take two hands."

She did as she was told. She reached down to open the bottom drawer of the cabinet, a metal tray long enough to hold a human body. The drawer pulls felt like ice in her hands. When the drawer slid out she found a long black vinyl bag inside with a zipper that ran its whole length.

"It was Harold who wrote to me recently to say the Mütter had a certain specimen that would interest me. When he told me it was dated from 1863 I thought it might do more than just satisfy my curiosity." He waved a folded piece of paper at her. "I did a little research before you arrived. Let me show you what I dug up. 'Item 67-c, Lot 1863a. The remains, in part, of a male. Believed to be a vampire.'" Arkeley looked down from the paper and nodded for her to unzip the bag. "I think we can confirm that."

Caxton thought so too. She'd seen enough vampire skeletons—especially after the ninety-nine in the cavern in Gettysburg, she knew to look for that jaw. Rows of translucent teeth jagged outward from the mandible, some sticking so far out that they looked like they would have shredded the vampire's lips every time he opened or closed his mouth.

"It's a vampire, alright." A vampire collected the same year as the battle of Gettysburg. The same year, presumably, that the cavern under the battlefield was filled with coffins. "You think this vampire knew our suspect?"

"It would be a surprising coincidence if he didn't. Vampires are few in number at any given time. They seek each other out, when they can." Arkeley read from his sheaf of papers. "'Bones of a believed vampire. Remains of one Obediah Chess, of Virginia.' You should recognize that name, I hope."

She searched her memory. "Shit," she said. She had it—

kind of. "Malvern first came to America when she was already too weak to get out of her coffin. She was sold like a fossil, sold to a guy named, um," she worked for it, "Josiah. Josiah Caryl Chess."

Arkeley placed a finger alongside his nose. "She killed Josiah, I'm relatively certain of that. He was found without any blood in his body. Not, however, before he had brought a son into this world. Zachariah Chess, whose life seems to have been quite ordinary. Zachariah begat another son. Whose name was Obediah. Meanwhile Malvern rotted away quietly in the attic of the Chess plantation. I don't know any details, but I will happily bet that it was Malvern who made Obediah what you see before you."

The cold that gripped Caxton then had nothing to do with air-conditioning.

Arkeley continued to read from the paper he held. "'Specimen obtained under unusual circumstances, donation of the War Department. Signed for by C. Benjamin, whom see for further particulars,'" Arkeley read. "Well, that would be tricky, since Dr. Benjamin died over a hundred years ago. But he was kind enough to leave us a few notes." With his one useful hand Arkeley picked a sheet out of the packet and read it in silence, his head moving back and forth slowly for long minutes while Caxton could only wait. Occasionally she looked down at the bones in the drawer, but that just made her feel cold.

"Can I see that when—"

"Done," he said. He handed the sheet to her. It was an old photocopy of a much older document, written out in a long sloping hand. Caxton read it twice:

Specimen prepared by Captain Custis Benjamin, surgeon. At the request of a Colonel Pittenger with the War Department I have undertaken a preliminary examination. Results follow. Remains removed to the College of Physicians at Philadelphia for study on June 25, 1863. After dinner that night I took possession of two wooden boxes personally, and moved them immediately to the dissecting theater. There I performed an autopsy on the subject, assisted by my colleague, Doctor Andrew Gorman, a fellow Member of the College. Examination began at half past nine in the evening.

Subject was delivered in a skeletal condition. Under separate cover heart arrived packed in excelsior. Heart examined first; found that it weighed twelve and one half oz. (slightly heavier than average human organ), had a blackish red coloration, and oozed a pale milky secretion when probed. Had no particular smell, nor showed any signs of corruption despite being separated from the body for several days.

When returned to the remainder of the body, heart began action almost instantly. Production of milky secretion increased dramatically. Steam and palpable heat arose from the area of greatest activity and some reconstituted flesh visible after ten minutes time. This despite removal of heart from body cavity for extended period.

As requested by Colonel Pittenger, then moved on to application of four oz. human blood, secured from Doctor Gorman's left arm. Reconstitution accelerated considerably. Muscle tissue began to knit together following one hour, at which time full suite of organs already visible.

Major Gorman expressed unwillingness to see body completely restored. I concurred. Heart removed at this time. Reconstituted flesh and structures collapsed rapidly, as an inflated bladder losing air through a puncture. Heart destroyed as per orders and male subject permanently deceased, as of one quarter past twelve, June 26, A.D. 1863.

When she'd finished she looked up at Arkeley. He was smiling like a cat with a mouth full of fresh mouse. "Would you care to say it first?"

She knew exactly what he was getting at. "No," she said. "I think you're jumping to a dumb conclusion. This vampire's heart had been removed for a couple of days. When they put it back, he started regenerating, sure. After a couple of days! Geistdoerfer found my vampire's heart lying on top of his coffin. He put it inside and the vampire came back to life. I see what you're getting at, but it can't be the same thing. Too much time passed for that." Surely the heart would have rotted away after a hundred and forty years. To think anything else was absurd. Yet how else could she explain her vampire's condition? He had cheated time.

Still she wouldn't believe it. She shook her head back and forth.

"Tell me, Trooper," Arkeley said, his face a patient mask. "If the doctors here had not destroyed the heart—if they had saved it in another one of these cabinets—would you be willing to reunite it with these bones, just to prove your point? Would you take that chance?"

Caxton looked anywhere but his face. Then she pushed the drawer closed with her foot, shutting the bones away, out of sight.

48.

With the vampire below, our only path of egress was UP. We must find stairs to get away. Thinking he had found the way to the cupola, Storrow rushed for the locked door, and burst it open. My heart was in my mouth, and I could not speak, though I knew that was the wrong door, and something of what lay beyond.

Eben Nudd was the first in. "Oh, Mercy," he said. It was the harshest language I'd ever heard him use.

It was not hard to find the seat of his discomfort. The room beyond the door was another boudoir, perhaps that of the lady of the house. The fittings might have been sumptuous once, but I had little time to study their decay. One feature of that room demanded all my attention. It was a coffin, a simple box of pinewood, tapered at the bottom, & it was open. Within lay a creature unlike any we'd seen before.

She had the pale skin & the hairlessness of a vampire, & the pointed ears. She certainly had the fangs. Yet she looked to be some sixmonth-dead corpse, her body ravaged by the worm, her face a mass of sores & pustulent blisters. She had but one eye in her head; the other having collapsed long since, & rotten away perhaps. She made no movement, nor rose from her place, but only watched us with her remaining eye.

"Another," Storrow breathed. "There is another?"

None of us had time to answer him. Bill, at that moment, slew German Pete with a single blow to the head. He had a massive truncheon made of the leg of a dressing table, and his hand did not stay a moment.

Eben Nudd did not wait for the hexer's body to fall before raising his musket rifle. It was too late, though, for Bill had run off, and I never did see him again. From the look of him & from the state he was in, he wasn't going to last too long.

—THE STATEMENT OF ALVA GRIEST

49.

"We know so little about them, really," Arkeley said. "No scientist has ever written more than a partial description. They can't be captured and put in zoos for schoolchildren to gawk at, and they're thankfully rare enough that no one has ever tried. We don't understand anything about their magic, their orisons, or even how their curse works. It defies everything we do know."

"But do you understand what you're saying? They're stronger than us and maybe smarter. We can barely destroy them when they do crop up. The one thing we can count on, the one real advantage we have over them, is that they get old even faster than we do. That they wither away." Caxton thought of the old stories of vampires who remained forever young, their looks and their strength bolstered by regular access to copious amounts of blood. That was the myth, the dream every vampire tried to make come true. It was what Malvern was still living for, the hope that someday she would be fully restored, if only she could get enough blood.

Now there was evidence—the bones in the drawer, the record of Custis Benjamin, Surgeon—that maybe it was possible. Maybe it wasn't perfect, but there was a way for vampires to live for centuries and not lose their power.

All they had to do was have somebody remove their heart from their bones and put it someplace safe. Days, years, centuries later the heart could be returned to the body and the vampire would reanimate, almost as strong as ever, weak and hungry perhaps, but ready to hunt again.

It wasn't quite eternal youth. But it was as close as they could get.

She thought of the way the vampire of Gettysburg—*her* vampire, she had come to think of him—had looked when she'd first seen him. Stringy, bad skin, limbs like sticks. His rib cage had stuck out prominently from his white flesh and his face had been hollow and depleted. That had to be what came of being denied blood for so many decades. Yet as soon as he started drinking again he had plumped out with surprising quickness.

"If you have a better answer, tell me," Arkeley said.

Caxton fumed in silence, unwilling to give up her denial. Knowing that he was right anyway. "Okay," she said.

"At the very least it's a working hypothesis."

"Okay!" she said again. She handed him the photocopy and he tucked it in his pocket. Caxton ran her fingers through her hair, her elbows out. Slowly she turned away from him. Exhaustion and fear caught up with her as if she'd been running down a dark corridor and smacked right into a wall she couldn't see. "I just—I can't—they're too strong already! They're too good at what they do. Now they have this power too. I guess they had it all along, but we were so in the dark we didn't even realize it. We can't keep up with them. I can't keep up with them." She started walking out of the room. Away from him, from the bones. She didn't want to see any more skeletons, didn't want to be around them. Ever again. "I can't do this," she said.

"Laura," he called out.

It felt like she'd been doused in cold water. She couldn't remember the last time he'd spoken her first name. She had no doubt he used it calculatedly, to get her attention. She turned and stared at him from maybe twenty feet away. "I'm losing my shit," she said.

"Then find it again. Now."

She nodded. Swallowed, hard, her throat still bruised and thick. She fought her swimming head and got her focus back. "What's our next step?" she said, finally.

His eyes widened a fraction. "You tell me."

Fair enough. This was her investigation. "We go see what Malvern's come up with, if anything. Then I'm going to go meet with the local cops. He's probably not going to attack again tonight—not here or anywhere else. He's already fed and he's smart enough to get off the streets. Tomorrow night is another matter."

He nodded and walked with her up the stairs, back toward

the museum. He was pretty slow going up—one of his knees just wouldn't bend sufficiently, so he had to climb the steps one at a time. He took a rest at the first landing, just stood there looking down at his shoes. She wanted to hurry him along, but out of respect she waited for him to catch his breath.

Upstairs Malvern had been busy. When they arrived at her coffin they found she'd written quite a bit on the laptop. Her hand still rested on the keyboard, but it was motionless, perhaps waiting for the next question, or maybe she'd just run out of energy.

What she had written, though, got a reaction out of them both.

> *the answers you seek i lack*
> *but there is one other who knows*
> *a dead man, in this house*
> *i can call him*
> *ye know my price*

Caxton read the words on the computer screen again. "She's saying she can raise Geistdoerfer as a half-dead. She's suggesting he knows something we could use. How could she know that?"

"They can communicate without words, you know as much," Arkeley said. "She sensed him coming. She must have sensed Geistdoerfer's death as well. I think we should do this."

"No, no, no. No. Absolutely not," Caxton said. "Never. Can't be done. There is zero possibility here and you should just stop thinking about it right now."

She said it to herself. Arkeley was back by the coffin, patiently asking Malvern questions and then waiting while she tapped out the answers, one painful letter at a time.

"No. We will never do that." She stood in a corner muttering to herself. It made her feel crazy. But she wasn't the crazy one. Arkeley was crazy for even considering this. He had changed. His wounds and his bitter regret had driven him insane.

"This is a nonstarter." She knew perfectly well that it was the only way. That she was going to do it, that she was going to help Malvern bring Geistdoerfer back from the dead just so she could question him, was almost a given.

There remained, however, some residue of her former self, some resinous discoloration on her soul that still looked like Laura Caxton, soldier of the law. Some particle of her being that still believed in human dignity and compassion for the dead. There wasn't much of it, just enough to make her feel extremely nauseous.

"It's not even possible," she said, aloud this time. "Malvern didn't drain his blood. My vampire did. Nobody can call back a half-dead except the vampire who killed him."

Arkeley tapped the laptop's trackpad. "I already asked that one," he said. Malvern's answer scrolled down onto the screen:

the curse is all of a part

"Which means what, exactly?" Caxton asked.

Arkeley shrugged. "It means it doesn't matter. Any vampire can call a half-dead. As long as the corpse has had its blood sucked, the curse is in it. The same curse they all share. I believe her."

"That's . . . scary," Caxton said. Malvern was an inveterate liar. A master manipulator. Believing her—trusting her—was absolute foolishness. "Look, we know her. We know she'll say or do anything if she thinks it gets her one step closer to getting out of that coffin on her own two feet. She said she needs blood to do this, more blood—"

Arkeley scrolled up a little on the page:

my strength has flown i require more

"Exactly. She gets blood out of this. What happens if we feed her and then nothing happens and she says, 'Oh gosh, guys, I guess that wasn't enough blood. Maybe if you gave me a little more . . .' I mean, how much are you willing to give her?"

Malvern had an answer for that, too:

one tenth part a woman's measure it will suffice

"Oh." The average person had about six quarts of blood. So Malvern was asking for a little over a pint. That much would revivify her considerably, but it would hardly be enough to bring her back to full health.

"If she demands more, she won't get it. I was quite clear on that," Arkeley said. "I've thought of all these things, Trooper."

Caxton shook her head. No matter what he thought he knew, there was a catch somewhere. There always had to be when Malvern was involved. "It's a trick."

"Yes," he said. "It is. It's a trick to get blood from us. That's the only thing she ever wants. The only thing any vampire ever wants. In exchange we get information we truly need."

"This is worse than the worst thing I have ever done," she said, talking mostly to herself.

"Shall we get started?" Arkeley asked.

She clamped her eyes shut and held her tongue. "Yes," she managed to say, though that tiny part of her, that last shred of who she used to be, was screaming no.

She went down to the basement, where Harold was waiting. The night watchman didn't ask any questions. He helped her as he had before, taking Geistdoerfer's body, getting his arms under the torso while she took the legs. The body felt dry and lighter than it had before. She was very conscious of the fact that at any moment, with no real warning, her vampire, the vampire of Gettysburg, could call to Geistdoerfer. Even while she was carrying him the vampire had the power to reanimate him.

It didn't happen in the time it took to carry the corpse up the stairs, nor while they tied his dead hands and feet together and laid him out on top of a wooden cabinet. From a display case nearby the shriveled head of a woman with a horn growing out of her forehead stared down at them, her mouth frozen in an eternal groan. Caxton turned away and saw a cat with two faces, one open and mewling, the other with its eyes and mouth permanently shut.

None of the room's skeletons pointed accusing fingers at her. No formless voice came out of nowhere to say "*Thou shalt not.*" The museum was as silent and lifeless as it had ever been. Caxton knew better than to expect divine retribution, of course. She knew what her real punishment would be: more guilt, to haunt her every quiet moment. More nightmares.

Well, she was starting to get used to those.

When she was finished feeling sorry for herself she turned to find that Malvern had left another message:

i will take laura's blood now

Steeling herself, fighting down all her instincts, Caxton started to unbutton her shirtsleeve. The physical pain, she told herself, would almost be welcome.

Then Arkeley stepped up and said "No," and she stopped where she was. "No, that's not necessary."

Malvern's hand began to move across the keys again.

"No," Arkeley said again. He grabbed the hand and moved it away from the keyboard. He turned to look at Caxton. "I'll donate the blood. I've already cut myself tonight. The wound hasn't had time to close properly."

In response, Malvern merely typed:

very well

But how thankful should we be to a merciful Providence that that awful tomb was not disturbed by anyone not having the knowledge necessary to deal with its dreadful occupant!

—F. G. Loring, The Tomb of Sarah

GRIEST

50.

"What of HER?" Eben Nudd asked, pointing at the thing in the coffin. No man made answer. We had not time for demons any more.

We made for the next doorway down, the one which led up into the cupola. Storrow nearly dragged me.

We made what speed we could. Chess was on his way up, through the house. We could hear him shrieking, though none could understand the words he spoke.

Our shoes rang on the iron gallery, which was suspended from the dome by rods. We pushed through the broken section of the cupola & out into the night air, & the light of one million stars. Around us the dark trees sighed & cast their limbs about. Storrow & Eben Nudd lifted me through the opening & then set me down on the slope of the roof, to hold on as best I might.

"We'll have to climb down. Try not to fall, is my best counsel," Storrow said. But then he turned. "Did you hear that?" he asked.

"Ayup," Eben Nudd said. We all had. It was the sound of feet falling on the iron gallery. It could be naught but Chess the vampire, hot on our heels. "I think—" the downeaster began, but we never learned what he thought.

Chess jumped up through the broken dome as if he'd been shot out of a parrot gun. He grabbed Nudd by the collar & twisted his head clean around, snapping his neckbones with audible sounds. He did not bother to suck the erstwhile lobsterman's blood, but only threw him off the roof to crash to the ground below.

"I'm not sure we've been properly introduced," Chess said. His eyes burned like coals.

—THE STATEMENT OF ALVA GRIEST

51.

"What time is it?" Arkeley asked. He held his arm over a white enameled basin and rolled up his sleeve. The gauze bandage around his wrist was brown with dried blood. When he removed it his arm was smeared red, the fine hairs turned dark and stuck to his skin. An ugly wound like a dried-up worm ran down the length of his wrist. "Trooper?"

Exhaustion passed through her like a cold wind. It had been a long time since she slept. "It's, uh, four-thirty." Clara would be asleep. "What—where is it? I put it down for a second." Harold met her gaze with questioning eyes. She looked down at his hands and took a paper-wrapped lancet from him. There were plenty of supplies in the museum basement for what they intended to do. On the table before her sat a graduated glass jar, a fresh roll of gauze, and a roll of surgical tape.

"We have to keep moving," Arkeley told her. "If the sun comes up before she's ready, we'll waste an entire day. And more blood than I want to spare."

Caxton nodded and bit her lower lip. Time to focus. She peeled the paper back from the lancet, a short rectangle of surgical steel with one sharp triangular end. She looked down at Arkeley's arm. It was the one with no fingers. The palm was a flat square of flesh, so thick with scar tissue it didn't even look human. It looked more like the paw of an animal. Caxton tried to drag the lancet across the wound but flinched away when Arkeley grunted and moaned in pain. A few dark drops of blood welled up out of the cut but nothing like the flow she'd expected.

"You can't hesitate like that," he said, gritting his teeth. "This isn't like cutting open a bag of frozen peas. You need to dig in. Deep."

Caxton got dizzy for a second just listening to him. Holding the lancet very tight in her fingers, she leaned over and stabbed it deep into Arkeley's arm. He shouted in pain but she ignored him and started reopening the wound with a resolute sawing motion. "Like this?" she asked.

"That'll do," Arkeley said. He moved his fingerless hand back and forth to work the muscles in his arm. Blood seeped vigorously from the wound and rolled across his skin. "Now, the jar," he said. Caxton brought it up underneath the wound to catch the blood. With his good hand Arkeley squeezed at his arm as if he were getting the last toothpaste out of a dried-up tube. Blood surged out of the wound, thick and dark, venous blood the color of red wine. It splashed and pattered on the sides of the jar, then started to fill it up. The meniscus of blood climbed up the white painted graduations on the side of the jar. Two ounces. Five ounces. Ten.

"Halfway there," she said, in what she hoped was a reassuring tone.

"God fucking damn it," Arkeley bellowed, pushing and squeezing at his arm.

Twelve ounces. fifteen. The wound wasn't closing up, the flow wasn't slowing down. Caxton gave silent thanks for that. She must have hit a big blood vessel. Would he need stitches? Seventeen ounces. Twenty.

"Okay," she said, and took the jar away. Blood splattered with a ringing noise in the white basin. Setting the jar aside, she wrapped Arkeley's arm tightly with the gauze and then sealed the bandage with surgical tape. Red dots appeared on the white gauze almost instantly. "I might have gone too deep," she said.

"Don't worry about that now," he told her. He put pressure on the bandage with the fingers of his good hand. "Feed her. It has to be warm to have any effect."

It has to be warm, and fresh, and human, she thought. As much as vampires scared animals, they would never attack them. The blood had to be fresh, too—if it clotted they couldn't digest it properly. She moved quickly to the coffin. Malvern was straining to lift her head. Her hands were at the level of her throat, reaching up, unable to grasp the jar. Caxton didn't want to get close enough to her toothy jaws to get bitten. There was no good way to do it otherwise, though. Hands shaking only a little, she tilted the jar over Malvern's open mouth. The blood poured through the air and splashed on the vampire's gray, shriveled tongue.

The effect was electric and immediate. Malvern's body started to tremble, then white smoke lifted off her tattered nightdress, tongues of it licking up from her armpits, blowing back over her ragged head. The skin started to grow over her half-exposed skull instantly, the old dry leather there inching across the yellow bone. Malvern's single eye grew wet and started to reinflate. Her hands reached up and grasped at the jar, tore it out of Caxton's hands.

Caxton took a step back. She watched in disgust as Malvern licked out the contents of the jar with a probing tongue. The skeletal hands fleshed out visibly, the prominent knuckles and veins smoothing out as new muscle grew in under the skin.

A noise sagged out of Malvern, a long, whistling moan of pleasure. She dropped the jar, now spotlessly clean, and it rolled across her shoulder. Her hands lifted in the air as if she were giving thanks. Before she had looked like a pile of bones wrapped in a too-big pelt of leather. As Caxton watched the ravages of time reversed themselves until she looked like she'd only been dead a few months.

"Do it," Arkeley commanded. "Call him."

Slowly, creakingly, Malvern sat up in her coffin, hauling herself upright with her hands. She brought her knees up and hugged them to her chest, her gruesome head resting on protruding kneecaps. Luxuriously, almost dreamily, she turned her face to look on Geistdoerfer, who lay only a few feet away. She opened her mouth and a rattling sound came out, a noise like a metal rake dragging through a pile of leaves.

Malvern hadn't spoken more than two words in over a century. And that was after she'd bathed in blood, her coffin filled with the life of half a dozen men. Twenty ounces wasn't about to restore her rotten larynx.

Caxton had watched a vampire named Reyes call a half-dead once. He had literally called the corpse back from death. "Will it work if she can't talk?"

Arkeley just shrugged.

Malvern tried again, this time managing a gargling rasp that sounded like she was choking. She turned to look at the three living humans behind her. Caxton grabbed for the charm in her pocket, expecting some kind of trick.

Arkeley's Glock came out of its holster and the muzzle pressed against Malvern's sunken chest in one fluid movement. Right over her heart. The old vampire hunter must have been waiting for just such a move.

Malvern's head turned from side to side, just a little. As if she were afraid it might fall off if she shook it too hard. Then she reached out a hand toward the laptop and typed a quick message:

if i had but a little more . . .

"No fucking way," Caxton said, and Arkeley nodded.

Malvern's eye rolled in her head. She nodded, however, and typed some more. She looked back at Geistdoerfer, very pale and very dead on top of the display case. She stabbed at the keys, making a noisy rattle as she typed:

come to me. come back to me. hear me.

The words were similar to what Caxton had heard when Reyes brought back his half-dead servant. She repeated them over and over, filling up the screen with her commands. Geistdoerfer's body didn't so much as twitch.

Malvern's bony fingers stabbed at the keyboard. The laptop jumped with every pounding keystroke. She seemed desperate. Maybe she knew that if this failed they would never trust her again. That she would never get a chance at more blood.

come back. come back. come back and serve.

Harold gasped in surprise. Caxton turned to stare at the night watchman, who pointed at the corpse.

"There! His hands, look!"

Caxton looked. Geistdoerfer's fingers were moving, it was true. His fingers were curling into tight claws that dragged across the top of the wooden case. His nails dug into the varnish and scratched across the surface, tearing at the wood.

Then his mouth opened wide and he screamed, a high-pitched, terrible scream that turned Caxton's blood to ice water.

52.

"Take this as my calling card, ya Southron bastard," Storrow spoke. He was lifting his target rifle to his eye & without further ado he fired, the recoil from the heavy weapon staggering him backward.

Now, that rifle was custom built for distant work, & could make twelve-inch patterns at some eight hundred yards. By necessity its balls were launched at some high velocity & with much power. This one took the top of Chess' head & his tarboosh as well & spread them over half Virginia. The vampire's body tottered for a while, sundered just above the bridge of the nose & thus unable to see, & his arms reached for us, but how could any creature that draws breath live long without the organ of sense?

It was over. We had won, & now were free to go. I thought of my Bill, & began to weep again, but there was naught for it. & even I felt some soaring of spirit when Chess' white body finally fell over & lay still, skidding some way on the shingled roof.

Our peril was ended. We were all but home.

—THE STATEMENT OF ALVA GRIEST

53.

Geistdoerfer struggled against his bonds, trying to drag his hands up to his face. He moaned like a starving kitten, cried out sometimes like a man in pain. He writhed on top of the display case until he could press his nose and cheek against the smooth wood. With his shoulder he shoved himself along the surface until his head was hanging over the side. For a moment he lifted his neck to stare at them, to see the strange collection of people who were mute witnesses to his revival. Then he brought his head down fast and hard, smashing the sharp corner of the display case with his nose.

Caxton winced to hear cartilage snap and part under his pale skin. She watched in mute horror as he brought his head back for another bash that tore open part of his cheek. No blood oozed from the wound, but the skin parted like torn silk, revealing gray muscle tissue underneath. A third time he reared up, but Harold was already rushing across the room, grabbing at the rope that bound the dead professor, pulling him back, away from the edge.

"He's gone crazy," the night watchman gasped. "He's trying to kill himself, again!"

"No," Arkeley told him. "There's not enough human left in him for that."

Caxton turned away in disgust. She knew exactly what Arkeley meant. Half-deads were not human beings. They weren't the people they had been before they died. The curse animated their bodies and it could read their memories, but their souls were already gone, their personalities completely cut away.

Half-deads existed only to serve their vampire masters. Beyond that they knew little but pain and self-loathing. The curse hated the body it possessed, hated it so much it took every opportunity to deface the physical form. Literally deface it, in fact—the first thing half-deads did on their rebirth was to tear and claw at their faces until the skin hung down in bloodless strips.

"Hold him tight. He won't be very strong," Arkeley said.

Harold grimaced. Caxton saw something in his eyes that hadn't been there before. Had they pushed him past his limit? "This is it, Jameson," he said. "After this I don't owe you nothing. You and her get out of here and I pretend like I never knew you. Got it?"

"Yes, yes, fine, but please," Arkeley said, "hold him."

Harold twisted the rope in his hands. Geistdoerfer loosed a pained howl. He shook and strained and tried to tear free, but the rope just cut into his deliquescing flesh. After a while he started to settle down, and then he turned his damaged face to look right at Caxton.

A chill ran down her back as his dead eyes studied her. "I was dead. I was happier dead," he said. "What have you done to me?" His voice had risen in pitch and become a perverted mockery of the professor's easy tenor.

Arkeley moved closer to the undead thing and crouched down to get on his eye level. "We have some questions for you. If you answer them nicely, we'll put you out of your misery. Do you understand?"

The half-dead spat in Arkeley's face. It was the kind of thing Geistdoerfer would never have done in life—the man had been cultured and refined. "I don't serve you," he whined.

Arkeley stood up and wiped the spit off his face with a

handkerchief. He looked back at Malvern in her coffin and cleared his throat pointedly.

The vampire's hand glided across the laptop's keyboard.

i have raised him and it has drained me
i have not the strength to compel him

Maybe, Caxton thought. Or maybe she'd gotten what she wanted out of the exchange and she no longer cared what happened next.

The half-dead stared at the thing in the coffin and laughed, a fractured, ugly sound that bounced around the corners of the room. "You're working with *her?*"

"Why is that so strange?" Arkeley asked. "She's the enemy of your killer. I'd think you'd want to help her."

"Then you don't know how it all works." The half-dead let out another laugh, this time almost giggling.

"Oh," Arkeley said, "I think I understand a little. I didn't really expect you to be reasonable, but I thought we'd give you the chance. It didn't work. So I guess we'll have to go the more traditional route." Without warning he grabbed a handful of the half-dead's hair and yanked upward, dragging his head up, wrenching his neck around. "What's his name?"

"Who?"

Arkeley bounced the thing's head off the top of the display case. "Harold," he said, "maybe you could find me a toolbox from somewhere. I need a hammer and maybe a pair of needlenose pliers."

"No," the abomination moaned, and bounced on the wooden case as he tried to break free of Arkeley's grip. As infirm and decrepit as he might be, though, Arkeley was still stronger than any half-dead.

"I think we'll start by pulling his teeth out. Then maybe his fingernails."

"Don't—"

"Don't what?" Arkeley asked. "Don't hurt you? I tried to be nice."

Harold let go of the rope and walked off into the shadows. Arkeley placed his good hand across the half-dead's temple and cheek and then leaned down hard, using all his weight, pressing Geistdoerfer's skull into the wood of the case. The thing screamed horribly.

Caxton licked her lower lip. It was suddenly very dry. "Arkeley," she said. "You're going too fast. Give him another chance, for God's sake."

The old man stared at her with pure anger burning in his eyes. Then one of his eyelids drooped down and flicked back up. Was that?—yes. Yes, it had been a wink, Caxton thought. A wink.

He thought she was playing a game. The oldest interrogation game: good cop, bad cop. That hadn't been her intention. She just didn't think she could bear to watch Arkeley torture even a dead man.

"Listen," she said, leaning over a little to look into Geistdoerfer's bloodless face. "Listen, maybe if you just tell me a few things, maybe this doesn't have to be so bad. I mean, is that something you might do?"

The half-dead's face writhed as if bugs were burrowing under his cheeks and lips. "I don't know his name," he said, quickly. "He never told me. He just said he was a soldier. And then he said he had been tricked, that he'd never wanted to be a vampire. That it was all a trick! Please!"

Caxton looked up and Arkeley let a little of the pressure off.

"Who tricked him?" she asked. She threw a thumb over her shoulder, gesturing at the coffin behind her. "Her? Was it somebody named Justinia Malvern?"

"I . . . I'm not sure. I think so."

Arkeley leaned on his head.

"Yes! Yes," the half-dead screamed. "It had to be! That was why—why he wanted to kill her so badly. Oh God! Tell him to stop!"

"I will," Caxton said, "but first I need something more. Something we can use. You have to tell me what he's going to do next. Will he try to kill Malvern again?"

"Y-yes. I think—I mean, I know he will. It was the one thing he wanted to accomplish. He knows you'll catch him eventually. He wants to kill her first. That's all I know—I swear!" His eyes swiveled to look past her. "Oh, God, please please please please please . . ."

Harold had returned. He had a long red toolbox in one hand. The other held a big power drill.

"You don't have much time left," she said. "You need to tell me something more. Just think, okay? Don't guess, but think. Will he come back tomorrow night?"

"I don't know—I don't know," the half-dead creaked.

"Think!" she shouted.

"Yes yes yes, he will, he'll come back, he'll—he mentioned something once, he just said it in an offhand way, but but but—"

"But what?" she asked.

"That night you chased him. When you chased him onto the battlefield, he came back, he came back and we talked a little. He said you were dangerous. He said he might not be able to do what he needed to do by himself. That he might need help."

"Help." Caxton made a hard line of her mouth. "You mean reinforcements. More half-deads like you?"

The thing on the display case managed to wiggle its head back and forth in negation. "No. He swore he would never make a half-dead. He swore it a hundred times—I think—I think there was something there, some story he didn't tell me. He seemed to think that killing people and drinking their blood could maybe be okay, but that calling them back from the dead was the real sin. I don't know why."

"Then where would he get reinforcements?" Caxton demanded. A high whining, grinding noise startled her. She looked up. Harold had stretched an extension cord across the floor and had plugged in his power drill. "We're out of time," she said.

"Other vampires!" the half-dead screeched. "He'll come back with more vampires. More—maybe lots more."

Arkeley grabbed his hair again and pulled his head back. "He's going to make new vampires? That'll take some time. At least another night. That's good, that's useful to us."

The half-dead stared up into Arkeley's hard eyes. "Why would he do that? Why make new ones when he already has ninety-nine of them waiting to strike?"

54.

A courier met me with certain papers, hastily-made copies of letters from the Ranger Simonon to his masters in Richmond. One of my spies had intercepted them en route and made the copies, then sent the originals on, as were his standing orders. I read the letters with a growing fear, that was not alleviated when I'd finished. I asked the soldier if he knew where this place was, the Chess plantation, and he said he did not, but could direct me on to Gum Spring, at least. I listened closely to the directions he indicated, and then was off again. My horse needed rest. I needed food, and perhaps a nice cigar, and time to smoke it. They say misery loves company, but I doubt the horse was capable of appreciating the sentiment.

—THE PAPERS OF WILLIAM PITTENGER

55.

"I," Arkeley admitted, his face blank, "may have made a mistake."

"What are you saying?" Caxton demanded. She knew, of course. She just had to confirm it.

"The other vampires—the ones in the cavern—" the half-dead spluttered out. "They're not dead. Just sleeping."

"And you think he can wake them," she said, speaking slowly to buy time. Time to think. Time to get her stomach under control.

"Yes, yes! He was quite clear on that." The thing squirmed in its bonds. It seemed to think this was the simplest, most logical thing in the world.

"But there were no hearts," she said, when she could speak again. "There were no hearts in the cavern—just bones. I checked every coffin. He can't revive them unless he has their hearts." At the time it had been reasonable to assume that the bones were dead. That the vampires were dead, permanently dead.

Her reasonable assumption was wrong. If a hundred vampires got loose—how much damage could they do before she could stop them? Could she even stop that many?

Arkeley was staring at her with a look of horror on his face. She didn't need to say what she was thinking, because she knew he was thinking exactly the same thing.

"There were no hearts there," she insisted again.

The thing that had once been Geistdoerfer was happy to fill her in. "When I entered the cavern there was a heart laid out on every coffin. Dipped in tar, wrapped in oilskin. I originally wanted to replace them all but he said no, I should let the others sleep. Together we gathered up the other hearts, to keep my students from disturbing them. We numbered them carefully and then we put them in a barrel."

"I've seen that barrel," Caxton said, turning to face Arkeley. It was in the specimen room of the Civil War Era Studies department of Gettysburg College. She remembered silver wood and hoops weathered down to rust stains. She had thought it was just one more artifact from the dig. "I've seen where it is. I know exactly where it is."

The two of them stood there, looking at each other.

"If I can get somebody there in time, they can destroy the hearts. We can stop this before it even begins."

Arkeley nodded as if he liked what she said. "This doesn't have to end badly. Not if we can get to the hearts before the vampire does. You can call the Gettysburg police, tell them where it is, tell them how to destroy the hearts."

She nodded and grabbed for her cell phone. Dialed a number she knew by heart. Finally someone picked up in Harrisburg. "This is Trooper Laura Caxton," she said. "Put me through to the Commissioner, please. No, wait, he won't be in yet. Just get me the duty officer in charge."

The dispatcher didn't ask any questions. After a couple of seconds a bored-sounding man answered from the operations desk. She explained quickly what she needed.

The duty officer grumbled, "We'll need a warrant for that."

That would take time. Maybe hours. They would have to wake up a judge—and the judge would want some paperwork. Some kind of evidence to justify barging into private property and seizing an old rusty barrel. It would take more than one trooper's panicked testimony. "There are exigent circumstances. The barrel is going to be used in the commission of a violent crime. Maybe a lot of violent crimes."

"That would be a first. I don't know, Trooper—"

"Listen," Caxton said. "Listen closely." She closed her eyes and tried to think of the words to light a fire under the OIC.

A hundred vampires. Caxton had once seen what just two vampires could do. They'd eaten the entire population of a small town, leaving only one survivor. A hundred vampires—vampires who had been starved for more than a century, vampires who would wake up emaciated and cold and very, very hungry—could depopulate Gettysburg in a single night. "Listen," she said again. "I will take personal responsibility on this. You get a patrol unit down there now and get that barrel. If you don't a lot of people are going to die. They're going to die painfully and all their families are going to grieve for years. Because you wouldn't trust me right now. Do you understand?"

"Yeah," he said, finally. "Hey—yeah, you're *that* Caxton, aren't you? The gay lady supercop they made that movie about. How much did you get paid for that?"

"Send the fucking unit right now!" she screamed, and flipped her phone shut.

Arkeley and Harold were both staring at her when she looked up.

"They're sending a unit to look for the barrel," she told Arkeley.

"It's still dark out," he replied.

"I know." She fumed silently. "They'll send one man in a patrol cruiser. He might think to take his shotgun with him, but probably not. If the vampire is there, if he's beaten us to it, he'll take our guy apart piece by piece. We just have to hope our man gets there first. I'll go there as fast as I can and try to stop anyone from dying, but I can't fly. It'll take me hours to get back. What could I have done differently?"

Arkeley shook his head. He didn't have a nasty comeback, didn't so much as call her an idiot.

She checked her things. Her Beretta, fully loaded, was back in its holster. She'd gathered up her pepper spray as well, her handcuffs and her flashlight, recovered from Geistdoerfer's pockets before they'd revived him.

She turned to look at the half-dead one last time. When she was gone she knew Arkeley would destroy the reanimated corpse, smash in its head and cremate the remains. He wouldn't bother trying to contact the professor's family, at least not until afterward. Fine, she thought. Let them sleep in. Let them get one last night of peace before they had to hear about how John Geistdoerfer had met his grisly end a second time.

She stepped over to where he lay on top of his wooden case. "I have one last question before I go," she said. "No torture this time, no threats. I just want to talk to the man who used to own that body."

The half-dead's eyes were dry and yellow in their sockets. They focused on her as if they were glued in place.

"When you searched me, Professor, you took my weapons away. You took my handcuffs, too. You found my cell phone, but you left it where it was. I don't understand why you did that. You must have known what you'd found."

"Oh, yes, Trooper. I knew what it was," he said in that irritating high-pitched squeak.

"Why, then? Were you trying to help me? Did you think that might have made the difference, and helped me stop the vampire?"

The half-dead licked his dry lips with a gray tongue. His nose crinkled as if he'd smelled something foul. "Maybe," he said, finally. "If I say yes, will you let me go?"

"No," she said, frowning.

"Then maybe I just didn't think you could call anyone. Not while we were both watching you." He turned his head away from her. "I'm a villain. If you're done with me, just kill me already!"

She shook her head and grabbed at his shirt and his jacket. He struggled to pull away, to get his face away from her, but she wasn't interested in that. Instead she shoved a hand in his pocket and pulled out his car keys.

Moving quickly, she went to the front door of the museum building and pushed it open. Outside a bright blue light filled the sky—the color of night just before the dawn begins. Everything that had happened since she'd gone to Gettysburg College to interview Geistdoerfer had happened in a single night, but now that night was over. A layer of frost lay over the cars in the street, on the wooden utility poles, ready to melt into morning dew. Nearby a bird was chirping, a repetitive, shrill little sound that made her scalp feel tight. She really needed some sleep.

Behind her she heard the rustling of clothing, and her hands twitched in paranoia. When she turned around it was only to see Arkeley filling the doorway. "I should be going with you, but I can't." His eyes burned in the blue light. Cold, fierce, angry. "This should be my case, but I was too frail to finish it. You need to be my hands on this one."

It was her case. Caxton was sure of that. Still she could understand his frustration. He'd been working most of his adult life on trying to drive vampires to extinction. He must have watched her failures and mistakes with growing dread, knowing he could have done a better job. If only his body still worked, if only he still had his strength.

"I'll get what I can out of Geistdoerfer—if he comes up with anything else I'll call you. I'll help as much as I can from a distance." His face fell. "Do it right," he said. "Be smart, and don't get yourself killed."

It was the closest thing he could manage to wishing her luck. She just nodded and moved on to the next task. That was how she would get through this—one simple decision at a time.

She hurried down the alley to the parking lot, where Geistdoerfer's car with its suggestion of tail fins waited for her. Its windshield was covered in a thin layer of white frost, which she wiped away with her sleeves. Then she climbed in and started up the powerful engine, listened to it purr. The sky was brightening by the minute. When she felt the car had warmed up enough she put it in gear and headed out, laying her cell phone on the passenger seat beside her. There were a lot of calls to be made.

Her stomach growled noisily. She hadn't eaten in a very long time. Her brain was fighting her, squirming painfully in her skull. Her body was breaking down. It needed sleep, and food, and peace.

Not a lot she could do about that. But maybe, something.

She couldn't sleep, not yet. Peace was an abstract. Food, though, was a possibility. There were few diners in that stretch of Pennsylvania—mostly there were family restaurants, the kind that didn't open until the farmers started their day. Not for a while yet. She found a fast-food place that was open all night, decided to waste a few minutes if it meant her body would calm down a little. If it meant getting some energy back.

She pulled up to the drive-through bay. Cranked down the old car's manual window and let cold air blast inside, across her face. It woke her up some. She shouted her order at the microphone, but nobody answered. After a while she tapped the horn. The big pneumatic noise it made drew tiny birds out of the trees across the road. Finally a sleepy voice croaked out of the speakers. "How can we help you?" it asked.

"Give me an egg sandwich and a cup of coffee," she said.

"Do you want milk and sugar?" the voice blurted. There was a bad feedback whine that nearly drowned out the words.

"No," she shouted back.

"Hash browns for only thirty-nine cents more?"

Caxton grabbed the bridge of her nose and squeezed. "People are going to fucking die if you don't just put a fucking sandwich in a fucking bag for me," she said.

The speaker cut off with an electronic belch. Then the feedback returned. "I'm sorry, I missed that."

Probably a good thing, too. Caxton exhaled noisily. "Yeah, give me some hash browns," she said.

"Thank you, pull through."

She drove up to the next window, took her food and paid for it. She tore into the greasy sandwich before she'd even gotten back on the Turnpike.

The road disappeared beneath her wheels. When she got to the toll plaza she pulled into the purple E-ZPass lane. The toll went on Geistdoerfer's tab and she was through.

56.

Storrow regained his footing & grabbed at the degraded side of the cupola. "No reason we can't go back the way we came, now," he said, a smile on his face. "It'll be a hard slog back through partisan country, but lackin' Simonon, them horsemen we saw'll be disorganized. Maybe we'll actually make it back to the lines."

I wiped my face with my hands. What would I do now? For what purpose should I go on? Bill was dead. I had my duty, I supposed, to my country. I could draw on that for strength, I told myself. I reached out a hand for Storrow to take. He did not accept my grasp, but instead loosed an anguished cry. I turned to look at him.

In that same instant all hope died. Chess rose up again with a fury I could scarce credit though I saw it myself. The vampire's head was fully re-formed, though he was hatless now.

"Sweet Jesu," Storrow barked. "We're done for!"

"Get," I told him, because suddenly I wanted him to live. We had argued, Storrow & I, & been at loggerheads, yet I wanted him to live so badly I would sacrifice myself to make it happen. Which is exactly what I thought I was doing.

I ran at the vampire with my head down, as fast as my hurt leg would allow. Under normal conditions this would have had all the effect of blowing on him with my breath. He was stronger by far than I, massively so, & invincible as far as I knew. Yet on the

pitched roof I gained momentum as I ran heedless of my footing, &
when I collided with the vampire we both were launched into light-
less space.

For one moment only I felt suspended between Heaven and
Earth, a spirit of the air. A moment after that I struck the dry
Virginia soil below, which felt much harder than I recalled.

Pain was my portion, but for one moment more only. Then all
feeling left my legs & aught below my chest. My back was bro-
ken. I needed no physician to tell me as much.

—THE STATEMENT OF ALVA GRIEST

57.

Leaves stirred up into the air, splatted across her windshield as she pulled off Route 15 and into the Gettysburg bor-ough limits. The streets were empty, the day's traffic not yet begun. It was well after eight and the sun was already above the treetops, a white glare in a sky full of dark clouds.

The Gettysburg College campus was just up ahead. She had not heard back from headquarters, did not yet know whether they'd beaten the vampire to his prize. She held her phone against the steering wheel, ready to answer it the second it started to ring.

She crested a low hill and eased off the gas as the car surged down into a dark hollow. The trees were buffeted by a stiff breeze and their half-naked branches lashed against each other, against the surging air.

It wasn't much farther to the edge of the college. She pulled into the parking lot below Geistdoerfer's old offices and jumped out, looking around for any sign of the patrol cruiser she'd had dispatched there. It stood a bit away, at the end of the lot, its lights off. She approached it carefully, not knowing what she expected to see. Occasionally she glanced at the tree-lined sidewalks of the campus, at the darker shadows. There would be nothing there, of course. Her vampire would be asleep now, hidden tight away in some stolen coffin, waiting for the newly risen sun to go away.

She got up to the car, bent down with a hand over her eyes to look inside. A trooper in a wide-brimmed hat sat in the driver's seat, hunched over. His hat obscured his eyes, but she could see his mouth was open.

No, she thought. Not another dead cop. Guilt skewered her kidneys like a thin knife. She put a hand on the door of the car, leaned down to get a closer look.

The trooper inside sat bolt upright, his mouth closing with a click she heard through the glass. He turned bleary eyes to look up at her, then frowned.

She fished out her state police ID and pressed it against his window. He nodded, then gestured for her to step back. Slowly he pushed open his door and clambered out.

"You Caxton?" he asked.

"Trooper Caxton, yeah," she said, frowning.

He gave her a weary smile that spoke volumes. She didn't impress him. He'd probably heard stories about her, maybe even seen the stupid movie. All he really knew about her, though, was that she had dragged him away from a nice warm bed and made him run a fool's errand before the sun had even come up.

Hoping for the best anyway, she glanced at the backseat of his cruiser. No barrels there. "I'm ready to receive your report," she sighed. "What's your name, Trooper?"

"Paul Junco," he said, leaning against the side of his car and stretching out long arms and legs. "I got here about six-fifteen," he said, pulling a notebook out of his pocket, "yeah, six-oh-nine A.M., to be exact, on report of a barrel stored at this location that you requested we take into police custody. I obtained entry at six-thirteen with the aid of a maintenance lady, name of Floria

Alvade, and proceeded to room 424, in the Civil War Era Studies department—"

"Where you failed to find any sign of a barrel. Come on, I need to see for myself." She led the way. Junco shrugged and kept up with her as she hurried inside. A woman in blue coveralls, presumably the same Floria Alvade, was buffing the lobby floor with a big metal waxer. Its furry wheel spat dust across Caxton's shoes. When she saw them coming she switched the machine off.

"Miss Alvade?" Caxton asked. The woman nodded, her face a cautious mask. Lots of people looked like that when cops approached them. It didn't mean anything. "I need to know, did anyone enter this building last night?"

The woman nodded at Trooper Junco.

"Anyone else? Anyone at all? Maybe a tall man, very pale skin, bald?"

"Like that vampire I seen on the TV?" Alvade crossed herself. "Oh, Mary preserve me, no! Just him, I swear. I been here all night, too."

Caxton nodded and turned to go up the stairs. "How about you, Trooper? Did you see anybody leave as you were coming in?"

"I think I would have mentioned if I saw an undead bloodsucker," he told her.

She whirled on him, fixed him with her hardest glare. Arkeley wouldn't have put up with that kind of insubordination. She had to get tougher, had to rise above her bad reputation. Had to make people understand just how serious things had become.

"If you have any more glib comments to make, Trooper," she told him, "I suggest you save them for your official report. Clear?"

His mouth hardened. "Yes, Ma'am," he said.

She turned without waiting for anything further and raced up the stairs two at a time. She was winded when she got to the top, but she pressed on, past the classroom where she'd met

Geistdoerfer, back to the specimen room where she'd seen the barrel. It was gone. She'd already known that. Seeing it for herself made a difference, though. It made her blood run colder, made her skin prickle.

The hearts were gone.

When she could think again, when her own heart wasn't bursting inside her chest, she headed back down to the parking lot. Three local police cars were just pulling in, lights on but no sirens. Officer Glauer stepped out of one. Dots of toilet paper flecked his throat where he must have just finished shaving.

"You got my message," Caxton said, by way of greeting.

"Yeah. All four of them," Glauer replied. He fingered his mustache, an obvious tell. He was worried.

Good. She needed him worried. She needed him scared.

"I just called exigent circumstances so I could search a room up there," she said, gesturing over her shoulder at the classroom building. "Turned up nothing. There are ninety-nine missing vampire hearts. Whoever has them can wake up ninety-nine vampires when the sun goes down tonight. I'd like to make sure that doesn't happen."

"I'd like to help you with that," the big cop said. He reached into his car and picked up his hat. "The chief, on the other hand—"

Caxton nodded. She knew Vicente was going to be a problem. "I'll talk to him, when he actually comes in to work." She looked up at the sky. The clouds were thickening and turning dark, but the sun was up there somewhere. "What time did the sun go down last night?" she asked.

Glauer placed his hat carefully on his head. He squinted for a second as he tried to remember. "Just before seven. Yeah, I'd say ten till—that's when I took my dinner break and I remember being very glad I was off the street. We kept our guard up last night, believe me, even if the chief thought we were safe. So we have until seven to find those hearts?"

Caxton shook her head. "There might be another way." She looked at Geistdoerfer's Buick and decided it wasn't the ideal vehicle for what came next. Her own Mazda was nearby, but it wasn't marked as a police car. "You're driving," she said. "Maybe we can finish this in the next hour."

He gave her a weak smile. "Christmas is still two months away," he told her, but he didn't waste any more time. He took her south through town, down the tourist lanes into the battle-field. Up Seminary Ridge and then down an unpaved road through a clump of trees. She remembered exactly where it was—in highway patrol she'd learned to make mental notes whenever she was called to a scene, to pick out the local land-marks so she could find her way back if she needed to, so she could give accurate directions to paramedics and firefighting units. The little dig site was still fresh in her memory from the last time she'd seen it, only two days before.

There were no cars at the end of the road. She got out and led Glauer and the four other cops down the path, about two hun-dred yards into the trees, back to where the dig site had been set up by Geistdoerfer and his students. The tents were still there and the campfire, but the ashes were cold and wet with dew.

Exhaustion and guilt formed ice crystals in her brain as she saw the place again. She should have known—somehow she should have known. She should have cordoned the place off, declared it an official crime scene. Of course she hadn't been on active duty when she'd first seen it, but there had been plenty of time afterward. It had just not occurred to her. Jeff Montrose, the grad student who showed her around, had thought the place was dead, a simple crypt.

It helped her conscience a little that Arkeley hadn't both-ered to lock the site down, either. It helped a very little.

Okay, she thought to herself. *My guilty feelings about the past help nobody. For the present: No more mistakes. Do this just like Arkeley would.*

She drew her weapon from its holster. Checked the safety. "There won't be any vampires down there, not now, but there could be others. Half-deads, or maybe deluded people who work for my vampire. They may have gotten the hearts but didn't have time to put them with their respective bodies. In that case they might be guarding the coffins right now." She stood silent for a moment, listening for any sign of activity inside the tent. The nylon walls stirred a little in a breeze, but she didn't hear anyone moving around. She stepped through the tall wet grass that left little dark ovals on her pant legs, and twitched back the door of the tent.

There was nobody inside. Not up top, anyway. She looked back at two of the cops who'd come with Glauer. Gestured for them to go around either side of the tent. There could be any number of monsters hiding in the trees around them—she did not want to go down into the cavern and have somebody pull the ladder up, trapping her inside.

She moved into the tent with just Glauer at her shoulder, half a pace behind her. He was so tall that the roof of the tent bowed outward around his head. She stopped and looked back at him, then down at his belt. He looked confused until she pointed directly at his gun. He frowned guiltily, then drew it.

His instincts, his cop training, had told him you didn't enter a place looking for a fight. You didn't draw until you were ready to shoot. In any other circumstance that would have been a good thing, proper firearms discipline. In the tent it was just dumb.

He drew his weapon, lifted it to shoulder height. The muzzle pointed up, through the roof of the tent. If he tripped or panicked his shot would go clear and not hit Caxton in the back. That made her feel slightly better.

She walked past the tables full of old rusty metal artifacts and whited lead bullets. The excavation at the far end of the tent was as she'd last seen it, with the ladder leading down into the cavern. One thing was different, but it took her a moment to place it. Somebody had turned off the lights down there.

She spun around looking for a generator, or a switch, or any way to get them back on. She couldn't see anything. Instead of wasting more time looking for a way to get the power back on, she took her flashlight off her belt and swished its beam around the bottom of the hole. Nothing jumped out at her.

"Cover me," she said, "then come down ten seconds after I get to the bottom."

Glauer nodded. His eyes were very wide.

There will be nobody down there, she thought. *There will be nobody down there except ninety-nine skeletons. We can spend the rest of the day grinding them down to powder and then burning the powder in a blast furnace. My vampire has the hearts, but without the bones that's nothing.*

It could be that easy. It really could. She knew better, though.

She put one foot on the ladder. Nothing grabbed her ankle. The rung held her weight. She put her other foot down and waited a second, then hurried down as fast as she could go. At the bottom she panned her Beretta back and forth at eye height, ready to shoot anyone who appeared. Nobody did. She scanned the cavern with her flashlight beam.

Behind her Glauer scampered down the ladder too fast. He missed one of the rungs and nearly fell.

She should have told him not to bother coming down.

"Remember the conversation we had that one time, about the worst things we'd ever seen?" Caxton asked him. "I think I have a new contender."

Her flashlight lit up stalactites and stalagmites, old dusty broken furniture, mineral deposits. The cavern was otherwise empty—no bones, no coffins.

Somebody had moved them while she wasn't looking. There could be only one reason why.

Back up top, she gathered the locals together and told them to start calling every name on their emergency phone tree, to get every available man out of bed or work or wherever he was and get them down to the police station. She asked Glauer to find Vicente for her, to start liaising there.

Her job had just become a lot more difficult. They would need to find the coffins, the bones, the hearts. All of them. They would need to find her vampire, wherever he was sleeping the day away. They might need to do a lot more than that. She glanced at her watch. It was nine-fifteen. She had less than ten hours and no leads whatsoever.

No—there was one person she could call who might know what had happened in the cavern. One person who was responsible for the coffins. Deep in the stored phonebook of her cell she found an entry for Jeff Montrose, the graduate student from the department of Civil War Era Studies. She called him and after four rings got his message:

"Welcome . . . to the dark lair of Jeff, Mary, Fisher, and Madison. We can't take your call right now, most likely because we're hanging by our feet someplace quiet and gloomy. If you'd like to leave a message, a prayer for salvation, or your darkest desire, we're just dying to hear from you!"

The phone beeped in her ear and she snapped it shut. She needed to talk to Montrose as soon as possible.

"Glauer," she shouted, "call your dispatcher. I need a street address right now."

58.

I looked to the side, which was all I could do, & caught sight of Chess rolling on his own ground, his hands clutching his sides. He, I knew, would not be slain by such a fall. He would be merely inconvenienced.

Storrow fired direct into the body of Chess, & then he loosed his second shell. The vampire curled like a moth that has touched flame, & shook, & screamed in anger & in pain. Not dead yet, & surely he would recover in a moment.

When he did Storrow fired again. Then he reloaded his weapon & when the vampire stirred he shot once more. Neither of us knew any way to permanently steal the vampire's strange life, but Storrow understood the creature could be kept stunned, at least for a while.

Storrow did not speak to me as he carried out this ugly work. I did not know how many shells he possessed. It could have still ended in both our deaths, & perhaps it should have. Yet before too long we both looked up for we had heard some great noise in the woods around us, as of many men approaching. Had I seen then dead Simonon's ghost riding a skeletal horse I would have not been so surprised as to see who led that host. For instead it was Hiram Morse, our cowardly deserter.

—THE STATEMENT OF ALVA GRIEST

59.

She spent the morning doing police work—real police work. Following up leads and examining crime scenes. There was plenty to find. The vampire had been busy.

By ten-thirty it started raining, a faint drizzle that felt more like mist. Water shook down from the trees and soaked the leaves on the sidewalks. Where Caxton's shoes brushed away the oak leaves they left brown spiky stains on the concrete, shadows cut loose in the silvery light.

The chief arrived in a car with a gold badge on its hood and just a single blue light on top. He stepped out and glared at her, not even trying to hide his annoyance. He wore a heavy yellow raincoat with reflective tape across the back. He rushed toward her while opening an umbrella.

"You told me you had this under control," he said.

"I told you to stay on your toes," she replied.

It wasn't what she'd wanted to say. It was a game she was playing, though, and she'd never been very good at games. This time she needed a solid win.

"I'd hoped we'd seen the last of you," he said. He had a tight smile on his face that was probably the closest he could manage to a look of patient concern. "That's why we brought you in. You're supposed to know how to handle these things."

The chief would have been briefed at least once by his officers. He had to know what was going on. Still he wanted to put the blame on her. To make her say it was all her fault. That wouldn't help anybody.

Carefully she laid out their shared problem. "There were ninety-nine more skeletons in that cavern. Our vampire has managed to remove them all to an unknown location. He has also come into possession of the hearts that used to belong to those ninety-nine vampires. If he puts the hearts together with the bones he can wake them up. All of them. Tonight, just before seven, they'll rise from their coffins and they'll be very, very hungry." She had to play this just right, she knew. Not step on his toes, but not kowtow to him either. "This is your show. You have some pretty tough decisions to make. I'll be happy to advise you if I can."

"You're saying he came back here." The chief just didn't seem to get it. She needed to fix that. "You're saying there are going to be more of them?"

Caxton nodded. "I'm sorry to drag you all the way out here. I just thought you should see this for yourself."

Arkeley would not have played this game, she knew. He wouldn't have had to. He would have bulled into town and demanded his due share of respect and power and he would have run things his way from the start. She'd already blown any chance of doing that—already squandered what goodwill the chief might once have felt toward her.

Glauer had filled her in on what had happened while she'd been in Philadelphia. Already Vicente had tried to undermine her. He'd made a big show of inviting her down to Gettysburg originally because he thought she could kill the vampire in one night and make all the bad things go away without putting any of his men at risk. She had been the famous vampire killer, the one they made that movie about—surely one vampire would be no problem for her to dispatch. It hadn't worked out that way. Instead she had scared off all the tourists—the town's lifeblood—and cost the local businesses untold amounts of money.

Everybody in this world has a boss, and the chief of police's boss was the mayor. There had been an emergency meeting of the chamber of commerce. The National Park Service, which was its own little fiefdom in a town with more history than people, had weighed in as well. They weren't happy at all. The mayor, who knew nothing about vampires, had come down hard on Vicente. Ripped him a new asshole, as Glauer put it (and this from a man who had trained himself never to curse in polite conversation).

Shit rolls downhill. Bureaucracy rolls faster. Vicente had put the blame on the state police and more specifically on Trooper Laura Caxton. It had been her misconduct that had hurt the town, he claimed. In short, he had covered his ass. His question the previous night, when he had asked her if his men could stand down, had followed immediately.

He knew the danger his town was in—knew it intellectually, but didn't really understand. He was a lot more worried about losing his job.

Which meant she had to convince him there were some

things more important than political advancement. He could still send her packing if she didn't get through to him. Send her away with polite thanks and say he would take it from there. She couldn't let that happen. *No more mistakes,* she swore. "Would you come this way, Chief?" she asked.

She led him down an alleyway between a bank and a dry cleaner's. More yellow police tape blocked it off from traffic. Halfway down the narrow lane stood a car, a Ford Focus with New Jersey state tags. It looked like three people were sleeping inside, one in the driver's seat, two in the rear seat leaning against each other.

"Jesus, no," Vicente said, staring. She could feel his tension in the wet air. "That's not—"

"I'm afraid so. Your people found the car early this morning, just as I was getting into town. At first they didn't even think to connect it to my investigation." Caxton took a key from Glauer and unlocked the driver's-side door. When she pulled it open a foul wave of stink rolled out of the car. The stink of death. "Officer Glauer heard the report on his car radio and put the pieces together. It's important you look, Chief," she said.

Vicente stared at her. She was pushing him hard, but she had no choice.

They had made a solid identification of Subject One, the woman sitting in the driver's seat. Her face was a pretty close match for the picture on the driver's license in her pocket. What was left of her face, anyway. Her name was Linda Macguire and she was—had been—a resident of Tenafly, New Jersey. The state police records and identification unit up in Harrisburg had contacted her husband and he was on his way to make an official identification.

The two kids in the back were Cathy Macguire, aged sixteen and Linda's only child, and Darren Jackson, also of Tenafly, aged seventeen. Cathy's boyfriend. According to Macguire's husband, Linda, Cathy, and Darren had been on vacation in Philadelphia the night before. They'd gone to see the Liberty Bell and Independence Hall.

Linda had most of her shoulder torn away, the tattered ends of her shirt wrapped around her neck. The kids had massive defensive wounds on their arms and both of their throats had been torn out. All three of them were exsanguinated, and only minimal bloodstains had been found on the car's floor mats.

"What did he do?" Vicente asked, very quietly.

"He needed someone to drive him here from Philly," Caxton answered. "Most likely he just approached the first car he saw and forced his way inside." The door handle on the front passenger's side showed signs of stress, as if the vampire had tried to rip the door open. "He kept them alive—at least, he kept the driver alive—so she could operate the vehicle. Times of death have not been established yet, so we don't know if he killed the kids in Philly or only after he got here. When he was done with the driver he killed her, too."

"You mean she could have been driving for hours knowing that her daughter and her boyfriend were already dead back there?" Vicente asked.

"He can be very persuasive when he needs a ride," Caxton said, her cheeks turning red with shame. If she had refused to take the vampire to Philadelphia, if she had just forced him to kill her on the spot, these people might still be alive—

She had more important things to do than feel guilty.

"Shall we move on to the next scene?" Caxton asked.

The chief wheeled around to stare at her. "Don't tell me there's more bodies."

Caxton looked over at Glauer. Glauer just shrugged and failed to make eye contact with anybody. He'd never worked a homicide case before. Neither had the chief. *Hell of a way to start,* Caxton thought.

60.

I lit out at once for *Gum Spring*. My orders were quite vague, which was hardly unusual, yet there was enough in them to chill me. A creature had been discovered there, a vampire. I thought such evils were banished from the earth. Yet this war had dug up so many ancient wrongs—fratricide, treason and espionage among the more mild.

At a field morgue in Maryland, I once saw teamsters fitting bodies for pinewood coffins. If the dead man in question proved too tall they would jump in with him, and trample on his feet and legs, until he became a shorter being and would fit better. Then there were the amputated limbs, stacked like cordwood, ripe with decay. When they found some man missing an arm or a leg they would place one from the proper pile in with his remains, taking no pains whatsoever to ensure the right man was matched with the right appendage.

I chastised such men when I saw their work, but only the first time. I learned quickly what every soldier knows. A man is counted lucky, who is buried by his mother back at home. For most a shallow grave on foreign soil is their only recompense for service, a grave dug deep as possible by the decedent's friends, so that hogs and other animals may not root it up.

Should dumb animals, should nature herself have turned against us, what surprise is there in a risen corpse come to prey upon the living? None. Yet a vampire—what the deuce could this have to do with me?

—THE PAPERS OF WILLIAM PITTENGER

61.

Bright yellow police tape wrapped around the house on Railroad Street leased to Jeff Montrose and three roommates. The house was a gray-painted clapboard affair with plenty of gables and a porch with white gingerbread details. Some of the carved wood had come loose and hung on rusty nails. Around the foundation clumps of ailanthus and hydrangea hung wilted and sodden. A basement window on the side of the house flashed with the trapped light of the police cruisers that filled the street.

Caxton shook out the collar of her jacket, spraying water everywhere, and hurried toward the house, gesturing at the white wooden porch with its loose gingerbread. "This house is rented in part to a graduate student at the college, one Jeff Montrose. I tried to contact him to ask him about the coffins but he didn't answer his phone. Officer Glauer and I came here to see if we could find him, or at least figure out where he might have gone."

Vicente went in first and then she followed. Glauer stayed outside. He didn't explain why, but she supposed he didn't have to. He'd already seen what was inside.

Vicente stamped his feet on a mat inside the front door. It was warm and mostly dry in the front room, a big living space with a pair of mismatched couches and a television on top of a plastic milk crate. Beyond, through a high archway, stood the kitchen—dishes in the sink, a refrigerator full of leftover Chinese food.

In any normal crime scene the room would be full of forensics cops taking samples, lifting prints, cutting fibers from the stained shag carpet. There was no need this time. Caxton had already learned what she needed to know from the house from her previous visit.

She led Vicente up a wooden staircase that creaked at every other step. The old woven runner that draped across the risers was faded and worn through in places. Silvery light from an exterior window brightened the wall ahead of them and dazzled their eyes. At the top a hallway split off toward four different bedrooms. Three of the doors were closed. Mary Klein, Fisher Hawkins, and Madison Chou Zhang owned those rooms. All three were accounted for, safe at the homes of parents or friends far away from Gettysburg. They had left town after hearing Caxton's press conference the day before, even though it meant skipping classes. Montrose had the fourth room, the farthest one from the top of the stairs.

Vicente paused with his hand still on the banister. He looked slightly out of breath. Caxton wondered if he'd ever seen a dead body before.

Together they stepped into the room where Jeff Montrose's life had ended at approximately five-fifteen that morning, several hours before Caxton arrived back in town.

The walls of the room were lined with posters from various concerts, black ink on vibrantly colored paper. Clothes and books littered the floor, were heaped up by the cot that had served as Montrose's bed. Videos and DVDs were stacked neatly on shelves, prominent among them a copy of *Teeth*. Caxton hoped Vicente didn't see it. A desk sat beneath the room's single window, mostly covered in a big beige computer setup and thick sheaves of printer paper. In a chair before the computer Montrose remained just as Caxton had found him. He wore a white shirt open at the neck and wrists and a black cape lined with red velvet. He'd told her about that cape when she'd met him—he wore it when he did ghost tours in town. His eye makeup was impeccable, but the dark mascara and kohl stood in high contrast to the near-perfect whiteness of his face. Most of his neck had been torn away, but there was not a drop of blood anywhere in the room.

Vicente took one look at the body and started to vomit. He turned around in a circle until he found a trash can and hugged it to him as his chest and shoulders heaved.

Caxton waited patiently until he was done.

"The killer was our vampire, the original one. There's no real question. He must have come here directly from the crime scene in the alleyway. He would have been told where to look for Montrose by Professor Geistdoerfer from the college."

"The Running Wolf?" Vicente stared at her with wild eyes.

"Professor Geistdoerfer was the one who woke our vampire in the first place. I don't think he understood what the consequences would be, at the time. Afterward the vampire controlled him through threats and intimidation. He's . . . dead now." Presumably dead again, and for the last time, she thought, but didn't say.

"And this kid." Vicente stepped a little closer to the body in the chair. He reached out and touched the cloth of Montrose's cape. "Was he some kind of—Satanist?"

"No. A student of dark history." Caxton frowned. "He was fascinated with ghosts and vampires and other unnatural things. That's why he came to school here, to study the darkest period of American history. The people of the nineteenth century shared some of his more ghoulish interests."

"So when a vampire came along he just jumped at the chance to help."

Caxton shook her head. "Just because he was interested in vampires, that didn't make him evil. My girlfriend was a goth, back in high school, and she read nothing but books on vampires. I can promise you she's not evil. Lots of kids play vampires and victims."

"Sure, we did that at my school, too. We'd tie black towels around our necks and run around pretending to bite each other, just like in the movies. Then we discovered girls and it all seemed kind of silly. This guy didn't grow out of it, right?"

Caxton shrugged.

"And now he's paid for it. Just a dumb kid."

She pushed some papers aside on the desk and showed him what lay there. A simple wooden stake, a piece of wood about a foot long, sharpened at one end. "He was a lot of things, but he wasn't an idiot," she said. "He knew something was up. I think he must have known all along, at least as soon as he heard on the news about how Officer Garrity had died. He must have known he was an accomplice, that he had helped bring the vampire back to life. He knew what was happening in this town." She touched the pointy end of the stake. Montrose had probably known it was useless against a vampire that had already fed on blood that night. He'd studied vampires enough, had watched *Teeth* probably more than once. The stake must have been the best thing he could get his hands on. "I don't think he was a bad person, at heart. He just couldn't seem to make up his mind which side he was on."

Vicente shook his head. "I don't understand, Trooper. Why did you want me to see this?"

Caxton leaned over the computer on the desk. "We found this when we discovered the body. He made no attempt to hide it." The computer was in sleep mode. When she tapped the space bar the screen lit up right away. It displayed the client for Montrose's student webmail account, with a message already opened:

Subject: A Humble Request for Aid
From: John Geistdoerfer
To: Jeffrey Montrose
Priority: Normal

My dear Montrose:

I'm afraid it's come to the worst. The police are going to seal off the site, well, we should have expected that. I believe you met Trooper Caxton. She's on her way just now to come interrogate me. Rubber hoses and the third degree. I think I'm man enough to take it, but what might be worse . . . Jeff, they're going to seize the coffins and other artifacts and I doubt we'll ever see them again. I know you share my passion for this find and I'd like to ask for your help.

What I have in mind may not be strictly adherent to the letter of the law. Don't worry. I'll take all responsibility, and pay whatever silly fine they want, if it comes to that. You will remember we discussed moving the coffins to a place where they could be better looked after. I'd like you to take the department van and start doing that today. Don't tell anyone what you're up to, though of course if you're stopped en route don't lie for my sake, either. Do it soon, Jeff, if you can.

I see big things for you, son, big things indeed. I see your name just below mine on the paper when we describe this find. There are times when the petty temporal concerns of we mortals must bow to the needs of history—I think in you I have found someone who shares that belief. You have my eternal thanks.

—John

62.

Hiram Morse had done his duty, according to general orders. When we first met resistance to our picket he had run back to the line as fast as he was able, & summoned aid, & much of it. He had brought the whole of the 3rd Maine with him, some twelve score men, & Colonel Lakeman at the front with his sword in the air. They carried lanterns through the wood to light their way, & it seemed like great fires moved through the trees there were so many.

They made short work of Chess. The men got a length of rope around his neck, & hanged him from the tallest tree in his own yard, & settled in to watch him struggle & try to break free.

Eventually he seemed to realize the futility of his efforts & he let his body slacken on the line, yet still he did not die. It was during this part of his destruction that I asked to look on him, the creature who'd so utterly corrupted my Bill. It was allowed, & I was brought close, & looked in his red eyes. I had thought to spit on him, but when I saw the expression & great intelligence in his face I banked my wrath. For a good minute I did naught but look on him, & he on me. In the end I could muster up not enough hate to curse him.

He lingered long through the night & up until the dawn, when the light of day touched him like the finger of God. Then his flesh melted away like candle wax, & his naked bones fell from the noose.

They made me a stretcher, for I could walk no longer, and carried me hence.

—THE STATEMENT OF ALVA GRIEST

63.

Vicente read the message over a couple of times, just as Caxton had before him. While she waited she wondered about Montrose. The day and night before, the student had taken on a truly gruesome task. Alone, unaided, he had moved ninety-nine coffins to a new location. She supposed that if you were studying to be an archaeologist you learned how to handle bones and not be creeped out by them. Still. It must have taken him all day. It must have left him exhausted.

Then he'd come home after all that hard and dirty work and put on his cape, the one he wore when he led his ghost tours. He had prepared his stake and sat down to wait and see what happened. He must have been so confused—wanting, desperately, to actually meet a real vampire in the flesh. Terrified because he knew he probably wouldn't survive the encounter. She wondered what the two of them had talked about. She wondered if Montrose had, in the end, learned what he so badly wanted to know.

When the chief finished reading he looked down at the body again. He seemed to have recovered from his squeamishness. "I don't get this. He helped the vampire. Why did it kill him?"

"Because Montrose could have told us where the coffins are. You'll notice Geistdoerfer was careful enough not to give the location away in his email. Montrose here would be the only living person who knew it."

"We need to find those coffins," Vicente said. "We need to find them before dark."

Caxton nodded. That was about half of what she'd wanted him to say. About half of what she'd wanted to get by bringing him down here and making him look at Montrose's corpse. The other half would take some more finesse.

She lead Vicente out of the murder scene, down the stairs again and out onto the sidewalk. While they'd been inside the rain had turned serious. Glauer stood at attention by the chief's car, the brim of his hat completely soaked.

"Officer, I want you to organize a house-by-house search," Vicente said, his face perfectly impassive. "I want you to bring in every man and woman we can get, have them check every possible place someone might hide all those coffins."

"Yes, sir," Glauer said, but he didn't move at once. Caxton had already rehearsed him in his part of the drama that came next. "I think we can get about thirty people together, each of them with a vehicle. We'll get right to it. There are hundreds of places like that in and around the borough. We'll do what we can."

"I sincerely hope so," Vicente spluttered. "Do you know what's at risk here?"

Glauer stood stock-still and said nothing. After a long, tense silence, he turned and looked across at Caxton.

Vicente broke the silence. "What is this? What aren't you telling me?"

"This scene is considerably more violent than others we've seen from this vampire," she said. She had thought, once, that this vampire was different. That he had some sense of honor or decency. Arkeley had known better—she should have listened to him. She should have known it herself all along. "I'm willing to call it a pattern. He started by wounding Geistdoerfer. He could have killed him then and there, but he had enough restraint to hold back. He moved up to provoked homicide with Officer Garrity, who tried to kill him. He then killed Geistdoerfer because he was hungry. The family from New Jersey," she said, pointing in the direction of the alley and the death car, "he did because he was in a hurry. From there he went directly to this house. Montrose was actively helping him. He spent his whole life wanting to be a vampire's best friend. The vampire killed him just because he knew where the coffins were—just to tie up one simple loose end. Human life has lost all meaning to this vampire, Chief. He's become a real sociopath now, capable of acting in cold blood. He's getting nastier and he's not done yet."

Vicente's face was already pale. He turned to look away, up the rainy street. He wasn't looking at her.

She moved around him, got right in his face. This was the dangerous part of the game, the part where she had to rely on him being a reasonable man. "Originally, he didn't want to wake the others. He wanted to let them rest in peace. That was before he started to change. I think he's more than capable now of bringing them all back. He won't just wake up one or two of them—he'll wake them all."

"Pure conjecture," Vicente said in a weak voice.

"Maybe so, but that's what we have to go on." Time to drive her point home. "Chief," Caxton said, "I'd like to make a recommendation, if you'll listen to it."

Vicente scowled, but when he'd stared at her for a while he eventually nodded.

"You should completely evacuate the town."

She stood her ground, waited for Vicente to start shouting. She didn't have to wait for long. While he told her just what he thought of her idea she waited patiently for the verbal storm to blow over. She barely even registered what he was saying.

"We'll search this town from top to bottom for those coffins," she said. "I will do everything in my power to find them before nightfall. But if the search fails—"

"—You have a recommendation for when that happens, too?"

Caxton stared into his eyes. Directly into his eyes—like a vampire hypnotizing a victim. She lacked the magical powers, but she hoped her sincerity and her fear would have a similar effect. "If we can't find the coffins before nightfall, we need to be ready. Ready for an army of vampires. Because that's what we're talking about. They'll wake up hungry and they will kill everyone they see. Chief, I need you to authorize me to start planning for tonight."

"Tonight? Tonight, when you're going to single-handedly take on a hundred vampires with your sidearm?"

"No. I need you to help me gather my own army. I need officers, I need guns, and I need you to stay out of my way. I need you to stop thinking in terms of jurisdictions. I need you to stop thinking of this as an investigation and start thinking about this as a war."

64.

I arrived in time to see Chess hang, and to watch his mansion burn. It should have ended there, with the vampire's second and final death. Yet like this war the tale has no conclusion yet; and like the unquiet grave, it seems, any finality it offers is temporary at best.

If the War Department wants my final assessment of what happened at Gum Spring, then let it have this: Private Hiram Morse should get a medal. Then he should be horsewhipped. The cur was good enough to search the burnt ruins of the Chess plantation and find the decrepit female still partially alive; or undead, or whatever the mot juste *may be; and then to bring her down to where the Army Investigators waited, where they were already examining what remained of Obediah Chess. I would guess he was drunk with the praise he'd already received for giving them one vampire on the end of a rope. He must have thought his rewards would be doubled when he returned a second, and this one still capable of interrogation. Surely he cannot have known what vital knot he was unraveling. By recovering her body he may have changed the course of this war; yes, and of history. But he has also given me the most profane duty I ever hope to receive, and robbed all my future nights of sleep, however many they may be.*

—THE PAPERS OF WILLIAM PITTENGER

65.

So much to be done. Caxton's weary body felt it piling up on her as if she were being buried alive.

Local police had to be rounded up, given cars, given maps that broke down their search areas. Radios had to be synchronized. The dispatcher, with an exasperated sigh, routed dozens of messages an hour to the unit in Caxton's car. Houses, museums, inns, tourist centers had to be searched. Schools, the hospital, every building of Gettysburg College (especially there, no stone could be left unturned there). The fire station, the old houses that were headquarters for ghost tours or guided tours of the battlefield. Restaurants, gift shops. The 7-Eleven. There were plenty of buildings that were too small to hold all the coffins, but they might have basements.

There were phone calls to be made. Always there were more phone calls.

Caxton called the state police barracks just outside of town, and the one in Arendtsville. She needed more eyes, more cops, more people to come and help look for coffins. She waited on hold for long minutes, far too many of them, just to talk to the Commissioner up in Harrisburg. She called the National Guard armory, only to be told that they couldn't mobilize without a direct order from the governor.

The governor wasn't available to take her call.

She oversaw roadblocks being thrown up across the major roads. Local cops from Harrisburg, Arendtsville, and Hanover could man those. She oversaw hospital staff, doctors, nurses, orderlies, and maintenance men as they packed up necessary equipment, spoke in low tones with administrators about moving patients out of their rooms, out to the available beds in nearby towns. Always someone wanted to argue, someone wanted to claim that a given patient couldn't be moved, that their condition was too delicate. The vampires wouldn't care, she tried to explain. They didn't care if somebody was dying of leukemia or brain cancer or pernicious infections. Blood was blood, and if the donor couldn't get up and run away, all the better.

She scared a lot of people. She saw their faces go white, saw their hands tremble as they failed to meet her gaze. Laura Beth Caxton's heart went out to them. Arkeley would have been pleased—if they were scared they would move faster. It would inspire them to get away. She needed to be more like Arkeley. When their voices broke, when they begged her to understand, she hardened herself and told them what was coming.

More calls. She called in school buses, talked to principals and superintendents, called the local Greyhound station. Called the National Guard again and asked if they could send troop transports. A lot of people had already left Gettysburg, including most of the tourists. A lot of the townies had stayed put. She needed to get more than five thousand people out of harm's way and she needed to do it before six o'clock, her absolute, positive deadline for the evacuation. The National Guard had a fleet of vehicles fueled up and ready to go, but they couldn't dispatch them without the approval of the governor, or, if he was completely unreachable, the lieutenant governor.

The lieutenant governor was away from his office at the moment. Did she want to leave a message? His personal assistant wasn't really sure how to get hold of him, even if it was an emergency.

Operations like this didn't just happen. They had to be obsessively planned. Everyone wanted oversight and everyone wanted to cover their respective asses. People couldn't be pulled away from necessary jobs, life-and-death-type jobs. There were authorizations she needed just to use the right kind of weapons—much less to requisition them. A police operation this size normally took months to organize, to get all the necessary people and equipment in place at the right time. She had just a few hours.

Not every piece of news was cataclysmic. The Harrisburg Police Department had a long-standing agreement with the borough of Gettysburg, a convenient blurring of jurisdictions that had never been legally questioned. They were happy to send some men down. Would ten suffice? Caxton wanted a hundred, but she took what she was offered.

"What about helicopters?" she asked. The coffins could be hidden somewhere out in the woods around the battlefield. They could be sitting on a rooftop somewhere, someplace her searchers couldn't easily get to. Aerial support would help the searchers coordinate their efforts, too. Harrisburg had two helicopters, though one was in for scheduled maintenance. It could be prepped and fueled and in the air within a couple of hours. They'd send them down as soon as possible.

The local Harrisburg PD had a special arrangement with the state police as well. They knew she was serious, and they wanted to help any way they could. She couldn't thank them enough.

Glauer called her several times. "Nothing," he always said. "Nothing. A couple people wouldn't let us search their houses, but these are good people, people I've known all my life."

"Make sure they get evacuated in the first wave," Caxton said. "Then search their houses after they're gone. This is an emergency."

They put an announcement on the radio, on TV and over the Internet. All citizens of the borough of Gettysburg should report to the closest school or government building and await transport out of town. Under no circumstances should they try to leave town in their own vehicles. Caxton had seen how bad the traffic could get on a normal day—the streets of Gettysburg would have been hopelessly snarled, the evacuation hopelessly gridlocked in honking horns and flashing lights and road rage and minor accidents and maybe major accidents too. The rain would make it worse.

Some of them tried. She got calls from all over town and had to send units to untangle the mess, to calm people down, to get them in line. Every officer she sent to chase down an unruly motorist was one less officer she had for the door-to-door search.

A call came in from the mayor. Did she think she would find the coffins in time? Did she think that this could be resolved without loss of life? Did she think the mayor and his staff should be evacuated by the helicopter they'd seen circling the town?

No, no, and no. Caxton closed her eyes for a moment and waited for the mayor to stop talking. She said no a few more times, barely listening to the questions.

"Nothing to report," Glauer said, over the radio in her car. "I'd estimate we've searched twenty percent of the buildings in town."

It was already three o'clock.

Caxton sat up straight, hung up on the mayor. So much time had passed and there was still so much to do. People were lined up around the block at the post office, at the town hall, at the visitor's center. Waiting for buses to take them away.

She called the National Guard again. Begged.

"The governor, or in an emergency, the lieutenant governor . . ."

She flipped her phone closed. Tried to breathe through her nose. Then she opened the phone again.

She called the state police again, got them to send every available liquor enforcement officer. Getting the LEOs onboard doubled the number of people she had who could work traffic details, man roadblocks, help search.

The press called her. Over and over. Did she think they would find the coffins in time? Did she really believe that Gettysburg was about to be overrun with vampires? Didn't she think that story was a little hard to swallow?

She did not waste time on the press.

More calls, more to do. She got through to the sergeant at arms at the Harrisburg headquarters. Outlined the equipment she needed as if she were ordering out of the L.L. Bean catalog. Except instead of sweaters and fleece vests she wanted patrol rifles and riot gear. The man hung up on her once, so she called back and threatened him, pulled rank. Then she pleaded: please, please, please.

"Even if I have that stuff I need a special order, in writing, from the Commissioner, and he's out of his office right now," the sergeant at arms told her.

The National Guard had everything she needed. They had piles of it, all kept in perfect working order, oiled up, ready to go. Mountains of ammunition, rack after rack of rifles. Plus plenty of people to carry them, including more than a few veterans from Iraq. Soldiers. Real soldiers.

The lieutenant governor was meeting with an educational task force and no, his personal assistant didn't think he could deliver a message right now.

"Do you understand what is going to happen? Do you understand how many people are going to die?"

He didn't have to understand. That wasn't his job.

She called the Commissioner of the state police in Harrisburg. Got put on hold. She didn't have time to wait on hold. She couldn't afford not to talk to him. She put her phone on speaker, borrowed Chief Vicente's cell, and kept making calls.

By four-thirty the Commissioner was available to talk to her. "Yes, I understand how serious this situation is. I know it's an emergency. You want to tell me what kind? I'm a little in the dark here. I sent you in there to chase one vampire, and you come back to me saying you might have a hundred of them. If this is a mistake, if you blow this——"

"I won't," she promised. If she did blow it, if she failed, she doubted she would live long enough to have to worry about losing her job. "You have to trust me. I have a chain of evidence as long as my arm, I have information from trusted informants, but I don't have time to write it up in a report and send it to you. I need you to just do what I say, and not ask any more questions. Otherwise a lot of people are going to die. Tonight."

"You don't think you'll be able to find the coffins before sunset?"

The last report she'd had from Glauer said that they'd covered maybe forty percent of the town.

"No," she said. "I don't. I'd like to say yes, but I can't afford to be wrong."

There was a long, deadly pause on the line. Caxton could hear the Commissioner breathing, but that was about it.

"Alright."

Caxton could hardly believe her ears. "You're saying yes?"

"I am."

She couldn't thank him enough.

The governor called her next. He apologized for taking so long getting back to her. Asked her how she was holding up, and what she needed, and what he could do to help. He would mobilize the National Guard immediately, send the troop transports she needed, send helicopters, soldiers, weapons. As fast as humanly possible. "A small force should arrive before sunset tonight. More will be sent out as they become available. Please, Trooper, I am asking you to please protect the Commonwealth."

"Sir, I'm truly grateful," she said, meaning it. "I just—I didn't expect you to—I didn't—"

"You have some interesting friends, Trooper," the governor said. "So—is there anything else you need?"

"Can you send any tanks?"

He laughed, in a good-natured way.

She ended the call. Dialed Arkeley. "I don't know what you did, but—"

He sounded distorted and weird. As if he were in a car moving under speed, or maybe it was just the rain interfering with the signal. She didn't know where he was or what he was up to, didn't have time to ask. His reply was to the point. "I've earned a lot of favors over the last twenty years, because I knew a day like this would come. I used up every ounce of political capital I had."

As a U.S. Marshal, Arkeley had guarded a lot of court-houses in his time and gotten to know a lot of judges. Politicians listened to judges. "Thank you," she said. "I don't know what else to say."

"That's enough." Arkeley was silent for a moment. "There's one more thing I might be able to do for you. It's drastic."

"These are drastic times," she said.

"Okay. Let me get back to work."

Caxton agreed and hung up.

One more phone call.

She dialed her own home number, waited for Clara to pick up. It took six or seven rings.

"Hello?"

I need to tell you what's happening, Caxton thought. *I need to tell you what's going to happen when the sun goes down.*

I need to tell you that I might get killed tonight. That I will probably get killed tonight. I need to tell you that.

"Hello?"

The words wouldn't come out of her mouth. None of them.

I need to say good-bye, she thought.

"Laura? I know you're there—I saw it on the caller ID. What's going on?"

Caxton opened her mouth. Forced something out. "I love you," she said.

Nothing from the other end. Then a low, soft sound. "I love you, too," so low, whispered so gently that it could have been an echo on the line.

Caxton flipped her phone shut. She couldn't say another word.

Shaking and dizzy with lack of sleep, lack of food, over-doses of caffeine and terror, she climbed out of her car for the first time in hours. She walked half a block down to the post of-fice, where a big white uparmored personnel carrier was loading the very frightened citizens of Gettysburg. National Guardsmen in full uniform helped them climb up through the rear hatches, smiled at them, told them it was going to be alright.

She looked at her watch: six-twenty-three.

66.

I hurried into General Hooker's headquarters as soon as I arrived and was directed to a room upon the second floor. Inside I found the female propped up by pillows in a comfortable bed. A single candle burned behind a silk screen, leaving the room in great dimness. Any more light would cause her physical pain, I was told. She was well provided with writing materials and much ink, and had already covered several pages with a fine and flowing hand. When she turned her singular eye upon me a chill flushed through me, as if the very marrow of my bones had been replaced with ice, yet I barely hesitated as I strode to the bed and kissed her rotten hand. I had been told she was a spy for the Union now, and had provided much useful intelligence, and was an honored guest of the general. I was also told she would drink my blood if she could. Yet she assured me she was sated, and that I should be at my ease. I did not enquire as to from whose veins she had drawn her rations that night.

She told me much of her history; how she had been brought to America in the last century (and by her considerable decay I believed it), and how she had been an ornament in the house of the Chess family that whole time, unable to climb out of her gilded coffin. She told me of how she came to know Obediah Chess when he was a child, forbidden to approach her but unable to heed his parents' good offices. It was only after the commencement of hostilities, however, that she had convinced the lad to join her in immortal unlife. He had honored her as a second mother (his first lost to a fever when he was a babe). He had fed her first from his own blood, then brought the vital fluid of others to her

upon reaching his majority and accepting her curse. He had
found it quite easy, she said, to procure the needed substance in
time of war, when persons could go missing without question, espe-
cially slaves who might be believed to have run off in the chaos.
She spoke fondly of that time, as others now speak of peacetime
and the prosperity and abundance we once took for granted.

I asked and learned at once her name, which was Justinia.

—THE PAPERS OF WILLIAM PITTENGER

67.

By six-thirty the town was empty of civilians. The weapons and the troops had arrived and were being offloaded in Lincoln Square. Approximately 65 percent of the town's buildings had been searched. Not a single coffin, heart, or vampire had been found. The sun was a yellow smear on the clouds, only partly visible through the dark net of tree branches that obscured the view to the west. It was time to stop looking for the coffins, and time to start fighting vampires.

Down in the square her troops had gathered. They stood in small groups, smoking cigarettes, or sat on the sidewalk, leaning up against historical buildings, conserving their energy for the activity to come. She'd rounded up about seventy-five, almost all men. Not enough, not nearly enough, but it was the best she could do. They were all trained in how to handle firearms. That was something. Liquor enforcement officers in navy windbreakers and baseball hats. Local cops and fellow troopers. SWAT professionals from Harrisburg and National Guardsmen in camo, heavy armor strapped across their chests, night-vision goggles dangling from their helmets. Many had brought their own weapons, mostly pistols and shotguns. She frowned at the latter—shotguns were almost useless against vampires. Luckily she had better weapons at hand.

The rifles and grenades sat in big crates hastily removed from unmarked trucks, piled high in a crushed flower bed, laid out end on end on the sidewalk between the parking meters. The grenades were individually wrapped in plastic, then buried in packing peanuts. The rifles lay in neat rows inside the box, secured by Styrofoam spacers. She picked one up and checked its action, made sure the modified barrel was firmly secured to the receiver. The plastic stock fit into the crook of her arm and she kept the flash hider pointing straight up.

"Listen up, guys," Glauer boomed out, loud enough to make her flinch. "Some of you know me, but most probably don't. I guess you all know who this is."

"Yeah," one of the guardsmen said, nodding happily. "That chick from *Teeth*."

Caxton stared at him. He couldn't be more than nineteen years old.

"She's the boss," a LEO with a silver beard but no mustache said. "Our designated field commander."

She'd never heard the term before. It sounded like something he'd read online or in *Soldier of Fortune* magazine. "I'm Trooper Caxton, that's good enough for now. You've all been filled in on why you're here, I'm sure, so I'll be brief." She looked around, made sure she had their attention. A few were still chatting among themselves, but mostly these men were professionals. They knew when to listen. "In a few minutes it'll be fully dark. They'll come out then and hopefully our air support will see where. We need to be ready to move as soon as we get that report. When we engage the enemy it is crucial that you have the right mind-set. This is not a raid. We are not here to take anyone into custody. You must shoot to kill, from your first shot, and you must not hesitate. Not a single vampire can be allowed to escape tonight."

She hefted her weapon, showed it to them. "Anyone recognize this?"

"It's a patrol rifle," one of her fellow troopers shouted, raising an index finger. "You point that end at your target and it goes boom."

A few of the others chuckled.

Caxton looked around and found a guardsman. "Give me your body armor," she said. The soldier hesitated, so she grabbed the straps of his vest and started pulling them loose. "These won't help, by the way," she said. "The vampires won't be shooting at us. Armor will just slow you down." She thought about ordering all the guardsmen to take off their armor, but she decided against it. It might give them some purely psychological comfort. The guardsman she'd grabbed shrugged out of his vest and she took it from him, then looked around again and found a big orange pumpkin that had been set up as part of a hotel's fall decorations. She wrapped the pumpkin in the vest, and set the armored pumpkin down on the asphalt and had everyone back away from it, made sure they were clear by twenty feet.

"This is a patrol rifle, yes. A Colt AR6520. A little heavier than you're probably expecting. The barrel has been upgraded to fire fifty-caliber BMG rounds. The magazine has a capacity of twenty rounds—remember that. Also, remember this." She sighted carefully on the armor vest, switched off her safety, and put a single round right through both the ceramic armor plate and the pumpkin.

Stringy orange glop erupted from inside the armor, splattering a couple of nearby cars.

"You'll want to avoid any friendly fire incidents," she said.

A lot of the men laughed then. She hadn't expected them to. It was good, though. The laughter would help bond them together as a unit. It would help take the edge off their anxiety. She knew she could use some of that herself.

She couldn't let it get out of hand, though. "I'm giving you this kind of firepower because the only way to kill a vampire is a direct shot through the heart." She put a hand over the left side of her chest. "Even then you can't be guaranteed of a clean kill. When we see them at first they're going to look mostly dead, very skinny and pale. A fifty-caliber round will take them down just fine. Once they drink some blood, though, they become all but bulletproof. These," she said, flicking the safety back on and then holding her rifle in the air, "may still work. Or maybe they won't." She pulled another crate open and gestured for the men to start arming themselves.

"They're faster than we are. They are much, much stronger. They have no compunction whatsoever about ripping your head off or tearing your guts out. How many of you have been hunting before?"

As she'd expected, most of their hands went up. They were Pennsylvanians, most of them born and bred between two ridges. They probably learned how to shoot looking down the sights of a .22-caliber rifle at a white-tailed buck.

"Clean shots, careful shots. Heart shots every time, just left of center mass. You have twenty rounds. Do not waste any of them on head or leg shots. You've probably been trained to try to incapacitate a victim without mortally wounding him. Forget that, right now." She looked around at the men under her charge. The National Guardsmen, many of whom had fought in Iraq, didn't need to be told as much. They numbered less than a third of her troops, however. The rest were one kind of cop or another, and cops were drilled and trained endlessly to not kill people, to not even take a shot if they thought it might lead to a death. It would take more than a stern warning to break them of that conditioning. Maybe, she thought, when they saw what they were up against, when the vampires came howling for their blood, they would just get it.

And maybe a lot of them would die before they learned.

Arkeley would have accepted that possibility without another thought. He would have recognized the importance of what they were doing, would have sacrificed anything, anybody, including himself, to stop the hundred vampires from getting out of Gettysburg. It was time to demand that kind of commitment from these men, she decided. It was time to demand it of herself.

"Okay, listen up," she said. In quick, sketchy strokes she outlined her plan. "They've got a lot of advantages, but we can beat them if we stay together." She held up a map of the town and the park. "I don't know where we're going to engage them, but regardless, the plan's the same. We make first contact and do as much damage as we can. They'll try to close with us—they need to be up close and personal to hurt you—but we won't let them. As soon as they start coming for us we split into groups and fall back to the nearest large buildings. Your group commanders will know where to go. We defend those buildings as long as we can, then fall back again—always moving toward the center of town. Then we regroup, surround them, and take out as many of them that are left. Any questions?"

There were none.

68.

When she had finished writing out her statement I had enough to smash the remainder of Simonon's mob, and put an end to much Southern brigandry forever. I thanked her profusely and said she'd proved a great friend to my country. This was what I had come for, and now it was done. I could leave at dawn, and be back in Washington before the day was through with my report.

Ye are well come to it, *she wrote,* but now where be my reward?

I professed ignorance of her meaning. "You've been fed well on rich blood. Did you wish for something more?"

Some peace of mind onlie, *she answered.* What is to come of me, friend of your nation that I now am? Walk on my own I cannot, and so cannot be released. What will be my fate?

What should happen to her next was none of my concern, though I imagined I could guess at it; a quick and painless execution, which would be a mercy to her and far moreso to us. "That is hardly for me to decide," I assured her, and prepared to make my adieu.

Yet she had more to say. So much more. In that graceful hand of hers she laid out the broad strokes of my future destiny, one fine letter at a time:

Mayhaps I can aid you further, good sir. I know little of war, though I have seen some few in my long years. It seems to me that in most great conflicts that which lacks is not the ability nor the will to fight, but the soldiers to engage. In short, I ask, have you not a need for men?

It was my duty to report Justinia's offer, whatever I might think of it. I went at once to the telegraph wagon. I composed my message, and encoded it, and sent it on, thinking then I was done. The operator cursed and struggled with his instrument, and had trouble sending. Yet the reply came almost instantly he was through, and was one word only when it was decoded:

PROCEED.

—THE PAPERS OF WILLIAM PITTENGER

69.

No more mistakes. She'd thought it so many times, it was written on the inside of her skull. No more mistakes. Slinging her patrol rifle over her shoulder, she pressed the spiral pendant into her palm and tied it there with its broken ribbon.

The last trace of yellow faded from the sky. A few stars peeked through the clouds that wheeled from east to west while she watched. She could hear the helicopters quartering the town, searchers with infrared and night optical cameras looking for any sign of the enemy.

Now, she thought, her nerves thrumming. *The call will come now.*

It didn't. Her radio crackled a bit, but nothing came through but the occasional check-in as the helicopter pilots kept track of each other. Caxton tried to breathe.

The vampires, she thought, *could split up and—*

She shook her head to clear away that thought, but the sudden motion made her neck hurt. She was so tired, hadn't slept in far too long. Occasionally during the day she had started to nod off but had managed not to lose any precious time. Now she was just waiting, waiting to hear something.

They could split up, go across the open ground. Avoid the roadblocks on the highways and just melt into the darkness.

No. No, that wouldn't happen, because it couldn't. If it did, she would have to spend the rest of her life tracking them down. Every night would be a bloodbath, every day a frantic search, and never any time for sleep. It couldn't happen.

She stared around at the men under her charge, watching them for signs that they were losing their edge. They were tough guys, most of them. Volunteers all. The LEOs tended to look the roughest. Liquor enforcement officers had to go into bad places all the time, had to deal with sketchy individuals who tended to own a lot of guns. The troopers were much the same, veterans of endless drug raids and meth lab assaults. They looked a little scared. That was how she could tell they were tough, because they looked scared. She remembered how terrified she'd been herself the first time she'd fought a vampire, and now when she looked around she saw fear in every face. Because they knew, they knew they could get hurt every time they clocked in to their jobs. They knew they could get killed.

The guardsmen, the soldiers, were a little harder to read. Some, the newbies, sat silently in groups of four or six, their rifles between their knees. They looked up every time someone laughed or the radio spat white noise. The veterans from Iraq looked a lot more casual. More Pennsylvanian guardsmen had been called up for duty in Iraq than from any other state in the union, and their casualties had been commensurately high. These men knew more than she could tell them about keeping themselves alive. They stood leaning against the trucks, not moving much. She saw them keeping their eyes on the four roads that lead out of the square, not alert so much as just aware, constantly aware of their surroundings.

Now, she thought, staring at her radio. Nothing.

Glauer came up beside her with a giant thermos of hot coffee and a sleeve of Styrofoam cups still in their plastic wrap. He tore it open and handed her one, poured it for her.

"How are your guys doing?" she asked.

He puffed air into his cheeks, let it out. "We're good, we're good," he said. He looked back over his shoulder. Of the twenty officers of the Gettysburg Police Department, eighteen were scattered around the square, waiting on her orders. All twenty had volunteered. This was their town—they wanted to be here, wanted to defend their home. She had sent two of them home. One was the only means of support for an autistic brother who couldn't care for himself. The other one was sick.

Chief Vicente had been moved to a safe location.

Glauer scratched at his mustache. "Listen, Trooper," he said, but then it was as if he'd forgotten what he'd meant to say. He smiled awkwardly, put his hand down.

"They'll do fine," she said, because she thought it was what Arkeley would have said. "They've had firearms training. They'll do just fine."

He nodded briefly but didn't look convinced. "Yeah. On the firing range. Some of them are hunters, too. I always preferred fishing. If I'd known what was coming, what was going to happen here, I would have done one of those counterterrorism courses the FBI offered. They would have paid my hotel bill and everything. I always figured, you know, that Gettysburg wouldn't need that. I mean, none of us went. We thought it was silly."

"They'll do just fine."

"Okay," he said, and chewed on his lip. "I, um. I've never fired a gun at a living thing. Not in my whole life."

"You won't tonight, either," she said. "The vampires are already dead."

He laughed, not the friendly chuckle she'd expected but a loud, embarrassing snort that made even a few guardsmen look up in surprise. He nodded again and moved on, handing out coffee to anyone who wanted it.

These men would succeed, she insisted to herself. She would lead them to the vampires and then it was all about the shooting. The vampires would stick together, they wouldn't split up. She wouldn't have to go chasing them. She would finish this, tonight, and whether she lived or died it would be over and then—

"Contact," the radio coughed. It sounded almost apologetic. "Can you confirm?" the helicopter pilot asked. Not speaking to her. "Affirmative. Contact." The pilot rattled off a string of map coordinates. Caxton went to her own map, laid out on the hood of a truck, and suddenly seventy-five men were crowding around her, pushing close, perhaps trying to see. The contact had been made just south of town, at the top of the battlefield. That fit her plan just fine.

"Okay," she said. Her heart was jumping in her chest, but she didn't let it show. "Let's not make any mistakes," she said. "I'm going to move fast so they don't have a chance to split up. Everybody keep up."

She ducked through the throng of men, headed south. The old buildings of Gettysburg, red brick with white trim, yellow brick with black trim, streamed past her. The noise of all the men moving together was a vast rustling like sails caught by the wind. Vampires had excellent hearing. They would hear her coming. They would see the men's blood, sparkling in the night.

She checked her rifle as she moved, checked the magazine, checked the action. Behind her she heard seventy-five safeties being flicked off.

The town's cemetery opened up on her left, darkness flooding in where the streetlights stopped. On her right the buildings grew farther apart. Their windows were dark. Up ahead the street rose to crest a low hill. She saw old painted cannon, memorials to the various battalions and regiments that had fought at Gettysburg. Open stretches of grass, stands of trees, and then she was atop the hill looking down into the valley, the open ground between the two tree-crowded ridges that flanked the battlefield. Seminary Ridge, to the west, and Cemetery Ridge to the east. In between was open grassland, studded with memorials and crisscrossed by roads and footpaths.

They called it the Valley of Death in all the tourist literature. In the brochures and pamphlets and the guidebooks. A hundred thousand men had fought down there for three days, and many of them had died. She craned her head forward, strained her eyes trying to see anything. A flicker of motion, anything. There was no moon to light the field and only a few stars shone down through gaps in the clouds. Nothing, she couldn't see anything—

—and then she did. Something white, paler than the dark field. Moving, almost writhing. Like a mass of maggots squirming on the grass. Coming her way, very slowly. Slowly getting bigger, resolving into separate forms.

She lifted her rifle to her shoulder, squinted down the sights.

Okay, she thought. *Now.*

70.

Bill, thou art aveng'd, for Chess, they tell me, is reduced &
destroyed. Yet I miss you so. Though justice be done memory is not
assuaged.

How many times have I dreamed of us returned to dear old
Maine, & feted well by family and friend alike. How many
dreams of that homecoming did we share? & now neither of us
shall see that blessed day.

I went to sit with HER *today, thinking only hatred would fill*
my heart. You served her like a slave at the end, did you not? I
said you had escaped her, but she told me (by writing on a paper)
that your body was already dead, & that within seven days your
soul would be loosed. Hardness in my chest afflicted me, & I began
to signal that I should like to leave. My attendants stepped for-
ward, to take up my litter. Yet before they could remove me I
asked them to stop.

She had changed, Bill, to take on your face.

It was the barest of illusions, & easily pierced, yet I knew if I
wished it she could speak with your voice, and hold my hands as
you once did. Disgust, first, consumed me, but not for long. In
time I came to understand she was giving me some gift, some
favor, & I admit, it was good to see you again.

Then it was she spoke to me direct, using thought in place of
word.

—LETTER OF ALVA GRIEST (UNPOSTED)

71.

The vampires came toward them in a square formation, lined up abreast in at least a dozen ranks. They wore nothing but rags, tatters of old uniforms, loose trousers torn at the cuff. A few had tunics on, colorless in the dark. Their skin was easier to see, pale, pale white even in the gloom. Their faces were hairless and gaunt, their cheeks sunken in.

They were big. They were fast and dangerous. They moved in an eerie lockstep, as if they were one being with many bodies. She could see their teeth glinting in the starlight, she could see their enormous, powerful hands.

One vampire could kill her. That was all it would take. One vampire had nearly strangled her. It would have been just as easy for him to tear her into little pieces. Now she was facing an army of them.

I can't do this, she thought.

I am going to die here, she thought. She couldn't move, couldn't breathe. She felt bewitched.

Still they came on. Their feet moved together. Left. Right. Left. Right. An army—not just a gaggle of them, not just a mob. A literal army.

Well, yes. Because that was what they'd been when they were alive. "They're soldiers," Caxton said, and it broke the spell. Breath plumed out of her. She drew oxygen into her lungs. "They're marching."

Arkeley would not have hesitated. Arkeley would have been braver. She channeled him, forced herself to think the way he would. Vampires were deadly, they were strong, but they were not invulnerable. She lined up her first shot, held it. One of the front rank, to the left of the center of the formation. She looked for her vampire among the ranks but couldn't find him.

She'd expected him to be at the front, leading the charge, but he must have been hidden in among them.

They were thin, painfully, horrifyingly thin. They looked starved and bedraggled.

Their eyes, however, were bright. Glowing like smoldering embers. Even in the dark they seemed to glow. She held her shot.

"Go for the hearts," she said, loud, so the others would hear her. "Every time."

Around her troopers and LEOs and guardsmen and local cops lifted their patrol rifles. Some knelt down, elbows on thighs to steady their aim. Others aimed from the shoulder, ready.

The vampires came on so fast, their feet barely brushing the ground. Their arms swung at their sides and their eyes stayed facing front, never looking to the side, never betraying them. If they saw Caxton and her troops they didn't show any sign of it. They certainly didn't show any fear.

She had worried they would split up. Worried they would head in a hundred different directions, that she would never catch them all. That wasn't going to be a problem. The vampires were soldiers, and they'd been drilled in nineteenth-century battle tactics. Which meant staying together and walking right into fire. That standard operating procedure hadn't worked so well during the Civil War, when men had marched right into cannon fire.

Closer—always closer. It was so dreamlike, so wrongly surreal that Caxton couldn't get a sense of how far away they were. She held her shot. Corrected her aim. They were closer, well within range.

"Fire at will," she shouted, and the night blew apart. Patrol rifles barked and jumped in the men's hands. Caxton took her own shot, felt the weapon kick her shoulder. The recoil wasn't as bad as she'd expected. She kept her eye on her target, watched a dark hole open in his chest. The vampire's arm flew up and he turned at the waist, his chin hitting his shoulder.

The formation stopped in place. The vampires stood there, still, perfectly still, as if in surprise. Their eyes burned.

The one she'd shot slumped to the ground. His eyes stopped glowing, stared upward, into the sky. Here and there in the front rank others fell. Two—no, three of them down. The rest stared down at their bodies, at the holes that riddled their chests and bellies and their faces, looked from side to side, to one another.

The three who were down stayed down. The others grimaced as their flesh filled in around the bullet holes, as their bodies healed. It couldn't have taken more than a second or two.

"Keep firing!" Caxton called. The rifles jumped and spoke. Another vampire fell, and then one on the end of the line spun around and grabbed at the vampire next to him. The rifles roared and vampires jumped, stepped backward, moved aside to let the ones behind pass.

They were moving again. Coming closer. So fast.

"Hold your positions," Caxton shouted as the men behind her wove back and forth, looking for shots, some of them walking backward, trying to keep their distance. "Hold on," she shouted, over the noise of the rifles. Vampires collapsed in the front line, but others moved forward, more of them. There were so many and they were so close, moving so fast. "Hold on!" she shouted again. She fired again and corroded brass buttons flew off a dark tunic. There was no blood; they had no blood in them to leak from the wounds. No way to tell if any given shot went true or wild. Some of the vampires who had fallen to the grass, their limbs wild and askew, started to get back up.

They moved fast. They were closer than she wanted them. She grabbed a pair of ear protectors from around her neck and pulled them on over her head, checked to make sure the others had theirs. Then she pulled a grenade out of her pocket and tore open its plastic wrapper.

It felt weird in her hand, like a can of soda more than a

miniature bomb. It was painted a matte black, cylindrical and heavy, with circular holes punched down its length. She'd never seen one like it before, but she knew what it could do.

"Eyes," she shouted, and pulled the pin. She threw it like a softball and it bounced harmlessly off a vampire's shoulder. The vampire turned to watch it drop to the grass.

Even as she pulled her rifle back around to a firing position, Caxton squeezed her eyes shut. When the grenade went off she still saw stars.

Normal fragmentation grenades would be useless against vampires. The burst of shrapnel might slow them down for a moment or two, but the shards of metal would never reach a vampire's well-protected heart. When the National Guard had asked her what kind of armament might be more useful she'd had a real inspiration, for once. She remembered the way Harold the night watchman's flashlight had bothered her vampire and she had asked for flashbangs—stun grenades, in other words. The guard called them XM84s.

The grenade she threw held only about four and a half grams of magnesium and ammonium perchlorate. That was more than enough. When it detonated it pumped out more light than a million burning candles and a noise nearly one hundred and eighty decibels, loud enough to leave an unprotected human being staggering and dazed. To Caxton, even with her ear guards on, it sounded like a bomb had gone off right next to her face.

When the flash and noise were over she cautiously opened her eyes again, praying the grenade had been effective. What she saw almost made her smile.

Vampires were nocturnal creatures, unable to stand any bright light. They were also predators with exceptionally acute hearing. They were also well over a hundred years old and could not have imagined what she was throwing into their midst. Many of them must have turned to look right at the grenade. All of them had heard the noise. Their advance had halted and the majority of them were down, rolling on the grass, clutching their triangular ears. The glow in their eyes had brightened considerably until the red embers looked like they were sizzling away painfully in their sockets. One, she saw, was reaching up toward the stars as if to fend off some unseen blow. One had dropped to his knees and was clawing his own eyes out with talonlike fingers.

They were no more than ten yards away. If she had hesitated for another second they would have been on her, all over her, devouring her troops. "Get around them," she shouted, looking back to see her men tearing off their ear protectors. She reached up and took off her own. "Circle them, now, this is the best chance we'll get!" She had another flashbang in her pocket, but she knew better than to underestimate vampires. They would know what to expect if she tried that trick again.

Her feet slipped as she ran through the long grass, but she didn't fall. She came around behind the mass of vampires and lifted her weapon. It hardly seemed sporting, but she was beyond caring about that. One shot, then the next she lined up, executing the monsters, blowing out their hearts. They writhed and moaned beneath her, their white bodies luminous in the dark. An absurd deadly chant rang through her head, syncopated with the reports of her weapon. *One vampire two vampires three vampires four.* She did not stop or slow down until Glauer grabbed her arm.

"What?" she demanded. "What now?"

He pointed and she saw one of the dazed vampires blinking his eyes rapidly. He was sitting up, slowly regaining his composure.

"Shit," she said.

She had known they would recover from the flash. She had really, really hoped it would take longer than it had.

72.

I thought it would be hard to find volunteers. Yet again I was wrong. It was a shock to me, as it must be to any man who had not seen this war at first hand, to learn just how many dying soldiers there were in Maryland, wounded in battle, victims of dread pestilence, or simply broken in spirit and in mind. How many who had so little left to live for, who would gladly welcome one last chance for glory before they must go on to meet their rest.

I was not stopped by dint of volunteers. In fact, I had to turn many away, men who still possessed some spark of life, and healthy frames, whose only infirmity was despair. Though I could not give particulars to any, though the word "vampire" never passed my lips, still, there were so many. Far, far too many.

Procuring the supplies I needed was easy enough as well. A few demijohns of prussic acid were requisitioned and readily available, for the troops used it to poison rats in their camps. Coffins were easily obtained, of a necessary quality and stoutness. This government has assured there will never be a shortage of coffins. A railroad car, fitted up for transporting dead soldiers home, was waiting for me in Hagerstown. And the most necessary item, Miss Justinia Malvern, I had accessed already. She was most tractable, and accommodating, as long as each night she received her ration of blood. More than once I provided this from my own veins.

—THE PAPERS OF WILLIAM PITTENGER

73.

"Damn it. Get back, get back," Caxton called.

Some of the men around her obeyed at once, falling back, some running. Others stood their ground and kept shooting vampires, their weapons pointed down, the muzzle flashes going off in stuttering bursts.

More of the vampires started getting up, getting to their feet. The ones still rolling around on the ground were getting picked off, but there were still so many of them.

"Get back!" The only advantage the humans had was range—if the vampires recovered too quickly they would make short work of the troopers and LEOs and guardsmen. "Get back!" she screamed again.

More of her troops peeled away and ran off into the dark. More than a few, however, didn't seem to hear her at all. Maybe their ear protectors hadn't protected them from the bang. Maybe they were deafened—or maybe they were just so scared that they didn't understand what she was telling them.

On the far side of the formation a vampire leaped up off the grass and tore into a trooper, tore his uniform shirt open and much of the skin beneath. Caxton raised her weapon and tried to cut the vampire down, but she couldn't get a clear shot. The .50-caliber bullet in her rifle could cut through an engine block; it would pass right through the vampire and the trooper as well. There was nothing she could do for the man.

Right next to her a rifle jumped and danced, spitting bullets. The LEO there had switched to automatic fire and was hosing down the vampires with .50-caliber rounds. He was wasting ammunition—the vampires he hit jerked in place as if pulled by strings, but he was firing blind and had little or no chance of getting a clean heart shot. She screamed at him, but she couldn't hear herself over the noise, could barely see from the muzzle flashes. She grabbed at his arm, trying to pull his hand off the trigger, but even as she did his weapon went dry.

"I'm out," he called, and turned around, to go back, maybe to get more ammunition, maybe just to run. She grabbed a spare magazine out of her pocket and brandished it at him, but then she heard a local cop on her other side scream.

Her heart stopped beating in her chest as she swiveled around to see a wave of white skin and moldering cloth crash over her head.

So fast—they moved so fast, even after a century and a half in the ground—they were—they were everywhere—

The men bellowed and fired wildly, their muzzles pointing in every direction, tracking, trying to find targets. Caxton ducked low as a hot flash hider swung over her head. The noise as it fired deafened her, but she looked up and saw a vampire not ten inches from her face, watched as his red eyes flickered out. His pale hands beat at her shirt, at her arm, but there was no strength there.

"Come on," Glauer said, right next to her.

Around her men were dying, left and right. Much faster than the vampires had. She saw a guardsman get torn in half, saw a white face bury itself in his red flesh. She saw necks twisted, saw vampire teeth ripping through navy windbreakers, digging through Kevlar vests. She heard screams all around.

She heard someone praying, a sound that ended abruptly.

Glauer grabbed her hand and she nearly dropped her rifle. "Regroup! Regroup!" she shouted, even as she danced away from a vampire running right at her, his shoulder down, his claws scooping at the air where she'd been. She managed to get her rifle back up, fired three shots, without aiming, into his face, his chest, his groin. The vampire jerked spasmodically and tripped over his own feet. She lined up a shot on his back, fired, watched him jump and fall face forward on the cold grass.

"Fall back," she shouted, unsure if anyone was listening. The field was a mess, a chaos of bodies struggling in the darkness.

"Spread out," one of the guardsmen shouted. "Get clear!" A vampire's fingers were tangled in the combat webbing of his body armor. He swung around, trying to get free, and the vampire's other hand snatched off his helmet. Blood fountained from his neck and Caxton saw his head dangle forward, attached by nothing more than scraps of flesh. The vampire leaned forward to lap at his blood.

"Help me!" someone barked. She turned and saw an LEO surrounded by three vampires. He was firing his patrol rifle from his hip, his other hand holding a big shiny Desert Eagle. He shot out a vampire's eye and the vampire smiled wickedly, then grabbed him up in a bear hug so tight that Caxton could hear the man's vertebrae pop inside his windbreaker.

She tried to go to his aid when a cold hand grabbed her leg and pulled her off her feet. It was the vampire she'd shot in the back, rolled over and facing up now. She had lined up a perfect shot—but now she realized her mistake. From behind she'd gotten her left and right confused. At worst she had shot him through a lung he didn't need anymore.

His face opened wide, his mouth enormous. He pulled her toward him, hand over hand. His eyes blazed and she felt her spiral pendant warm up in her hand. He was trying to hypnotize her.

A vampire leaped over her head, deeper into the fray. She looked back down to see two bony white hands dragging her ankle up toward that gaping cavern of a mouth. She struggled to spin around, to get her weapon up. Swung the flash hider down between her knees, jabbed it like a bayonet into his flesh even as the teeth sank effortlessly into her calf.

She squeezed the trigger and the vampire screamed, releasing her leg. She rolled away from him and onto her knees, her weapon pointed right at his chest, right at his heart. He was already dead. It didn't matter.

There were plenty more all around.

Two came at her, one from either side. Their hands came up, ready to tear at her, to pull her apart. She shot one in the chest and he fell away, screaming, but the other collided with her, his fingers grasping at her tie, her shirt. He yanked and her throat closed up, her own tie crushing her windpipe. She tried to pull her weapon around, but he was right on top of her. She could feel his cold flesh against her own, smell his stink of putre-faction. She started to scream but the noise couldn't get out of her throat. White spots drifted across her vision.

She heard gunshots. They sounded as if they'd come from far away. She could barely connect the sounds to the fact that the vampire's head had split open in a white, pulpy mess, brain and bone flicking away in pieces. The vampire let go of her and she slid out from underneath him, tore open her tie. But even as she tried to get her feet under her the vampire was healing, his head knitting back together, his eyes glowing with pure rage.

Glauer grabbed her arm and helped her up. He brought his patrol rifle up and ready. He brought his arm up, sighted, and shot the vampire right through the heart.

74.

This is the sworn affadavut of Rudolph Storrow, of the 1st US Sharpshooturs, and all of it tru. On 27 Joon I came to Maryland to visut with my old pal Alva Griest, who was sick and in bed. Cornel Pittenger sent me.

They gave Alva a littul room at the garrisun and it was clean and it was bright with windas and nice enuff, yet full of stink, for his woond had ternd gangreenus, I am told. I sed noth-ing of the smell, for me and Alva are old frends.

We sat and talkd one quartur of an hour on what we seen and did in Virginy at the vampier's house like I told Cornel Pit-tenger. We even laffd, a litul. Then I askd Alva if he was sure, and if he still wantud to go threw with it as he had said he did.

He told me he was not long for this life anyhow, with his woonds and all, and that he wantid to help his cuntry howevur he culd, and that he was reddy. He askt me if I thot it was a sin he did, and I sed no, I did not think so. Lots of othur men

have volunteerd for this dutee, I sed, and the Cornel asshured me
they wuld go to the good plase, and not to Hel after. So the Armee
says its alrite.

He sed that was good enuff for him.

I had my canteen with me which I had filt with Prussic
Asid, which I got from the Cornel, and I pored him a cup. The
stuff smells over strong of almunds, if you ask me, and does not
recumend itself for drinkin.

He sed he was tierd and missd his friend Bill. Then he drank
his fill, which was not much. In a cuple minits he died. Then I
rote this out as I am sposed to, and now its dun, and I am goin to
pore myself a cup, and be dun too. God sav America, and Mis-
tur Lincon, and all our boys.

—AFFIDAVIT OF RUDOLPH STORROW

75.

Glauer got Caxton on her feet, but she was already moving. There was no time to talk, no time to thank him for saving her life. They moved fast, crouching low, heading for a big round building she could just see in the dark. Behind them the vampires were feasting on the dead and the dying and they didn't bother pursuing them. She cast the occasional glance over her shoulder and saw bodies strewn across the field. Some were pale in the starlight, their heads hairless and their eyes dark. Many, many more of those bodies belonged to her troops.

She would feel guilty in the morning, if she lived that long. She kept running.

When they had gotten far enough away that she dared to make a sound she said, "I thought you'd never shot anybody before."

"On-the-job training works wonders." Glauer favored her

with a short-lived grin that transformed into a rictus of pain. Was he hurt? She couldn't see. It didn't slow him down if he was. How many vampires had he killed? She had no idea.

As tight as her plan had been, as disciplined as she'd made herself, she'd seen very little of what had happened on the field. She'd been fighting herself, too focused to keep an eye on anyone else. She had no idea how many of her troops were still alive.

Up ahead the dark curved mass of the Cyclorama building blocked out the stars. She needed to get there, as fast as she could. Holding on to the sleeve of Glauer's jacket, she pumped her legs to add more speed. A vampire could be right behind her, or directly in her path. They could move fast enough to get around her, to get in her way—

If that were the case, of course, she was already dead. Nothing she could do about it. She poured on more speed. Her feet hit concrete and she gasped in relief as she dashed up the handicapped ramp of the Cyclorama.

The front doors opened and a pair of guardsmen stepped out, weapons up and aimed at her. She lifted her own patrol rifle and they stood down. "You," she said, pointing at one of the guardsmen. He had his night-vision goggles dangling in front of his face, a pair of shiny lenses staring back at her. "What do you see? Is anyone behind us?"

"Negative," he told her.

"Okay. Get this door shut once we're in."

As badly as the first stage of the battle had gone, regardless of how many people had died, her plan was still operational. She led Glauer inside, into a building with electric lights and warmth.

The Cyclorama Center was one of the big tourist attractions of the military park—or at least it had been. It had been closed to the public for renovation for over a year. The police had been kind enough to open it up for her so she could use it as her preliminary fallback position. It was a round building with no windows, so no vampires could come crashing in from the sides. Inside was mostly open space so that people could see the cyclorama itself, an oil painting twenty-seven feet high and hundreds of feet around, a 360-degree vision of the battlefield during Pickett's infamous charge. The painting was badly faded, but restoration work had already begun and the smoke and cannon and hordes of struggling men were depicted with eerie realism. The subject matter was too close to what Caxton had just fled for comfort.

Some of Caxton's troops—mostly guardsmen in camouflage-pattern uniforms—had gathered inside, keeping close together. They had their rifles in their hands, ready to fight again at a moment's notice. None of them spoke, none of them smoked or even gave her a second look. They knew what was still out there in the dark. Falling back had bought them a few moments' respite, but nobody would call it peace.

In the middle of the floor a table had been set up on sawhorses. A big man-portable radio rig took up half the tabletop, and the rest was covered in small-scale maps of the park and the town. A guardswoman with chevrons on her uniform was holding court down there, craning over the radio and shouting heated questions into her mouthpiece.

"Lieutenant Peters," Caxton said, rushing up to the woman. "You made it."

"By the skin of my ass, Trooper," the guardswoman said. She was one of only three female volunteers in Caxton's slapdash army, but she was also the highest-ranking of the National Guard contingent. She was a little older than Caxton, maybe thirty, but she already had streaks of iron in her dark hair. She'd been to Iraq and come back from that alive. Caxton wondered briefly if she would live through the night. If any of them stood a chance, she supposed it had to be the lieutenant.

"Any word from the visitor center?"

Peters frowned and looked at her radio. "There are some men there. They don't sound well organized. The mass of the opposition went after them."

"As long as they're holding their ground," Caxton said. She drew one of the big maps toward her. The visitor center was just across the Taneytown Road, only a few hundred yards away and slightly farther north than the Cyclorama. Caxton's forces had split in groups to occupy the closest buildings, just as she'd planned. Every group had orders to abandon their positions as soon as things got too hot and move to tertiary locations farther up the road. The plan was to draw the vampires farther and farther north, into the town, where it would be easier to box them in. If they headed south instead, into the open ground of the park, they might get away. She had a contingency in place if that happened—the helicopters would try to herd them back toward town with powerful searchlights. She didn't know if that would actually work.

"If I were them I'd cut my losses and run," Peters said, as if she'd read Caxton's thoughts. The lieutenant pointed at three places on the map. "The roadblocks we set up couldn't hold these assholes for more than a minute or two. If they made contact here—"

"They won't," Caxton said, suddenly sure of it. "They'll come for us first."

"For God's sake, why? We hurt them. They hurt us worse, but they took some hits."

Caxton nodded. "I should hope so. No, they'll come toward us. They want our blood. They've been starving for so long in darkness, waiting, dreaming about blood. They'll go for the nearest supply. And that's us." She looked up at the front door of the building. "Are your people ready? They'll be here in minutes."

"I saw how fast they moved. My people are ready," Peters said, fixing Caxton with her eyes. Caxton started to look away—but the lieutenant didn't. She just stood there studying Caxton, not blinking.

"Something wrong?" Caxton asked.

"We didn't expect this kind of resistance. Over in the desert," she said, shifting her weight slightly, leaning against the table, "our SOP when we found ourselves this badly in shit was to withdraw. Live to fight another day. That's what we know."

And that's why I couldn't just turn this job over to you, Caxton thought. She would have loved to let the soldiers take charge of Gettysburg. She could have gone somewhere and gotten some sleep. She knew better, though—Arkeley had taught her better. Soldiers didn't just stand around waiting to get butchered. They moved strategically and only held positions they knew they could adequately defend. They worked that way because they knew their enemies were following the same model.

Vampires didn't fight that way. They were too arrogant— they never backed down. "Lieutenant, if we just bugged out now, the vampires could do as they pleased. Like you say, the roadblocks couldn't hold them. You saw what they did to heavily armed soldiers. Do you want that kind of threat getting out into the civilian population?"

Peters scowled but shook her head. Good enough. Arkeley had never asked anyone to approve of his orders. Just to follow them.

76.

The procedure for creating our new troops was simplicity itself, and was accomplished without hindrance or delay. A man was carried, or wheeled, or walked into the room where Miss Malvern reclined on her bed. She did not speak with them, or rather she wrote them no kind words, no gentle assurances. She told me that what she did must be accomplished in total silence. Instead she only looked into the eyes of the volunteer. In some cases their heads had to be held up so she could see them properly. Some short time would pass, whilst who knew what communication might pass between the two. Then the man was removed to another room, where his cup of poison awaited him. Very few of them balked at this time. Only two refused the cup, and both of them returned a short while later and asked for it again. I had some men under my command, hard-hearted fellows, who took the bodies and put them in the waiting coffins. The coffins were loaded into the funeral car. And then it was done; until nightfall.

I waited by the car, waited for the sun to go down. I did not drink liquor, or play cards, or do any other thing as a pass-time. I simply sat on a camp stool and waited, perfectly alone. Just me and my conscience. When night had properly fallen I heard them stirring inside, moving around. I heard them talking amongst themselves, in low and emotionless voices. Then there came a rapping on the steel door at the end of the car. I rose and threw back a narrow portal in the door, little more than a spy-hole, and saw red eyes, so many red eyes staring back at me.

—THE PAPERS OF WILLIAM PITTENGER

77.

They had a moment's downtime, maybe no more than that. Still there were priorities to consider. Caxton placed her patrol rifle on the floor and plopped down to roll up her pant leg. Dozens of red chevrons dotted her calf, places where vampire teeth had just touched her flesh. The wounds weren't deep and though the leg felt like it was stiffening up it still held her weight just fine. She'd been lucky—incredibly lucky.

When Glauer took his uniform jacket off she saw he'd gotten it a lot worse. He was a big guy and he could take a lot of punishment, but the wound looked very bad. A chunk of flesh was missing from his bicep and he could move his left arm only with halting pain. There was surprisingly little blood in the wound.

Caxton was afraid she knew what that meant. He was breathing heavily, he complained of excessive thirst, and his face was pale—the symptoms of anemia. The vampire that bit his arm had sucked out some of his blood. Maybe too much. Someone passed him a canteen and he sucked at it greedily. Caxton took off her tie and made a tourniquet above the wound. It would help keep the rest of his blood in his body and it would also help stave off infection. He needed more help than she could give, though. He needed a doctor. He needed to be taken to a hospital.

That wasn't going to happen. Not yet, anyway.

He wasn't in shock, she could at least be thankful for that. One of the guardsmen had a bandage and some surgical tape. She wrapped it around Glauer's arm and then helped him shrug back into his jacket. It hurt him to put the garment back on, but it would keep him warm—crucial in a case of massive blood loss.

When she was finished she stared into his eyes. "The one who did this—"

"I got him," Glauer insisted.

Caxton bit her lip and nodded. There would be others, though. Other vampires who had drunk hot human blood. It didn't just feed them. It made them stronger and tougher. She passed the word around, through Lieutenant Peters. The next wave they faced would be harder to kill. A single shot to the heart might not be enough to take down a well-fed vampire.

"Jesus," one of the guardsmen said when he heard the news. "What's today, my birthday? I didn't want this. I wanted a pony."

A few of the soldiers—far too few—laughed. The tension in the Cyclorama Center was thicker than road tar. Everyone knew the vampires were coming, but they were taking their damned time about it.

Caxton's radio crackled but before she could answer it Lieutenant Peters stood up straight, without warning, and every eye in the room turned to look at her. The guardswoman touched the earpiece of her radio set. "Report," she said. Caxton guessed she was talking to the pilot of one of the helicopters. The Cyclorama building had no windows, so that was the only way they had to know what was happening outside without poking their heads out the door and taking a personal look. Nobody was about to volunteer for that duty. "Okay, received," the lieutenant said a moment later. She turned to look at Caxton. "Definite signs of movement. Under light enhancement these things show up pretty good, and—"

The doors of the Cyclorama Center slammed open before she could finish her thought. A single vampire strode through them, his arms wide, his mouth open in a wicked grin. He was shirtless and Caxton could make out his ribs below his tight white skin, but his cheeks were glowing pink. He must have just fed, moments before.

The guardsmen were ready, had been ready since they'd taken shelter in the building. They opened up with single shots, peppering both sides of his chest. White meat splattered from the impacts and a thin black tendril of blood oozed from a wound in his cheek. He took a step forward and new holes opened all over his body, but the older wounds were already healing over.

Another step forward—and then white shapes burst out from behind him, flashing left and right, other vampires coming in right behind him.

No, Caxton thought, but yes—they were that well organized. They had planned this attack, they had gorged one of their number on blood until he was nearly bulletproof and they had sent him in first. While he drew fire the weaker vampires had crept inside without resistance.

The round room's weird acoustics made every rifle shot echo and repeat, and the muzzle flashes fractured Caxton's vision as she jumped to her feet. She grabbed Glauer and shoved him toward the rear exit, a fire door at the northern side of the building. She felt a cold breeze on the back of her neck and spun around. It felt as if her Beretta jumped into her hand. Before she'd even registered the pale shape looming at her shoulder she lifted and fired three quick shots. The vampire there curled around his emaciated limbs and tumbled at her feet. Had she hit the heart? She doubted it—she'd been firing blind. Hurriedly she brought up her rifle and shoved the stock into the crook of her shoulder. The vampire struggled to get his knees under him, then one foot. She waited, holding as long as she could, until his pale body loomed up and over her again.

Then she pressed the muzzle of her weapon against his chest and fired a .50-caliber round right through his heart. He died before he could even look surprised.

Safe—for the moment—she spun around to see what was happening.

Elsewhere in the room the guardsmen were dying faster than they could acquire targets. She saw one screaming and pounding at the floor as a vampire tore into his back with razor-sharp teeth. His legs had already been torn off by another. She saw Lieutenant Peters wrestling with a vampire that could have bench-pressed her, body armor and all, smacking the monster across the head again and again with the heat shield of her patrol rifle.

"Break contact," Caxton shouted, and a few of the guardsmen heard her and ran for the fire door. Those few who weren't already in the process of dying. She tried to line up a shot on the vampire wrestling with Peters, but there was no way to avoid hitting the lieutenant as well. A moment later it didn't matter—the vampire got his face into her throat. The guardswoman tried to spit out one last curse, but it came out as a gurgling, plaintive moan. In moments she was dead, and her vampire assailant was that much stronger.

78.

I thought we would have time to train, and devise special tactics for the use of vampires in wartime. We did not.

No one expected Gettysburg to happen. Neither side was prepared. Once it began, however, like a fire in a fallow field, it could not be stopped.

I was near Hagerstown with my rail car at the time the news came. I was on my way toward Pipe Creek, to join up with Meade's army; a trap had been laid there, to draw Lee south again. Clearly Lee had failed to take the bait. My orders changed in a moment and I linked up with a troop train to take us across the border. I was not ready. My men, such as they were, were not ready.

It didn't matter. None of it mattered. I moved about the troop train once we were under way and saw men praying, some wailing to the skies. They believed the End of Days had come. The soldiers knew this battle would be a "good 'un," a last desperate fight to try to stop Lee before he could capture Philadelphia and force a peace. The men sang songs, "John Brown's Body," which I hadn't heard since the great muster when all Washington was an armed camp, or the "Battle Hymn of the Republic." By God, it was stirring.

As we approached the little market town of Gettysburg the singing stopped abruptly. There was another sound, an abominable sound, an unbearable sound that rocked the train car beneath me, shifted the coffins back and forth in their racks. I had never heard real artillery fire before. I had not heard guns ring like bells and the earth roar as it was torn open. From twenty miles away the noise was loud enough to tear the breath out of my mouth. They say those guns were heard as far away as Pittsburgh.

—THE PAPERS OF WILLIAM PITTENGER

79.

"Go, now," Caxton said, grabbing a guardsman's arm and shoving him toward the exit. He went. The door flapped open and closed on its spring-loaded hinges as one after another of her troops pressed through. Caxton searched the Cyclorama for any more survivors, but all she saw were torn and bloodied corpses—and vampires.

Twenty or so of them had pushed inside the vast round space. They stood in the middle of the floor, looking up at her. Their tattered uniforms—one even wore the moldering remains of a forage cap—echoed the look of the painted soldiers on the walls. They were old, these vampires. So old—and so hungry. She could only imagine how hungry they must be, after lying asleep in the ground for a hundred and forty years.

Caxton cursed herself. Arkeley would never have given that thought time to form. They weren't people, these vampires. Not anymore. They were killers, wild animals that needed to be put down.

One of them stepped forward, toward her, arms up. Beseeching, begging her for her blood. Behind him others started moving.

She lined up her shot perfectly. The vampire took another step. He had fed—she could see a slight tinge of pink in his cheeks, could see his chest where his ribs weren't quite as prominent as they were on the others. Her first shot only ripped open his skin and splintered a few bones. Her second shot spun him around until she could see only his arm and his side. She waited for him to turn back, to face her again, before she fired a third shot that sent fragments of his dark heart spinning out through a hole in his back.

The others were still moving, still coming closer. Some of them tried to fix her with their gaze, but she was able to avoid eye contact. She could feel her skin rippling, her body curling in revulsion. Adrenaline—pure, liquefied fear—coursed through her body. Every fiber of her being just wanted to turn and run, to escape. Somehow she held her ground.

Caxton couldn't take them all on. That would be suicide. She could buy a few moments for her troops, though. They were out there in the dark, running for the visitor center. The longer she kept the vampires inside the Cyclorama the better chance the guardsmen and Glauer had to make it. She wanted Glauer to make it. She owed him this chance.

"Who's next?" she asked, raising her rifle to a firing posture.

The vampires seethed forward, all of them at once. Like vaporous white mist they rushed toward her, so fast they seemed a single mass of death hurled at her. Caxton had expected as much. They were too smart to try for her one at a time.

She dropped the rifle, letting it fall back on its sling, and shoved her hand in her pocket to pull out her second and last flashbang. She'd already peeled off the plastic wrapper, so it took only a fraction of a second to rip out the pin and let it tumble out of her pocket. She didn't have even enough time to throw it—

She hurled herself backward, her eyes screwed shut. Her back hit the push bar of the fire door even as the flashbang went off and the vampires howled in pain. She hadn't had time to pull on her ear protectors, and the noise of the explosion ripped through her eardrums, deafening her, filling up her head with a high-pitched whine so loud it made her teeth hurt, made her guts vibrate.

She couldn't think, couldn't breathe. Her body was wracked by the noise, her senses completely scrambled. She was just marginally aware that she was falling, falling backward, then she felt a new wave of pain as she hit the grass hard, her arms flying up reflexively to protect her head. She opened her eyes, but all she saw was darkness. She'd passed from the well-lit Cyclorama into the near-total darkness of the overcast night, and her eyes were still adjusting.

Someone grabbed her arm. She lashed out, terrified that a vampire would tear her apart while she was still deaf and blind, but the hand just held on to her and eventually she realized it was a warm hand, a human hand holding her. She blinked her eyes rapidly, trying to force her pupils to dilate. Eventually she saw a gray shape looming out of the darkness above her, a gray shape bisected by a darker bar. A face—a face with a thick mustache. It was Glauer.

"—hear me? The . . . through . . . door . . . bolt . . . how . . ."

His voice was a distant rumbling, a bass-heavy noise trying to fight through the ringing in her ears. She could hear only a fraction of what he was saying. Frustration surged up inside of her and she sat up, then climbed to her feet. She could see Glauer a little better then and she noticed that he was jabbing his index finger at something behind her.

She spun around and saw the fire door she'd just crashed through. It had closed on its hinges, but now it was rattling in its frame. As if the vampires inside were trying to get it open but didn't know how to work the push bar. Well, maybe that was even true—they'd probably never seen one before. It would take only seconds before they figured it out, however, if only by trial and error.

Glauer had been asking her if there was any way to bolt the door. She'd lost precious time while she recovered her senses. Urgently she cast around her, looking for a lock, looking for something to push up against the door. The door had no knob on this side—it was meant to be opened only in emergencies, and to keep out trespassers who might try to break in. There was a small lock plate with a narrow keyhole, presumably to be used to seal the door shut. They didn't have the key, though. Glauer ran his fingers across the plate, wincing back every time the door jumped in its frame. If a vampire so much as leaned on the door, if his hip caught the push bar, it could fly open at any moment. They had no more time. Caxton grabbed his sleeve, tried to pull him away, but he was intent on the lock plate.

"—in the movies. Open the . . . but maybe it'll . . . the lock," he said, staring at her.

She could only shake her head. What was he saying?

Looking as if he'd lost all patience with her, Glauer finally drew a bead on the lock plate on the edge of the door with his rifle. Grimacing, he squeezed the trigger before she could stop him. The enormous bullet pranged off the lock plate and Caxton felt its wind as it ricocheted past her cheek. It could have killed her, could have blown her brains out.

"You idiot," she shouted, and was surprised to find she could hear herself. Then she looked at the lock plate. The bullet had smashed in the keyhole, deforming the lock mechanism altogether. More importantly, the door had stopped jumping.

Maybe Glauer's stupid move had actually jammed the lock. Or maybe the vampires were afraid of being shot through the door. It didn't matter.

She shook her head and pushed Glauer toward Taneytown Road, which ran past the side of the Cyclorama building. He'd bought them a few more seconds, but that was all they were going to get.

80.

This was the first battle I'd ever directly witnessed. I suppose I had imagined men in pressed blue uniforms whirling sabers in the air, calling other men on to a glorious attack. It was nothing like that at all. At Gettysburg I saw soldiers pressed forth into withering fire, muskets popping and blasting, the oncoming men knowing not which way they should run. I saw the guns chew the land up and spit out corpses, flinging them high in the air. I saw much blood; and many dead men, far more than I could stomach. They lay in heaps, or strewn about the field as if they'd been lead soldiers, tossed aside by a bored and impatient child. They were hauled back behind the line when it was possible, which was rarely, and there stacked like cordwood. The wounded far outnumbered them, but the sight of these was almost worse. So many men begging for water, for a surgeon, and so few of those to go around. There was always some man screaming his last, and some other begging him to shut his mouth and be quiet.

This was the second day of the battle, which had been running hot all day. Lee held the northwest, and all of Seminary Ridge while we faced him across a sunken roadway from the top of Cemetery Ridge. Rebels came roaring up that incline, their weapons high, their packs swinging, and they were chopped down like wheat at harvest. As they ran they screeched and hollered and bleated out the worst noise I have ever heard. This was the famed "Rebel Yell," and its design was to strike fear into our hearts. It worked well enough on me.

—THE PAPERS OF WILLIAM PITTENGER

81.

er hearing came back, but not perfectly. A dull grinding buzz filled her head and it didn't diminish over time. Repeated exposure to the noise generated by the flashbangs could permanently deafen someone, she knew, and she worried she was already halfway there.

She could hear her own clothing rustle, though, which had to be a good sign. In the distance she could hear gunfire— patrol rifles, some discharging in short, careful bursts, others going wild with pointless automatic fire.

She ran behind a tree and signaled for Glauer to come up next to her. "Some of our guys are still out here," she said. "They must have been trapped—unable to get to the next fall-back point."

"We could go find them, try to help them," Glauer suggested. He sounded like he was shouting at her from a far-off hilltop, even though he was only a few feet away. "They'll get slaughtered out here."

She shook her head. She had to think like Arkeley, do what Arkeley would have done. The old Fed would have known better than to go racing blindly into the dark in the hopes of rescuing his troops. He would have considered them disposable. For Arkeley the only thing that mattered was that the vampires died.

She couldn't reconcile that with her own conscience. But her rational mind was willing to accept it for the time being. "We need to stick to the plan," she said. She looked up at Glauer. "You should have stuck to the plan. You shouldn't have waited for me out here in the open."

He shrugged. "We're partners, right? You don't abandon your partner in the middle of a firefight."

She scowled and looked away, toward the road. Partners. Glauer's old partner, Garrity, had died at the hands of a vampire. Glauer had refused to give chase, instead sticking with Garrity even though he was already dead.

Caxton had been Arkeley's partner, once. At least she'd thought of herself that way. Arkeley had only ever meant to use her as bait.

"Come on," she said, and hurried out into the road. The streetlamps lit up the dark asphalt but nothing beyond the edge of the road. They ruined her night vision, but still she squinted into the shadows, ready for any threat that came toward her.

It was Glauer who saw the danger when it came.

"Something moved," he said, raising one hand to point at a cannon sitting by the side of the road. The streetlight dripped from the rim of one of its wheels. "There," he said again, much louder.

A vampire launched itself from behind the cannon, streaking across the asphalt. For a second Caxton thought she saw his red eyes. She swung her rifle up and fired three shots, but she knew she wouldn't hit the vampire. It was just suppressing fire.

"Run," she shouted, and then booked across the road, her knees pumping madly.

The visitors center, their next fallback point, sat low and massive directly in front of her. It was a sprawling pile of yellow brick with plenty of doors, much less defensible than the Cyclorama building. She rushed up to the front entrance, a row of glass doors, and shoved her way inside, Glauer pressing up tight behind her. Behind the row of doors lay a narrow entrance foyer and beyond that the main access point to the building. She crouched down and stared through the glass, trying to see the vampire she'd shot at. For a few panicked seconds she waited, trying not to move too much, trying not to breathe.

Apparently the vampire was too smart to try a frontal attack. Or maybe he'd just been after somebody else all along.

"Okay," she said, finally. "Let's move in."

Glauer went first, his rifle cradled in his good arm. He kicked open an inner door and ran through, then jumped back hurriedly as bullets tore out of the darkness. The noise in the enclosed foyer was like the ringing of giant iron bells, and the muzzle flashes dazzled Caxton's eyes. She understood what was happening instantly, though.

"Stand down!" Caxton shouted, grabbing Glauer's belt and pulling him back, away from the door. "We're on your side!"

A scared-looking face popped out of the inner door. It was one of the guardsmen, one of the troops she'd seen at the Cyclorama Center. The one who had wanted a pony.

"Shit," he said, looking at Caxton and then Glauer. He chewed on his lower lip. "We thought you were—"

"Vampires. Yeah," Caxton said. She cursed herself for nearly getting Glauer killed. "Well, we're not. Can we come in?"

The guardsman stepped back from the door and she pushed past him into the main lobby of the visitor center, a cluttered space of display cases and signage. A ticket counter lined the wall on her right, while a darkened gift shop stood on her left. At the far end of the room exits led into gloomy hallways, posted with signs for guided tours and the "famous" electric map.

Three guardsmen sat on the floor, their weapons across their knees. They stared up at her with terrified eyes. The guardsman who had shot at them leaned against the ticket counter, looking into the shadows, specifically not meeting her gaze. He had corporal's bars on his uniform and a name tag that read HOWELL.

"Four of you," Caxton said. "That's all that got out?"

"I've been trying to raise the others on my radio," Howell said. "No fucking dice."

Caxton let out a long uncomfortable breath. Four of them—that was horrible. That was devastating. Only four left? She shouldn't be too surprised, she thought. She'd seen the others die, back in the Cyclorama building. She'd seen Lieutenant Peters die. The contingent of soldiers from the National Guard had been expertly trained, heavily armed, and well organized.

Arkeley had told her a million times never to underestimate vampires.

"What about the others?" she asked. Her plan had been to keep the various units of her army together as best as possible. The guardsmen had been responsible for the Cyclorama. The liquor enforcement officers had been assigned to fall back to the visitor center and hold it until all of her troops could regroup there. "Have you made contact with the LEOs?"

Corporal Howell looked right at her then and she knew she wouldn't like to hear what he was about to say.

"We found them, anyway," he said. He gestured with his chin at the gift shop.

Caxton took a few steps toward the shop, but she didn't have to go far to see what he meant. In the cluttered aisles of book racks and souvenir stands a number of human bodies—how many in all she didn't know—lay strewn about like broken toys. They wore navy blue windbreakers, some of them torn to shreds.

82.

My coffins were disguised as crates of rifles and were stowed away carefully in the appropriate magazine behind the line. I stayed with them all the rest of the day, even as the Confederate guns hammered at the earth all around me, and though I feared for my life at every moment. A tightness grew around my head, as if some circlet of iron had been placed there, and through cunning design been made so it could be tightened slowly, almost imperceptibly. By the time the shelling stopped my ears were ringing and my skull felt it might split. I could smell nothing but spent gunpowder and the stink the dead made and my eyes ran freely with water, for the smoke was much irritating.

At sundown the battle halted for the day. Tents were thrown up, so many of them. I could not see very far, despite my position atop the ridge, for the smoke dulled my eyes to everything. Yet the white canvas stood out in that murk and for the first time I saw just how many men surrounded me. Why, there was a whole city's population on that field, almost all of them armed. It was something I shall never forget, to look out on that sea of canvas, and feel it must go on forever.

—THE PAPERS OF WILLIAM PITTENGER

83.

"You should have told us," Howell said. His face was wracked with hatred. "You didn't tell us it would be this bad."

Caxton knelt down to touch the arm of one of the dead LEOs. It was cold and the hand at the end was very pale. She rolled him over on his side and got a shock. The man's head was missing.

Stepping backward, unable to see anything except the raw bloodless stump of his neck, she barely heard Howell complaining.

"We need to pop smoke right now," he said.

"What?" Glauer asked.

The soldier stared at him wide-eyed. "Pop smoke. Bug out. We need to leave!"

She looked up at him with a sudden measure of anger that surprised her. The LEOs had given their lives to stop the vampires. Now this idiot wanted to just leave, with the job unfinished? It was the kind of reaction Arkeley would have had. *Feel free to step outside, the door's just there,* she thought, smoky rage billowing in her chest. *See how far you get.* She managed not to say it out loud. "We just need to hang on," she said, instead. "The guard will send more troops."

"Oh my God, how many times have I heard that?" Howell held up his radio, his thumb on the receive button. Only crackling static came through. "Nobody's going to come save us! We're the last of your task force, lady. Haven't you figured that out yet? They took us to pieces!"

"We heard others outside, others who are still alive."

"Not for long," Howell replied.

She ground her teeth together and hit him with her best cop glare. "A lot of my people have died, yes," she admitted. "But their sacrifice wasn't in vain. We killed a lot of vampires. But there are more of them—"

"No fucking shit!" Howell shouted.

She began to reply, but Glauer grabbed her arm. He lifted his free index finger to his lips. "Has it even occurred to either of you that the monsters who did that," he whispered, pointing at the dead LEOs, "might still be here?"

Howell shut up instantly. He looked away, down the dark corridors leading into the building, and lifted his weapon to a firing position. Caxton could see the flash hider on the end of his rifle shaking in the air.

She drew her own weapon, pointed it. She half expected a horde of vampires to come running out of the darkness that second. When nothing happened after a long, tense interval, she raised her rifle to point at the ceiling.

Howell spun around, his face white and his eyes wide. He had nothing clever to say this time.

Caxton wanted to mock him—but she caught herself. He was just scared. She understood that perfectly. He knew Glauer might be right, just as she did. She needed to get control of herself. Needed to keep it together, just as much as Howell did.

"Good thinking," she told Glauer, her voice barely audible to herself.

"What do you want us to do, Trooper?" one of the other guardsmen asked, quietly. His name tag read SADLER. Slowly, careful not to make too much noise, he climbed to his feet and the others followed.

There were two corridors, one for guided tours and the other for the electric map. There was no reason to choose one over the other. Whichever one she chose, though, could be the wrong one. If she took her people to the guided tour office, a vampire could sneak up behind them and kill them before they even knew he was there. Assuming there even was a single vampire still in the visitor center. They might have devoured the LEOs and then left.

She needed to think.

"We need to secure this place. We'll split up, just for a little while. Howell, you take your people down the hall on the left. Glauer and I will take the one on the right. If you make contact don't wait for us to catch up, just engage." She looked at her partner. He was pale and breathing hard, but he was still mobile, and his right arm—his shooting arm—was okay. He saw her sizing him up and gave her a reassuring nod.

"Okay," Howell said. He looked at his own troops. "Guys, get your asses up."

With Glauer at her back she headed down the dimly lit corridor toward the electric map. The way turned around a number of corners, almost instantly hiding the guardsmen from view. It led them past glass display cases full of artifacts from the battlefield—cannon, racks of antique rifles, a whole wall of white-corroded bullets and black tarnished uniformed buttons. She turned another corner and brought her weapon around, her breath catching in her throat. Before she fired, though, she saw what had scared her so badly—a posed group of mannequins wearing replica uniforms both blue and gray. The mannequins' faces were as white as plaster.

"Jesus," Glauer said from behind her. "Don't scare me like that."

"I'll do my best," she promised.

A few moments later, the corridor opened into a waiting area. There were turnstiles and a ticket taker's podium and several broad double doors leading into an auditorium beyond. As they watched one set of doors slowly creaked inward, just an inch or two.

Caxton's blood froze. She dropped to a firing crouch and held out an arm to keep Glauer back. She waited for the doors to crash open, for dozens of vampires to come bursting out, but nothing of the sort happened.

The doors just stood there, slightly open. It could have been nothing. The building's furnace might have switched on and a sudden puff of hot air could have pushed the doors open.

Not likely, she thought.

"Cover me," Glauer said, moving in. She stayed in her crouch, her weapon ready. He pushed his back up against the wall just to one side of the slightly open doors and peered through the crack. "I don't see anything," he told her. He held out his rifle and used it like a stick to push one door open all the way.

Caxton could see something of the room beyond—a big open space lined with rows of seats. The doors opened on the top level of a square amphitheater. Anything at all could be waiting below, hidden from view.

Duck-walking forward, she moved closer to the doors. Glauer stepped through them, his rifle moving from left to right as he covered the room. "Clear," he said, and she got up to her full height again and moved in, her own rifle still at the ready in case he'd missed something.

She scanned the blue seats and the flights of steps that ran between them, made a note of all the fire exits from the room, then looked down. The electric map lay at the bottom of the amphitheater, an enormous topographically correct rendering of the town of Gettysburg and the battlefield to the south. An operator could switch on and off a series of lights to indicate where various regiments and battalions had stood on each day of the battle. It was hard for Caxton to see much of the map, however, because it was obscured by coffins.

Lots of coffins. Some were broken open but most remained intact. They lay without any real organization on top of the map or on the floor around it. A lot of them had been laid across rows of seats or stood propped up against the steps. She didn't need to count them to know there must be ninety-nine in total.

She had finally found the coffins. Too late to do any good.

84.

While I was off to war, much transpired behind me, at my previous lodgings. I was only to learn much later of how sorely I'd underestimated my new friend. I was able to reconstruct most of what happened. The following I took from the official record of the special court martial of Private Jack Beecham, transcribed from his own words:

"It was right after midnight, right after her night's feeding, that it happened.

"I really have no explanation for it, sir, other than it seemed right. The man who came had a bad wound on his face and he looked sickly, but we just thought he was some poor casualty bastard put to use by the quartermaster 'cause he wasn't fit to fight anymore. Some of the men working as cooks here have worse injuries and ailments, as I'm sure you know. This fellow said his name was Bill something. He was a yank soldier and he used

Colonel Pittenger's name, said he had orders to pick up a coffin and take it away for burial, that's all I know. No, sir, he hadn't any papers, but that's not so rare in wartime, when things aren't often done to a nicety. He had a wagon with black bunting, you know, a funeral hearse, and a team. Oh, how those horses got themselves up when we brought out the coffin, as if they'd been at by a whole nest of hornets. We was all glad to see him go, as you might imagine, for it meant getting rid of those maddened beasts.

"It seemed alright, honest. I didn't know Miss Malvern was inside that coffin, or I'd have put up a real fight. He said he was going to take her home and bury her proper, but where he actually got to, I have no notion.

"I'll take my punishment now, if that's alright."

Private Beecham was made to ride a donkey backward around the whole of the camp at morning rolls, with a dunce cap over his eyes. Then he was flogged, given six stripes, and had his week's pay taken away. It was lucky for him I was so far away; my punishment would have been far graver. Perhaps I'd have introduced him to my new acquaintances.

—THE PAPERS OF WILLIAM PITTENGER

85.

Glauer headed down the steps toward the map. She circled around the top of the amphitheater, scanning the exit doors. She tried one, found it locked. Moved to the next one. That was a dangerous game, she knew. To try the doors she had to lower her weapon, leaving her vulnerable. She needed to do this the way she'd been trained—which meant she needed help. She needed Glauer to cover her while she opened each door.

"Glauer, let's keep together, okay?" she called out. The big cop had made his way down to the level of the map to stand in the middle of a group of coffins. Though she was sure they were empty, she didn't want him down there. "Glauer?"

He didn't even seem to hear her. His rifle was pointed down at the floor, but his face was turned upward, his eyes focused on a glassed-in booth above her head, where the map's operator would have sat.

His jaw slid open as if it had come unhinged. His massive arms fell lifeless at his sides.

"Glauer!" she shouted, but he didn't even flinch.

Oh shit, she thought, even as his rifle lifted, even as he brought up the hand of his bad arm to grip the heat shield. She recognized the look on his face just fine—she'd worn the same expression often enough herself. There had to be a vampire up there in the booth. Glauer had made eye contact and now the vampire had him hypnotized. She rushed down toward him, thinking she could snap him out of it.

Then she noticed that his rifle was pointing right at her. Still he looked upward as if transfixed by some religious vision. He wasn't aiming at her. He probably didn't even know what his hands were doing. She saw his finger slip through the trigger guard and just had time to drop to the floor as his rifle spat bullets across the wall behind her.

"Trooper?" she heard him call, his voice watery and indistinct. "Where are you? I can't . . . I can't see you."

Caxton crawled forward on her elbows and knees, protected only by the row of seats between Glauer and herself. He fired another burst that tore at the upholstery of the seats, sending yellow fluff into the air.

She had no idea what she was going to do next. He had her pinned down—if she stood up he would blow her away. If she moved forward or backward too far she would come to one of the sets of steps that ran down to the map. To the side there were two doors, the locked fire exit she'd just tried and the door she'd intended to investigate next, a total unknown. It might be open. There might be fifty vampires waiting behind it. It didn't matter much, since to get to it she would have to dodge bullets.

"Trooper . . . did you say . . . something?" Glauer asked. His voice sounded different, and she realized he was moving. Coming toward her, climbing the steps.

She couldn't move—but if she didn't move he would just come to her and kill her where she lay. Her only choice was to try the mystery door. He would have plenty of time to shoot her while she reached for its handle, but she was out of options.

No—she had one option. She could shoot him first. Arkeley would probably have done just that, but she didn't know if she had the nerve.

So instead she waited for his next burst—just two bullets this time, one of which knocked chips of plaster out of the wall right over her head—and then jumped up and ran as fast as she could for the door.

She glanced back as she ran and saw him six feet away, his rifle barrel trained right on her. His face kept looking up at the booth. She slammed into the door with her hip, hoping to trigger the push bar and propel herself through in one motion. There was only one problem: there was no push bar.

The door was narrower than the fire exits she'd seen, painted the same color as the walls. A sign at eye level read ELECTRIC MAP PERSONNEL ONLY. PLEASE! Instead of a push bar it had a brass knob. She grabbed the knob and tried to twist it, but found it locked.

In the next moment, she knew, she would be shot in the back. She drew her Beretta and tried to point it at Glauer, but her arm couldn't complete the motion.

He took a step closer and squeezed his trigger. The patrol rifle clicked, but there was no round in the chamber. He had emptied his clip. It would take only seconds to reload, seconds during which she could still shoot him. She raised her pistol. If she shot him in the arms it would keep him from shooting. He had already lost a lot of blood, though. There was no guarantee that new wounds wouldn't send him into shock or even kill him. It was her or him, though—

His hands worked at the rifle, moving the fire control selector back and forth pointlessly. He held the weapon by its heat shield and looked right down the barrel.

What the hell was he doing? But then she understood. Glauer could have ejected the spent magazine and slapped a fresh one in place with a blindfold on. But Glauer wasn't in control of his own body. The unseen vampire was—a vampire who knew how to load a musket rifle and even a breech-loading Sharps rifle, maybe, but certainly not a Colt AR6520.

"Caxton?" he asked. "Did you—did you leave me here alone?"

Ignoring him, she smashed at the door with her hip and shoulder. If she could get through she could get up to the control booth. She could get to the vampire who had Glauer hypnotized. She could kill said vampire and break the spell.

Behind her the local cop took another step toward her. He threw the patrol rifle away, let it clatter on the ground. Reaching down to his belt, he took out his ASP baton and extended it to its full length.

"Laura?" he called.

The door failed to collapse under her repeated attacks. As Glauer lifted the baton to strike her, he looked like a bear coming at her.

"Oh, fuck this," she said, and kicked him right in the chest. The air went out of him and he fell backward, hitting the ground like a big sandbag.

She turned back to the door—and that was when the lights went out.

86.

General Hancock, who had nominal charge of me and my wards, came to me just as the dark of the battle was turning to the dark of night. I had a tent of some bigness within which my coffins were propped up on sawhorses. From within them already I could hear my men stirring, getting ready for their baptism in fire.

"By Judas Iscariot," the general swore. He was a young man, no more than forty years in age, with a long full beard but his cheeks were clean shorn. He waved his hat at Griest and took a step back. Could any man blame him? The first time one sees a vampire is always hard. One does not expect the protruding teeth, nor the red eyes. One feels immediately the suspect coolness, the prickling of the hairs on one's arms. I rushed forward to assure him.

"Secretary Stanton sends his warmest regards, sir," I said. "Does the battle go well?"

Hancock's eyes lit up. "We have not yet lost, and Lee is on the field, so I shall count this day a victory. I've come to tell you to stand down for the night."

Griest's face fell. I could see he longed to speak but he was still a corporal, even if he was no longer human. Instead I spoke for him.

"The men are ready to fight, sir. They've made a great sacrifice, all of them, to be here."

"I know it well. Yet I cannot loose them on the Rebels tonight. I'm counting on a grand surprise from your fellows, and I dare not spring it too soon. Stand down, man, but be ready."

He could not seem to get away soon enough.

—THE PAPERS OF WILLIAM PITTENGER

87.

It was dark—so terribly dark. There was no light anywhere, not even a glimmer of starlight. The electric map auditorium had no windows and no light could even sneak in around the edges of the fire exits.

She was trapped in the dark with a vampire and her partner, who was hypnotized and trying to kill her.

Caxton staggered backward, blind and terrified. She fought down a scream and then dug in her coat pocket for her flashlight. She held the Beretta straight upward—without light she had nothing to shoot at.

The door she'd been pressed against a moment before flapped open and something cold and inhuman shot past her, into the dark. The vampire had come down from the booth.

Glauer was still down on the floor, she thought. He was a sitting duck. The vampire would have had to break his hypnotic connection with the local cop to come down, but most likely Glauer was still dazed and unable to defend himself.

Well, there wasn't much she could do for him if she couldn't see. Even less if she was dead. She found the flashlight and switched it on before it was even out of her pocket. The beam twitched in her hand and she realized just how scared she was. Fighting to control herself, she pointed the flashlight down toward the electric map. Her light barely gleamed off the broken coffins down there, the beam illuminating nothing of use. She moved the light slowly across the floor at her feet, toward where she'd left Glauer. She didn't worry about giving his position away—or her own. She knew the vampire could see their blood glowing in the dark, a fine tracery of red where arteries and veins pulsed faster and faster.

The vampire laughed at her, an animal noise like a hyena

would make. A cold and violent growl. She shuddered, her whole body shaking. Then she went back to looking for Glauer.

She found his ASP baton, abandoned on the floor. There was no sign of the cop. She thought about calling out his name but couldn't seem to get her voice to work.

It was just too much. She'd been shot at, grabbed, even bitten. She was operating on no sleep and little food and there were vampires everywhere, vampires who had already killed most of her army. And now they were coming for her.

A sound leaked out of her throat, then. It sounded a lot like a whimper.

Stop this, she told herself. *You're a trooper of the Pennsylvania State Police and you have killed more vampires than this asshole has killed humans.*

She willed her hand to stop shaking. Her chest was shivering as it dragged more and more oxygen into her lungs. She would start hyperventilating soon. She would get that under control too, but first she needed her hands. The flashlight beam steadied, moved slowly across the metal seat backs. She had to find the vampire.

She was covered in weaponry, but she didn't think that would scare him off. In the dark he was at a distinct advantage. He could have killed her already, several times over. If he hadn't attacked yet it meant he was toying with her. Playing with his food. Vampires were like that—real assholes. She concentrated on the fact that she was still alive. That was good, and useful. It meant she could still, possibly, save herself. She could worry about Glauer later.

The flashlight lit up another row of seats and then bounced off a white face. She saw squinting red eyes and a very toothy grin, and she yelped in fright.

The vampire leaped out of her light even as she brought her pistol around to shoot him. He moved with an awful grace, his limbs contracting and then extending like finely machined springs. She heard him land with a gentle thud, somewhere to her left. She spun on her heel, tried to follow him with her light, but she had lost him.

From very close by she heard him laugh again.

She tried desperately to remember her training. She needed to try to control the scene. That was something they'd taught her in the state police academy, in almost every class she took. You didn't run into a dark alley until you knew who was waiting in the shadows. If someone was shooting at you, your first instinct should not be to return fire but to find cover.

Arkeley had taught her that sometimes those rules didn't apply when you were fighting vampires, but at that moment she was willing to trust time-honored police procedure. She kept her back to the wall and started moving slowly to her left, toward the door to the control booth. If she could get a barrier between herself and the vampire, well, that would considerably extend her life expectancy.

She put her foot out, let it touch the floor. Another foot, another step. She reached across her body with her right arm—her gun arm—and waved the barrel of her pistol into empty space. The door was still open. That—that was good. She turned slightly and started to slide herself into the doorway.

Instantly cold hands descended on her shoulders and pulled her back. She screamed, a full-throated shriek of terror, as the vampire hurled her through space. She plummeted through the dark, sensing rows of seats passing beneath her, her arms and legs spinning, trying to find something, anything to hold on to.

She collided belly first with a pile of coffins and stopped screaming at once. All the air in her body was forced out as if she'd been wrung out by a giant hand. Her stomach burned with pain and her legs felt battered.

Desperate, panicked, she rolled over onto her back and pointed her flashlight back the way she'd come, back toward the top of the amphitheater. The vampire was right there, moving toward her, his hands up as if he intended to jump down right on top of her. She brought her gun hand up, but found it empty—the Beretta had fallen out of her grip on the way down. She threw the arm across her face instead in a purely reflexive gesture—there was no way the arm would protect her against the vampire's attack. She waited out the split second it would take him to land on her, to kill her, waited it out with nothing but fear inside her, waited—and waited—

From up above she heard a surprised grunt. Then a noise like leather being torn. The vampire roared, but still he didn't pounce on her, still she was alive. She decided to risk a quick glance.

Up top, on the walkway behind the topmost row of seats, the vampire was waving his arms furiously. It looked like it was waving for her to come help it.

Its chest was torn open. The skin hung away in flaps from exposed ribs that glistened with clotted blood. Her light went right into its chest cavity and she saw—without understanding—that its heart had been torn out.

It collapsed with a mewling noise she found almost piteous.

She could find no sign of what—or who—had destroyed it.

88.

I have changed so. It feels wrong, somehow, even to hold this pen with my new white hand. The pen is a tool of the living & I have put behind me all such things. Tonight we are at rest, though it is unwelcome, & unsought for. Tomorrow surely we will be loosed. It is quiet here, though they say a battle raged all day. I was asleep, & heard nothing of it. I do smell the smoke now.

My heart longs to go out into the night, to fight, & serve again. I have gained new powers, both of my body, which walks again (& I thought it never possible!), & of the mind. Such

*things I see now. I see ghosts, Bill, everywhere now about me, yet
am not much frightened. Like me they have passed the vale of
tears, & we are as comrades . . .*

*One power I now possess, which is to raise the dead. Just as
you were raised. I will not do it. Yes, even if I am ordered to do
so . . . I cannot bear to see the faces torn, the bodies broken, as
yours was.*

Beyond this I promise no mercy, to any man I meet.

Tomorrow there must be BLOOD. *I did not know, before, that
I would dream of it, & in such quantity, & of its taste.*

—LETTER OF ALVA GRIEST (UNPOSTED)

89.

It was over. For the moment. Caxton was alone again, still
alive, lying on a pile of broken timber that had once been
some vampire's coffin.

She had no way of knowing if Glauer was still in the room
or not. She flashed her light around the corners of the amphitheater, looking for any trace of him, but found nothing.

She lay back for a while, uncomfortable but unwilling to
move. Her body protested every time she lifted a limb or even
moved her eyes too rapidly. She could be dying, she thought.
The fall onto the pile of coffins had hurt—a lot—and for all
she knew, she had internal injuries. She might have punctured a
lung, or she could have a cerebral hemorrhage just waiting to
bleed out if she tried to sit up.

You're fine, she thought. It was what Arkeley would have
said. He wouldn't have even bothered with looking her over. In
Arkeley's world if you were capable of standing up, then you
were capable of continuing the fight. And if you weren't spurting
blood from a major artery or looking down at a compound frac-
ture of your own femur, then you were capable of standing up.

She sat up slowly, determined to have at least a few more seconds when she wasn't under the immediate specter of death. She brushed splinters and dust off her arms, then she used her hands and knees to roll up to a standing posture. She hurt all over, but nothing was broken or even sprained. She was exhausted beyond all human capacity, but adrenaline would keep her going for at least a little longer.

She was alone, it was dark, there were enemies all around—such things were too abstract compared to her aches and pains to be even worth thinking about.

She waved her flashlight across the floor until she'd found her Beretta. It looked alright. She checked the magazine and found four rounds inside. She had an extra clip in her coat pocket. Her patrol rifle lay next to her on the floor. There were six rounds in the clip, big .50 BMG bullets capable of passing through an engine block. Those six rounds were all she had left for that weapon.

She'd started out with two flashbangs, but those were gone. She had a can of pepper spray, a big four-ounce police model, but she had never actually tried pepper spray out on a vampire and she had no idea if it would incapacitate one. She didn't know if it would even annoy a vampire.

She had no idea where to go next.

An answer came, then, though she knew better than to trust it. The red sign over one of the fire doors came on, flickering red. It said EXIT, and it dazzled her eyes when she looked at it.

She'd played their games before. She knew the only sane course of action was to lock herself in the control booth and wait for morning. She also knew that was not an option, not when she still had work to do.

She headed for the door marked EXIT and took one last look back at the auditorium. The red buzzing light lit up the whole room, once her eyes had adjusted to its demonic glow. She couldn't see Glauer anywhere, not in the seats, not down by the map, not cowering in one of the long shadows. She called his name a couple of times but got no answer. So she turned to the exit and put her hand on the push bar.

The corridor beyond was dark, but a light shone at its far end. She moved forward slowly, trying not to make too much noise. There could be anything down there, she knew, anything at all. As she approached the light she saw it was another exit sign. She moved toward it, trying not to hurry, and lifted her patrol rifle just in case.

The sign didn't flicker off. No other lights came on. The sign's glow filled the hallway with pinkish light that did little to dispel the shadows in the corners.

She was being led around by someone, led into what was probably a trap. And she wasn't going to be allowed to go anywhere else.

The darkness in the corridor slowly gave way to dull light. She squinted into the half-gloom and saw a plain ordinary emergency light box high on a wall down there. It had two big spot lamps mounted on it, throwing light around a corner. Just beneath it was a sign with an arrow, pointing toward the guided tours area.

The place she'd sent Howell and his guardsmen. She sighed, wondering if she was going to be able to meet up with them, regroup and at least not be alone anymore.

She had a very bad feeling that the answer was no.

Moving carefully, her rifle at the ready, she headed around the corner and down a short hallway that ended in a closed fire door. There was no sign on it, just chipped enamel paint. The paint around the push bar had been worn off entirely, leaving bare silver metal beneath, as generations of tourists had pushed it to go through. A narrow rectangular window was set into the door, chicken wire suspended in the glass. She peered through but could see only shadows.

She told herself to buck up, and then she pushed the door

open. A breeze poured through the open door, carrying a trace of a foul smell she didn't waste time trying to identify. She moved into the room beyond, a sort of waiting room with lots of chairs and a reception counter.

On the carpet, lined up next to each other, lay Howell and his guardsmen. They had clearly been dragged there, perhaps arranged just so she would find them. Their empty faces stared at the ceiling. One of them—Sadler, she remembered—was missing his arms. The wounds at his shoulders were bloodless and pale.

Howell had a series of cuts on his face, four thin scratches that Caxton figured had to be claw marks. The edges of the cuts were translucent, but she could see severed pink muscle tissue underneath. No blood anywhere.

The other two showed no sign of violent injury. All four were still wearing their full battle dress, including their helmets. Their patrol rifles were missing and none of them had any personal firearms.

Howell had a single grenade dangling from his combat webbing. She pulled it carefully off its metal clip and studied it. Green and cylindrical, with holes on its top rather than down its sides. It wasn't a flashbang, nor a fragmentation grenade— it must have been part of the guardsman's regulation kit. She studied the codes stenciled on its side—M18 GREEN—and realized that it was, in fact, a smoke grenade. If she pulled the pin it would billow out thousands of cubic feet of smoke that would do exactly nothing to any vampire she threw it at. She shoved it in her pocket anyway, on the principal that you never left weapons lying around an unsecured crime scene. Basic cop procedure.

She stood up but couldn't stop looking at the four men. They were younger than she was, but they would never get any older. They'd already served their country once, in Iraq. Then they had come home and in less than a year they'd been sent into danger again, and this time they hadn't made it. She told herself that they were soldiers. Sworn, just as she was, to protect the Commonwealth of Pennsylvania. She told herself that two or three times. It still didn't sound as good as she'd hoped.

She had to keep moving. If she stopped, if she stood still and thought about how the guardsmen had died, or where Glauer was, or how many of her troops were still alive, she knew she would break down. She would lose her resolve. So after one last look at the dead men she turned away.

Behind the reception desk she found an office, a cramped little space full of filing cabinets. At the far end she found an exit door that let out into darkness. It was past time, she decided, to get out of the visitor center. Exhaustion was starting to catch up with her and she knew she could only go so much farther without getting some rest. Outside the cold air on her face would help keep her awake, keep her sharp.

Beyond the exit door she could see an empty parking lot, and beyond it a line of trees. She had studied various maps of Gettysburg long enough to know that past the trees was a gas station and a street full of the tackier sort of tourist industries—T-shirt shops, novelty photographic studios, cheap theme restaurants. Her next fallback position, by contrast, was a two-hundred-year-old tavern and inn off to her northeast. It was some distance away, a very long distance to cover with vampires on her tail. She had to stick to the plan, though. If there was any chance of meeting up with other units it meant following her own instructions as closely as possible.

Patrol rifle cradled in her arms, ready to shift it to a firing position at the slightest provocation, she rushed for the trees and then out of cover, across the open concrete of the gas station. Nothing jumped out at her, nothing pale and fast came running toward her. She couldn't help but wonder if she was being watched, though. A high wind had blown most of the clouds away and she felt exposed under all that starlight. She had to reassure herself that it was an advantage for her. The vampires didn't need the light—they could see her in perfect darkness—so the stars were on her side.

Every second out of cover, though, every moment she spent without a wall at her back, made her more scared. She pushed through the doors of the gas station's little store and sank down behind the abandoned counter just to catch her breath. It was quiet down there, almost perfectly quiet. She could hear nothing but the humming of the chiller cabinets that flanked the counter, their lights turned off but their contents still kept at a perfect low temperature. In the dark she let that hum run through her, a droning sound that calmed her nerves.

She switched on her radio and whispered a call for anyone still on the main channel. She held down the receive button and waited, hearing nothing but static. Electrons whizzing through empty space, voiceless, pointless. Her soldiers were under strict orders to answer her radio calls whenever possible. Either they were pinned down in places where it would be dangerous to make any noise at all—or they were all dead.

It seemed impossible that she was completely alone. There had been so many soldiers under her command. They couldn't all be gone. Could they?

"Chalk One, Chalk Two, come in," she said into the mouthpiece. She waited for the helicopter pilots to reply. They didn't.

That was all wrong. Vampires couldn't fly. That was one power they lacked. They couldn't have taken out the helicopters. That was just impossible. "Chalk Three, come in," she said again, louder this time, turning up the gain and the volume in case interference was blocking her call.

The radio emitted choppy static, louder but no more meaningful than before.

She came out of the gas station moving fast, keeping low. Her rifle was in her hands, ready to fire at the first shadow that moved. It was a stupid way to cross open ground—she was as likely to fire at nothing, or at another human being, as she was to actually target a vampire. It was all she could do to keep her fear from overwhelming her, however, and she didn't think about it too much.

The Taneytown Road crossed Steinwehr Avenue ahead of her, a broad, open intersection, an expanse of concrete and grass and terrible sight lines. She hurried across, leaving on the lawns dark wet footprints that anyone could have followed. Ahead of her she saw the old buildings of Gettysburg, including the oldest of all, the Dobbin House Tavern. It was her next stop.

A sign out front claimed the tavern had been standing since 1776, long before the Battle. It was a long, sprawling complex rather than a single building, added on to over the years and surrounded by tree-lined parking lots. The main building had thick, defensible-looking flowstone walls pierced by dozens of windows with broad white shutters. Redbrick chimneys stood up from the shingled roof and a white picket fence ran around the structure, leading up to a broad red door like a target that she hurried toward, certain she wanted to get inside as quickly as possible, sure as she could be that the intersection was better off behind her.

90.

July 3rd dawned and at once the guns were on again, hurling death against us as we hurled destruction at them. My troops slept through it all in their coffins, through the fighting at the Devil's Den where men stumbled on the bodies of their compatriots, and could gain no result. I saw it all, and came to envy them. The feeling, as if my head were stuck in some invisible vise, continued throughout that day, and vexed me sorely. I complained of it to a surgeon, who had so little time for my aches and pains that he did not even spit out a reply. When I asked about it I was told every man felt the same. They knew this sensation well. Some felt it was from the noise, that the very sound of mortar shells bursting all around us was enough to physically harm a man. Others claimed it was from our inability to sleep.

One man, a volunteer from Kentucky, offered to pray with me. "That feelin' ya got, that's God speakin', tellin' ya to git right now, for ya ain't got so much time left to make up for bad behavior!"

I will leave it to others to describe the content of that third day of battle, to list the regiments who fought with such valor and to sing the plaudits of those generals who finally outwitted Master Lee. I could only watch in terror as the Southron horde came on in waves, again and yet again, as we fought them back, with muskets and in some places with bare bayonets. My mind was not capable of making sense of the general horror, the appalling loss of life, the noise, the smoke. The smoke, the smoke! In my memory that place is all made of ash, and flecks my cheeks and nose with its feathery powder, and all I breathe is smoke. I smell it now!

—THE PAPERS OF WILLIAM PITTENGER

91.

Just before she reached the door, the hairs on the back of her neck stood up and she stopped, motionless, like a rabbit paralyzed by fear.

Someone—some thing, some unnatural thing—was nearby. She'd been fighting vampires long enough to know the feeling. It had to be close. It could be hiding in any of the broad shadows around her. It would be within striking range, she thought. It would be waiting for her to turn her back, and then it would attack.

She lifted her rifle and turned on one foot, pointing the

weapon at nothing and everything. Ready to shoot the second something moved.

Then as quickly as the unnatural feeling had come, it disappeared.

There had been a vampire nearby. She was certain of it. It could have attacked her. It must have wanted to. But for some reason it had changed its mind and left her alone. That made no sense.

It didn't need to. It was a good thing, she told herself, and she could use some more of those. She thought about the dead vampire above the electric map. Something had torn out its heart. Something was—protecting her? That wasn't something a vampire would ever do. They didn't see human life as possessing any significant value. They certainly wouldn't go out of their way to save a human being. Yet something had done just that. Then again, perhaps it wasn't protecting her at all. Maybe it was just laying claim to her. Maybe one of the vampires had decided she was its personal prey. Maybe it had killed the vampire at the electric map so it could save her for itself.

Again she told herself it didn't matter. She was still alive, and that did matter. She wanted to stay that way.

"Okay," she said, to center herself. Then she turned, pressed the thumb latch on the door, and stepped inside into darkness.

Closing the door behind her, she let her lungs heave and strain to get her breath back. She felt like she'd been punched in the gut. It was freezing inside the tavern. She detected no sign of life inside the big stone building.

"Okay," she said again. She wanted to sit down for a while. She wanted to get a good night's sleep. She didn't have time to be exhausted, though. Nothing had changed. No matter how many vampires were after her, no matter what they might have wanted, she still had to follow her own plan. She needed to hook up with any remnants of her army of cops and guardsmen. She needed to find more ammunition for her weapons. If nothing else she needed to get somewhere safe, somewhere she could defend, and hold it as long as she could. Hopefully long enough for the National Guard reinforcements to arrive.

There was a light on inside the tavern. She hadn't expected that. A single candle stood on a table in the middle of the room, flickering with a yellow light that dazzled her eyes.

She was expected, she realized. Someone was waiting for her in here.

In the light of just the candle the room was full of dancing shadows. It was worse than darkness, she decided, so she blew out the flame and watched its orange spark dull and finally die. She didn't turn on her flashlight immediately—she wanted her vision to adapt to the darkness first. So she stared into the dark and listened to nothing but her own breath. For a while that was all there was.

Then she heard music.

The sound of a fiddle playing a lively tune. It was so appropriate a sound for the ancient tavern that for a moment she wondered if she'd been sent back in time.

If only, she thought.

She climbed to her feet. The music was coming from above her, from some room higher up in the building. She heard another instrument as well—a flute? A recorder? No, it was a fife. And underneath, pounding out an uncomplicated rhythm, she heard a bass drum.

There was nothing forcing her to investigate the music. If she wanted to—and she really did want to, she knew that it was herself thinking this—she could just stay downstairs until dawn. She would be safe enough there in the tavern. She could defend herself. Shoot anything that tried to come through the door. Keep her back to a stone wall that even vampires couldn't break their way through.

She could just sit there and listen to the music all night. If she wanted to. And she wanted to.

There was only one problem. Arkeley would have wanted her to go upstairs. She knew exactly what he would do in her situation. She knew he was right. Vampires loved to play tricks with your brain. It was one of their chief joys. It was also one of their few weaknesses. If you walked right into their traps, if you defied the obvious logic of their illusions, more often than not you could catch them on a bad footing.

So she switched on her flashlight, found the stairwell, and headed up.

The room at the top of the stairs was maybe fifteen feet on a side, with a low ceiling and lots of windows. Beyond that she had no idea what it really looked like. What she saw up there, in that room, couldn't possibly be real.

Men in blue uniforms, well tailored and lined with polished brass buttons, stood against the walls holding steins of beer or cups of punch. Their faces were ruddy with health and good cheer. A few of them were playing the instruments she'd heard, making a raucous, happy sound. Along one wall stood a groaning board loaded with roasts and cakes and an enormous punch bowl. Bunting hung from that wall, golden cloth printed with the message:

WELCOME BACK, ALVA
"our hero return'd"

The floor of the room had been cleared away—a thick rug had been rolled up and shoved in a corner. On the bare floorboards two soldiers danced a spirited turn to the fiddle's tune. Their faces were bright with sweat and excitement and they laughed as they turned and kicked around each other.

One was dressed in a tattered uniform of dark blue cotton and his face was torn and bloody, the skin hanging in ragged strips. He didn't seem to mind, judging by how he laughed and clapped to keep time. His partner looked in far better shape. He was a giant of a man, maybe seven feet tall. He was dashing in a green frock coat and tight gray trousers, his shoes shined to a high luster. The chevrons on his sleeve were picked out in gold embroidery. A shaggy mane of hair and a thick beard shot through with traces of gray framed a tanned, slightly lined face. His eyes were deep and soulful and very brown.

None of the room's occupants seemed to notice Caxton as she clomped up the last risers and into the square room. They were too busy watching the wild dance, too absorbed in drinking and eating their fill. Even as she raised her patrol rifle and tried to get a bead on one of the dancers' hearts, not a single eye tracked her.

Then she fired—and everything changed.

92.

They came at us all at once. That is called Pickett's charge now, but at the time we did not know who had called the advance. At the time it was only a wall of gray, sweeping toward us, as if some dam had been burst open and floodwaters were rushing uphill right at us. They screamed as they came, even as our mortars blew them to bits, even as General Berdan's Sharpshooters picked them off one after the other. Still they came, our muskets blazing, and still they came, with banners flying. They pushed up against us, spun and died as they ran athwart our bayonets and still they came!

They broke our ranks. We pushed them back and they pressed us harder. The guns spoke volumes, the smoke so thick I could suddenly see nothing, and wandered mazed through a world that had lost all color and definition. I brushed up against the flank of a horse and muttered a pardon. The rider leaned down to get a look at me. It was General Hancock. "Have your men ready, sir," he said, his eyes wide. "Make them ready!" He dashed off into the gloom and a moment later I heard him cry out. Had he been struck by enemy fire? I learned later that he had, and most grievously, but that he refused to leave the fighting. By God, even the generals were not safe that day!

I rushed back to where the coffins lay, watched over by a small guard of wounded men. I would have thrown them open at that very minute, and bid Griest and his men come forward and do battle, but time was against me. Despite the black pall over the sky the night was still far off.

—THE PAPERS OF WILLIAM PITTENGER

93.

Instantly she understood the trick.

Her burst of three shots tore through the small room, ripping away the illusion. The bunting, the banquet table, and the well-dressed revelers broke apart like a plate of glass as her bullets ripped through the air, leaving nothing but a cold and empty room. The white plaster on the far wall erupted in puffs of dust, but she failed to hit anything. The soldiers had all been part of the illusion. The dancers had never been there. Caxton was alone in the room.

At least it felt that way, for a moment. Then a vampire, huge and pale and fast, rushed at her and knocked her hard into the door frame, pressing all the air out of her. Her rifle's barrel came up and nearly smacked her in the face. The vampire grabbed her around her waist and hurled her through the air, sending her smashing against a wall of framed photographs.

She couldn't get her footing, couldn't breathe. She sank down to the floor, unable to catch herself, unable to think.

Smart—so smart. Caxton understood that this was how she was supposed to die, that she had wasted her one chance shooting at phantoms, hallucinations the vampire had put into her brain.

"Nice trick," she managed to hiss out. "With the music and everything."

The vampire squatted down next to her. Peered into her eyes.

Caxton tried to ignore him and focused on staying alive. Her breath was coming back, but it hurt as it surged into her chest. Had she broken a rib? Had it punctured her lungs? It felt about that bad.

"There are so many things I've learned to do, since Malvern made me thus," the vampire replied. He grabbed her patrol rifle in both of his hands and tried to pull it away from her. The nylon sling was still wrapped around her arm and she jerked like a broken doll as he tugged. She felt his cold hands slide along her neck and shoulder as he freed the weapon. She could only watch as he bent it over his knee, ruining the barrel. The rifle would never fire again.

She still had her Beretta in its holster at her side. Had he seen it? It was pretty dark in the room. Then he leaned closer and she got a good look at his face. His cheeks looked almost flushed. He had fed, and recently—which meant he would be all but bulletproof. The pistol wasn't going to make a lot of difference.

She saw something else, too. She saw eyes she recognized, a certain angle of his cheekbones. This wasn't just any vampire. It was her vampire, the one she'd chased through Gettysburg and Philadelphia. The mastermind. She hadn't seen him since he'd fled the Mütter Museum, but she would never forget his face.

"You—you're the one. Why," she said, the word making her whole chest twinge. The pain was bearable, and there were things she needed to say. Questions to ask. "Why did you wake the others? You hate what you've become. Why not let them sleep forever?"

His hand went back, the fingers curled like talons. Ready to snatch her head off, maybe. Then the arm slackened and his eyes met hers. "Malvern had to be destroyed. You proved to me

I couldn't do it on my own. In a way, this is your fault, isn't it? If you hadn't stayed my hand—"

"Bullshit," Caxton said.

His face flared in outrage. Maybe he wasn't used to hearing women speak like that.

She shook her head. "Fine, you needed some help. Why wake all of them?"

For a long dangerous while he just stared at her, his hands at his sides. He could kill her in an instant if he so chose. They both knew it. Instead, he sat back on his haunches. She could tell he wanted to talk about this. He wanted to explain himself. "How could I choose which should live again? When they put us in that cave we were promised it would be a few days only. That we would get our chance to fight, and soon enough. Did you think all that time could pass, and we wouldn't feel it at all? We did, Miss. Oh, we had dreams to measure our captivity by. Dreams of blood. Those men—my men—deserved to walk again. They deserved a chance no one else could give them."

Caxton's teeth ground together. A chance to kill, he meant. A chance to slaughter. "A chance you didn't want to take, yourself."

"I beg your pardon?" he asked, fluttering his eyelids.

"You weren't with them when they came to. You woke them up but you didn't stick around to lead them. Have you been hiding here the whole time?"

"They knew where I was. They were to come to me. I knew they would never rise unopposed."

"So you kept yourself apart, out of danger."

The vampire smiled, showing lots of teeth. "Like any good general, who is worth more behind the lines where he can issue orders, than in them, where he is just one among many. You disapprove? You, I know, led your men from the front. For a woman you've a certain measure of intestinal fortitude, I'll allow. Now, if you please, hand me that sidearm and we'll finish this."

"I thought you were different," she said, ignoring his request. "You weren't like the other vampires I've known." Arkeley had known better, of course. All vampires are the same once the bloodlust takes them. Whatever noble principles they might possess in life, in death they become monsters.

"I can offer only my regrets, Miss, but the time has come. Your sidearm, please."

"What, this?" Caxton asked, pulling the Beretta out of its holster. It wasn't exactly a quick draw and she wasted a fraction of a second slipping off the safety. Still she managed to start shooting before he could tear her arm off.

He leaped up and backward, away from her. It was a movement far faster and more graceful than anything a human being could have managed. Her four shots, lined up perfectly with where his heart had been a moment earlier, passed into the soft tissue of his abdomen. The cross-point bullets shattered inside his body, each fragment tearing its own wound track through his muscle tissue, through his stomach. The skin flapped and puckered and tore until she was looking right at his cold intestines, dripping with a few stray drops of somebody else's blood.

The wound was grisly and frightening and it would have dropped a human being right in his tracks. The pain and the shock of it would have killed many people. The vampire stared down at his own body with a look of surprise and—humor.

He started to laugh even as his body started to knit itself back together, the tatters of skin stretching across the gap like pale fingers weaving together. She hadn't hit his heart at all, hadn't even come close. A wound like that wouldn't even give him pause.

The Beretta was empty. She had fired every bullet in the magazine. With her left hand she reached deep into her jacket pocket to get her spare clip, even though she knew she'd never have time to reload. He was done talking.

In her desperation she put her hand in the wrong pocket.

The extra ammunition was in her right pocket and she'd reached into her left, which held a pack of gum, her miniature flashlight, and the grenade she'd taken off Howell's dead body.

The grenade, her subconscious mind thought. She yanked the pin and tore it out of her pocket. It was a weapon—that was all she was thinking. She reached up and shoved the grenade deep inside the vampire's exposed guts. The white skin of his stomach closed over the gap so quickly that it nearly caught her fingers.

All this took less than a tenth of a second. Far less time than it took her rational mind to catch up, to remember that the grenade she'd just shoved inside the vampire's body wasn't a fragmentation grenade, nor a concussion grenade, nor even a flashbang. It was an M18 smoke grenade. She might as well have thrown her car keys in there.

94.

I could do nothing but cower among my wooden crates, and listen as the guns came closer, and shake in my boots whenever I heard the Rebel Yell come from close by. I could think of nothing but defeat. If Lee overran my position, if the boxes were taken before sundown, I would be hanged, I knew it; when the South learned of what we'd done, there would be a noose for me, if I was not destroyed by cannonade or musket fire first! My head felt as if it were crumbling, as if the pressure on it was too great to bear. I was sure I would die of the noise, of the damned smoke!

And then the ringing in my ears grew louder. Or rather, all other sounds slipped away. Had I gone deaf? I leapt up and ran through the smoke to find some man, to ask him what had happened to me. I stumbled on a Major with a face stained black by powder burns. "What is it? What has become of us?" I demanded.

"Why, we've turned them back," he said. He sounded as if he could scarce believe it. I matched his emotion.

Yet as I ran forward, to the very top of the ridge, I saw that it was true. The wave of gray was sweeping back, away from us. The guns chased them, and many men on the line were still firing their muskets, taking targets of opportunity. Yet the blaring of the bugles, and the great exodus of gray, showed it plain.

There was much confusion still, and many movements of troops and skirmishing. But it was over. By four of the clock it was over, the battle was done. And won.

My vampires had not been loosed. There was some discussion with General Hancock about sending them after Lee's retreat, to harry him from behind. But General Meade, who had approved of my operation, sent personal word down: there would be no counterattack.

The Battle of Gettysburg was over. My men, my monsters, who would have been heroes, remained unused, and unfed.

—THE PAPERS OF WILLIAM PITTENGER

95.

The vampire stood up straight, an easy movement, as if he were an origami sculpture unfolding limb by limb. Caxton pushed against the wall behind her, shoved herself upward in a far less graceful manner. Her Beretta hung useless in her hand. She had the urge to pistol-whip him, to fight her way free, but she knew better. She could not escape him, not now.

He placed a hand on either of her shoulders and pressed her against the wall. It felt like she was being crushed between stones. He leaned in close, as if he wanted to kiss her, and she turned her head to the side, but she couldn't stop looking at his teeth, at the rows of them, sharp, triangular, glistening. His jaws spread wide and his head tilted to one side. He was going to tear her throat out.

Then, instead, he coughed. A small, dry noise in the dark room. His eyes widened a little and his grip on her let up, just a bit. He coughed again, from deeper in his chest, and a trickle of green smoke worked its way out of his nose.

She turned to look at him head-on and saw he looked as confused as she felt. Then he vomited a huge gout of smoke and spit and blood right across her eyes and she reeled to the side, blinded momentarily. The hands on her shoulders were gone and she slipped sideways, ducked under his arm. He didn't bother trying to catch her, though it was well within his power.

She got clear, spun around, her hand going for the extra magazine in her pocket. She watched him from a place of pure fear, with no idea why he had released her. The smoke—that she could explain logically, sure, the smoke grenade had gone off inside his abdomen. The smoke was expanding inside of him, hundreds upon hundreds of cubic feet of it boiling inside his body. It would burst out through the handiest orifice, which in this case was his mouth. But surely that wasn't enough to hurt him. He had just laughed off four nine-millimeter bullets to the stomach.

In his face she read what was actually going on. His eyes were so wide that she could see white all around the pink pupils. He wasn't in pain—it was confusion that wracked him. He couldn't understand at all what he was feeling, but he knew it was bad. His hands clawed at his stomach, tearing at his own skin. As she watched, her own hands still working at the clip release of her pistol, he doubled over and vomited up a vast plume of dark green smoke that filled the ceiling of the small room. He tried to close his mouth, to swallow down what was so intent on coming out, but the smoke shoved his jaws open again and he coughed out another vast cloud of the stuff. His hands gripped a stomach that had grown distended and convex.

His whole body heaved as he threw up one more time. Caxton shoved home the magazine of her pistol with her palm. He turned to look at her, his expression pleading. Or maybe it was just surprise.

It didn't matter. She fired once into his gut and half his belly burst open, green smoke pouring out of him, his arms jerking wildly. She stepped closer and held her pistol out directly from her body. It ruined your aim to fire from the shoulder like that, but she couldn't risk inhaling a lungful of the smoke and losing the initiative. She fired into his chest once, adjusted her aim, twice, thought she saw his dark heart light up in the muzzle flare, and fired a third time.

He fell down, one leg kicking at a wall, smoke still billowing up from his torn innards. Was he dead? She couldn't be sure. She didn't want to waste any more bullets, but until she knew he was dead she couldn't move on. She bent low—the room was full of smoke to the level of her shoulders, only its lower half still full of breathable air—and bent to study his eyes, her pistol pointed always at his heart. His pink eyes told her nothing. She looked down and into his chest. His heart was in shreds. Good enough.

She let out a long breath and thought about what to do next. She wanted to sit down. She wanted to lie down, actually, to finally get some sleep. The smoke was too thick, and soon she wouldn't be able to breathe in the small room. She headed back down the stairs, down to the dark tavern room on the ground floor. Before she got even that far, however, her radio squawked for her attention.

"This is Caxton, go ahead," she said, relief washing through her. Finally she was getting a signal.

"Chalk Two here, what is your position?" The voice was faint and blurred by static, but it sounded very real.

"I'm at the third fallback. The, uh, the Dobbin House."

"Copy that," the radio said. "There's movement in your

vicinity. We're tracing multiple suspects. Estimate nine, maybe as many as twelve suspects on foot. Go ahead."

Caxton bit her lip. Suspects in this case meant vampires. Maybe as many as twelve. She thought she knew what they were up to, as well. "I copy you. What's their bearing?"

"Headed right for you, Caxton. They're converging on your twenty. They just came out of nowhere about a minute ago and lit out right for you. No information yet as to why."

"I have a theory," she said, but there was no time to go into it. She thought the vampire she'd just killed must have sent out some kind of telepathic distress call. Rallying the troops to assist him or, now, to avenge him.

As many as twelve vampires, headed her way. She'd finished off their leader. That should have been enough. It looked like her night wasn't over, though. Not quite yet. "Chalk Two, do you have any other confirmed sightings?" she asked.

"Negative at the moment, Caxton. Go ahead."

Caxton tried to think. Did that mean her army had gotten the rest of them? Were these twelve all that remained of the vampire battalion? She doubted she was that lucky. "What about our people? Have you made contact with anyone else?"

The helicopter pilot was silent for far too long.

"Did you copy my last?" Caxton demanded.

"I copy. No recent contact with friendlies," Chalk Two said. He made it sound like an apology.

"Out for now," Caxton said. Then she started to move.

96.

Ninety-nine hearts for ninety-nine coffins. I buried them myself in a natural cave on Seminary Ridge. I placed ninety-nine men at their quietus, and they did not resist. Across the cave from me, the one hundredth and the last, stood Alva Griest. He looked thin, thinner than I remembered him, and his cheeks were sunken, his eyes hooded by fatigue. Yet he spoke with great animation.

"Make us partisans," he said, gesturing boldly in the flickering light. "Send us behind the Southron lines. We'll make such mischief down there they'll be forced to surrender. By Christmas we'll have Jeff Davis chained, and dragged down Pennsylvania Avenue. Or just send me and I'll drain him myself. You have to give us something!"

"Alva," I said, softly. "Corporal. It is no use. The Secretary has given me my orders. This isn't the end, though. We'll wake you when the need is there again."

"And now we sleep. You call it sleep."

I shook my head. "I have no better word." I waved a hand at the men sleeping in their coffins. "What else can be done? We cannot leave you wakeful, with your hunger growing every night. Do you understand? You need not suffer, longing for blood that is forbidden to you. For you it will be a rest. How I envy you!"

Griest stood over me then. He had moved so quickly it might have just been a wavering of the light. Yet now I could feel him, his cold body, cold as the grave, so close. His hands moved before my face as if he would grab my neck and choke the life out of me.

"You understand nothing! We need blood!"

It took all my manly strength to turn my head and look up into his eyes. "Southern blood, you mean."

The fire in his red orbs banked visibly. His hands fell to his sides. "Yes," he said, "of course."

"Your time will come," I promised him. As I had promised him before.

—THE PAPERS OF WILLIAM PITTENGER

97.

What would Arkeley do in her situation? He would run. She moved as quickly as she dared through the dark tavern, the beam of her flashlight bobbing in front of her. From behind, near the front door, she heard glass breaking and wood splintering. She did not slow down.

The Dobbin House had seemed sprawling from the outside. From the inside it was a maze. She dodged tables and chairs and ducked through low doorways, slipped past stacked crates of liquor and canned foods, looking for an exit. She was scared to go outside—there was no cover out there; it would just be her and the vampires—but if she got trapped in a back room with no exits she was assured of a quick and unpleasant death.

Down a short flight of stairs. Around a tight corner. Windows everywhere, but they were all locked and she didn't want to make any noise by breaking one open. She was grateful enough for the starlight that streamed through them in slanted silver beams.

How many of them were there behind her? As many as twelve, her air support had said. Unless there were more of them he hadn't seen, which was possible. She had lost her patrol rifle—it had been empty anyway. How many bullets did she have in the Beretta? There was only one meaningful answer to that question.

Not enough.

She passed out of a large dining area and into a kind of gift shop. Tight aisles wound between displays of Civil War books and memorabilia, potpourri, and soup mixes based on original recipes from the tavern's kitchens. She banged her hip badly on a table full of stuffed animals wearing forage caps and toting miniature plush rifles. The toys slid to the floor in a rustling avalanche. The pain was bad enough to make her stop for a second, to squint and wince and try not to call out.

Lucky it wasn't broken, frankly. As fast as she was moving through the dark, she deserved a twisted ankle at least.

She wasn't moving as fast as the vampires, though. While she stood there trying not to stamp her foot in pain, she heard movement behind her. The agony was forgotten instantly as she craned her senses in that direction, desperate for any information.

If the vampires were already there, they didn't give themselves away. What had she heard? A door creaking open?

Keep moving, she told herself. Do not wait here, do not wait for someone to kill you. She hurried on, forcing herself not to hobble on her hurt leg. Arkeley would have laughed at an injury like that. He had no time for any physical ailment unless it kept you from walking. Even then, he would have pointed out, you could shoot a gun while sitting in a chair.

At the far end of the gift shop she found a fire exit. No alarm went off as she pushed through. It spilled her out into a parking lot. What next? What next?

A piece of rough, weathered wood slid down to crash on the asphalt, having come skittering down off the roof.

She glanced up, saw pale shapes streaming across the shingled roof of the tavern. No—not yet, she thought. They were almost on her. She lifted her weapon, fired into the mass of them. The shapes scattered like frightened birds, though she was sure she hadn't hit anything. She turned and ran—flat-out ran—toward the street.

She remembered very clearly how her vampire had nearly outrun a patrol car. There was no way she could outrun her pursuers. Maybe it was better to turn and face them, to try to fight. She slowed down, her hurt leg screaming with relief. She drew herself up to her full height and spun around.

They stood in a semicircle, nine of them, looking as if

they'd been waiting there all along. One of them wore a forage cap. Most of them were naked or wore just mud-stained trousers. Their chests were skeletal, each rib clearly defined even in the faint light. Their faces were emaciated, cheeks and eyes sunken, full of shadows.

She wanted to scream. Instead she raised her pistol and shot one right through the heart. He fell down, screaming. The rest of them tensed up but didn't run away. She swung around, found her next target. Shot again. The vampire spun around on his heel, but she must have missed his heart, because he didn't go down. As if in slow motion he turned back to face her, his bony face split by a wide grin.

"Had your fun yet, dearie?" one of the others said. He was much taller than the others and not nearly as decrepit. He turned to look at the vampire standing next to him. "Call the rest. Ain't a reason they should miss this bit."

The one he'd spoken to closed his eyes for a moment and tilted his head back. Then he looked at her again and his face was bright with mischief.

She fired again, but the vampire she'd aimed at feinted to the side even as her finger was squeezing the trigger. The bullet didn't touch him. The rest of them took a step forward, toward her. None of them wanted to be the next one to get shot, but they knew she had only so many bullets left.

Nothing she could do would end this well. She fired blind, not even looking where each shot landed before taking the next. The vampires did back up then, if only a few feet. One more of them went down before the gun ran dry, completely empty. She had no more extra magazines. She'd taken down two of them, though. Maybe that was worth the cost of her life.

Caxton closed her eyes and dropped the gun to the ground.

Light blasted through her shut eyelids, dazzling her. A moment later she heard the chopping cacophony of helicopter blades directly overhead. She clutched a hand over her eyes and then opened them slowly.

Before her the vampires were down on their knees or rolling on the ground. They were clawing at their own eyes, tearing them out as if they were on fire. Above her one of the helicopters floated in midair, its thirty-million-candlepower spotlight pointed right down at her head like a sunbeam from heaven.

She could barely see anything herself. The light hit her dark-adapted eyes like a beam of pain. She could make out a few details—for instance, she could see the tall vampire rising slowly to his feet. His eyes were dark holes in his face, already filling with white mist as they grew back. Could he see her without eyes, could he see her blood?

As if he'd read her mind he spoke, words she could barely hear over the helicopter's roar. "I can still smell you, gal."

Oh God. She had to get away. She ran up the street behind her, away from the vampires. One direction was as good as another. She heard the helicopter's whine change pitch and knew it was following her. The spotlight stayed on her, blinding her but offering her some scant protection.

Ahead lay the center of town. The houses on either side got taller and closer together. It was exactly the wrong place to go—she could easily get boxed in up there, if the vampires were smart enough to flank her. They had been soldiers. Would that kind of maneuver be second nature to them?

She wheeled around a corner, intending at least to get to a stone building, somewhere defensible. How she would defend it was a question she would answer when she found it. The old town hall rose up before her and she crashed against its doors, intending to rush inside and lock them behind her.

Then she realized, far too late, that they were already locked.

"Oh, no," she said, out loud. She pushed again and again on

the door's latch. Nothing happened. She turned around, looked from her left to her right. Back to her left.

In that moment of time, that blink of an eye, he was on her.

"A pleasure to meetcha, Miss," the tall vampire said. He was not five feet away from her. He bowed deeply from the waist. "I owe Alva plenty," he told her. The words meant nothing to her. "But I have never had such pleasure in fulfilling an obligation."

He reached for her and his fingers sank through her flesh as if it were water. She could feel the tendons and sinews in her shoulder coming apart, could feel her own blood hot and wet on her chest. She felt her bones wrenching apart and she knew he was going to tear off her arm at the shoulder and then drink from the wound.

She wanted to close her eyes. To give up, to just drift away. The pain wouldn't let her, though. It was screaming in her head, a wild animal trapped and desperate inside the hollow of her skull. She could see nothing but the vampire's white face as it loomed up before her, as it came to suck her life away.

Time seemed to slow down—then to stop. Then to reverse. She watched the vampire float backward, away from her. She was confused. Was this what death meant? But it wasn't as simple as time moving in reverse. The vampire was being pulled away, off of her. Someone bent his arm behind his back and twisted him, grabbed his chin and pulled it savagely sideways. She heard vertebrae exploding like gunshots going off. Then a white hand reached down and tore open the vampire's chest. Skin, muscle tissue, ribs all split and fell away. The white hand reached inside and pulled out a black heart still rubbery with tar and shreds of oilcloth. The heart flopped forward, fell at her feet.

She didn't have time to understand what had happened. Someone had saved her, but there were more important issues. She reached up and felt the wound on her arm. It was slick with blood.

Her savior walked toward her, his face twitching. He was staring exactly where her fingers were. At the wound.

"Please, Trooper. Cover that up."

She frowned. Shrugged her jacket over the injury. "You're one of them," she said. And yet he wasn't anything like the others. He was muscular, his body full and healthy and strong. His cheeks were almost burning red with heat and life. He wore dress pants and a white shirt buttoned almost all the way up. No shoes. No tie. "Who—"

"Malvern," he said. "It was Malvern's idea." He held up his left hand. There were no fingers on it.

"Never," she swore. That could never be right. It could never happen. The face was all wrong, and the way he stood, his posture was just—just—

"I told you there was something I could do, but that it was drastic."

"You didn't say it was unnatural!" She stepped forward and slapped him hard across the face. It was like striking one of the town hall's marble columns—it hurt her hand a lot more than it hurt his cold skin. "This is perverted. It's obscene."

"Yes." He looked up as if he were sniffing the wind.

"You—you saved me. At the electric map. Then again at the door of the Dobbin House. You were . . . there."

"Yes."

Rage exploded in her chest. "I didn't ask you to!"

He turned his face away. "There are more of them, close by. We can stand here arguing, and I can get drunk on the smell of your blood, or I can go kill them. Every last one."

"And then what?" she demanded.

"Then I come back here. Right here. And you shoot me through the heart." His face changed. She wouldn't have said it softened—but then she wouldn't have recognized tenderness on that face, before or after death changed it. "I was worthless to you before. My body was worthless. What the hell good is a vampire hunter who can't even dress himself? This way I could actually be of use, if only for one night. This was the only way."

She would have argued with him. She would have said a million things, if he had stuck around to hear them.

98.

I had the cave blasted shut the following day. Sealed. Even then, even as the powder went up and the earth heaved, I believed what I had told Griest. That I would be back for him before long.

Then the strangest thing occurred, one that seemed impossible at the time: the war ended. There was no need at all for the dreadful trove, no reason to dig up old secrets. I did not return. I will not say I forgot what I had buried, for that would be a lie.

Over the years I thought of the cave, though, less and less. Even secrets fade.

I have before me all the papers I collected. Griest's statement, laid out as a narrative, and the papers of my own account. Even Rudolph Storrow's half-legible "affadavut" is here. I have every scrap of proof, every shred of evidence that could implicate me in what was done. It has taken me twenty years to gather them all and now I am unsure why I bothered. Should I follow General Hancock's advice, and burn them all? Or place them in some dusty Washington archive, with strict orders they are not to be examined for fifty years? Or mail them to the editor of Harper's Weekly? *Let all America know what was done in its name?*

I think not. The secret is mine. The duty of silence mine to keep.

In a moment I shall put down this pen. Then I shall feed this sheet, and all the others, to the flame, as the general recommended.

Alva Griest and his dead compatriots shall never wake,

until the final Trump, and that is a blessing on us all. The world need never know what I did, though God saw. He alone shall be my judge.

—THE PAPERS OF WILLIAM PITTENGER

99.

D awn came up and found her sitting outside the town hall, alone. Half an hour later the National Guard arrived, hundreds of men and women in full combat gear, trucks, helicopters. Even a small tank tied down on a flatbed trailer.

They brought plenty of medical personnel and equipment. They erected a field hospital in Lincoln Square with beds for two dozen patients. One by one the patients showed up, men with patrol rifles slung across their backs and sheepish looks on their faces. Some of them had gone to ground when the plan fell apart. Some had locked themselves in supply closets or public restrooms and waited out the night. Others had just gotten separated from the main group and had wandered out onto the battlefield, looking for vampires to fight and finding only ghosts. She counted twenty-three survivors—nearly a third of the men she'd brought to the fight. It wasn't the kind of number that would help her sleep, but it was honestly more than she'd expected.

Every one of the twenty-three was injured. Most of them had lost blood. All of them had lacerations and contusions to treat. By midmorning most of them were cleared to go home. Then the dead started to arrive. Guardsmen carrying stretchers brought them up from the charnel pits of the Cyclorama and the visitor center, from the bloody patch of earth where the battle had begun. There were far too many of them for the field hospital's limited beds.

By that time Caxton was the only patient still being treated.

She was going to have her arm in a sling for a while, they told her, and she would need orthopedic surgery on her shoulder. There would be all kinds of drugs to take and physical therapy they promised her she would hate. But she would live.

Once she'd heard that, she got up and walked right out of the tent. There were a lot of things she still needed to do.

Teams of guardsmen combed the town looking for evidence. When they found some they brought it to her. By noon she had counted seventy-nine hearts, matched up with seventy-nine skeletons. The hearts looked charred or smashed or cut in half by rifle fire. She had each one put in a heavy-duty biohazard bag, which she planned to throw into an incinerator herself. She planned to watch each one burn until it was nothing but ash. Skeletons were notorious for not burning completely, so the bones went into a wood chipper. It was grisly work, but she did most of it herself, feeding femur after pelvis after phalange into the machine until dry yellow dust coated the legs of her pants. Someone was kind enough to give her a surgical mask and safety goggles.

She wanted to sleep. She wanted to see Clara. She wanted a lot of things she was not going to get until she had accounted for exactly one hundred hearts and one hundred skeletons.

Occasionally someone would call her cell phone. The Commissioner of the state police called and congratulated her on her amazing success. She wasn't sure what he was talking about. He said her job in the Bureau of Criminal Investigation was secure, that he should never have doubted her. She thanked him and hung up.

Most of the calls she screened out. She felt she needed to answer when the governor called, though she kept the call short and told him she'd write up an official report for him. When Clara called she just said she would be home soon.

About four o'clock in the afternoon two guardsmen came toward her carrying a stretcher that didn't have any bones on it.

Instead there was a man, a living human, lying on the canvas. She frowned, annoyed at this interruption, until she realized it was Glauer. He looked pale and his face was streaked with dirt, but he was alive.

"I don't know what happened—I don't remember much," he told her. "I woke up lying on somebody's desk, bleeding all over their paperwork."

She smiled then, though she didn't have the strength to laugh. "I'm glad you made it," she said. "You were a big help back there."

"Listen," he said, reaching out one weak hand to grab her good arm. "I know this looks pretty grim right now. But you saved my town. You saved seventy-five hundred people. Can I buy you a beer?"

Another smile. "Maybe," she said. "Maybe tomorrow. I have to wait here until nightfall, at least."

She could see the doors of the town hall from where she stood. Arkeley hadn't come back, even though she'd waited until the sun rose. She promised herself that he was just caught out by the sun, that he had been unable to make it back in time.

She knew she was wrong.

All vampires are the same, he had taught her. They could start out as noble and compassionate people or total scumbags. Once they got their first taste of blood it didn't matter—it made them wrong. Unnatural. Once they tasted blood they wanted to live, just to get some more. They wanted to live forever.

The sun set at seven o'clock that night. She had destroyed exactly one hundred hearts by that time. She'd found them all, just as she'd known she would. Arkeley had always been thorough. When the last pink light of dusk left the sky over Gettysburg, she was waiting by the town hall doors once again, her Beretta reloaded and in her hand. If he didn't show up she would have to hunt him down. She figured she would give him one more night before she got started.

Acknowledgments

John Geistdoerfer is a real person, who does like vampires, but not *overly* much. His generosity earned him a place in this book, and his good humor earned him a very *weird* place in it. "Have fun with it," he said, and so I did.

I spent a lot of time doing research for the portions of this novel set during the Civil War. A lot of people helped with that, answering my questions and keeping me honest. The staff and the reenactors at the Gettysburg National Military Park were extremely generous with their time and their knowledge. So too was Craig Young, who compiled a detailed account of what the Third Maine Volunteer Infantry did, where they slept, and what equipment they had for every day of the war. His work was of inestimable help in creating the timeline for my story.

Thanks also must go to Carrie Thornton, Jay Sones, and so many others at Three Rivers Press who helped make this book possible.

My wife, Elisabeth, showed me unwavering support during the writing process and deserves a lot more gratitude than I can express here.

About the Author

DAVID WELLINGTON was born in the South Hills of Pittsburgh, Pennsylvania, in 1971. He attended Syracuse University, Penn State University, and the Pratt Institute. In 2003, he established the website www.monsternovel.com, where he began serializing novels online. Mr. Wellington currently lives in Manhattan with his wife, Elisabeth, and his dog, Mary.